JAKOB EJERSB~~O~~ 1983-4.
When he published his first novel, *Nordkraft*, in 2002, it quickly became
one of the most successful and talked-about Danish novels of recent times.

EXILE

...lived in Moshi, Tanzania from 1974–7 and from...

He spent the next six years working on a trilogy of novels based on his experiences in Africa, but died of cancer in 2008 before they could be published. The Africa Trilogy, of which Exile is the first part, proved to be another remarkable critical and commercial success.

METTE PETERSEN's previous translations include My Friend Jesus by Lars Husum.

'The first volume of this Danish writer's ambitious and original African trilogy, exploring the lives of rootless Europeans in post-colonial Africa. This fine epic of loneliness and alienation in a beautiful land that seems to be sinking shows that he was a writer of huge talent.'   SARA SANDERSON, The Times

'Exile offers a shocking insight into the state of Africa in the 1980s and the failure of Europeans to save it, or themselves, from the downward spiral.'   ROWENA MACTOSH, Slundy

'The first part of a powerful trilogy.'   CHARLOTTE VOWDEN, Daily Express

'Jakob Ejersbo's Exile shows there is more to contemporary Scandinavian fiction than thrillers . . . Set amongst a group of European expatriates in Tanzania in the mid-1980s, whose callous, hedonistic behaviour recalls that of the Happy Valley set in Kenya fifty years earlier.'   MICHAEL ARDITTI, Daily Mail

'With its unemotional spare style, the tone of this novel about troubled ex-pat teenagers is hard-hitting. Bleak, yes, but also an intriguing portrait of a former colonial society facing unprecedented social and political change.'   Bookmus Translated Fiction

'Seldom has anyone written anything so insistent and impassioned, so glowing, hot and ice-cold, so heartfelt and so cynical.'   KLAUS ROTHSTEIN, Weekendavisen

Jakob Ejersbo

EXILE

BOOK ONE OF
The Africa Trilogy

Translated from the Danish by
Mette Petersen

MACLEHOSE PRESS
QUERCUS . LONDON

First published in Denmark as *Eksil* by
Gyldendal, Copenhagen, 2009
First published in Great Britain in 2011 by MacLehose Press
This paperback edition published in 2012 by

MacLehose Press
an imprint of Quercus
55 Baker Street
7th Floor, South Block
London W1U 8EW

A CIP catalogue record for this book is available
from the British Library

ISBN 978 0 85705 110 3

10 9 8 7 6 5 4 3 2 1

Designed and typeset in Collis and Quadraat Sans by Libanus Press
Printed and bound in Great Britain by Clays Ltd, St Ives plc

A big thank you is due to my first reader Christian Kirk Muff for stoking the fire and kicking my arse to bits. Thanks are also due to Ole Christian Madsen for tune-ups.
And to Morten Alsinger for a thousand coffee breaks.

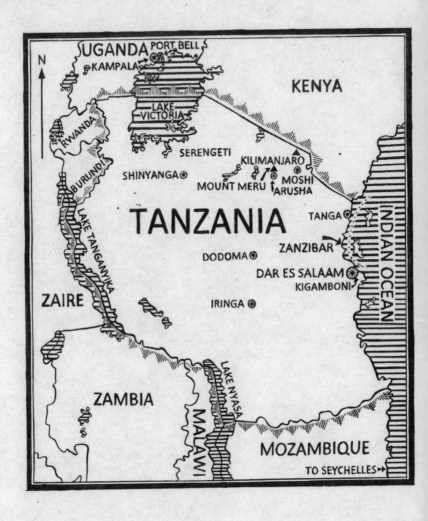

1983

Blue silver

The surface of the water is like a sheet of vibrant blue silver a metre and a half above me, and I am kicking my way along the sandy bottom with my flippers. I turn onto my back and look through my goggles at the shiny underside of the little waves. The tiny fish flee towards the corals at the bottom as I approach. It is over. The summer holiday is over. We are driving my big sister Alison to Kilimanjaro Airport – she is flying back to England. In a few days I am going back to boarding school, without Alison. Flipping my feet, I surface and gulp down air. The world is one big noise. I take off my goggles and blink with my eyes in the water. Salt water – that way no-one can see I've been crying.

I head up the slope. Baobab Hotel is quiet – the main building with its reception and restaurant areas, the bungalows spread among the baobab trees. We don't have a lot of guests. Inside the house Alison is packing. She is going to live with my dad's sister and study hotel management for six months at a school in Manchester, and after that she is going to work as a trainee at a hotel. I lean against the door to her room.

"Are you going to leave me here alone with the folks?" I say.

"Yes," Alison says.

"They'll be the end of me," I say.

"I have to get a qualification some time," Alison says. Dad passes in the hall. I turn my head to watch him as he goes.

"I haven't been to England for three years. We've lived here for twelve – I'll end up a Tanzanian," I say loudly. He continues down the hall.

"You'll get to England soon enough," he says without turning.

11

"I bloody well need to," I say. Dad stops, looks at me.

"That's enough from you," he says. "I've told you not to swear at home. You can go and visit Alison next year."

At home

Mum serves lobster for dinner, and afterwards Alison makes *crêpes suzettes*, which she flambés in Cointreau at the table.

"The first bird to flee the nest, Mrs Richards," Dad says to Mum.

"Yes. Sad, isn't it?" Mum says and smiles – slightly tipsy.

Alison puts her arm around my shoulder.

"I hope they behave while I'm away," she says.

I nod.

"Who?" Dad says.

"You two," Alison says.

"Luckily I'll be at school most of the time," I say.

"We're not that bad, are we?" Dad says. I pluck his cigarette out of his hand and take a drag.

"Samantha," Mum says sharply.

"Oh, let the girl," Dad says.

"She's only fifteen," Mum says.

"I did worse than that when I was fifteen," Dad says.

"Yes, but we don't want her to turn out like you, do we?" Alison tells Dad.

"Samantha's a tough customer like her old man," Dad says and looks at Mum. "The children are almost leaving home. Job well done. We can split up, then."

"Dad," Alison says.

"Why do you have to be such a boor?" Mum says.

"*Tsk*," I say.

Mum starts snivelling.

Africa

I wake up early with blood on the sheet, a headache and aching joints. I can hear the maid in the kitchen. We have to leave by mid-morning. I scrunch up the bed linen and dump it in the laundry basket. Then it's into the sitting room. Alison is standing in the middle of the room in an oversized T-shirt, looking sleepy.

"Where's Dad?" she asks.

"I don't know," I say. I look outside – his Land Rover is gone. Only clues: toothbrush missing, toothpaste, gun. Not a word, not even a note. Just gone. How long? Who knows? Mum sits on the patio drinking coffee.

"He can't face saying goodbye to Alison," she says.

I leap down the slope and into the boathouse; then I sail out to fish, bringing only a mask, a snorkel and a harpoon. I hang about three metres below the surface, and it starts raining, even though the short rains aren't due for several months – it's scary. The surface of the water is whipped to foam. I hurry back ashore. Everything's a grey blur.

Mum is still sitting on the patio. The rain has stopped.

"Don't you have anything to do?" I ask.

"Why?" she asks.

"Because . . ." I say.

"You girls have almost left home, and Douglas is always away, and I have chased the staff every single day for years and told them the same things over and over. And they don't do it – not unless I stand over them, glaring at them. I'm sick of it. I'm sick of the humidity, of the mosquitoes, of the hotel, of . . ."

"Of Douglas, of us," I say. Mum looks startled.

"Not of you," she says. Alison appears in the door leading into the sitting room.

"You're sick of yourself, really," she says.

"Yes," Mum says. "And of Africa. Africa is doing me in." She looks up at me. "If I went back to England, would you come, Samantha?" she asks.

"You want to go on holiday?" I ask.

"No, to stay."

"In England?"

"Yes."

"No," I say. England? What would I do there?

"We have to be off soon," Alison says.

Dengue fever

The road west is shoddy almost all the way to Road Junction, and it takes us six hours to drive the 350 kilometres inland to Moshi where the school lies at the foot of Kilimanjaro. Fortunately there's a couple of days left until the holiday is over, so we drive on for another hour westward, almost all the way to Arusha. It's lovely to get inland after the humid heat of Tanga.

A couple of kilometres before we reach Arusha, we leave the tarmac road and head up the dirt track to the slopes of Mount Meru and Mountain Lodge. We're visiting Mick, who is two years above me. Four months ago he fell ill and went to hospital right before sitting his exams. I'm looking forward to seeing him.

Mountain Lodge is an old German coffee farm dating back to 1911. It has been done up as a high-end hotel. Mick's mother is running the lodge and a safari company with Mick's brother and his wife. Mick's stepfather has a travel agency in Arusha.

Mahmoud comes out and tells us that Mick is the only one home. The others have gone on a safari in Serengeti with some Japanese people. I had really been looking forward to seeing Mick's sister-in-law, Sofie; she is so much fun. "But come in and have a cup of tea," Mahmoud says and walks ahead of us in his Arabic get-up with a turban and a scimitar in his belt – anything for the tourists. Mahmoud is a dignified man; he rules the local staff with an iron fist. We follow him to the patio surrounding the large, whitewashed house. A thin man in a deckchair is staring at us.

"Mick?" Alison says. He smiles so broadly that the skin on his skull creases as he slowly gets up.

"Is that really you?" Mum says.

"It's me, Mrs Richards," Mick says. He looks like a dead man. We hug him and are careful not to hug too hard. "Don't worry," he says and presses me close. "I won't break."

"How much weight have you lost?" Alison asks.

"Sixteen kilos," Mick says. "At first it was just the dengue fever: raging fever for a fortnight, a red rash all over my body, terrible muscle aches, internal bleeding. At the hospital in Arusha they had to try to bring down the fever with ice and plunk in an I.V. because I was so dehydrated."

Mick lights a cigarette and smokes it slowly – even his fingers are thin. It's a good job he was chubby before, otherwise he'd be six foot under by now.

"But with the I.V. came typhoid; I sweated, threw up, almost shat myself to death. The hospital was killing me. So Mum arranged to have me come home and hired a nurse to look after me."

"It's dangerous to be ill here," Mum says and shakes her head. True. The corporate ex-pats are flown home if they fall ill. None of our parents can afford health insurance, but we know how to bribe the doctors.

"So, what now?" Alison asks.

"I have to do some retakes and then I'm off to Europe," Mick says. "I don't know where exactly." Mick has a German passport because of his mother – I think she is really Austrian, but she used to be married to a German. Mick doesn't speak any German, and his stepfather is French. His real dad was English, but he died years ago of some sort of malaria.

"Mind you come and visit if you do go to Europe," Alison says.

"Oh, I'm going," Mick says. Mahmoud brings out tea and cakes.

"I'm afraid we've no room for you," Mick says. "We're having a load of Japanese in tonight."

"Oh, don't worry," Mum says. "We've arranged to stay at Arusha Game Sanctuary."

All of us white ex-pats are old friends, and when we go around the country, we stay at each other's. Arusha Game Sanctuary belongs to Angela's family, who are Italian. Angela is two years above me, and I've known her since I was a little girl – she was in Mick's year at the Greek school in Arusha until they came to the school at Moshi. But I'd rather stay at the lodge.

"How about you, Samantha?" Mick asks.

"I think I'll be at Arusha Game Sanctuary until I go back to school. There's not much point in going home to Tanga with Mum."

"Come and see me," Mick says. "We can always fit you in."

Saying our goodbyes

After tea, we drive down to Arusha Game Sanctuary, which is run by Angela's mum. It's like Baobab Hotel, with a restaurant and bungalows for the guests. But they also have a little zoo with all sorts of creatures from birds to lions.

Angela is staying with friends in Arusha, but her mum is at home and gives us our rooms. She says that it's no problem: I can stay with them until the new term starts. I go down the footpath with Alison to Hotel Tanzanite next door to swim, but it's disgusting – too much chlorine in the water.

We sit, drinking Cokes, smoking cigarettes, not saying much.

"You're upset – don't be," Alison says.

"You are too," I say.

She nods.

The next morning we take Alison to the airport, which is halfway between Arusha and Moshi. I can tell from the way Mum looks that she had a few too many last night.

"I'll talk to your dad," she says. "Then we'll see if me and Samantha can come see you for Christmas."

"Yes," Alison says, and then she says nothing for a while. It doesn't seem likely that we'll be able to afford any more airline tickets. There are swallows flying about inside the airport terminal. We say our goodbyes at the check-in counter. Mum is crying, Alison is gritting her teeth, I clear my voice and swallow.

"Now, don't you go doing anything stupid while I'm away," Alison whispers in my ear. She lets go of me and starts walking but turns around. "You will come up and wave, won't you?" she asks in a small voice, and I swallow again, and Mum nods, and Alison disappears behind the doors. We take the stairs to the roof, which is used as a viewing platform.

"I'm going to miss her," Mum says.

"Yes," I say and light a cigarette.

"You shouldn't smoke, Samantha," Mum says.

"Right now I should," I say.

"If you say so," Mum says, and we wait in silence, staring at the passengers walking towards the plane until Alison comes out of the building below us.

"Bye now, Alison – take care," Mum shouts.

"*Take no prisoners; kill 'em all,*" I shout. Alison doesn't say anything – she kisses her fingers at us and waves and stops at the door to the plane, and a queue forms behind her while she looks up at us one last time. And then she's gone. We stay there silently, trying to stare through the little windows of the plane to see her, but no such luck. Nevertheless we remain there, waving, while the plane taxies out. We wait as it rumbles down the single take-off and landing strip, turns around and gathers speed. We wave again as it takes off. We've flown from this airport several times. We know that you can see the people on the platform as the plane rises. We know that she's sitting there looking for us and thinking about when she'll be able to come back.

"Mum, you can just drop me off on the main road," I say as we leave the airport, because Mum is going east while I am going over to Arusha Game Sanctuary to stay for two days until the new term starts.

"No, of course I'll drive you."

"I'll just get a bus, Mum. That way you can be back in good time."

"Alright then," she says and hands me some money. "Remember to call home, Samantha." I hug her and get out – then watch her drive off. I eat barbecued cassava with a mustard dressing at a wooden shack, drink tea. Then I get on a bus towards Arusha. I'm squashed between the Maasai girl on my lap and the goat between my ankles until I can get off at Arusha Game Sanctuary.

Big game hunter

Angela is back. She is in their garden, working on her tan. I don't really know her, although she's quite cool and doesn't take shit from anyone. When she went to the school at Arusha, she was a day pupil, and at the school at Moshi she's in a different House from me. Angela is thin, gawky, small-boobed, hawk-nosed. Alison has always thought that Angela wasn't "all there". I walk up to her.

"Hey there, Angela," I say. She lifts her sunglasses and looks at me. Her eyes are red-rimmed as if she's been crying.

"Me and my mum had a row," she says.

"What about?" I ask.

"She says I've been flirting with her boyfriend," Angela says.

"And have you?" I ask.

"A bit." She put her sunglasses back on. "He's a big game hunter from Arusha. Italian."

"And your mum's boyfriend," I say.

"For now. But it won't last," Angela says. What am I supposed to say to that?

"Do you want to go swimming?" I ask. She doesn't, so I go alone. When I return, Angela has disappeared, and her mum doesn't know where she is – she doesn't seem to care either. I eat and go to bed and cry. I miss Alison. I wish I had gone home with Mum to Tanga. I don't want to go back to school.

The pearly gates

In the morning Angela is gone, so I tell her mum that I'm going to go up to Mountain Lodge to see Mick, and that I'll get a bus from there to school the next day.

Mountain Lodge is only two kilometres down the main road and then a good stretch up the slopes of Mount Meru. It's not so far I can't walk, because it's only morning, and the Arusha area is so high above sea-level that it's still cool up there. I walk up to the lodge. Between the trees I see the garage where Mick keeps his Bultaco motorbikes and his beach buggy, which is resting on its flat tyres. In front of the lodge there is a small stream coming from the mountain, and right by the bridge there are reservoirs, trout ponds. Mick is standing there next to a worker who is fishing out rainbow trout with a net on a bamboo pole. Mick hasn't seen me. He is shirtless, scrawny.

"Mick," I call out. He looks up and smiles. Comes up to me on the bridge, gasping for air. He puts his arm around my shoulder.

"Will you help a sick man get home?" he asks.

"Of course," I say.

"Alison – did she get off alright?"

"Yes. And Angela was at home, but . . . I don't really know her," I say.

"A bit of a wild one, she is," he says.

"Maybe you fancy her," I ask.

"No, I don't like her," Mick says. "Far too much dirty talk in that mouth of hers." We reach the house. Mahmoud serves us lunch and tea on the patio. We smoke cigarettes. "I have to go lie down for a bit," Mick says. "I'm still feeling a bit dodgy. But you can come along." He winks at me.

"You'd like that, wouldn't you?" I say and stay where I am.

"You will stay until tomorrow though, won't you?" Mick asks. I nod. He goes inside. I walk around the garden. I am fifteen. Mick is seventeen. I haven't lost my virginity. I go into the main building. The ground floor has a large room with an open fireplace and a dining room for the tourists, filled with trophies and furs. The family lives on the first floor. I go up the stairs. The door to Mick's room is ajar. I walk over to it. "Come in," Mick says, and I do. It's very gentle, very sweet. I get goose bumps when Mick undresses me. We go slow until Mick uses his hands and his tongue on the special spot, and then it's more than just sweet. He raises his head and looks at me. "The pearly gates," he says.

Smoking in the morning

First day at school. At 7.30 I dash out of my house, Kiongozi House, towards the dining hall. The boarders live in houses according to their age and sex. Some of them are quite some way from the school, but Kiongozi House is placed right next to the playground where the younger pupils play. I always arrive at the last minute – hair tousled and books under my arm – giving myself fifteen minutes to shovel down the grub.

"How are things, Samantha?" Shakila is already leaving the dining hall. She is the daughter of a professor who runs a private hospital in Dar. Shakila is two years above me – she was my "mentor" when I was sent to boarding school at Arusha in Year Four. All the new pupils are teamed up with an older pupil who is supposed to show them the ropes, teach them how to make their beds, tidy up, do their prep. Shakila was mine, and even though it's been four years, she still sometimes asks how I'm doing.

"Good. And you?" I say.

"Good," she says. Why is she asking? Because Alison has gone. I'll be alone at school from now on. For the first time I have neither my parents nor Alison around. The dining hall is half empty – the older boys are in Kijito House and the girls in Kilele and Kipepeo Houses have their own kitchen for breakfast, while the oldest of the boys in Kijana House and the ones from Kishari House eat at school.

I spot Panos, who is sitting at a table with Tazim, Truddi and Gretchen, who I share a study with. We're all starting Year Eight today. Panos is polishing off bread and juice – he is a mulatto, and his dad is a Greek tobacco farmer in Iringa. Out of the corner of my eye I see Jarno from Finland staring at me with his piss-coloured eyes behind the pale dreadlocks he has started sporting.

"Are you alright, Samantha?" Tazim asks.

"Of course she's alright," Panos says. "She's eating, isn't she?" I've known Panos for seven years, ever since I started school in Arusha in 1976 – Year Four, when Alison was in Year Seven. Panos is as strong as a horse, barrel-shaped, with a fervent hatred of books. We have to be out of the dining hall by 7.45 – the first lesson starts at 8.00. "Cigarette?" Panos asks without looking at me, as he gets up and scans the room.

"Absolutely," I mumble through the food in my mouth.

"At Owen's," he says and leaves. Owen is the Headmaster and his house is right behind the dining hall. It was Panos' idea to smoke right behind his house because that's the one place no-one will look for offenders. And Owen is already at the office – his wife has gone down to the teachers' common room. I sprint out after Panos, flitting between trees while I look up at Kilimanjaro. The snowcap on Kibo's peak is still visible – it won't be covered by clouds until some time in the mid-morning when the sun makes the water evaporate from the rainforest further down the mountain. I've never been up there, even though you can climb the mountain with school – I just can't be bothered. But Panos has, even though he was sick repeatedly on the way to Gilman's Point and didn't make the trip round the edge of the crater to the highest point, Uhuru Peak. Before the first white people climbed the mountain, the Africans believed that the white crown was made of silver.

Panos has stopped in the dense bushes behind Owen's house.

"Are you alright?" he asks.

"I hate being here," I say.

"Tell me about it." We light up, smoke so fast it makes us dizzy, share a piece of Big-G gum to cover up the smell, trot down to our classrooms; it's 7.55 now. The entire area is swamped with infants – day pupils. I.S.M., that's the name of the school – International School of Moshi. It offers twelve years, and then you're ready for university.

The day pupils know nothing about life. Home every afternoon to have their bottoms wiped by Mummy and Daddy. Most of the boarders are white – children of diplomats or people who work for aid organizations, or families who run farms or tourist businesses in Tanzania. And then there are the black boarders – sons and daughters of corrupt businessmen or politicians. Among the day pupils are a lot of Indians. The school started out as a Christian school when a group of whites built the large hospital K.C.M.C. – Kilimanjaro Christian Medical Centre, which is reportedly the best hospital in the country. There are still plenty of teachers who are holier than thou, but there are also loads of Hindus, Sikhs and Muslims, and at least you don't have to wear a uniform here the way you did in Arusha.

The first lesson starts. Another day of our lives is about to be wasted.

Pancontinental Mick

Everyone is running around saying hello to each other in break time that first day. I look for Panos' friend, Christian, but he's not in school. Christian lives at the sugar plantation T.P.C. just south of Moshi. Almost a year ago his little sister died in a traffic accident – maybe his family have gone home. For a while afterwards he went out with Shakila, but it didn't work out, and he was suspended for a week for constantly smoking cigarettes everywhere.

Savio comes over in the lunch break and asks about Mick. It makes me feel all warm inside, just hearing his name. Savio is thickset, originally from Goa, now from Arusha, and a Catholic.

"He'll be here soon for his retakes," I say.

"Is that you, Mick?" Savio says and looks over my shoulder. I turn around. Mick is coming down the corridor.

"Savio, my man," he says. "Samantha."

"Christ, you're thin," Savio says and slaps his hand. Savio stands shoulder to shoulder with him and lifts up his T-shirt. Savio is pot-bellied and Mick is worn to a shadow. We laugh. Shakila comes running and hugs Mick. They went out for a while last year before he fell ill.

"You're back," Shakila says. At the same time Tazim is standing some way off, looking sad – she fooled around with Mick once, but nothing came of it.

"I'm not back," Mick says. I swallow.

"What's going on?" Savio says.

"They can't be bothered set up a retake for me until November. Actually they'd rather I retook Year Ten," Mick says.

"Bastards," Savio says.

"What are you going to do?" I ask.

"I'm getting out of here," Mick says.

"And going where?" Savio asks.

"Germany," Mick says.

"What are you going to do there?" I ask.

"I know a German bloke who is signing up for a Technical School in Cologne, but it'll be me showing up with my friend's exam papers."

"Cool," Savio says.

"What are you going to live on?"

"I have a small inheritance from my Austrian grandmother, and then I mean to buy used cars, do them up and sell them at a profit," he says. Mick has been taking motorbikes apart since long before he could ride one. And he does it the African way – with whatever is to hand.

"But do you speak any German?" I ask.

"Enough to have a German passport," Mick says and laughs. "I can order two beers." Aziz comes over – a greasy Indian from Mick and Savio's year.

"Do you have any Arusha-*bhangi* on you?" Aziz whispers to Mick – Aziz smokes far too much weed.

"No," Mick says.

"Come on, be a chum, Mick. I know you've got some," Aziz says. He is always trying to make some deal or other.

"Piss off," Mick says. I wish he'd just kiss me.

Mangy dog

Lesson after lesson. I drag my bag behind me as I leave the classroom and cross the concrete decking stretching along the classrooms under the eaves of the roof that stops us having to wade in mud during the long rains.

"Samantha," Mr Harrison says behind me. I stop, standing still without turning around and without answering. "You should carry that bag properly." I turn around slowly.

"How do you carry it properly?" I ask.

"Pick it up," Mr Harrison says.

"That's for me to decide. It's my bag," I say.

"But it's the school's books," Mr Harrison says.

"Are you sure?" I ask.

"Do you actually want to be sent to the Headmaster?" Mr Harrison asks. I shrug. What else can I do? Lose face? I'm standing still, waiting. Quite a few people are now watching us. Then Mr Harrison starts smiling. He comes over to me, takes the strap out of my hand and lifts it over my head, taking my arm and moving it, so that it rests on the bag, which is now hanging with the strap between my breasts. "There you are," Mr Harrison says and pats me on the shoulder before he hurries towards the teachers' common room without looking back. I stay where I am for a moment. Then I grab hold of the strap, lift it over my head and lower the bag onto the concrete decking.

"Samantha," Gretchen says, shaking her head.

"Would you carry a mangy dog like that?" I ask and start walking again, dragging the bag behind me. The bag is jerked – Svein is giving it a hard kick, making it lift off and fly into the wall. The strap is still in my hand.

"Idiot," I say, swinging the bag forward sharply. Svein jumps out of the way, making me miss my mark, but I bulldoze on and let the bag swing a full circle over my head until it slams into the back of Svein's.

"Samantha!" That's Mr Thompson's voice – he's the Deputy Head. Everyone stops in their tracks. I turn my head and look. "My office, now," Thompson says, jerking his head. "You too, Svein." Svein protests. I shrug and head towards Thompson's office. The bag is trailing along the concrete decking behind me.

Silver cross

I bump into Stefano at running practice. Some of us girls are standing waiting for the runners to come back from their ten-kilometre run. Me and my study mates: Tazim, who is from Goa, vivacious and sweet, and Norwegian Truddi, who is standing with her friend Diana, the daughter of a corrupt Member of Parliament who people have named Mr Ten Percent.

Italian Stefano is first man back, blasting into the far side of the playing fields, encircled by 400 metres of running track. All he needs to do now is cross the finish line. We cheer him on. Baltazar comes into view only a short distance behind Stefano. Baltazar is tall and black as coal, the son of the commercial attaché for Angola. Stefano is short and powerfully built, topless . . . No, he's just pulled his head out of the T-shirt and pushed the front of it behind his head; it covers the back of his neck so he doesn't get sunburned. I can see how the muscles on his chest and stomach shift; there isn't an ounce of fat on him. His upper body glistens with sweat. He looks over his shoulder, allows Baltazar to catch up a bit but keeps a distance of a couple of metres. Stefano reaches the finish line first, arms in the air. Dark hair is visible in his armpits. The cross in his silver necklace has been stuck to his chest with tape so it won't jitter about when he's running.

"God, he is so dishy," Truddi says next to me. Stefano comes over to us spectators.

"Hi, Samantha," he says.

"Hi," I say. He comes up close and takes my hand, lifting it.

"Can you peel this tape off for me?" he asks.

"Of course," I say and, taking a careful hold of one corner and feeling the warmth of his skin, I pull it off.

"Thanks," Stefano says.

"Why don't you just take it off when you go running?" I ask.

"My mum gave it to me when I was born," he says. And I think that's the most beautiful thing I've ever heard.

That night we're snogging away behind the stables.

Sistah, sistah

"Are you feeling better?" I ask Christian when I bump into him on the Friday. He looks a bit the worse for wear.

"Feeling better?" he says. "I haven't been ill."

"Then what have you been up to all week?"

"All sorts of things . . . It's been bedlam. We've moved to Moshi. I got a motorbike."

"Right then, you can give me a ride," I say. "And I can come by on weekends if you provide some decent grub."

"Of course," he says and tells me where it is. It's right on the road from school into town.

That Saturday I am puttering about with Tazim in the city centre. She wants to go to the Moshi Bookshop and buy writing paper. Afterwards we go through the Kibo Arcade to Zukar's and buy *samosas* and *mandazi* – a sort of doughnut, a blob of batter cooked in oil and tossed in sugar. And Tanzanian tea, which is boiled with milk and sugar. The white girls won't come here. "Oh but it's so dirty, it'll give us tummy upsets," they say.

We forget the time and miss the pickup and haven't got the money for a taxi, so we have to walk.

"We can visit Christian on the way; he can give us a lift," I say.

"Yes, alright then," Tazim says, sighing. We're walking towards the

Arusha roundabout. A bit further ahead there is a group of fairly large blokes – early twenties, black – five of them. They see us coming from miles away.

"Can't we go some other way?" Tazim asks.

"We have to go this way," I say.

"But . . ."

"They won't hurt you."

"Are you sure?" Her father is a businessman in Mwanza – he ships goods across Lake Victoria to Uganda. She was born here, but the Indians and the blacks don't interact much.

We are getting closer to the five men. They go to it.

"*Sistah, sistah.*" When we've passed them, they start following us. I can tell that Tazim is panicking; she is gasping for air and moves stiffly. There's no-one else around. One of the guys reaches for my hair, touches it. Tazim looks like she has just received a death sentence. She is going to be raped now, and mutilated, and murdered, and raped again, and mutilated even more, and then finally eaten raw. I turn around:

"I'm not your sister. Don't touch me," I tell them in Swahili. Bloody annoying, and unpleasant too, but it's still light; they're just trying to rattle us. The five blokes laugh and stop. We walk on, round a corner. Tazim starts sobbing.

"What's the matter?" I ask, holding her close.

"I was so scared," she says.

"They're just idiots."

"Yes, but I thought . . ."

"You didn't think anything would actually happen, did you?"

"Yes. It . . . It could happen, you know."

Colonialist

We reach Christian's. Mick's Bultaco 350cc is parked outside. Mick's here! No . . . He left for Germany. Mick has sold his best bike in order to have a bit of money for when he gets to Germany.

Christian is home alone. He immediately gives Tazim a ride up to school. He comes back, turns the bike around in the courtyard. I'm sitting in a chair just outside the door. "Do you want a lift?" he asks.

"I'm in no hurry," I say.

"O.K.," he says, switches off the engine, and gets off, flicking down the kickstand. "Can I get you anything?"

"Cigarettes and whisky," I say. He laughs.

"The old man locks the bar cabinet, but cigarettes I can manage. Coke?"

"Yes." He goes inside. I follow him. I stand behind him as he opens the fridge and gets out a Coke. "I want to see your room," I tell him.

"O.K.," he says and, handing me a Coke, starts walking down the corridor. The cook's in the kitchen, ironing. I pop in my head and say hello. He asks if we want something to eat. "Are you hungry?" Christian asks.

"Always," I say. The fridge is amply stocked.

"Yes, we'd like something to eat, please," Christian says in very passable Swahili.

We go to his room. He has his own hi-fi – a big one. A nice stack of L.P.s and loads of cassettes. He puts on Eddy Grant. "Cigarettes," he says and points to the big cowhide drum that serves as a bedside table. "Help yourself," he says. It's Marlboro. I light one. They're much better than the Tanzanian cigarettes, which always make your throat hurt, have been too loosely rolled and are too dry.

"Mmmmm," I say and lean back until I'm lying flat on the bed, taking a drag so deep it makes my breasts rise. I'm aware that he is looking, even though I am looking up, letting my eyes follow the smoke rings I am blowing. "Nice ones – these Marlboro," I say. He doesn't say anything. "Where are your parents?" I ask. A couple of months ago there was a rumour that Christian's mother was seeing a man who wasn't Christian's father. Christian still isn't saying anything. I look at him. He is standing by the window, looking me with dead eyes, taking such deep puffs of his cigarette that the smoke is billowing around his head.

"My mum's playing at being a colonialist at some Dutch farmer's up on West Kilimanjaro, and my dad is drinking."

"Has your mum . . . moved out?" I ask. I've seen her a couple of times, when she came to the school – a tall, beautiful woman with large breasts – aristocratic. Christian takes one last puff of his cigarette and comes over to the table.

"Yes. She's done a runner," he says as he squashes his cigarette in the ashtray. "She thinks he . . . what the hell do I know? I suppose she thinks that the farmer is more . . . something . . . than my dad. More . . . human. Or just more of a man."

"Is he?" I ask.

"How would I know?" Christian says. "I'm seventeen years old – I'm just a kid."

"Has your dad gone native then?"

"Native?"

"Started seeing black women?" Christian shrugs:

"I don't know," he says.

Engine

I can hear a Land Rover coming to a screeching halt in the drive. The engine is turned off, the door slammed. Christian looks up at me and, smiling faintly, starts counting: "One, two, three, four, five . . ." The front door is opened and someone yells in Danish.

"Translate," I say.

"How many times do I have to tell you not to park that sodding motorbike in the middle of the yard? One of these days I'll end up running it over," Christian says while steps are coming down the corridor. The door is opened, it's his dad – angry – until he sees me, and then he suddenly looks baffled.

"Hello," he says and takes two steps into the room, holding out his hand.

"Niels," he says. I raise my upper body from the bed and say hello. Christian says something in Danish. I put out my cigarette. Niels is a member of the school board. They're the ones who decide whether you're going to be suspended for a week, or a fortnight, or forever. Do I have a smoking permit? No. But he probably doesn't know that – or at least he doesn't say anything – he merely looks at us; his skin is sallow, his eyes looking knackered – heavy drinking, hangover, tiredness.

"*Karibuni chakula*," the cook says in the hall – please eat.

"Are you staying for supper?" the father asks.

"Of course she is," Christian says.

We go to the kitchen, sit down at the table and eat. Conversation is laboured. Something about school work, the hotel in Tanga, golf. The food's good, though.

Afterwards we set off on the motorbike. I'm better at riding a motorbike than he is, but I don't tell him that. We approach Lema Road. I don't want to go back to school.

"Want to go to the Moshi Club?" I shout. Christian slows down and stops at the T-junction where Lema Road veers to the right.

"You know, I really don't," he says. "Any minute now my dad will be going there to get plastered."

"But can't we go for a ride then?" I ask.

"Alright," he says and revs the engine, continuing straight ahead. We pass the exit to Moshi Club and go down the twisting roads to the old railway bridge across the Karanga River. The lane is made up of several uneven layers of wooden boards that have not been stuck down properly, and in several places you can look through the cracks and see the water ten metres below. Christian drives slowly until we reach the tarmac on the other side; then he revs the engine. My body is jerked backwards, and I make sure to lock my fingers in front of his stomach very quickly so I won't fall off; I can feel his stomach muscles through the thin fabric of the T-shirt.

His dad, my mum. Everyday drunkenness.

We're speeding along – the engine and the wind, it doesn't make sense to say anything. We dash past Karanga Prison, heading west. We pass a herd of inmates in their white, washed-out overalls with a couple of guards in their dark-green uniforms, carrying rifles. The prisoners are filling in cracks by the side of the road. The floods create hollows under the tarmac during the long rains, which makes the tarmac break under the weight of tyres when heavy traffic passes. White prison overalls – easy targets in the midst of the greenery. If we continue long enough, we'll reach the road north to West Kilimanjaro, where Christian's mother is living now.

White kings

After a couple more kilometres the road cuts through a village. Christian stops at a kiosk.

"Have you got any money?" I ask, because I haven't.

"Yes."

"You've always got money."

"I steal it from the old man."

"Aren't you worried he might find out?"

"He's too hungover. I nick a few dollars and a few pounds he has lying about – Phantom does the exchange for me; he's the one with the small kiosk down by the market."

"The Rasta bloke?"

"That's the one."

We drink fizzy drinks and smoke cigarettes.

"They're not even here," Christian says.

"Who?"

"My parents. The . . . whites. It's got nothing to do with Africa. They move between their houses, their jobs, their clubs and all the other white people's houses. If someone really pushes the boat out, they go to the market with the cook or gardener in tow so he can lug their shopping back to the car."

"What's wrong with that?" I ask. It sounds like our life in Tanga.

"It's . . . They're in Africa – they know fuck-all about the Africans," he says.

"Do you think they miss out on something?" I ask.

"Yes, well . . ."

"Well, what?"

"They might as well stay at home then."

"No, because they live like kings here," I say.

"Yes, but then it's really got nothing to do with aid for Africa, has it?"

I make no comment. I'm not here to provide aid for Africa.

"Have you seen your mum?" I ask.

"I got a friend of mine to drive me up there – Marcus."

"And?"

"She's a white farmer's wife these days. Super-colonialist. She's really going for it," he says and lights another cigarette – probably so he won't have to look at me. He smokes for a while without saying anything. Should I tell him about my parents? He seems to have enough on his plate as it is. He is sitting hunched on the bench with his elbows resting on his knees. When he speaks again, he looks straight ahead:

"All of a sudden your parents turn out to be idiots. I mean . . . They're children. Stupid children, even, mindless."

"Yes," I say. "I don't want to be like that when I grow up – I'd rather not grow up, then."

"Yes," he says in a flat voice.

"Drag me all the way down here, and now – so many years later – they start talking about sending me to England. Do you want to go to Denmark?"

"I don't know, actually."

"Hard to know what it'd be like, isn't it?"

"Cold," he says.

"Yes." He turns his head and looks at me over his shoulder, smiling:

"Shall we?"

"Absolutely," I say.

32

This time it's his fingers that are locked around my stomach. I give it my all up Lema Road; if you go fast enough, the tyres don't have time to pitch down into the potholes – you fly right over them.

The river

I'm sitting with Panos where the bank slopes down to the river, smoking cigarettes on a Saturday afternoon.

"Stefano treat you alright?" Panos asks.

"Alright?" I say.

"Is he being pushy?"

"No," I say.

"That's alright then," Panos says.

"Why would you ask if he's being pushy?" I ask.

"I've known Stefano all my life. When he's not being a complete arsehole, I always put it down to divine intervention," Panos says and leaves.

On the way back to Kiongozi House, Stefano comes over to me from the playing fields where some of the guys are playing. He caresses my hip and kisses me.

"See you tonight, love," he says.

"Yes," I say. Out of the corner of my eye I see Truddi standing, staring at us.

"We'll have a good time then," he says. I don't say anything. "I don't want you running around with Panos and Christian all the time," he says.

"Panos is my friend," I say. Panos' parents' tobacco farm borders on the one Stefano's parents own.

"Yes, but you're with me now," Stefano says.

"Yes, of course I am," I say.

Later, while we're having dinner in the dining hall Owen comes over and stands right next to me, putting his palms on the table and leaning forward so he can look me in the face. Everyone around goes quiet so they can hear what he says.

"Samantha," he says. "I saw you on that motorbike today. I'm letting you off with a warning. Next time you're study grounded." He is looking at me; I am looking at him.

"Alright," I say, looking back at my plate, spearing a piece of roast potato on my fork, popping it into my mouth and chewing. Owen is still standing next to me. I won't dignify him with a look. I won't stoop to tickle his pathetic, power-hungry balls.

"Next time you're study grounded," he says.

"O.K.," I say. He steps away.

A warning for riding a motorbike. How banal.

Hormones

"Come on, Samantha. Just touch it a little bit," Stefano says. We're lying in the darkness in the middle of the playing fields and can only just make out the lights from the school.

"Why?" I ask.

"I love you if you'll do it."

"Only if I do it?"

"No, but only . . . come on."

"Do you want me to . . . with my hand?"

"Yes, grab on to it."

"I don't want to touch it."

"Why not? It's clean."

"Then you touch it. I'd rather have another cigarette," I say and sit up with my back turned to him. Why can't Stefano just hold me? Kiss me? All he cares about is shagging, groping my tits, getting me to touch his cock. It's got nothing to do with how he feels – I know that.

"A cigarette," he says and twists to sit next to me on the scorched grass of the playing fields, fishing a cigarette out of his pocket. "Alright. Here you go," he says and grabs hold of my wrist.

"Where is it?" I ask.

"For crying out loud," he says. "I'm giving it to you." He is guiding my hand.

"Christ, that's so disgusting!" His stiff cock against my fingers: he's pulled down his trousers – that was what I heard. I get up. He's lying on the ground, laughing.

"Damn it, Samantha. You said you would."

"I never said anything of the sort," I say and stay where I am with my arms folded. I bloody well didn't – wishful thinking is what it is. "Light that cigarette for me," I say. Why can't he be nice to me? I need that. I've got no-one to talk to. Dad is always on one of his so-called business-trips, mum is falling apart in Tanga – when they're together, they row. And Alison's in England, Mick is in Germany. Mick, he knew how to do it. He touched me, said lovely things to me, turned me on. Stefano is a fool.

The crackle and hiss of the match is loud in the night. I look down at Stefano in the light of the burning sulphur. He's pulled his trousers back up again. Then the cigarette's lit, he shakes out the match, and then it's dark again. I wonder if you could see the glow from afar. If a teacher comes down, I'll be study grounded – I already have one warning. So what? The glow probably just looks like a firefly.

"Here." He holds out the cigarette to me with the lit end hidden in the palm of his hand. I take it. Stefano, I think. He's got shit for brains and an equally shitty personality, but he is really good-looking: squat and strong, with pitch-black hair – a year above me. Something's moving in the dark. Stefano is quiet, immediately putting his hand on my inner thigh; I can't say anything now, or even move – we'll be found out then. I exhale a puff of smoke quietly. Darkness is dense – I can only make out the shapes of the two people because they're moving in front of the lights in the distance. Their steps are coming closer.

"He keeps asking me if I'll go out with him," I hear someone saying. It's Truddi – we are study mates, and she is in my year, but there's no love lost between us.

"But you like him, don't you?" I hear another girl ask her. Diana from her year.

"I suppose, but he shouldn't be asking me if I want to go out when he's already seeing Samantha," Truddi says. Stefano removes his hand from my thigh.

"Samantha's such a bitch," Diana says.

"Hang on," Truddi says. "I smell smoke."

"Get lost," I sneer.

"Ooh, sorry," Diana says, and she and Truddi snigger when they walk away. I don't think they recognized my voice. I get up, taking a drag on the cigarette. Pull my foot back and kick Stefano somewhere on his body.

"Ow! That fucking hurt, Samantha," he moans. "Bloody psycho."

"Bastard," I say, throwing the cigarette at him and walking off. I spit at him over my shoulder. Tears are running down my face. I have to take a detour behind Kijana House so I won't approach Kiongozi House from the playing fields, because Truddi and Diana may be there and then they'll be able to guess that it was me on the playing field just now. We have to be indoors soon.

Truddi and Diana are lounging about on the steps outside the door.

"Hi, Samantha," Truddi says brightly. "Where have you been?"

"None of your business," I say, pushing past her, and go to my room.

Gretchen, who is from Germany, smart, pale and self-effacing, wearing thick spectacles, is lying on her bed, reading – she's always reading.

"Hi," I say and go over to pick up my toothbrush.

"Are you having a row with Truddi?" she asks.

"Maybe."

"Why don't you two get along?"

"She's so bloody . . . well-adjusted," I say.

"You can't say that."

"I know. It's just . . . I want to be sick all over her."

Sunday I stay indoors while I wait for Stefano to ask someone to come in and fetch me outside so he can apologize. The boys aren't allowed in the girls' houses. But no-one comes for me.

Ebenezer

Every evening from seven to eight we do prep in our studies. I tell the houseboss Minna that I need to go to the library to look something up for a social studies paper. Minna marks it down on her list, and it will have to be registered at the library that I'm there, not in my room studying. But they don't cross reference the lists, as I've found out – I certainly haven't been caught yet.

I don't see anyone in the hall heading for the library, so I turn down Breezeway – the passage between the three blocks of classrooms – and once I turn the corner of the furthest building I stand and light a cigarette. I hide the lit end of the cigarette when I hear steps in the dry leaves.

"*Nani?*" the voice says – who? It's Ebenezer, one of the guards.

"It's me – Samantha," I say. "Come and have a cigarette with me." He comes over and stands next to me in the dark; there's a sharp smell of rancid sweat and wood smoke.

"You are very bad," he says and laughs softly, making his teeth light up in the dark.

"Yes," I say and hand him a cigarette – he lights it using my lit one. We're standing, talking in low voices about his family, his fields. Ebenezer was a soldier during the Tanzanian invasion of Uganda in 1979. As a security guard he has a Maasai club in his belt, a bow hanging over his shoulder and a quiver on his back. "Can you hit anything with those arrows when it's dark?" I ask.

"Maybe. Maybe not. But the thief will be afraid because the tip of the arrow has been dipped in poison," Ebenezer says.

"Really?" I ask.

"Really," Ebenezer says. "If I hit the thief in the arm, he may still run away, but the poison will make his arm rot, and the doctor will have to cut it off."

"Can it kill?" I ask.

"Maybe, if I hit him close to the heart," Ebenezer says.

"I'm sick of this school," I say.

"School is important."

"I want to leave," I say.

"That would be sad," he says. "Then you wouldn't be here, and we wouldn't smoke cigarettes together."

"Alright," I say. "Then maybe I'll stay a little bit longer." It's important to be on a good footing with the security guards so they don't tell on you if you're out and about at night. But I'm not going anywhere. After prep I stay inside Kiongozi House – I can't deal with Stefano pressuring me right now.

Respect

In Art we're told to look at one hand while we draw it with the other without looking at the paper. It's a complete waste of time.

"Can't we do croquis instead?" I ask Mrs Schwartz.

"Please just draw your hand, Samantha – it's a very important exercise in hand-eye coordination."

"Croquis is so much more exciting," I say.

"You'll have to wait a few more years for that."

"What's croquis?" Svein asks. He's one of the Norwegian glue-sniffers.

"Nudes," I say, sticking out my chest and pulling down at my neckline so the top of my tits become visible. The Indian girls tut while all the blokes stare. Some of the older girls have Art with us at a more advanced level. Parminder, one of them is called. She says something in Hindi, and the other Indian girls nod. She's their leader, because she is the prettiest of the lot – completely feminine with a plait so long it reaches her anus.

"Is there anything you'd like to say to me, Parminder?" I ask.

"*Tsk*," she says.

"It's my body – I can do with it what I want," I say.

"I know what you need," Gulzar says in a low voice – he's an Indian bloke who has been kept back a year because his brain isn't working. His twin sister Masuma is in the year above us. Gulzar takes a firm hold of his crotch under the desk. "You need to be ripped apart by this big, hard thing I've got for you."

"Shut it, you smutty fool," I say.

"How much? – for a quick one?" Gulzar asks.

"What?" I shout.

"What?" Mrs Schwartz says.

"He's got no business talking filth to me like that."

"Samantha, really – you're acting up as much as he is," Mrs Schwartz says.

"That doesn't mean he gets to talk to me like I was a whore," I say.

People stop their work.

"You should both speak nicely to each other," says Mrs Schwartz, who didn't hear what Gulzar said.

"He's sitting there asking me how much I am going to charge him for a fuck," I say. Mrs Schwartz sighs. I keep going, "He thinks that women are his slaves – his mum and his sister must wipe his arse from morning to night. And he thinks I'm a whore – that he can treat me like dirt. And you're telling him it's alright." People have started smiling now. Panos, Tazim and the Norwegian glue-sniffers are doing so openly. Gretchen is trying to hide it, because she thinks I'm out of line. The Indian girls are looking at their desks, but my guess is that they're enjoying every minute of it.

"Samantha. You're always trying to stir up something. You wear such revealing clothes."

"And?" I say. "Surely there has to be something nice to look at around here?"

"Do you think that's nice to look at?" Mrs Schwartz asks.

"Ask Gulzar," I say.

"Samantha. Off you go," Mrs Schwartz says and points at the door.

"What?"

"Headmaster."

"Why?"

"Off you go." I get up and leave. Mrs Schwartz walks past me and walks down the hall. I follow her.

"What did I do this time?"

"I've had it," she says without turning around. I have to stay outside while she speaks to Owen; she comes out and tells me to enter.

"We can't have this behaviour," he says.

"Ah well," I say. He sighs.

"We respect each other at this school. We have different religions and cultures, and we must all feel welcome. You can't hurt other people's feelings. I know that you enjoy provocation, but you can't overstep the mark," he says.

"I do respect them. I don't tell them to be like me, but I don't intend to be like them either."

"You wilfully offend them, Samantha. I can't tolerate that. Is that understood?"

"They're offending me as well when they won't speak to me just because I snog a boy every now and again."

"Yes, but you don't have to offend them to their faces," Owen says.

"But I don't. No-one says they have to stare at me. Don't you think I find it offensive when they think they're so much better than me that they won't even speak to me? Don't you?"

"They have a different culture. You have to respect that. It's an important part of this school – learning to respect each other's culture."

"No. It's about my having to respect their culture while they're allowed to look down their noses at mine. The Indian girls think I'm a whore, and the Indian guys are convinced of it." He doesn't know what to say to that. "But I'm not, because I don't charge them for it," I say. He allows that one to pass unchallenged.

"You already have one warning, Samantha. If I hear so much as a squeak from you, you're study grounded for two weeks. And if you do more than squeak, you'll be suspended for two weeks. Is that understood?"

"Yes." He signals that I can leave. I'm on my way out of the door. "And Samantha," Owen says behind me. I turn around.

"Yes?"

"It's not considered terribly clever to smoke when you don't have a smoking permit – least of all if it's behind my house."

"Point taken," I say and leave. How annoying. How can he know? Maybe his gardener has blabbed. Ah well – he let me off the hook, that's cool. There's only a few minutes left of the lesson, so I'm not going back to class. I sit down on a bench by the dining hall. Angela walks past me.

"Hello there, Samantha," she says and sits down. "Why do you look so glum?" she asks, looking at me with her head tilted.

"Skiving off, are you?" I ask.

"Yes," she says and smiles. "And so are you by the looks of it. But you don't look too happy?"

"Stefano treats me like dirt," I say.

"You go out with a dog, you get treated like a bitch." She gives me a hug. "But he is good-looking – I'll give him that," she says and gets up.

"Yes," I say while she walks away.

Owen comes round the corner.

"Samantha. That's two week's study grounding starting today," he says.

"Why?"

"Enough's enough. You're going too far. You know you have to go back to your lesson. I'm not having any more of this."

"O.K.," I say, shrugging.

"Get back to your lesson."

"But you've already study grounded me," I say. Owen takes a deep breath, but then the bell goes.

41

"Two weeks," he says and leaves.

Idiot.

Study grounded

I'm only allowed out of my room for meals and lessons. The rest of the time I have to stay in my study in Kiongozi House. I go to the toilet to masturbate. I'm bored and hankering for a cigarette. Knowing what goes on is impossible when I'm not outside in the afternoon. And I miss Stefano, even though that's absurd.

Never before have I done so much homework – there's nothing else to do. Tazim comes in.

"Er, Samantha?" she says.

"Yes?" I say from my bed where I am lying, reading.

"There's something I have to tell you."

"Tell me."

"Truddi is going about snogging Stefano," Tazim says. I bury my face in the pillow, and Tazim sits down on the edge of my bed and strokes my back.

"Never mind," she says.

Truddi comes in.

"Hi," she says and throws herself down on her bed, lying on her front, hugging her pillow, saying nothing.

"How's it going with you and Stefano," Tazim asks. Truddi answers curtly:

"He's such a baby." Her voice is unconvincing. I snort. Truddi looks at me huffily:

"You're welcome to him, Samantha."

"Oh, too much of a handful for you, was he?" I say. "All that messing about can be quite the turn-on, you know." Anger makes Truddi's face contract, then turns into pure misery – she buries her face in her pillow:

"*He cut himself*," she wails. Tazim gets up to comfort her and manages to

42

get her to talk. Stefano has cut himself all over his chest to convince Truddi that he will kill himself if she doesn't touch him.

"He's a psycho," I say.

"But . . ." Truddi says.

"It's not like he's dead or anything," I say. Tazim goes outside to look at Salomon, who is the son of the Ethiopian ambassador in Dar, has dreadlocks and – obviously – is more Rasta than everyone else because he hails from Zion, the land of Haile Selassie. Tazim fancies him. Truddi leaves as well – most likely because she thinks I'm going to tease her. I sit there, staring at nothing in particular, desperately needing a cigarette. I can go to the toilet and smoke, but it's too risky. Or, I can wait, tell them I have to go to the library and perhaps sneak a quick smoke with Ebenezer. But I haven't got any cigarettes. The bushes outside my window shake.

"Samantha?"

It's Panos.

"Yes. Hi," I say. Brilliant. A visit. He's snuck in between the bushes along the outside wall and is sitting under the window. No-one can see him; all we need to do is to speak softly.

"Still hanging in there?" he asks.

"Is Stefano talking?" I ask.

"Nope. He's got a split upper lip," Panos says.

"How come?" I ask. Panos shrugs.

"He fouled me in rugby yesterday."

"And you punched him?"

"Hey, it fucking hurt," Panos says.

"Yeah well, it's fine by me," I say.

"Yes, I thought it would be."

"Didn't any of the teachers see?"

"Smith," Panos says. "He just stood there. I mean, to him violence is the only way to communicate." Smith is your bog-standard English working-class bully. He used to play for Coventry, he says, and these days he's

43

supposed to be a P.E. teacher while his wife is houseboss at Kilele and Kipepeo House.

"I'm dying for a cigarette, Panos," I say. He hands me two Rex though a hole in the mosquito net.

Plaits

I've been study grounded and am pulling a sickie. I'm sweating. It's too hot to be lying in bed, and I need to pee. If I pretend to be ill tomorrow as well, they'll send me to the sickbay, and I can't be bothered to go there, because *mama* Hussein will see right through me. I get up and traipse to the toilet, sit down and am about to pee when I remember that my knickers will have to be pulled down first. I look at my cunt – a deformed cockle with hair surrounding it: is that really so interesting?

The others will be back from their lessons soon. I go back to our study, get out my hairbrush, sit down on the chair with my legs pulled up under me and press the hairbrush against my inner thigh, making small marks on my skin. Outside the room I can hear voices in the hall. Gretchen comes in.

"Hi," she says. "Are you feeling better?" I don't say anything. She looks at me. I look up at her. "So, what's the problem?" she asks. I look out of the window again, holding the hairbrush up. I want her to plait my hair. Gretchen takes the brush from me.

"What do you want me to do? Shall I do your hair?" I nod. "What do you say?" Gretchen asks.

"Yes, please do my hair?"

"And how do you want it?"

"Like . . . plaits."

"Right you are," she says and starts brushing it.

"When are you leaving?" I ask.

"What do you mean leaving?"

"You know, leaving because your parents have to go somewhere else."

"I don't know." No, but it probably won't be long. "But we'll write to each other," she says. How naïve is that? The number of people passing through this school is legion. I make friends with someone, and then they leave. And I stay in touch for a while, but then it peters out. And I think . . . I keep thinking that it's like when people die – it's the same thing. A way of coping. They're dead. I know better than to think that I will see them again. "Won't we, Samantha? – keep in touch?" Gretchen asks.

"Yes," I say. When she's gone, she's dead. "Aren't you going to get yourself a boyfriend, Gretchen?" I ask. "I can find one for you."

"No thanks," she says.

"Why not?"

"All boys are scum," she says.

"I didn't think you ever swore."

"I'm not swearing."

"Then what are you doing?"

"I'm simply stating a fact."

"Hmmm," I say.

"Anyway, I'd rather read," Gretchen says and starts plaiting my hair.

Freedom

After being locked up for two weeks I am free. I go straight over and find Panos, who is sitting outside Kijana House. We head off, passing Sandeep – a horrible swot who's constantly studying because he wants to go to the West on a scholarship. He looks at Panos nervously.

"Don't worry," Sandeep says. "It won't happen again."

"I shouldn't bloody hope so – for your sake and Mister Jones'."

"What?" I say to Panos while we're walking. Mister Jones is Sandeep's cat, and Sally has allowed him to keep it in their study.

"That filthy beast pissed in my bed the day before yesterday," Panos says. I look at him while I wait. "Yeah well, I threatened to kill the cat."

"Let's go down to the river," I say.

"What for?"

"For a smoke, damn it," I whisper.

"Right you are," he says. We walk along the river and scamper down the slope until we're out of sight, except from the boys who are herding the flocks of goats around, looking for a bit of dry grass.

"We can go swimming," I say, pointing, "Over there where the water falls over the rocks – it's got to be pretty deep on the other side."

"And shit ourselves to death? It's full of bilharzia – I went swimming there last year."

"Were you ill?" I ask.

"Lost four kilos – shat them off." We light cigarettes, smoking them without speaking. I look straight ahead; I know him too well. There's something he wants to say, but he can't seem to get it out.

"What is it you want to tell me?" I say. Panos turns his head and looks at me, then turns his head and looks straight ahead again, taking a deep puff of smoke, sighs and exhales.

"Truddi," he says. I don't get how that girl can hold any sort of attraction for him.

"Just ask her," I say.

"That's bloody easy to say – what if she says no?"

"Then you'll know. I can ask her for you." We both laugh.

"Yeah, right, she'll definitely say no then," Panos says. We head down to Mboyo's *duka* to buy fizzy drinks. Sit ourselves down outside. Then Christian shows up on his motorbike.

"I thought that motorbike had been banned," I say. Christian points to the ground:

"Is this the school? No, it's a private enterprise." He points at the road: "And it's a public road. It doesn't belong to Owen."

Mister Jones

The snowcap of Mount Kibo shines brightly against the dirty-blue sky. Looking up and seeing it I stop in my tracks. From a distance the mountain seems hazy, because there's so much dust in the air. A bleeding mountain. And here I am – a girl who knows nothing about anything. Who is being pushed around. I make for Kijana House, hoping to find Panos. Outside the entrance to the quadrangle building that houses the male boarders from Years Nine and Ten, sits a small group of boys. In the middle of the inner courtyard is Philippo, one of the gardeners, cutting the grass with a *slasher*, a flat bar, three centimetres wide and one metre long, the bottom ten centimetres of which has been bent to a blunt angle and sharpened. He is holding the wooden handle in his right hand and lifting the tool in something that resembles a half-hearted golf swing, before he lets it swirp down just above ground, making the cut grass fly about as he swings his *slasher* back. Philippo is rocking slowly forward with tiny steps while the beads of sweat grow larger on his black-blue back. Even though he's sort of old, he is so fit that I can count every muscle. I force myself to nod at him in European: jerking my head abruptly in a motion going from up to down – he nods back in African by lifting his head in the same sort of jerk, only less abruptly, while at the same time raising his eyebrows. The thought that I'm probably going to end up in England has made me think about it: the ways we say hello; my soft wrists; the fact that I shake out my shoes before putting them on to avoid creepy-crawlies. The negro in me.

I knock on Panos' door.

"Yes," he shouts. I open the door. Panos is sitting on the floor and is taping a cigarette to Mister Jones' mouth.

"I won't hear any crap about being kind to animals," Panos says with the cat trapped firmly between his knees. I hold up my hands in a resigned gesture.

"That damned Hindu's cat has pissed in my bed . . . *again*."

"Why haven't you rolled it a spliff?"

"I thought about it, but no."

"Too much of a sacrifice?" I say, while Panos forces the tape onto Mister Jones' nose. The cat is struggling to escape.

"There's that, but frankly I'm afraid of living next door to a cat that has reached enlightenment," he answers. "It could be dangerous," he adds as he lights the cigarette.

The cat's nostrils have been taped over as well so the animal is forced to smoke. Mister Jones' eyes look mad, he tries to cough and that makes small clouds of smoke eject from the lit end of the cigarette.

Panos pops his head out of the door while holding the cat pressed against the floor and whistles at the gardener.

"Hey, Philippo," Panos says. "*Mama* Sally – *yupo?*" He wants to know whether Sally, the houseboss, is around: converting Mister Jones to the joys of smoking could easily get him two weeks' study grounding.

Philippo gives his *slasher* a rest, turns around and smiles broadly at the prospect of Panos making mischief.

"*Ah-ahhh, hapana,*" Philippo says and shakes his head. Svein appears from out of nowhere.

"Well, fuck me," Svein says cheerily when he sees the cat, but then his eyes become worried.

"*Tsk,*" Panos says. "I deserve a medal for not killing the cat." Panos gets up and walks outside with the cat. Philippo starts laughing with a clucking, guttural sound when he discovers the cigarette in Mister Jones' mouth. Tanzanians have no respect for animals' lives, except if the animals are intended for food or work. If it were up to them all national parks would be razed to the ground – what exactly is the point of having lions roaming free? It's only the tourists who are mad about wild animals. The tourists, on the other hand, are not so hot on black people in their natural state.

Panos holds the cat by the scruff of its neck and its tail and shouts at Sandeep to come out. I lean against the wall to watch.

Sandeep drops his pencil from its horizontal position in his mouth when he steps out of his room. The air stands still as the pencil hits the schoolbook that's glued to his hand as usual, continues its flight to the concrete decking that runs outside the doors to the rooms, and then rolls a bit further before coming to a halt. Sandeep says nothing, does nothing – he's in shock. A few more blokes have appeared in their doors, called there by Philippo's laugh.

Panos goes out in the middle of the lawn in the courtyard where he lets go of the scruff of the cat's neck and, with a firm grip on its tail, starts swinging it slowly round and round above his head, making rings of smoke.

"The next time your cat comes into my room," Panos says calmly, "I will kill it."

Sandeep starts begging in a whining voice in his broken English with its thick Indian accent:

"Oh, please stop. No, no, no. Panos, my friend, never again, I promise. Won't you please put Mister Jones down?"

The cat sputters as smoke is pushed through the cigarette – it's the only way the animal can breathe.

Tears are running down Sandeep's cheeks while the cat's sputter increases in intensity – its eyes are rotating in its skull. Maybe it'll choke soon. Panos lets go of the cat's tail and it flies three or four metres before it hits the grass. Sandeep is there in no time at all.

"Ohhh, Mister Jones," he says and falls to his knees next to the animal. "Don't *ever* go into Mr Panos' house." He tears the tape and the partly smoked cigarette off the cat's nose. Convulsions shake the little body, and vomit gushes from the animal's mouth. It tries to get up to escape, but the nicotine and the swinging were too much. After only three doddering steps Mister Jones falls onto his side and gives up. The cat just lies there, breathing heavily, while Sandeep clears away its sick with his bare hands. Philippo is laughing and slapping his thighs; Sandeep looks at him tearfully.

49

"Why does it always have to piss in *my bed*?" Panos asks while he shuts the door to his room and leaves Kijana House. I follow him.

"That cat loves you, that's why," I say. I wonder what Truddi would say if she knew what it costs Mister Jones that Panos is in love with her.

Compulsory tennis

We have compulsory games in the afternoons. I do tennis. Tubby Sally is our tennis instructor. I go over to the tennis courts where Sally is standing with five Indian girls. They're dressed in saris, long trailing scarves, high-heeled sandals, with polished nails and golden bracelets. Their culture and dress must be respected. My culture tells me to flash skin and smoke cigarettes – I'm not allowed to.

I'm told to play a vain little puppet who staggers about in her high heels. She doesn't hit anything – but then she doesn't actually want to. Sally can't show us how it's meant to be done, because she is too fat to run. I thwack the balls over the tall fence surrounding the two courts; fetching them back takes forever. I need a cigarette. The Indian girls are just standing there, waiting for it to be over. International school – my arse.

Panos and Christian come over to us. They sit down on the grass outside the tennis courts and look at us. I go out to them, slumping on the grass.

"What sport did you pick?" I ask Christian.

"Badminton."

"Cool – who do you play?" He hesitates for a bit.

"Masuma," he says.

"Is she wearing a sari as well?" He smiles:

"No, full length white trousers, white T-shirt – very British," he says. Sally returns. I make a date with the boys – we're going to meet up later behind the dining hall for a smoke.

In the end Panos is the only one to show up. He doesn't say anything.

"What's the matter?" I ask.

"Truddi," he says.

"Did you ask her?"

"Yes." I wait. Panos takes a deep breath: "No," he says.

"Why not?"

"How the hell would I know? I get bad grades, I'm fat, I've got no dress-sense – something." We go back to smoking. Panos laughs and sighs at the same time.

"What?" I ask.

"She had heard about the cat," he says.

"For crying out loud, it was only a bloody cat."

"Yes, that's what I said to her. But then she said I was the most evil person she had ever met." Panos gets up from the ground. "I have to go – I owe Sally two hours' worth of ditch digging for unlawful smoking in bed of an evening."

Making love

That night I play table tennis with Tazim on the patio in front of Kiongozi House. Stefano has moved to Kijana House. I become aware of him when he's standing by the steps. I keep playing.

"Samantha?" he says. I look at him and serve – play. "I'd like to talk to you," he says. I continue playing.

"Talk then," I say.

"Please?" he says.

The next day I sit, slumping, by myself on a bench by the dining hall. He begged. I fell for it. It was the same as before. He took my hand and put on it on his cock through his trousers. "I've missed you so much, Samantha," he said. I missed Mick. I squeezed Stefano's cock – rubbing it through the fabric of his trousers. I was so happy to be close to him again. That's how stupid I am. He's coming back tonight. We are going down behind the stables.

"No, I don't want to do that, Stefano," I say, when he tries to pull my trousers down.

"Why?" he says. "Don't you love me?"

"It's . . . not safe," I say; I can't really think of anything else to say. Love him? What is he talking about? He's the one who doesn't love me. He reaches over a hand, showing me three condoms.

"I've taken care of everything," he says.

"Stefano, I'm a virgin," I whisper. "I'm not ready." He pleads and he begs, gets his cock out, puts the condom on it, kisses my breasts and touches my thighs. "Stefano," I say. "I can do that thing with my hand, but you have to promise that you won't tell anyone."

"Yes," he says.

"Promise me," I say.

"I swear on my mother and the holy virgin Mary that I won't tell anyone," he says and makes the sign of the cross.

"Lie down on your back," I say and, sitting next to him on the ground, I lean over and wank him while we snog.

He's completely euphoric afterwards. It was over in no time flat. Not that I think he's a virgin – he's probably paid for it in some shack.

"How is it that you girls are always more keen up by the stables?" he says when we're walking back towards the playground.

"What are you talking about?" I say.

"It's just strange that it's so much easier to get your knickers off when there's a neighing horse around." Stefano laughs.

"You haven't got my knickers off, Stefano," I say.

"No, but it won't be long," he says.

"You're so stupid," I say, letting go of his hand and going inside.

Tip of the arrow

One night behind the stables Stefano tries to force his hand between my legs, and I slap him hard across the face. Next thing I know he pushes me up against the board wall, really hard, and starts tearing at my jeans.

"You little whore," he says.

"Stop it. Please, stop," I scream.

"Don't you slap me," he says and pushes me to the ground with him. The horses neigh.

"Help, help," I shout. He's opened the button in my trousers and yanked down the zip, but he can't pull them off altogether because then I'll get away. I gasp for breath. Suddenly it smells funny – wood smoke? The tip of the arrow is the first thing I see – the metal is shining dully in the dark. It's probably about twenty centimetres from Stefano's neck.

"Get out of here," Ebenezer says. Stefano has frozen with his hands on my arms. He stares sideways at the tip of the arrow. Stefano whispers into my ear.

"Tell him it was a joke." I cry but without making a sound.

"Right now," Ebenezer says.

"We were just having a laugh," Stefano tells him.

"Shoot him," I say. The arrow quivers next to Stefano's neck as he lets go of my arms and carefully gets up while the tip of the arrow follows his every movement.

"You're mad," Stefano tells Ebenezer.

"Yes, I really am," Ebenezer says. Stefano leaves quietly in the darkness.

"*Tsk*, he is not a well boy," Ebenezer says, and I start sobbing. Ebenezer pulls me up from the ground and puts an arm around my shoulder. "I'll walk you back," he says.

"Yes," I say, and we walk towards the lights. I pull the T-shirt out of my trousers so no-one will see that the zip's open – luckily they're so tight they won't fall down.

"Wait," Ebenezer says and fumbles in his pockets for something, taking out a half-smoked cigarette, lighting it with a match and handing it to me. It's coarse black tobacco from the market, rolled up in newspaper – it rasps my throat and makes me dizzy. I take a deep drag.

"Thanks," I say and hand it back. We are almost by the buildings now and have reached the faint light. "I'll go inside now."

"I'll stay here and watch you until you're inside," Ebenezer says.

"Thanks," I say and leave. Panos is sitting on the merry-go-round in the playground.

"Samantha?" he says. I walk past him. "What's going on?" he asks behind me.

Slut

The next day Stefano comes over during our lunch break to apologize.

"No," I say.

"I can't live without you, love," he says.

"Then don't."

"I will cut myself, if you won't see me," he says.

"Cut away," I say. He grabs hold of my arm really hard.

"We can't not be together," he hisses.

"Let go of me," I hiss. He tightens his grip. But then one of the teachers comes down the hall, and Stefano lets go and leaves.

That night I sit in the toilet – I've no reason to; I just want to be left alone. Someone – or someones – comes in to clean their teeth.

"Did you hear that Samantha got back together with Stefano?" Diana asks.

"She's *such* a slut," Truddi says.

"You don't mean that – she's not a slut," Tazim says.

"Everyone knows that he'd rather go out with Truddi," Diana says.

"Why does that make Samantha a slut?" Tazim asks.

"He only goes out with her because she . . . gives him handjobs," Diana says.

"You don't know that," Tazim says.

"He's boasting to the other boys that Samantha masturbates him," Truddi says. "Isn't that right, Gretchen?"

"I'm brushing my teeth," Gretchen says. I open the cubicle door ever so quietly.

"If you weren't so sexually inhibited, Truddi, maybe you'd get a boyfriend as well," I say. Truddi swallows and takes a step back. "You think your cunt is a beautiful flower, but a flower is only beautiful if there's someone to admire it," I say as I walk up to her, raising my fist.

"Don't!" Diana screams.

"Stop," I hear someone saying behind me. It's Minna, our houseboss. I turn around. "What are you doing, Samantha?" she asks.

"Nothing," I say.

"I'm giving you a warning," Minna says.

"I haven't done anything," I say.

"She keeps threatening to hit me," Truddi says in her plummy voice.

"You just called her a slut," Tazim tells Truddi.

"We don't speak to each other like that," Minna says and gives us a lecture on compassion. We walk down the hall to our room. Truddi is in there in her nightie. I walk over as if I want to fix something on my bed, but at the last moment I turn and kick her arse. She shrieks:

"I'm going to tell Minna."

"Tell her what?" Tazim asks. "I haven't seen anything."

"Gretchen?" Truddi says. Gretchen comes through the door.

"What?" she says.

"You saw Samantha kick me, didn't you?"

"I was in the hall," Gretchen says. "Strictly speaking I didn't see anything."

Underhand

Gretchen and Truddi are breathing rhythmically and peacefully. I can't hear Tazim. I creep out of bed quietly, grab my cigarettes and matches from under my pillow and tiptoe out of the door and down to the toilets. I light a cigarette and, standing by the window, blow smoke out between the bars and the mosquito net while I watch a security guard cross the playground. It's not Ebenezer. I sense something.

"Samantha?" It's Tazim.

"Over here," I whisper. She comes over. I hand her the cigarette.

"Is anything the matter?" she asks.

"Stefano tried to rape me behind the stables."

"No!" Tazim says.

"Yes," I say. "But nothing happened."

"Why don't you report him?" Tazim asks.

"I don't know," I say, and she gives me the cigarette back.

"Then everyone would be talking," Tazim says.

"Yes," I say.

"Shush," Tazim whispers.

"What?" I whisper. Tazim tiptoes to the door. She stands there for a while, listening. "Anyone there?" I say.

"I'm not sure," Tazim says. We smoke another cigarette. Then we go back and sleep.

As we go back to class after lunch the next day Panos appears next to me.

"Are you going to report him?" Panos asks.

"Who? For what?" I ask – suddenly feeling cold. Panos doesn't say anything – he merely looks at me in a strange way.

"No," I say. "Nothing happened." There must have been someone there last night when we were smoking in the toilet. "Who have you talked to?" I ask.

"Everybody's talking," Panos says. "It's just that there's not very many people who actually know what they're talking about." He goes over and sits down at his desk. I can't sit still that lesson. When the bell rings, I go over to him.

"Nothing happened," I say.

"Something happened," he says.

"We're not together anymore," I say. "Never again."

"He's an arsehole," Panos says.

56

"You couldn't be more right," I say. "Who's talking about it?"

"Diana," he says.

"To you?" I ask.

"To anyone who will listen," Panos says. I'm standing about with Gretchen and Tazim that afternoon when Truddi and Diana walk by.

"So, how does it feel to be a fallen woman?" Diana asks, and they snigger as they continue walking.

"What?" I say. Tazim sighs. "What?" I say again. Gretchen puts her hand gently on my arm:

"Stefano has told everyone that you've done it with him – gone all the way. That that's why he's left you, because you're so cheap."

"*Tsk*," I say. "It's not like he can leave me when I've already left him."

That night I stay in my room after prep, despite Truddi being in there as well. Luckily she's too scared to talk to me. Tazim comes back and says that Stefano is outside and wants to see me.

"Tell him I don't ever want to speak to him again," I say. Tazim goes outside to tell him. As I stare at my book without being able to see the words, I hear Truddi get up from her bed – she bustles out of the door and down the hall. Knock yourself out – he's all yours.

Passenger

The school year has three terms, and the first is an exercise in futility, eighteen interminable weeks' worth of it. But after seven weeks we get a week off: half-term. I call Mum. She wants me to come home.

"Can't you come up to Mountain Lodge?" I ask.

"Dad isn't home, so I have to be here," Mum says. "And you can't go up to the lodge – they're fully booked at the moment."

"But I could sleep in the house," I say.

"No, Samantha. They're too busy to have friends staying," Mum says. And I'm simply not up to a week alone with her. She's a passenger – a deadweight – if Dad were to throw her off the cart, she'd be helpless.

"But Angela has invited me to stay at Arusha Game Sanctuary," I lie. "I just can't be bothered to go about kicking the sand for a whole week in Tanga," I say.

"Oh well," Mum says. "I'll try to see if I can stop by."

We say goodbye. Should I spend a week with Angela? – the thought alone is almost too much to bear. I call Mountain Lodge hoping that Sofie will answer the phone, because Mick's sister-in-law is nice and will probably let me stay even if they are very busy. But it's her husband, Pierre, who picks up:

"I mean, of course, if you've got no place else to go, you can come. But we'll all be busy and that's never much fun, is it?" he says.

"No. Alright then," I say. "I'll just go to Arusha Game Sanctuary."

"O.K. then. Take care," Pierre says. Oh no. I walk up to Angela.

"Can I stay with you for a couple of days during half-term?"

"How many?" she says.

"Just a couple," I say.

"O.K.," she says and shrugs, and I have no idea what that means.

That Saturday there's a party in the school's dining hall. I don't go. I play table tennis with Gretchen in Kiongozi House even though she's hopeless at it. Where do you go to smoke on a night like that when there are herds of teachers trawling the darkness between bushes and trees to find pupils drinking, smoking or doing what comes naturally? I go out and climb over the locked gate to the swimming pool and sit myself against the hedge at the furthest corner. Very quietly. I miss Alison.

Lover-to-be

The week before half-term is finally over and we're sitting in a Range Rover that has come to pick up a Danish girl from Angela's year. The girl's parents teach at the Danish Volunteer Training Centre by the Usa River, so we're dropped off right by the drive to Arusha Game Sanctuary. Angela's mum isn't home, but they give me a bungalow and then I have dinner in the restaurant with Angela, who seems very on edge. She wants to go to Arusha city, but there's no-one who can give her a lift. We smoke cigarettes on the patio, and then Angela's mum returns in her Land Rover.

"Where have you been?" Angela asks.

"At Sebastiano's," her mother says and smiles.

"It wouldn't hurt you to be home when I get back from school, would it?" Angela says.

"I thought you didn't care," her mother says.

"We'll take the Land Rover and go out," Angela says.

"No," her mother says and walks past us into the reception. "Hello, Samantha," she says over her shoulder.

"Hello," I say to her back, looking at Angela, who sits down next to me, looking mopey.

"I'm going for a swim," I say. "Do you want to come?"

"No," she says. I go to get my swimming gear before taking the path down to Tanzanite Hotel, getting into the water, doing laps. Too much chlorine by far. I should have gone to Tanga.

The next day a driver takes us to Arusha, and we walk around the city centre, eating ice cream at Arusha Hotel, before going up to the residential area north of the city centre.

"He lives in there," Angela says as we approach a small, well-kept house.

"Who does?" I ask.

"Sebastiano – my soon-to-be-lover," she says.

"Your mother's boyfriend," I ask.

"It won't last," Angela says.

"Come on, are you serious?" I ask.

"Serious as cancer," Angela says and shakes the gates, calling to the gardener.

"*Bwana* is out on a safari," he calls back.

"*Tsk*," Angela says.

We have dinner at an Indian restaurant, and afterwards we take a taxi to the Hotel Saba-Saba where they have the best disco. Entrance fees are cheap. There are white tourists here and a load of Tanzanians in their most colourful get-ups. We're sitting at a table drinking K.C. – *Konyagi*-Cola.

"Look at all those cheap whores," Angela says and looks at the bar where a couple of middle-aged white men are standing chatting to young black women. There are some young black men as well, wearing flashy clothes and boisterous attitudes, buying large bottles, a woman on each arm.

"Who are they?" I ask.

"From the tanzanite mines," Angela says. "People who have hit a rich ore."

"Don't you think we should go back soon?" I ask.

"Wait," Angela says. "We'll be asked to dance any minute."

"By who?" I ask

"There are always a couple of white men who are afraid of the blacks," she says. And sure enough – shortly after we're asked to dance by two youngish white men who are in Arusha to evaluate some German irrigation projects. When we've danced, we sit back down at the table, and one of the men asks what we want to drink.

"Or we could go to our rooms and raid the minibar," the other one says.

"O.K.," Angela says.

"I am fifteen," I say.

"Fifteen?" one of the men says.

"Fifteen."

"We're not doing that," he says and, getting up, goes back to the bar. The other one follows him.

"Why did you say that?" Angela asks.

"Because it's true," I say.

"You're such a spoilsport."

"Maybe, but I'm not going with strange men to their rooms."

"Tsk," Angela says. "We could just drink their booze and tease them a bit."

"You don't know what they'll be like when they're teased," I say.

"I thought you were cool," Angela says. "They say your dad picks his teeth with dead men's bones."

"Well, he doesn't," I say. We get a taxi back. Tomorrow I'll go up to Mountain Lodge. Maybe Sofie will be there – her I like.

Muscles

The next day I hitch-hike down the main road and walk up towards Mountain Lodge, but just then Mahmoud comes down in his car and tells me that there's no-one home – they're all at Tarangire National Park with a group of Japanese tourists. He gives me a lift back to Arusha Game Sanctuary, and there is Dad's Land Rover.

A very white man with remarkably short hair is sitting on the patio with a beer. Angela is sitting on her chair with her legs pulled up under her and her dress pulled up to show her knees – she is leaning forwards so you can see her hard little tits, throwing her head back, laughing at something he has said. He gets up when he sees me. Tall, handsome, muscular – perhaps just over thirty years old. His shirt is open, giving me a good look at the strawberry blond hair on his freckled chest.

"You must be Samantha," he says.

"Yes, hi," I say, and pointing at the Land Rover, "Where's my dad?"

"He'll be down in a minute," the man says and comes down towards me, the colour of his eyes – a watery blue. "Victor," he says, holding out a hand. "Your dad picked me up at the airport." He holds my hand in a firm grip, not shaking it – just holding on to it.

"Er, are you going to stay, or do you have to leave?" I ask.

"We're leaving tomorrow, but I'm sure we'll all have dinner together tonight," Victor says and lets go of my hand, putting his hand on my shoulder instead. "I've heard so much about you," he says. "Your dad tells me you're very good with a harpoon. I hope you can teach me, if we meet in Tanga." Angela has got up. Even at this distance I can tell that she is miffed.

"I can do that," I say. "Well, I am going to go over to Hotel Tanzanite for a swim."

"Can I tag along?" Victor asks.

"Yes, of course," Angela says. "I'm going there as well. Let me know if you need to borrow a pair of swimming trunks," she says.

"No, I've got some," Victor says.

Angela prances about by the pool in her teeny-weeny bikini. She swims up to Victor and gets him to let her stand on his hands and flip her back in an arc into the air.

"Do you want a go, Samantha?" he asks.

"No thanks, I want to swim," I say. Angela pretends to have swallowed some water and throws her arms around Victor's neck, panting. I have no doubt at all that she can easily reach the bottom. Victor removes Angela's arms.

"I'm going to do some laps," he says and swims parallel to me. Angela tries to do some laps as well, but she can't keep up, so in the end she leaves the pool sullenly and sits down in a deckchair.

"Let's do a race, what do you say – two laps?" Victor asks.

"Ten," I say.

"Whatever you say," he says. We do it. I make sure to be just behind him so that he can see me out of the corner of his eye the whole time and I keep pushing him until we turn for the final lap. Then I race past him and cross the finish line. He nods.

"Nice one," he says.

"Longest time under water?" I ask.

"Measured in time?" Victor asks.

"And distance," I say. We do that as well. I make it 54 metres. Victor does 25.

"Wow, you're good," he says. We're standing in the shallow end. Angela has left. "What's with her?" he asks.

"She's just huffy," I say.

"She does seem a bit highly strung," he says.

"She is," I say and move in front of him towards the steps. He is right behind me when I get out of the pool – he must be staring right at my bottom. He grabs and squeezes the back of my thigh. What is he doing? I stop on the ladder, turning my head.

"They're strong," he says and lets go of my thigh, smiling up at me. Does he think I'm hot? Should I say something?

"Like you wouldn't believe," I say and get out of the pool. We're talking about muscles, nothing more. He could be my dad, if he had made an early start. But he touched me. Maybe he fancies me? He looks me up and down as we walk back to Arusha Game Sanctuary, and I can't help wriggling my arse, even though I blush as well, but he can't see that in the growing darkness. I wonder what it would be like to do something with a grown man. When I get back to my room, I go to the mirror, twisting and turning in front of it. I *am* hot.

Thirst

We have dinner with my dad. He and Victor are going to go up to the great lakes the next morning. After dinner I sit with Dad and Victor on the patio. They're having beers. I'm having a Coke and sip from Dad's glass.

"Stop that," he says. "Is everything alright at school?" he asks.

"Everything's fine. Have you heard anything from Alison?" I ask.

"Your mum spoke to her – she's fine," Dad says and, emptying his glass, gets up. I look at Victor's glass.

"Have a sip," he says. I take it, drinking it down in one gulp. "You're a thirsty girl," he says. "Cigarette?"

"Yes," I say, taking one of his Marlboros. He lights it for me. And then Dad returns with a fresh round of beers.

That night I dream of Victor. In the morning when I get up, they have left.

Angela has gone to Arusha without asking if I want to come. But that morning Sofie from Mountain Lodge comes over. She's brought a large group of Japanese so that they can spend the day swimming at Tanzanite and looking at the animals at Arusha Game Sanctuary.

"Samantha," she says and gives me a hug. "I didn't know you were here."

"I wanted to come up and visit you," I say.

"But where's Angela?" she asks.

"I don't know," I say.

"You're coming back with me today," Sofie says. "You're staying with us until you go back to school."

"I'd like that," I say. Sofie is half Greenlander, half Danish. She and Pierre, Mick's older brother, have a son, Anton, who is four and a half.

I've known that family for as long as I can remember. Sometimes I spent my weekends there with Alison when we went to the school at Arusha. Mountain Lodge is a lovely place.

Late that afternoon we set off with the Land Rover crammed full of twittering Japanese. The men are smoking non-stop, and the women are lovely but strange – giggling and smiling as they continue to hand me Japanese sweets wrapped in colourful wrappers.

The fields of coffee bushes in front of the main building are mostly for show, only there to allow the tourists to dream of days gone by. It would make better financial sense to cut down the coffee bushes and keep livestock on the field, or smuggle the coffee to Kenya, the way they do on Kilimanjaro – but it's too far from here. Many of the farmers cut down their coffee bushes, so now that's been made illegal. These days they leave four rows of coffee bushes by the road and cut down the ones in the middle of the field, using it for grazing, or growing bananas, beans, sweet corn.

We cross the river at the ponds where the family raises rainbow trout to sell to the hotels in Arusha.

Golden Cunt

I'm playing with Anton who only speaks Swahili mixed with a few English swear words.

"Fancy a swim?" Sofie asks when we've had dinner and she's tucked him in. It's already dark.

"Do you want to go to Tanzanite now?" I ask.

"Not at Tanzanite – in the trout pond."

"O.K." The trout pond is lit by lamps on the small bridge across the stream. Sofie wears golden rings on her toes. We barely notice the fish as we swim – they dodge us. It feels really weird; the water's alive with silver-blue flashes of lightning.

We haul ourselves out of the pond.

"Let's have tea," Sofie says.

"Yes." We walk up to the patio that stretches the full breadth of the house, facing the rows of coffee bushes.

Mahmoud comes out, carrying tea in an old silver teapot on an Arabian copper tray, where he's put little glasses with golden swirls painted on. He pours it the Arabian way – from up high. A Land Rover is coming up the bumpy tracks – Sofie listens, and then she smiles.

"Is that Pierre?" I ask.

"Yes," she says and suddenly she can't really sit still.

"Go out and say hello to him," I say as the car passes round the main building.

"No, he'll be out in a minute."

"Where's my Golden Cunt?" we hear him shout inside the house.

"Golden Cunt?" I giggle. Sofie shakes her head, smiling.

"We're out here," she calls back. He comes out. She gets up, they hug, kiss. Having to watch them is crap.

"Samantha," he says – looking a bit sheepish, I think. "Hello – I didn't know you were here."

"I'm just hanging out with Golden Cunt," I say. He laughs.

Sofie slaps him. "You can't say that in front of strangers." Pierre laughs. He goes inside to have a shower. I look at Sofie questioningly.

"It's golden," she says, laughing.

"O.K.," I say.

"Alright then . . . It was before I met Pierre in Serengeti. I went to Kenya with a French bloke who was an ex-soldier. Jacques. We went to Congo to buy gold, which he was going to smuggle to India where the price was higher. But before we could go, we had return to Kenya, and the nearest airport was Kigali in Rwanda – have you ever been?"

"No," I say.

"Oh well. The landscape is absolutely stunning – it's the most beautiful country I've ever been to. And the gold wasn't much of an issue before we were about to get on the plane. Luckily the airport was fairly basic, so there wasn't a metal detector, but obviously we could still have our bags searched, so Jacques told me to stick the gold up my cunt – wrapped in a condom, of course. And I did – it fit quite easily – it was about as big as a medium-sized cock. But gold is heavy; I had about a kilo's worth up there, and I wasn't actually strong enough to hold it in. So that caused some trepidation."

"But . . . did it fall out?"

"No, no, I tore a hole in my pocket so I could hold on to it while I was walking. I went about with my hand thrust into my pocket like I was having a bad itch."

"Couldn't Jacques stuff it up his arse?" I ask.

"I suggested that as well," she says. "He didn't think it was funny."

The days at the lodge are lovely. But then it's back to the treadmill.

Mum's trick

They've told Christian he can drive his motorbike to school again because his father isn't able to drive him in the mornings. Right before the last lesson of the day we pull it out of the car park and down Lema Road, so no-one will hear us. He starts the bike, I get up behind him, and we tear away, driving down a side street, taking the back road – less chance of bumping into a teacher that way.

"Can I make a call from yours?" I ask.

"Yes, of course," he says and drives us to the house.

"Is anyone in?" I ask as we get off.

"The old man's at work," Christian says.

"Is your mum still at . . . that farmer's up at Kilimanjaro?"

"She left a couple of days ago," he says, looking away.

"Where to?"

"Europe."

"But what about . . ." I start, but then I stop because I don't actually know what I'm going to ask.

"I don't know," Christian says and, opening the door, points: "The phone's in there." He goes through to the kitchen and opens the fridge, shuts it again, stands with his back to me, looking out of the window. I try to call Alison in England and the line connects quickly, but no-one picks up. We go to Moshi club and sit on the wide patio that stretches the length of the club's main building. We're not old enough to sit in the bar. Originally it was an English bar, built in colonial times; these days Indian businessmen, high-ranking, corrupt government officials and politicians come here, as well as a lot of European corporates and their brats.

"Beer?" Christian asks.

"Oh, absolutely. But a Coke as well," I say. He goes and fetches both.

"Maybe we should sit in the pool room," he says. "You never know, one of the teachers might drop in. Owen plays golf here. The Indians invite him whenever there's a building contract going at school and they want to butter him up."

"No, we're staying put," I say and split one beer between the two glasses and pour a glug of Coke into mine so that the beer takes on its colour. Then I carry the empty bottle back to the bar and organize things on the table so that Christian is left with the beer bottle and I with my Coke.

"Clever, that," Christian says.

"Cheers," I say. He lights a cigarette and lets me smoke it. We talk about hit-and-runs; that's what we call the teacher-rejects who can't find work in Europe and the States. Then they come here to bother us, but they soon work out they can't live the good life on their measly pay, and after a very short time they're off again, and we're left to the mercy of another hit-and-run.

"Give me that cigarette," Christian says and jerks his head towards the golf course. Owen is walking in front of the caddie who is pulling the golf bag. Owen pays the lad and pulls the bag the final few metres up the ramp to the patio; his spiked shoes click against the paving as he comes towards us.

"So, did he steal your balls?" Christian asks.

"Or did you just lose them?" I ask.

"Samantha," Owen says. "Christian." He nods at us. Reaches for my glass, lifts it, looks at it. "O.K.," he says. "I had to check, Samantha."

"Check away," I say and take the glass out of his hand and drink. Owen looks at Christian:

"Does your father know you're sitting here drinking beer?"

"Yes," Christian says.

"Hmmm," Owen says and heads towards the changing rooms.

"That was a close one," Christian says.

"One of my mum's lunchtime tricks," I say. Christian gives me a ride back to school – he has football scheduled. There's nothing going on between us. I think he's fooling around with a new, slightly sad-looking Icelandic girl called Sif.

"So, is she up for it?" I ask when we're standing in the car park again.

"What are you talking about?" Christian says.

"Sif. Is she up for it?"

"Wouldn't *you* like to know?" he says.

"I would, but she's not talking to me. Maybe she thinks I'm going to try something on with you," I say.

"Sif's cool," he says.

"I suppose she does what you tell her to," I say.

"It's not like I have to make her," he says.

"Carnal urges," I say and walk away so he can't see my face. All he can see is my wiggling arse. It's a better arse than Sif's.

Perv

Mama Kalimba is down with malaria, so instead they give us this little French maggot as a French teacher: Voeckler. He's disgusting. When he explains something to you, he leans over you from behind and touches you. It's terrible for the Indian girls, and they're afraid to say anything. In no time flat they stop asking for help. Then he slinks about behind the girls, leaning in across them, touching their shoulders, asking them how they're doing. A real slimy bugger. I am simply waiting for him to try it on with me. But he doesn't. He carefully selects the victims who are going to be too afraid to resist.

I borrow a strap dress from Gretchen. She's slighter than me, and I give my bra a miss, so the fabric is stretched tightly over my tits and my nipples are about to pop through. That's all it takes: he's mine. We're given an assignment. In a matter of minutes he's standing behind me, putting his hands on my shoulders and leaning his head forward to peer down the valley between the hills. I hiss:

"Get your hands off me!" Everyone can hear it. He stands up with a jolt. Everyone stares. The Indian girls are wide-eyed with wonder.

"Er, I just wanted to check that you had got it right, Samantha," he says hesitantly.

"You don't see with your hands, do you?" I say flatly, looking right ahead of me.

"Someone's a bit touchy today," he says, walking towards the teacher's desk.

"Not just today," I say. He stands behind the desk without turning around, fumbling with his papers.

"You have five minutes to finish up," he says without looking up. The Indian girls smile at me. Tazim gives me the thumbs up. Voeckler slinks around the teacher's desk and sits down; he's terribly preoccupied with his papers. The bell will ring any minute now. Voeckler gets up.

"You can leave your responses in my pigeon hole," he says and leaves the classroom; his steps disappear down the hall. The bell rings. Gretchen smiles.

"So, that was why," she says and looks at her dress.

"What a perv," Panos says.

"Well done," Tazim says. Right now the other Indian girls agree – they show me respect.

Smoke tunnel

R.E. – I skive off with Christian. I take him to the school's old swimming pool behind Karibu Hall. The walls of the small pool are cracked and its bottom is covered with dirt, leaves, weeds. We sit down with our legs dangling over the edge.

"What are your parents like?" he asks.

"Why?" I say.

"Oh well, it's just . . . you know, your dad has the hotel, but . . . What about your mum? Is she O.K.?"

"Parents," I say. "They're all restaurant, cash-box, hotel, shuttle service and endless blithering." I don't want to talk about them.

"But what does your mum do?" he asks.

"Who cares what she does? She lives in Tanga, half a day's journey from here. Suits me just fine. Where's that cigarette?" He gets out our one cigarette, lights it and hands it to me. He seems tense – maybe he's worried that someone will come. We're sitting here all alone, just me and him. But he doesn't do anything.

"Fancy a recycled puff?" I ask.

"A what?"

"Come here," I say and grab on to his neck. "Open your mouth." He opens it. "Smoke tunnel," I say, taking a drag and blowing the smoke into his mouth – almost like a kiss. He inhales the smoke. Right in front of me. I kiss him, sticking my tongue into his mouth. Our tongues are moving, warm and wet. I pull away. "You're not half bad at that," I say. He doesn't do anything. I've started it now. I don't know what he's supposed to do, but I can't do everything myself. Surprise me. He doesn't do anything. "Get back here," I say and blow smoke into his mouth. He tries to kiss me. "Stop it – I'm trying to smoke here," I say. But then I kiss him back, hard, with my tongue in his mouth. "Cop a feel," I say, putting his hand on my breast. He caresses it.

"Mmmm," he says, leaning forward, licking my neck. I giggle. Why doesn't he tell me he thinks I'm gorgeous? I can tell his cock is ready to burst through his trousers. I move his hand to my naked thigh; he immediately starts moving it upwards. I push it away.

"We're friends," I say, handing him what's left of the cigarette and getting up. "I'm going back." I look down at him. He takes a deep drag of the cigarette and says nothing.

I shrug and leave.

I catch malaria and am freezing and sweating in the sickbay for a week. I'm even more behind with my schoolwork now. Angela doesn't speak to me anymore. I try to write my essays and do my maths papers. Smoke cigarettes with Panos. Swim. Christmas is fast approaching.

Every afternoon I sit with Gretchen and Tazim in our study. They do their homework to get good grades. I do it hoping madly I'll survive.

"Does he live all alone with his dad, then, that Christian?" Gretchen asks.

"Yes," I say.

"Does he have a girlfriend?" Gretchen asks.

"Gretchen?"

"Yes?" she says.

"Did you just ask if he had a girlfriend?"

"Yes," Gretchen says, blushing.

"I'll ask him if he likes you," I say.

"No no, please don't," Gretchen says, blushing even harder.

"Yes, I will," I say, getting up.

"No," Gretchen says. I go outside. But Christian isn't there. It's almost Christmas. The first Christmas in my life without Alison. In a couple of days I'll be sixteen, and I don't even have a boyfriend. I change direction because I see Stefano approaching. I keep an eye on Baltazar at a distance – I think he's hot. But more than anyone else I am thinking about Victor. A man – not a boy.

Smoke tunnel II

It's my sixteenth birthday, but no-one knows. Mum hasn't even called. That's typical. It's my birthday a month before Christmas, and they always end up giving me all the presents in one go. But it wouldn't hurt them to give me a ring.

That night there's a power cut. I'm standing, smoking, with Christian down by the changing rooms by the swimming pool. I stand very close, so close that we touch. He ought to grab hold of me, but he's shy. And I did kiss him yesterday down by the old pool, just for the fun of it . . . It upset him, and now he doesn't want to do anything; now we're just friends. He was a good kisser. He's got the cigarette.

"Smoke tunnel?" I say – I think my voice is sounding really small.

"Samantha. I don't think . . ." He doesn't finish the sentence; he takes another puff of the cigarette. You really have to do everything yourself these days. He takes the cigarette from his mouth, and I grab on to him, planting my mouth on his, but he doesn't blow smoke into my mouth. He pulls his mouth away to exhale, and then we're kissing again. Deep kisses.

72

"Quick," I say, because someone's coming – another couple. I pull him through the door to the boys' shower room. We touch. He pulls my T-shirt up and kisses my nipples. It's not happening fast enough for me. "Here," I say, taking his hand and guiding it up between my thighs – my knickers are wet. He pulls up my skirt, kneels in front of me and licks me. I put my fingers on the bean. "Right there," I say. "Your tongue." I grab him by the hair. "Come here," I say. He stands up – his face all wet. I open his trousers quickly, his cock juts out. "Come into me," I say. He bends a little bit at the knee, I lift one leg – up and slightly to the side, reaching one hand down, guiding him towards paradise.

"Uhhhnnn," he whispers when the tip of his cock slips into me. Yes. Footsteps? We both stiffen.

"Shh," I whisper. Christian pulls out of me, and I lower my leg slowly.

"Who's in there?" Someone's at the door. One of the teachers. I don't say anything while Christian quickly pulls his trousers up, and I pull my skirt back in place, straightening my T-shirt. "You, guard," the teacher calls. "Bring your torch here." It's Voeckler. Judging by the sound of the voice, he has taken a few steps away, walking towards the security guard. I should have brought Christian to the playing fields or down behind the stables. But then I didn't know we were going to . . . and the playing fields are a minefield. My heart is racing. I quickly whisper into Christian's ear:

"Go into one of the cubicles." The toilet cubicles are opposite the door, and the shower room is to the right of it. He can't sneak through the door – even in the darkness, Voeckler will see him. And even if he doesn't see who it is, he is going to find me alone in the boys' shower room. Christian slinks through the dark and into one of the two toilet cubicles.

"Light, here please," Voeckler says. But no light comes on.

"It doesn't work," the security guard says. Ebenezer – I recognize his voice. Maybe he's seen me go in. I've given him many a cigarette in my time.

"Give it to me," Voeckler says.

"Here we go – it's working again now," Ebenezer says, and I see a cone of light dance towards the cubicle doors. Ebenezer's salary is so low he can't afford to risk his job for a few cigarettes. But he did what he could. I go over and stand in the door and see Voeckler take the torch from Ebenezer's hand, making the cone of light dance over his grey stubble, threadbare khaki clothing and the sandals made of old car tyres.

Old desire

"Can't a girl pee in peace?" I ask. Voeckler points the torchlight at me, blinding me. I shadow my eyes with my hand. "Don't do that," I say, stepping through the door.

"Why didn't you answer when I called?" the teacher asks.

"I was having a pee," I say. "That's a private matter." He's standing, pointing his torch at my breasts. My clothes are rumpled.

"What are you doing in the boys' toilets?"

"The girls' toilets were busy," I say.

"No," he says. "I've just been there."

"Wow, they've been quick about it then," I say. "Did you need a pee as well?"

"Don't be cheeky," he says.

"I'm not."

"You were coming out of the showers – I saw that."

"I was peeing down the drain," I say. "Anyway, it's past my bedtime."

"You're not going anywhere," he says, walking towards the door and through to the toilets.

"The sick white man fancies me like mad," I tell Ebenezer in Swahili. His teeth light up the darkness as he gives a silent grin. Voeckler turns around.

"What did you say?"

"I am speaking to the guard in Swahili. We're in Tanzania. Don't you speak the language?" I ask.

"Watch it," he tells me, pushing open the first door, shining his light into the cubicle. Nothing. Christian must be in the cubicle next door. Even if we were in there smoking or snogging, that's hardly a crime . . . or, I suppose smoking might be, but we weren't – not in there at least. I wonder what Christian is going to tell Voeckler in a few moments? Voeckler opens the other door, pointing his flashlight at Christian. Nothing. Christian isn't there. Where is he? Voeckler steps into the shower room. I lean through the door to see what he finds. I hear a faint sound.

"What?" Voeckler says, turning around. I look around, feeling baffled.

"I don't know," I say. Voeckler points the flashlight at the ceiling and just then Christian slinks out of one of the toilets, past me, past Ebenezer and out. He's been sitting on top of the divider separating the two cubicles. All Voeckler had to do was to raise his torch.

"Samantha," Christian calls from the other side of the building where the changing rooms are. "What's going on?"

"Can I go now?" I ask. "That's my boyfriend calling."

"You're not going anywhere," Voeckler says and comes back out. Christian comes round the corner.

"What took you so long?" he asks.

"He won't let me leave," I say.

"Why not? What's all this about?"

"Don't be clever with me," Voeckler says.

"Clever?" Christian says. "I'm going home – I'm just trying to say goodnight to Samantha."

"The two of you have been . . . naughty," Voeckler says.

"You wouldn't believe how naughty," I say, and Christian laughs. Voeckler walks up to him.

"You smell of smoke."

"I smoke," Christian says.

"You don't have a smoking permit."

"As a matter of fact, yes I do," Christian says.

"You're to leave school premises right now," Voeckler tells Christian.

"Why?"

"Because I say so – otherwise you can report to the Headmaster first thing tomorrow. And you're coming inside," he says, grabbing hold of my upper arm with his hand.

"Don't touch me," I hiss and try to pull my arm out of his grip. He won't let go.

"Off you go," he says and pulls at me. People show up in the darkness around us. They're standing, watching the spectacle. Voeckler still has the torch in his hand. He shines the light at them.

"What's going on here?" Panos says, suddenly standing next to Christian. This is it: I start crying and shouting:

"Let go of me. You're sick," I shout. "All you want is to feel me up. All the girls say you stare at them during lessons."

"What?" Voeckler says, letting go of my arm.

"Hmmm," Christian says, nodding.

"It's true," Panos says. Voeckler takes two steps away from me. Oh no – Gretchen is standing there, looking miserable; she's my best friend, and she can tell I've got up to something with Christian who she has a secret crush on. How could I be so stupid?

Voeckler shines the light at me and at Christian and Panos. I cry so hard my shoulders are shaking. I've so many things I can think about that will make me cry – it's not convincing, it's real.

"Everybody inside, now. Otherwise you can all go see the Headmaster tomorrow morning," Voeckler says and shines the light on Christian: "And you, get out of here right now."

Christian shrugs.

"See you," he says and walks off. Tazim has appeared next to me. She puts her arm around my shoulder, and we start walking back towards Kiongozi House.

Friends

Next day down by the old pool:

"No but . . . I don't really want to," I tell Christian.

"But . . . I thought that . . ." He looks shaken.

"No, it's just that . . ." I say, but he's already turned around – now he's walking off. But I don't want to be with him, because now he's exactly like Stefano: all he wants is to grope and fuck. I'm the one who made him like that, I know, but it was a mistake. Yes, maybe he loves me, but what good is that going to do me?

Panos gives me a look when we meet.

"What?" I say.

"That was uncalled for," he says.

"What was?" I ask.

"Christian," he says.

"No, but . . ." I say.

"It was," he says.

"I know," I say. Back in our study Gretchen is crying, stuffing things into her bag.

"What's the matter?" I ask, putting my arms around her. She is sobbing.

"I'm going home," she says.

"To Mwanza? What happened?"

"To Germany," she sniffles. "My dad's ill."

"Is it serious?"

"Cancer," she says. And two hours later Gretchen is gone – she's not coming back. Her father is going to need radiation for a long time. Maybe he'll die. Gretchen has gone. Now Tazim is the only one I've got left.

I'm going down to Karibu Hall. It's time for their badminton practice. Christian is playing, looking glum, winning almost all his rallies – Masuma can't keep up. He doesn't look at me. When they're done, they shake hands, and Christian walks past me and sits on a bench outside. He's gasping for breath and drops of sweat drip from his chin. I walk over and sit down next to him.

"You like me," I say.

"Yes," he says, looking straight ahead.

"But we're friends, Christian. We can't go out," I say.

"Then why did you take . . ." he starts but stops without finishing his sentence.

"But," I say, and then I sigh. "I need a man." He doesn't say anything. He stares straight ahead. "Not a boy," I say. He gets up and leaves.

Alison

I'm lying on my bed in Kiongozi House, feeling bored. Christian still isn't talking to me. The Christmas holiday is only a few days away. Four interminable weeks with my miserably dull parents and no Alison. The thought is almost too much to bear. The phone rings in the common room. I'm listening.

"*Samantha?*" Truddi shouts. I jump up and run out.

"Yes?"

"It's Alison for you," Truddi says, handing me the phone. I yank it out of her hand.

"Alison!" I cry. "Come home – I miss you." I hear the line crackle and Alison's sparkling laughter. "How's England?" I ask.

"I'm not in England, Samantha," Alison says.

"Then where are you?" I ask.

"I landed at Kilimanjaro Airport last night – got on one of the Aeroflots. I'm coming to pick you up when school finishes. Then we'll go down to Tanga," Alison says into my ear.

"Oh, I'm so happy. But . . . what about England?" I ask.

"I gave the internship a miss," she says.

"Do the folks know you're back?"

"They're about to find out," she says. I ask a lot of questions. She cuts me short. "We'll speak when we see each other."

*

Two days later there she is, on Mick's Bultaco motorbike. I run over and throw myself into her arms.

"Alison," I shout, kissing her cheeks, hugging her close.

"Easy does it," she says, smiling. She fishes a Mars bar out of her pocket and hands it to me.

"I've brought loads of sweets," she says. I kiss her again, tearing off the wrapping, biting off a big chunk, and say:

"You're a good sister, you are. Dad is going to kill you."

"He doesn't get to decide what I can do any longer," she says.

"Do you have a return ticket?"

"Nope," she says.

"Why didn't you want to be there?"

"It's so uptight. People are dull, and it's cold, and . . . they don't know anything."

"So what are you going to do?"

"Let's just go," she says. I cram the rest of the chocolate into my mouth, getting up behind her. At Road Junction we stop for tea.

"How's school?" Alison asks.

"It's O.K.," I say.

"And the boys?" she asks.

"I toy with them," I say, giggling, because I don't feel like telling her about Stefano, and I don't want to tell her about Victor because she'll tell me I'm being ridiculous. And that thing with Christian was stupid of me – I can't bear to have Alison tell me when I already know.

We switch places so that I'm driving when we're going over the bad bits of road – I'm a better motorcyclist than Alison.

The trip takes us six hours, and we reach home as the sun is setting. Mum and Dad come out, and Dad stares at Alison.

"How did you get money for the ticket?" he asks.

"That doesn't matter now, does it?" Alison says. "Seeing as I didn't get caught."

"Not from your aunt, was it?" Mum asks.

"No, of course not," Alison says.

"What did you do?" Dad asks.

"Are you sure you want to know?" Alison asks.

"Tell me."

"I robbed a corner shop," she says.

"How?"

"Balaclava and Granddad's Luger."

"Alison!"

"I ought to give you a good thrashing," Dad says, shaking his head and turning around, but I see his face as he walks away – that little smile. Mum is still standing there staring at Alison.

"You didn't really. Did you?" Mum asks.

"No. I danced."

"Danced?"

"Yes. In a strip club," Alison says.

"Alison!" Mum says.

Black holes

What is Alison going to do in Tanzania with no money, no man and with no education to speak of?

"I'll think of something," she says over dinner with the folks that night.

"And what if I don't want to support you?" Dad asks. But of course he will. She can work at the hotel, because Mum has completely let go of the reins in order to concentrate on her gin and tonics.

We head out for a swim in the dark. Afterwards I start gathering twigs for a bonfire. I say:

"What are you going to do?"

"Find myself a husband who is also human."

"Where do you get one of those?" I ask.

"I have no idea."

"England?"

"No – they're such bores," Alison says.

"Go native, then?" I ask.

"I'm not having any of that, thank you very much," Alison says.

"A bit of both: Ricardo?" I ask; he lives in Tanga and is a mulatto – his dad is white and came to Tanzania from Mozambique when the Portuguese were kicked out in 1975.

"He's an idiot," Alison says. I laugh. Ricardo kept calling last summer to ask Alison out. She was standing with the phone, writing notes to me, telling me to put on loud music and misbehave, so she would have to hang up. Alison smiles at me grimly: "You're very welcome to him," she says and sighs: "He drinks like a drain and he's got no idea what colour he is. His mother's a witch. You can't go there for a cup of tea without having her put all sorts of gunk in it to make you fall in love with her son. I've seen her collect dust in the garden where I've walked in order to cast some sort of weird spell on it."

"But . . . how are you going to find a man? Here? Most of them are busy pumping black holes."

"Yes. But I've got a couple of tricks myself. Like having a conversation. Not everyone wants to be seen as someone who's bought a Tanzanian whore for a wife."

"Do you have anyone lined up?"

"Not really. But Dad's suggested that I try to get the hotel up and running so he can sell it at a profit. I've promised him a year."

"Sell it . . . Then where will I live?"

"I don't know, Samantha," she says.

"But it's my home," I say.

"You don't want to live here," Alison says. "Not once you've finished school anyway. What would you do here?" The question gives me the shivers. I can feel everything fall apart. I mean – if they sell the hotel, then what? Where am I going to live? I don't say anything though.

"There's always the house at Dar," Alison says. Dad has a small house a bit further out than the cinema in Dar es Salaam, but it's completely run-down. Right now Juma lives there – my Dad's right-hand man. And what would I do there?

"Where are the folks going to live then?" I ask.

"Don't you think they've been together for long enough?" Alison asks.

"But . . . Mum says she thinks I should go to England in two and a half years, when I've finished Year Ten. Maybe she'll come as well. But I don't . . . I just don't want to at all."

"Then what *do* you want to do?" Alison asks. "Stay in school and finish Year Twelve?"

"No," I say. "But they can't just drag me here when I'm three, and then like a hundred years later suddenly send me to England."

"No, that really is wrong," Alison says and opens the two beers I have nicked from the fridge, while I light a couple of dry palm leaves and add twigs. The flames catch. I sit down close to Alison, light a cigarette and put my arm around her. In England all the houses have the same type of windows that the British colonial houses do here in Tanzania. But the English climate is hardly tropical. It's as cold as hell, and you can't get a room warm, because the wind comes through every crack.

"But what about that man you're going to find?" I ask her again. Alison leans her head against my shoulder.

"I'm going to go down to Melinda in Dar on holiday to check out the options, find myself someone nice and marry him when we've been going out for a year. End of story."

"What if he doesn't want to marry you?"

"Do you think that's up to him?" Alison asks and turns her head to me. The light from the flames is billowing across her face, allowing me to see that look of hers, which men think means all sorts of wonderful things.

"No, the man is going to have no say in it whatsoever," I say. Alison has tried to teach me how to make your eyes sleepy, sweet, saucy and vivacious all at the same time, but I can't keep a straight face – it seems utterly ridiculous to me. When we go to Dar together, men circle Alison like flies do a turd. They don't find me interesting until they've had a drink.

Happy families

When we return, the folks are on the patio with their drinks.

"It's a good job our big girl has returned to save the hotel," Dad says as we sit down ourselves down in the chairs.

"I'm sure Mum's going to help me," Alison says looking at Mum.

"Of course I am, darling," Mum says.

"Your mum has decided to focus her attention on her gin and tonics," Dad says. Mum looks at him and snivels.

"I've given it my all," she says.

"Yes," Dad says. "It just hasn't been good enough." Mum clips him on the shoulder. I hold my breath.

"You mean bugger," she says, crying, and, getting up, walks unsteadily inside.

"*Tsk*," Alison says. "Why do you have to get plastered and be like that?"

"I have to be drunk to sleep with that old hag," Dad says.

"I'm not going to sit and listen to that," Alison says, getting up from her chair. I get up as well.

"Are you also not going listen to that, Samantha?"

"No," I say.

"And here I was, thinking you were a tough customer like your old man," he says to my back.

"Yes, but I'm not a meanie," I say, going inside.

"Phew," Dad says behind me. Alison has already got into the extra bed in my room. I go and brush my teeth.

"Why doesn't she just bin him?" I say. "Get a grip, run the hotel. He's never here anyway. She clings to him like a baby."

"Samantha. She brought us up. She had to, while he brought home the bacon," Alison says.

"With the help of a host of nannies and servants. It's not like she's worked herself into the ground. And it seems to me that it's been years since we were shipped off to boarding school."

"Do you think there'd be any home to return to if it wasn't for her?" Alison asks.

I don't say anything.

"If you're impressed with your dad and hate him at the same time, you really are a mess," she says.

I still don't say anything.

"Even if she did kick him out, the hotel wouldn't fix it, unless you want to go to a local school here in Tanga."

"What do you mean?" I say.

"This hotel makes next to no money. Certainly nowhere near enough to pay for your school and holidays in England."

"*Tsk*," I say.

"Besides, she drinks too much to be able to look after anything."

"Yes, and why does she drink? Because he's such a bastard," I say.

"She's scared," Alison says.

"Of what?"

"That he won't come back when he leaves. That he dies."

"He couldn't go fast enough in my opinion," I say.

"You know you don't mean that, Samantha."

"But he's back now," I say.

"Yes, but he's going to be off again."

"So?"

"She loves him," Alison says.

I don't say anything.

It's raining non-stop, even though the short rains ought to be over and the

84

long rains aren't due till February. But rain is tipping down, and water seeps through the restaurant roof, making the tablecloths soggy and forming puddles on the uneven concrete floor. No guests, neither at home nor at the hotel. Christmas is miserable. I think we ought to go to Dar es Salaam, but Dad says he hasn't got time.

"What about that Victor character – where's he going to be for New Year?" I ask.

"Why?" Dad asks.

"I'm just trying to make conversation," I say.

"We don't talk about my work – you know that," he says.

"Yes. Damn it," I say – he never wants to talk about his work.

"And you don't swear at home," he says.

"Jesus!" I say, going off to my room. The man swears like a sailor whenever something makes him angry, but the rest of us must keep up a polite front.

Alison is lying on my bed with a paperback. There's water coming through the ceiling in her old room. I sit down at the desk and make a start on the four papers that are due the day after my return to school. Whenever I'm not sure what to write, I ask Alison. She dictates – I write it down.

We spend New Year's Eve at Tanga Yacht Club. Welcome to 1984. It's tedium personified.

1984

Mud

And then I'm back at school. The little ones are shouting, running up and down the corridors – you have to kick your way through them. I spot Christian. White T-shirt, blue jeans. I stop to look at him. His eyes are dead as they glide over me – or does seeing me register? I'm not sure. I turn to follow him, but then I stop myself.

There are no cigarettes to be had at Mboyas'. I go into town after school with some Swedes; I tell them that I'm visiting a classmate who is ill. I can't find any cigarettes anywhere. I go to Kibo Coffee House and ask a guy who's sitting there, smoking.

"You can buy a puff," he says. I get myself a taxi. When it reaches school, I see Christian shovelling dirt out of the deep concrete ditches around the school's drive – it has to be done before the long rains start in February. Jarno is there as well. I pay the driver, get out and stand there looking at them, my hands at my sides. They're both wearing white T-shirts and blue jeans.

"How's it going?" I ask.

"How does it look like it's going?" Jarno asks. Christian looks at me with dead eyes.

"*Tsk*," he says, spits and continues digging.

"What did you do?" I ask. Jarno looks at Christian who looks into thin air and doesn't say anything. Jarno smiles:

"Christian keeps saying, 'I don't know – I don't care,' whenever Mrs Harrison asks him anything. It drives her round the bend."

"And you?"

"Behind with my homework," Jarno says.

"What about your clothes?" I ask.

"That's our look," Jarno says. "The Carlsberg Twins." I've heard the glue-sniffers call them that. Christian steals Carlsberg from his dad – the white corporates have all the short-supply goods imported and bribe the customs officers to let it through. There's no beer to be had on the market because the brewery in Arusha has run out of bottle tops, and they won't be getting any more until they've paid for the last shipment.

"Jarno, Christian," I say. "See you later."

"Right-o," Jarno says and starts loading the wheelbarrow. Christian doesn't say anything.

"See you later, Christian," I repeat. He looks at me, silent.

"O.K.?" I ask again.

"O.K.," he says, smiling just a little, thrusting his shovel into the hardened mud at the bottom of the ditch.

Connection

Today's lessons are over. I ought to be doing . . . something. What am I going to do with myself? I go in and call Tanga. There's a connection! The maid fetches Alison.

"I don't want to be here," I say.

"What's wrong?" she asks.

"I just can't stand it."

"Come on, Samantha – it's not that bad, you know."

"Yes, it is. I hate it."

"I can come up for your long weekend – then we can visit the Durants together," she says.

"But that's weeks from now," I say.

"Come on, Samantha."

"Yes, alright," I say. "How are you?"

"You know . . . Mum and Dad, things aren't going so well."

"Is he home?" I ask.

"Yes. I think he's actually . . ." The line goes. I try ringing her again – no luck.

Black market

There are almost no Indians left at school today. They're afraid. The homes, shops and factories of the Indians are being searched, and people are being arrested and detained without conviction.

I catch sight of Masuma in her white badminton get-up, getting out of a chauffeured car in the car park.

"Masuma?" I call. "Are you alright?"

"I want to play badminton," she says.

"Has something happened at home?" Masuma looks nervously over her shoulder. "Come," I say, putting an arm around her shoulder – we're walking down towards Karibu Hall. Masuma start snivelling but pulls herself together – no tears.

"They've been to my father's factory in Hime, but they didn't find anything. But we've had word from Kerbala – our sacred town – there's been a vision of blood and violence in Africa. And my mother's had a vision – it was an omen of war. Things are really dangerous right now."

"But what's happening?"

"Tanzania has shut its boundaries to us, stopping all international flights. All the Shia Muslims in the world have heard of the vision – our family call us to check that we're O.K., but what can they do? We're living on the mercy of the Africans until the day when that mercy runs out – and then we die."

She starts snivelling again.

"In all likelihood nothing will happen, you know," I say. "Tanzania isn't like that."

"You don't know that," Masuma says. Christian isn't at Karibu Hall.

"He probably thought you weren't coming," I say. Masuma shakes her head, goes back to the car and is driven home.

In the course of the day, pupils hear from their parents in Dar that the beaches at Oyster Bay are loaded with stereos, video recorders, T.V. sets and all sorts of other things that can only be had on the black market. People are throwing their stuff into the ocean because the mere fact that they own something implies that they have broken the law. The authorities are coming down hard on illegal financial activity; that's why they have been targeting the Indians – they're the ones who operate much of the black market.

Friday afternoon our lessons are cancelled. The government has called out the general public; they want demonstrations against the black market. The government are digging their own grave – if the black market were to disappear, it would become blatantly obvious to anyone and every-one just how inept the socialist economy is. The Indians keep the country ticking over. Obviously, we are not invited to the demonstration: after all we're foreigners and eager participants in the black market.

Monitor lizard

Alison writes that she can't come up to see me at half-term after all: the hotel is too busy, and she has to go to Dar es Salaam. But she is looking forward to my coming back on holiday. Shit.

"Are you coming to the party tonight, Samantha?" Baltazar asks me outside the dining hall Friday after lunch. He is two years above me. Great at sports. He takes my hand. "I'd like to dance with you." He's blue-black and sinewy. I notice Stefano standing close to Truddi and trying to be cool, but keeping a constant eye on me. I smile at Baltazar.

"Yes, of course," I say. Baltazar has to go, football practice. Stefano passes me and Tazim.

"So, you're whore to the locals now," he says casually.

"She's got no arse, Stefano," I say.

"What do you mean?" Tazim asks.

"Truddi," I say. Tazim shakes her head at me. She promises me that I can borrow her yellow T-shirt tonight, and then she leaves to go to her priest – confession. I should have been a Catholic; all Tazim has to do is tell him what's she's been up to, say a Hail Mary and that's that sorted. But, as it happens, she never does anything wrong. "What have you done this time?" I ask.

"It's my thoughts," Tazim says. "I have wicked thoughts."

"Is that it?"

"Plans," she says. "I've got wicked plans as well."

"Do they involve Salomon?" I ask. She smiles a wry little smile and leaves. I can't find Panos, so instead I go and get the cigarettes I've taped under Truddi's bed – sometimes they do a house raid. And then I walk across the playing fields, leaving the school grounds and turn right towards the river, down a path on the steep slope. It's been dry for a while now, so I can skip from one stone to the next all the way over to the other side where I walk up stream a bit until I sit down and light up. I stare at a monitor lizard chasing a gecko on the other side of the river. Its eyes are devoid of feeling. I wipe a tear from the corner of my eye. I suck hard on the cigarette, making the filter go warm and soft between my fingers. I hear a sound further down. I quickly squash the cigarette under my foot and throw the butt down the slope. I sit and wait, looking at the place where the path curves. It's probably only a woman on her way to the market . . . Jarno – running. His T-shirt in his hand, his stomach muscles hard under a thin layer of skin, glistening with sweat.

Mama mbege

"Sam the Man," he says and stops, smiling, huffing and puffing – his long hair is hanging down over his piss-coloured eyes.

"What's the rush?" I ask.

"I'm off to the *pombe*-house, *mama mbege*," he says.

"Are you running up to get some *mbege*?"

"A couple of times a week I am," Jarno says. *Mbege* is the local beer, made with millet – it leaves you both drunk and feeling full; it's thick and luke-warm.

"O.K.," I say and go with him. We reach the edge of the little village and the *pombe*-house – *pombe* is simply a collective term for alcoholic drinks. A couple of local men are squatting in the tidily swept courtyard. We sit down on the benches at one of the tables. Jarno greets the men and the mama, and we are served drinks in a calabash that has been stuck on to a stick. Jarno drinks, lights a cigarette. I take a gulp. It's not easy to get down if you're not used to it. There's a laugh – Ebenezer, the security guard, steps through the opening in the hedge.

"Samantha and Jarno," he says, nodding. "You two are proper *waswahili*."

"Too right," Jarno says and asks the mama for *gongo* – a potent moonshine. The locals buy molasses from T.P.C. – it's a residual product of sugar production – to mix it into their animal fodder. But in reality they use most of it to make alcohol. *Gongo* – it's like being hit over the head with a club.

The party tonight is complete with a barbecue at Kishari House – the house where the oldest boys live, and Jarno has just moved there as the youngest of that lot.

"You alright?" he asks, looking at me sideways.

"I'm fine. Are you playing tonight?"

He nods and looks blindly ahead of him through his hair. Hands me the cigarette and then says nothing. That's what you get for spending time with a Finn.

"See you around," I say and wriggle away in my shorts. It's getting darker by the minute. I empty my cigarette pack of the last cigarettes and keep matches at the ready so I can set the paper on fire in case any wild dogs come running – dogs are afraid of fire, and the wild ones may have rabies.

Jarno doesn't have time to catch me up as I walk home along the river. Maybe he's taken a different route. The others have gone to the party already. I shower. Pull on my jeans and Tazim's yellow T-shirt, popping on my flip-flops. I head towards Kishari House. Aziz is minding the barbecue with two other of the oldest guys – they only need to pass their exams, and they'll be done. I find Tazim. They're playing the worst kind of English rock. I look through the window into the common room, which has been cleared of furniture to make room for dancing. It's not Jarno at the stereo.

"Did you get absolution?" I ask Tazim.

"Yes," she says. "Now I can start afresh." But she doesn't look too happy.

"Did you get absolution for your sinful plans?"

"No, God didn't like those."

"Are you going to give them up then?" I ask.

"God doesn't get to decide everything."

"Has anyone seen Jarno?" Aziz asks.

"No, but that's no reason not to put some decent music on," one of the older girls says.

"It's locked inside his cupboard," Aziz says. And just then Jarno comes running through the garden gate, a fine layer of dust on his sweaty skin and a big smile on his face. He runs through the crowd. They grin, applaud, saying, "Here's Mr *dee-jay* – the man with the music." Shortly after, the first crisp notes are heard. Baltazar has seen me – he brings me a glass of fruit punch. We should have got a bottle of *Konyagi* to spike the punch.

"Thanks," I say, taking the glass. I can still feel the effects of the *mbege*.

"Shall I get you something to eat?" he asks.

"Yes, please," I say and feel happy. I watch him as he walks over to get me something. Freshly ironed, tight-fitting shirt. I taste the punch; some-one *has* spiked it with *Konyagi*.

Dance

Later we move inside where Jarno is gearing the music up for dancing. He has changed into his uniform. White T-shirt, blue jeans, hair flopping down over his eyes. Several people have moved onto the floor. Panos is standing by the wall with Christian – he is dressed in the same way as Jarno.

Stefano is dancing with Truddi. Diana is dancing with a glue-sniffer. Shakila is standing next to Jarno, looking at his tapes. Some of the older pupils are out on the floor, dancing – among them Sharif, who is from Yemen but who looks exactly like Michael Jackson and has practised his moves. Sharif is dancing with Katja – a Finnish blonde from Jarno's year. Afterwards he dances with Shakila, and I see Christian following her with his eyes – when Christian's little sister had just died, they went out for a while, but it didn't work out. Stefano glares at me but keeps looking away every time I look at him. Baltazar pulls me out on the floor. Eddy Grant is singing "Electric Avenue", and afterwards there's a slow song, Hot Chocolate: "It Started With a Kiss". I lean into Baltazar; I can feel how toned the muscles of his back are through the fabric of his shirt.

"Shall we pop outside for a smoke?" Baltazar asks when the music is coming to an end.

"Yes," I say. We leave the floor. I am aware of Stefano looking at us. We go into the garden and out of the garden gate. Baltazar lights a cigarette. Only, it's not actually a cigarette.

"I see," I say.

"We need some *Jah-power*," he says. I smoke it.

"I don't want to go back to the party," I say.

"Why not?"

"Because . . . Stefano is telling lies about me."

"I'll deal with him," Baltazar says.

"How?"

"I'll tell him that if he doesn't stop it, I'll beat him to a pulp."

"Here," I say, handing him the spliff and leaning up against him.

"You're very beautiful, Samantha," he says, embracing me, kissing me, grabbing my bum a bit too hard. I can feel his thingy up against me. Why isn't he caressing my breasts? I slip a hand down and grab on to it through the trouser fabric. He moans. He opens his belt, the button, pulls the zip down.

"Hold your horses," I say.

"Please, just do it," he whispers and catches my hand. Of course I want to feel it, but . . . He guides my hand, and when it gets to where it's meant to be, I feel the softest skin. I allow my hand to circle his cock and press it. He's making sounds – like a puppy. It's grotesque. I pull at his cock.

"Do you like it?" I ask.

"Ohh, yes." He shudders; I can feel something wet on my hand. Sperm.

"Thanks," he says, taking a step back, doing up his trousers. Thanks? Here I am, nowhere near satisfied. What's he going to do about that, I wonder. I wipe my hand on a tuft of grass.

"Let's go inside," Baltazar says.

"Why?" I ask.

"I'm thirsty," he says and starts walking.

Monday Christian and Jarno are sent home for a week. One of the teachers caught them drinking beer at Moshi Hotel on Sunday afternoon. When you've been suspended for drinking once, people look up to you. But you have to be pretty stupid to get caught. If you're not stupid, you have to want to be caught. Maybe to impress someone. Christian isn't stupid. Christian wants to impress me. But what kind of impression is it he wants to make?

That night I disappear into the darkness with Baltazar. I'm not in love with him. He's not in love with me either. We snog. He puts my hand on his thingy, and I touch him, and he moans and pulls at my tits until I tell him to stop. It is what it is – it doesn't really matter. I go back to Kiongozi House. Truddi is standing at the door, hanging about.

"Who was it this time, Samantha?" she asks with a sigh. I stop.

"Sam," I say. "*Sam the Man* – call me Sam."

"Why? It's ugly. It's a boy's name," Truddi says.

"My point exactly," I say. "A man among sheep."

"Where have you been?" Truddi asks again. I push past her, not bothering to answer.

The finger

Monday all the boarders are informed that there's rabies in the area. Some of the girls from Nikele House were attacked on their way back from the party Friday night – one of them was bitten and is now being treated. For now, the boarders who live in houses outside the normal perimeter of the school must be escorted by a guard and have to go together when they go back to their houses in the evenings. We're also told to make sure we go as groups when we leave school grounds during the day.

Baltazar opens my jeans and sticks his finger into me that night between the eucalyptus trees at the end of the playing fields, and I give him a hand job.

"Stop. No, I'm not having any of that," I tell him when he tries to pull off my trousers.

Stefano has stopped talking to me. Baltazar has threatened him. I don't really talk to anyone. Tazim is flirting with Salomon. Tazim's wicked plan is to have Salomon pop her cherry.

One afternoon I'm running about, trying to find Panos – to ask him if he wants to go smoke a cigarette with me. He's on the playing fields. I see his barrel-shaped body from a long way away. He's strong. The boys in Kishari House have a tradition of catching the younger boys, sticking their heads in the toilet and flushing. Aziz got his arm broken when he tried that on with Panos.

We head out behind the stables and almost bump into Sharif with his hand up Finnish Katja's shirt and his tongue all the way down her throat.

"Excuse me," I say.

"Let me show you something," Panos says and pulls me along between the stalks of sweetcorn to the edge of the field. He points at something. *Bhangi* – six great, big plants.

"How did you find those?"

"They're mine," Panos says. "I planted them."

"How?" I ask.

"All you have to do is root about a bit in the soil with a stick and dump a handful of seeds into the hole right before the long rains, and Mother Nature sees to the rest. It just comes rushing up. The only problem is how to dry the stuff," Panos says.

"What are you going to do?"

"I keep it in the attic above the room next to mine – Sandeep's room – the one with the cat."

"In Kijana House?"

"Yes, you can lift out one of the ceiling sheets and climb up between the rafters. I've put it right above Sandeep's bed."

"Aren't you worried you might get caught?"

"I'm fed up with paying through my nose to Emerson or Alwyn." Emerson is in direct competition with Alwyn over control of the *bhangi* market at school.

Black man's skin

Stefano has got hold of a black 1950s leather jacket with zips everywhere. He's always wearing it in the evenings. Baltazar and I are standing under the eucalyptus trees at the end of the playing fields. I see Stefano as he passes the lamp on the end of the changing rooms – the boys have to leave now if they are to get back to Kijito House on time.

"The idiot is wearing a leather jacket in the tropics," I say.

"He's a bastard," Baltazar says, and it's true, but . . . Baltazar says something when Stefano passes us:

"You're such a pansy in that jacket," Baltazar says. Stefano stops. It's impossible to see his face in the dark.

"Do you know what my jacket is made of?" he asks.

"Pig's skin, to go with the rest of you," I say.

"Little black children from Angola," Stefano says. Baltazar gives a jolt – he lets go of me and, disappearing from between my hands, is running.

"Baltazar – no," I shout. Stefano makes a run for it, dashing round the corner of the playing fields where the road leads to Kishari and Kijito Houses. Baltazar is on his tail. Baltazar is fast, long-limbed. Neither of them says a word. I follow them. I'm almost at the corner of the playing fields, and in the light coming from the nearest villa. I see them pass – Baltazar is catching up. Then there's the sound of feet skidding on the ground. Stefano screams. I'm still running. There's the sound of punches.

"You stupid fuck," Baltazar says. The darkness is shifting quickly.

"Stop it, Baltazar," I shout. He's sitting on top of Stefano, who is lying on his front. Baltazar is grasping Stefano's thick black hair and slamming his face into the sun-baked earth. Stefano is screaming. I am crying. Baltazar gets up, spits on Stefano. He turns to me.

"You still want him? You can have him." He leaves.

"No," I say. Stefano groans and gets onto his hands and knees – blood and snot dripping from his face. I can hear a group of boys coming across the playing fields. I start running – back – past them.

"What?" they say as I pass them in the light from the house. They hear Stefano's groans. "What happened?" they ask, hurrying over to him. I run up to Kiongozi House – I go straight to the toilet, where I sit, trembling, in one of the cubicles. Stefano has told everyone that I went all the way with him when we were together. Baltazar thinks I'm turning him down because I miss Stefano. How grotesque is that?

Half an hour later Seppo comes for me – to take me to the Headmaster. Apparently Owen wants to see me.

"I don't know what happened," I say. "It was too dark." Stefano is at K.C.M.C. with a broken nose – but he refuses to say who did it. Baltazar is being watched – everyone knows it was him.

"Go away," I say when he speaks to me.

Ringworm

During break at 10.00, snacks, juice and tea are served to the boarders outside the dining hall. I take a doughnut and some tea. Baltazar is standing with Aziz. I go over to them with Tazim.

"Here's my woman now," Baltazar says, and I smile the way I'm meant to.

"Has she made a man of you yet?" Aziz asks, idiot that he is.

"I became a man a long time ago," Baltazar says. I don't think so.

"But is she any good?" Aziz asks.

"Oh shut up, will you?" I say and allow Baltazar to put his arm around me.

"But you have done it, right?" Aziz says and pretends to be shocked by the possibility that we might not have had sex.

"Of course we have," Baltazar says.

"Of course we bloody haven't," I say and let go of him, taking two steps away.

"It's nothing to be ashamed of," Baltazar says.

"It's nothing to lie about," I say.

"Why won't you admit it?" he asks.

"I have not had sex with you," I say. "And I'm not going to either." I turn around.

"You're a slag and a liar, Sam," Baltazar says. I turn around and look at him.

"And you're a dreamer," I say. "Your cock's no bigger than a ringworm and your brain's even smaller." I walk off, holding it in all day. It's only when I'm standing under the shower that evening that I allow the tears to come.

Christian is mad at me for going out with Baltazar. Panos is being made a fool of by Truddi or by himself. Most of the boys feel intimidated by me. Tazim says I'm too full on, but that's what they want, isn't it? She, on the other hand, has started holding hands with Salomon.

"Tonight is the night," she whispers to me in our study when we've finished prep and have a couple of hours to ourselves before bedtime.

"What?" I ask. Tazim raises her eyebrows. "But have you thought about protection?" I ask.

"Yes, of course I have," she says. "Now wish me luck."

"Good luck," I say, and Tazim goes outside where Salomon is waiting for her in the dark. The Pope is aggrieved – not only is Tazim going to whore, she is going to do it with a heretic from the Ethiopic Orthodox Church, who are not proper Catholics. And they mean to use those satanic condoms. Whoring, heresy and condoms – a triple sin. An hour and a half later Tazim returns and heads into the shower. I go out there with my toothbrush. I look at her.

"Not all it was cracked up to be," she says.

"Are you happy you did it?" I ask. Tazim shrugs:

"Can't take it back now, can I?" she says. "Yes, I suppose." I go over to her.

"Did he nibble your bean?" I ask.

"Samantha!" Tazim says and splashes water on me.

"You should make him do that. It works a treat."

The Breezeway List

The Breezeway List is hung on the noticeboards on the way to the dining hall. It's people from Year Twelve who write it: Who is the best looking, who is the most romantic, the most talkative, the most generally liked, most athletic, most bookish? Who might reasonably be expected to achieve success? And finally, who is the most likely to end up in prison?

Sam the Man.

O.K., I am the loser, bound for prison. But I'm on the list. I am a character. What about the rest of them? They mean nothing – they're just padding, filling out the list.

Most of the girls don't speak to me. The guys are cross that the girls won't shag them when I was willing to – with both Stefano and Baltazar, or so people think. And both Stefano and Baltazar are disappointed that I'll have nothing to do with either of them. The girls are nothing to me. They build a fort for a few select people and oppose everyone else; me. They'll climb as high as they like and push anyone else down in order to stay up there themselves. It's fine by me.

Sam the Man – can count on going to prison; O.K., I can handle that. But life could be better. I hang out with the glue-sniffers and with Panos.

Stefano gets together with Shakila; it's the broken nose that does it – she feels sorry for him. I almost can't bear it. Christian isn't talking to me. And Baltazar is with Angela of all people. Panos can't give up chasing Truddi even though he's getting nowhere with her. And in the end, Diana gets in there, swapping spit with Panos in the middle of the playground one evening because she is angry with Truddi for going about with some new trollop from France who everyone thinks is so exciting just because she wears fancy clothes and uses lots of make-up.

Jarno and Christian return from their two-week suspension. They have been to Morogoro and Dar es Salaam on a binge.

"It was brilliant," Christian says, and Jarno smiles and nods slowly so that his long hair flops into his eyes, and then they both walk away without telling me anything. Christian has stopped caring about me. How is that possible?

Going home

In a week we'll finally be halfway through the second term. I am lying on my bed facing the wall. I wish Alison would give her trip to Dar es Salaam a miss and come here instead. We have a long weekend with Friday and Monday off, but Mum tells me over the phone that she is unwell. At all events going to Tanga by bus is too far when it's only for a few days. Dad is away on business – no-one knows where. And there's no-one in Arusha I can stay with. Who can I ask? It's awkward. I can't bring myself to call Mountain Lodge because Mick is in England, and why would they want to have me come and stay with them? In the end, I go all the way down to tell *mama* Hussein that I have nowhere to go and can I stay with her?

But then I can't bring myself to go inside and ask, so I go all the way back.

Thursday Minna gives me a lift to the bus station.

"Bye," I say and jump out of the car and into the smell of rotting rubbish drying in the sun. There's the usual jumble of black-marketeers, taxi drivers, street vendors and pathetic conmen. Yes, I am white, but everyone can tell that I am from these parts and consequently a waste of time – only the most stupid of them would try to con me.

"Get lost," I tell a couple of little boys who try to guide me onto a particular bus to make a teensy commission. I check all the buses for Tanga and find one that is almost full but which still has a few empty seats – that way I won't have to wait so long. The buses leave when they are full, and then they pick people up as they go. I pick an aisle seat on a seat for two where two people are already seated. But they're slender people, and as you have to sit three on each seat, being three slender people is definitely best. Otherwise you might get some big mama with a baby on her back who squashes in to be the third person, making the other two sit in a sweaty vice between the lady's abundant arse and the body of the bus. I have been on a bus bound for Arusha with a big child on my lap and a goat between my ankles licking the salt from my sweaty toes. I am thirsty – I have had almost nothing to drink because the bus only stops once on the way. We wait. A street vendor pushes away another vendor who tries to undercut him. The cardboard box of goods goes flying through the air – biscuits and juice and nuts are spread on the ground. They're both just boys. They fight, African style: total aggression but no coordination – their arms are swinging all over the place but only hit arbitrarily and without any force. The bus is parked in the sun, the temperature is rising; the air is stinking and humid. Well, go on then – get us on the move – so we can have some air let into the bus. There are seventy-six seats. I count them to pass the time. We are one hundred and twenty-five people, plus children and all the luggage that wouldn't fit up on the roof. I've only brought a small bag, which I've got on my lap. Finally, we're moving; a waft of a breeze reaches me. On the way out of town we pick up more people who push their way down the aisle, while the conductor has to make his way through the bus to collect money. A young man in the aisle is pushed over towards me – a faint, sweetish smell of shit is coming from his arse. I push back. "That's enough," I say in Swahili.

"I'm sorry," he says.

"That's alright," I say – it's not his fault that he can only wash his arse in water when he's had a shit – soap is a rare luxury in a Tanzanian shithouse. First we go over a short patch of good tarmac until we reach Road Junction at Himo, and then all hell begins, because from here on the dirt road has been wrecked by floods and heavy traffic.

I try to relax in the bus – to vegetate. Dad's away on business, and Mum's not well. It's not going to be much fun.

Piss in the air

A man is struggling to get down the aisle and presses himself onto a seat two rows ahead of me where three men are already seated. And then he disappears again. Has he sat down on the floor? I sit up straight. Soon after he reappears with a Coke bottle in his hand and starts opening the window. Oh bugger. I reach across the two slumbering people next to me, hitting one of them on the shoulder with my elbow, because the window is stuck, and I need to get it shut, while telling the people behind me to close their windows.

"Sorry," I say to the man I hit. He looks confused. And then the urine from the Coke bottle splashes against the window I just closed.

"Would it be too much to warn people before you start pouring piss out of the window?" I say loudly in Swahili. The man has got up to straighten his clothes. He looks at me with dead eyes, before struggling down the aisle again. Several of the women tut loudly – we have to go without water while he splashes his piss about.

"Thanks," says the man next to me, and we drift back into a haze until we reach the petrol station in Mkomazi that means we're about halfway there; it's time for a pee. Street vendors throng around the bus to sell various snacks and drinks. People get on with live chickens and the stink becomes more complex because some of the passengers have bought dried fish and the fishy smell mixes with the smells of stale sweat, dirt, oranges, shit and pureed baby food. We go on with the Usambara Mountains on our left-hand side. People at the roadside are selling sacks of charcoal. Pillars of smoke are rising even though it's illegal; without the shadow of the trees the rainwater evaporates too quickly from the ground, which is then eroded by heavy rainfalls because there aren't any roots to hold on to it.

On we go, down the bumpy road – the driver maintains a steady pace while also keeping the bus from going into some of the worst potholes, to avoid wrecking the shock absorbers. Through Mazinde, Mombo, Maurui, Korogwe, Segera, Hale, Muheza, and finally Ngomeni – the last real town before Tanga. It's getting dark when we finally reach the bus station. I take a taxi to Baobab Hotel. Mum is lying sweating in her bed. That night I dream that I'm drowning. I wake up in the dark, and the bed is soaking wet – it's bucketing down and rain is coming through the roof. I push my bed into a different corner of the room and go and lie down on the sofa in the sitting room, but there's no mosquito net so the mosquitoes have a field day. While I'm home, I sail and swim, and drink gin and smoke cigarettes, and am bored all day Friday, Saturday, Sunday, and then I take the bus back to Moshi Monday morning. Whenever anyone asks, I tell them I had the best time ever.

Eroticism

I am making myself faint. I squat, and then I hyperventilate. Svein and Rune are standing there, ready to catch me. I get up, everything goes black. I like it. I feel myself falling before I am completely out.

Lying down, there's a light on the other side of my eyelids. Something's touching me. Someone's touching me. I open my eyes.

"Cut it out," I say. "Who was that groping my tits?" I am looking up at Christian, who is standing next to me, looking irked.

"Hey, don't look at me," he says. Svein and Rune are looking at him angrily.

"I know you didn't do it, Christian. You think it's wrong. It's one of those damned glue-sniffers."

"We didn't do anything," Svein says. "We just caught you." Rune sniggers.

"Rune," I say. "You're such a baby. The only time in your entire life when you're going to be totally covered in cunt juice – do you know when that is?" I get up.

"Next weekend in Arusha," Rune says. "Black cunt."

"Not bloody likely," I say. "You'll have to make do with the time your mummy squeezed you out."

Svein grins.

"Shut up," Rune says. I start hyperventilating again. Christian sneers as he turns around and walks away. He is disgusted with me. He wishes it were him groping my tits.

Winemaker

I am sitting on the stairs outside Kiongozi House, so that I can go inside if Baltazar shows up. Instead Panos comes over with Gideon, Emerson Strand's twelve-year-old little brother – he has just started school and is so tanned he looks like a blond Arab.

"Ask her," Panos says when they're standing right in front of me. Gideon looks from Panos to me.

"Do you want to buy some wine?" he asks.

"Are you kidding?" I ask. Where can he have got wine from unless he's stolen it from his parents?

"When I say I have wine, I have wine," Gideon says and nods with a shrewd look in his eyes.

"*Dodoma*?" I ask; it's the local wine, named for the town in the middle of the country that the authorities claim is the seat of government instead of Dar es Salaam. Dodoma is made up entirely of dust, only concrete buildings and dying vines that yield a fluid that will burn the skin off your tongue.

"Homebrew," Gideon says.

"Did *you* . . ." I start. And he's the brother of the *bhangi*-pusher Emerson. "What did you use?"

"Sugar cane."

I laugh at him, "I value my eyesight too much for that."

He looks at me arrogantly.

"I see you perfectly clearly."

"And?"

"I'm not blind," he says and looks at Panos. "Do you see me?" he asks. Panos smiles:

"Perfectly. And my hangover's perfectly real as well."

O.K., then. I order a bottle. We arrange to meet down by the old swimming pool where I'll bring my school bag.

"How did you make it?" I ask Gideon when we meet.

"You're asking for secrets of the trade, you know," he says.

"Oh, go on," I say.

"Alright," the boy says and starts explaining how he bought the sugar cane on the market in town three weeks ago, cut them up and mixed the pulp with water and cane sugar and a dash of dried yeast in a big white bucket he had stolen from the school's kitchen. He buried the bucket in the banana plantation behind the dining hall, with a plastic straw sticking up to allow the wine to ferment. "Next time I'll make apple wine," he says.

"I'm impressed."

"How about a pipe?" he asks.

"Do you want to smoke as well? What do you think your brother will say to that?" I giggle.

"No, man. Do you want to *buy* a pipe?"

"A pipe?"

"Made from a stick of bamboo that's cut in half on each side of a joint, with a pipe of stainless steel for a mouthpiece," he says.

"And what would I do with that?"

"Smoke dried elephant's turd. What do you think?"

"I have a perfectly good meerschaum pipe."

"Do you have *bhangi*?"

"You sell that as well?"

"My brother does," Gideon says. I smile at him.

"Off you go," I say and go back to Kiongozi House. What am I going to do with the bottle? Maybe Tazim wants to share it with me over the weekend, either around the back or at night in the toilet. The toilet! Of course. I go in and lift the lid off one of the cisterns, putting the bottle in it – that way it'll be nice and cool when we're having it.

Study raid

I haven't said anything to Tazim about the wine – I'm just going to wake her up when everyone is asleep as if we were going out for a smoke. I'm lying there quietly. Truddi gets up and goes to the toilet. I hear the faint sound of the toilet flushing and something clattering. She comes back not long after. I'm going to have to wait until I'm sure she is asleep, but Truddi is tossing and turning. What is she doing? Is she masturbating or what? A door is slammed in the hall.

"Minna, Minna," Diana shouts, and someone's knocking on a door somewhere. Truddi skips out of bed. Tazim wakes up as well. We all go out into the hall. The floor is flooded. Minna emerges from her flat in her nightie, with her hair all rumpled.

"What's happened?" she asks.

"One of the toilets is broken," Diana says. Bugger. Minna goes out to have a look at it. Almost everyone has got up by now. We follow her. The cistern of my toilet has broken, and water is gushing out. Minna fetches

Seppo who comes and turns off a tap. He fishes the broken wine bottle out of the cistern and sniffs it.

"Wine," he says. Minna turns around, giving us all a harsh look – her eyes seem to look at me especially.

"Who put it there?" We all stand there, looking at each other, but most of them are looking at me.

"It was Sam who had the wine," Truddi says.

"What are you talking about? That's not my wine," I say.

"Samantha," Minna says. "If it's your wine, you have to come clean."

"It's not mine. Truddi's just mad at me because she doesn't know how to be with Stefano because she's such a frigid cow."

"Samantha!" Minna says.

"Go to your studies and stay there," Seppo says. Soon after he returns with Minna. It's a midnight study raid. Minna finds my cigarettes taped to Truddi's bed, but Truddi gets off because Minna thinks they're mine.

"Then you'd better punish me, even though you have no proof," I say. "Apparently I'm to blame for everything that happens here."

"Come off it, Samantha," Minna says.

"Then you stop protecting that bitch."

"I'll have none of that language at this school."

"I will," I tell her. Afterwards Minna and Seppo go straight to the boys' section of the house and carry out a raid there as well.

Catnip

There is an uneasy atmosphere at breakfast. In the boy's section they found cigarettes, *Konyagi*, condoms, a little *bhangi*, pipes, dirty magazines, girls' underwear and superglue; of course the glue belonged to a Norwegian – they're constantly sniffing the stuff. Everyone wants to know who had the underwear and who it belonged to, because we all have nametags sewn into all our clothes. Gideon tells everyone that it was Truddi's knickers, but they were found in the toilets so no-one can tell who had nicked them.

Panos and I go up towards Kijana House. Seppo is standing in the opening to the quadrangle building in front of the students.

"You have to wait here until Sally comes for you one at a time – we're conducting a house raid." Panos shrugs and leans against the open metal gate that's locked at night, making it necessary to climb over the wall in one of the corners of the courtyard if you want to get out and about. Salomon is standing by himself, muttering about how it's like living in a police state. Then we hear Sally's voice, and everyone falls quiet.

"Sandeep, you can't have your cat with you if it pees in your study," she says and steps out into the hall. Sandeep follows her:

"It doesn't pee," he says. "It's housetrained."

"The house reeks of cat pee," Sally tells him and looks over at us, the people standing outside the gate. Panos speaks up:

"Maybe there's some dead squirrel lying rotting in the attic – that can be quite smelly. I've sometimes heard them scurrying about up there at night."

Sally calls for Phillippo and instructs him to take down the ceiling sheets. He finds three *bhangi* plants above Sandeep's bed.

"Panos," Sally sighs.

"What?" Panos says. "I don't smoke that stuff. Too Hinduist by far for me. It's subversive – they say so in *Daily News*." The newspaper often writes proclamations to the young, encouraging them to not smoke catnip. We use the pages as toilet paper from time to time when there's no paper to be had.

"Salomon?" Sally says.

"It's not mine," he says.

"And I had you down for a proper Rasta," Panos says, laughing.

"I am Rasta," Salomon says. Sandeep is sent out – Panos is called in. But of course there's nothing in his room – he kept it all above Sandeep's bed.

"I blame the Americans," Salomon says.

"What for?" I ask.

"The weed is illegal in the States because it was the drug of choice for the

111

black slaves: cheap, healthy and clean. And it blesses the user with divine insight. The white man has always feared the sacred weed because he doesn't understand the spirit world and the communion of natural man with the spirits. That's why the imperialists force the African states to make the use of the weed illegal – they make it a condition for helping us overcome the damages that their own slave hunts and colonialism inflicted on our continent, while the exploitation continues with them luring our best minds away with the promises of great salaries and stealing our natural resources but paying us only pennies. And instead of the sacred weed they want us to dumb down our minds and bodies with Babylonian fluids." He's talking about alcohol. It's a non-stop flow of pseudo-religious Rasta-babble with him. What Tazim sees in him, I really don't know.

Arousal

We have to be indoors early. *Mama* Hussein – the school nurse who is houseboss at Kijoto House – is coming to see us. We're excited. *Mama* Hussein is one of the two locals who are employed by the school, not counting of course the gardeners, cooks, security guards, cleaning staff and all that. Hussein is half Arab and half African from Zanzibar; she is a rather large lady, a single mother with two boys and very abrupt in her ways.

"I'm not supposed to talk to you about reproduction – sex – because you're not supposed to have sex at school," she says. "But you might have sex in your school holidays, and it's important that you know about these things, because boys don't care what happens. They don't think when they're aroused." Some of the girls titter. "And you don't want to ruin yourselves." She explains everything so that everyone can understand it. Minna comes through the door from the flat she shares with Seppo, which separates the boys' and the girls' sections of Kiongozi House.

"You can't tell them these things," Minna says, blushing.

"Never you mind what I do. Don't interrupt me," *mama* Hussein says and continues. Minna traipses quickly back into her flat, slamming the door behind her.

"Truddi?" I say when we're lying in our beds with the lights turned off that evening.

"Yes?" she says.

"You be careful you don't get pregnant when you put your knickers on, yes?" I say.

"Why?" Truddi asks.

"Because all the boys have used them as a wank rag," I say.

"You're such a cow," Truddi says.

Tazim sniggers into her pillow.

The next day *mama* Hussein has a stormy look on her face. Seppo told Mr Owen about yesterday, and *mama* Hussein has been called to his office for a serious talking to.

A visit

The Headmaster's secretary comes in in the middle of my last lesson and tells me to go to his office.

"Why?" I ask as I walk down the corridor with her.

"I don't know," she says. What can I have done? Smoked cigarettes? – yes, all the time. Drinking? – not recently. Stolen? – no. Handed in my papers? – haven't done that either. Maybe it's just my personality that is a matter for dispute. We walk through the door, and there he is.

"Victor!" I say.

"Hello, Samantha," he says and gets up to give me a hug. "I'm your uncle," he whispers in my ear before saying out loud, "I brought you some things from your mum."

"Oh, lovely," I say and look at Owen. "Yes, well, this is my uncle Victor then." I look back at Victor. "How long are you staying?" I ask.

"I have to leave later today. But I can take you out for lunch," he says.

"O.K.," I say.

"So long as you're back in time for prep," Owen says, smiling.

"O.K.," I say. And off we go in Victor's Land Rover to a place called the Golden Shower Restaurant, which is just to the east of the town. "What did you bring me from my mum?"

"I've never met your mum," Victor says. "It was just something I made up to get to see you. No-one knows I'm here." What am I supposed to say to that? I ask him where he's been. In a training camp in Uganda for Tutsies from Burundi. We order.

"And two beers, yes?" he says, looking at me questioningly.

"Yes," I say.

"So, how's life at that school of yours?" he asks. "How are those boys?"

"I can't really tell *you*, can I?" I giggle.

"I'm not easily shocked," Victor says.

"They're babies, the lot of them," I say.

"I bet they're gagging for it," Victor says. I'm actually blushing. "Aren't they?" he says.

"Yes, absolutely gagging," I say. "Boys are like that."

"Yes," Victor says and smiles at me.

"Are you like that as well?" I ask.

"I used to be. But these days I can wait," he says. We eat and drink our beers, smoke cigarettes, go for a stroll in the garden where there are clusters of little orange trumpet flowers absolutely everywhere. I pick one and suck the sweet nectar out from the bottom of it. "Is that good?" Victor asks.

"The best," I say. He picks one and, winking at me, pops it in his mouth, sucking it and smacking his lips.

"Yes, that *is* sweet juice," Victor says and smiles at me in a way that makes me look away. He drives me back to school when it starts to get dark. We get out of his Land Rover in the car park. I go over to his side. "It was lovely seeing you again, Samantha. I hope we'll meet in Tanga soon and then you can teach me how to dive."

"Oh, I'll teach you," I say and throw my arms around his neck, pressing him close against me.

"Careful now. You're just a schoolgirl," he says and keeps his hands on my back – doesn't try to move them anywhere else. I plant my lips onto his mouth and push my tongue forward. He gives a jolt, and opens his lips, but I let go of him and walk away. Oh yes, I can shock him.

Holiday under lock and key

Between the second and third term we only get two and a half weeks' holiday. I'm banking on Alison's being home and on it being great. Maybe we can go to Dar together. But in the end it's nothing like that. Mum leaves a message for me, telling me that Dad is coming to pick me up. The day before the end of term I am called to the Headmaster's office. Dad is sitting there with Owen. I start sweating. Maybe Victor has told Dad that I kissed him.

"Hi, Dad," I say.

"Samantha," he says. "Sit down." I sit down and look at Dad, then at Owen, then at Dad again. Owen clears his throat. "I've had a letter from school about your bad behaviour, your bad grades and all the papers you haven't handed in," Dad says. "So the two of us are going to go home to Tanga, and you are going to do your homework for the next two weeks."

"But . . ." I start, but then I stop myself.

"I've got a complete list here," Dad says and pats some papers in front of him. "You run along now and pack, and we'll get going as soon as possible."

Owen is sitting there, across the table, nodding.

"Righto," I say and leave. I throw my clothes into one bag and my school things into another. The bell rings for break as I make my way to the car park. Tazim sees me and comes running over. I tell her what is happening. Tazim gives me a hug.

"You take care now," she says. Dad doesn't say anything. Neither of us says anything all the way to Road Junction where he stops the car and gets out. I get out as well. He starts yelling at me.

"You useless bitch," he yells. I start crying. He continues yelling at me until he's blown his steam. Then he lights a cigarette and hands me the pack. "It's like this," he says: "All you have to do is get through school and pass Year Ten. Then we'll see what happens. This holiday you're going to catch up on everything you've left undone. Alison and your mum are in Dar. They're not coming back while you're on holiday, but I will be there all the time. You're going to start at eight and work until lunch, which we'll have together. You're going to continue at one o'clock and work until four. Then, you can have the rest of the day off. When you've completed all the papers I have on my list, you can enjoy your holiday. Got it?"

"Completely," I say. We drive on. And that's how it is. I get up at seven and go for a swim, have breakfast and get to it. Dad's going about doing repairs on the hotel's main building and the fourteen bungalows for guests. He fixes the roofs, the walls and the whitewash, changes door handles, puts new hinges on the windows or replaces entire window casements. We don't say that much to each other, and I don't understand why Dad bothers to keep an eye on me. The days drag on. My pile of finished papers is getting bigger.

Juma shows up. He is Dad's right-hand man – an ageing *chagga* whose teeth have gone brown because of all the fluorine in the water at Kilimanjaro.

"*Shikamoo Mzee*," I say politely.

"Samantha," he says, hugging me. "You have become a very beautiful lady."

"What are you doing here?" I ask. "Are you two going off to work?"

"I'm here to help your dad with a few things," Juma says. I've noticed that Dad calls the harbour master's office in Tanga, introducing himself and asking if they have any news. I know better than to ask him what about.

I have lunch with Juma on the patio, and I ask about his family – his grown-up daughter.

"Samantha has to work now," Dad says, and I work on until 4.00 in the afternoon when I am close to collapsing. There have actually been days when I've fallen asleep as soon as I've finished working, but most days I go fishing. I put on my bikini bottoms and a mouldering T-shirt to stop my skin from burning, find my harpoon and go outside. Juma is sitting in the shade, resting.

"Won't you come out fishing with me?" I ask.

"I'm not a good swimmer," Juma says.

"But you can sail the boat," I say and he gets up, smiling.

"I'd like that." We sail out a small distance, and I jump overboard and hunt, throwing the catch into the boat. "You're very good at that," Juma says.

"I want us to have a nice supper now that you've come to see us," I say. When I've got enough fish, I spring into the boat. Juma rolls me a cigarette, and we sit there smoking. Here it comes.

"Your father is worried," he says.

"He doesn't have to be."

"It's important to him that you do well at school, so you can do well in life."

"I'll be alright," I say. Dad's complained about me to Juma – that's not like him. We sail back to the shore and give our catch to the maid who fries the fish for supper. Dad and Juma go into town for a drink that night. I am bored stiff, drink gin and smoke cigarettes. I'm thinking about Victor and am afraid to ask where he is.

I manage to finish my papers. Every time I've finished one, I give it to Dad. He leafs through it.

"You're not supposed to read it," I say.

"Just checking that it is what it's supposed to be," he says and continues leafing page by page. "Right then. Next one is the Social Studies one. Describe the impact of oil on the political order in Iran since the 1930s."

"How am I supposed to do that without a library?" I ask.

"Just do the best you can," Dad says and makes a call to Tanga. He speaks to an old Brit, George, who used to be consul in Mombasa and who is now retired. Dad has a servant drive me there in the Land Rover the next morning, and George turns out to be very nice. Sitting behind his desk with its dictionary and piles of *The Economist*, he slowly dictates the entire paper to me.

"Did you get it?" he asks.

"Yes," I say.

"Then all you do is write it up in your own words," he says. "Anything else I can do for you?"

"No thanks. But thank you," I say.

"Always happy to be of service," he says.

Wooden crates

That afternoon I catch some squid and talk Dad into taking them to George as a small thank you for all his help. The next day Dad is gone all day, and late in the afternoon he returns followed by a lorry full of wooden crates, which are stacked in the garage that has been built into our house. I don't ask him about it.

Early next morning and it's chilly. I am out of my bed and getting into my swimming gear. A lorry drives up behind the hotel's main building, and three black men get out – one of them is Juma. Dad comes out of the kitchen door to meet them. He shakes hands with the leader. I stare out between the bars and mosquito net of my window. The men aren't Tanzanians; at least I don't think so. I can tell the different tribes apart if there's no mixed blood. They're wearing combat clothes with no military distinctions, and the leader is oozing confidence, so much so it's almost arrogance. Maybe they are Zulus from South Africa. The African National Congress, A.N.C., who are fighting apartheid, have training camps in Tanzania.

"Help us with the crates," the leader says to Dad and Juma in English. Dad and Juma start to carry the crates out of the garage and load them into the lorry. I can't hear what they're saying. The leader of the strange blacks points at one of the crates, asks a question, takes up a jemmy and a hammer from the lorry and opens the crate. Dad looks worried. The black man starts saying something:

"This is not what we agreed," he says loudly. I can't hear what Dad says. "Don't try to cheat us. If you were to disappear, no-one would ask any questions," the man says. I am waiting for the reaction, but Dad stays still, his shoulders slightly stooped, and answers in a low voice. The black man is in his face, and Dad's hands are hanging limply down his sides. "I'd very much suggest you do," the black man says and walks away from him. He's threatening Dad, and Dad is just taking it. He's afraid of the black man. Dad seems old. The lorry starts and drives off. I hurry out of the patio door and down to the beach, throwing myself into the waves. Dad hasn't stayed home to make sure I wrote my papers. He has been waiting for the shipment to land in Tanga harbour.

When I return, we have breakfast, and not a word is said about the lorry, but Dad is chain-smoking restlessly in his chair. He goes to his desk and gets his list, which he puts on the table in front of me. He points at it:

"You've got two papers left to do," Dad says. "You're going to do them well, even though I have to go."

"You have to go?" I ask.

"We're leaving in a minute," he says.

"What am I supposed to do then?" I ask.

"Enjoy your holiday until school starts again," Dad says. "I'm going to call your mum before we go." He puts his hand in his back pocket and hands me an envelope. I look at him questioningly. "Smoking permit," he says. "For school. Take care."

And an hour later they've gone. I write the last papers – really badly. The next day Mum returns from Dar but without Alison. There are only a couple of days left of the holiday. I hand in my papers. It feels ludicrous not to be hopelessly behind with things.

Exodus

A lot of the girls who matter are invited to a sort of hen night at Parminder's that Saturday, because she is about to get engaged – all the important girls except for me; after all I'm not a proper person. Shakila and Tazim are both going.

"Never mind," Tazim tells me on Friday. "I'll stay here."

"Oh no, don't," I say.

"O.K.," she says without hesitation, because she really does want to go. "But then we have to do something tonight."

"What?"

"It's a surprise," Tazim says. I'd like to go as well. Indian girls dancing in beaded robes. Flower wreaths, and henna patterns on their hands, and polished nails, and clanging bracelets. Sipping tea and nibbling fragrant Indian biscuits, sitting on opulent floral sofas covered in thick see-through plastic to stop them from going grey with dust in the dry season. Your thighs stick to the plastic making getting up a noisy business, and there are little crocheted nylon-lace covers on the armrests and backs of the sofas and all the little serving tables. I know it from the children's birthday parties at the school in Arusha. There's something fascinating about Indian girls, whereas the boys simply have their heads too far up their own arses to hold any allure.

"This is it," Tazim says on Friday night. She's made tea in the kitchen and has some powder in a bag – henna.

"Are you going to do it on me?" I ask.

"Yes," she says and mixes the pulverized bark with tea, making a thick mush. She uses a thin stick of rosebush to put it on.

"It would have been easier with a piping bag," I say.

"No, this is good."

"But Tazim . . . I really don't want any Indian patterns, O.K.?"

"Why not?"

"Then it's like . . . I'll be sad I'm not invited. Like I'm . . ."

"What do you want then?" I dig out a sheet of parchment where I've copied the title of the Bob Marley L.P. "Exodus" – I meant to paint it onto a T-shirt. Tazim punches tiny holes in the parchment so she can put it on my arm and press the tip of an orange felt-tip pen through the holes, tracing the outlines of the letters. She puts the henna-mush onto my arm, and I sit there for a long time to allow the colour to seep in. I'm going to wear sleeveless tops all of next week; "*Exodus – movement of the Jah people. Oh yeah.*"

Dreadlock

"That's so cool," Jarno says when he sees my upper arm.

"Thank you," I say and sit myself down on the bench outside Kijana House. When you have a smoking permit, smoking here is allowed.

"Why do you have that on your arm?" Salomon asks.

"I think it looks good," I say.

"Exodus isn't an adornment – it's a serious business to us Rastafaris," Salomon says.

"That's a load of bollocks," Jarno says. Salomon turns around and looks at him:

"Do you think your pale dreads make you a Rastafari?" Salomon asks.

"Am I not allowed to have dreadlocks?" Jarno asks, shaking his little lion's mane and sinking his piss-coloured eyes into Salomon.

"Sure you are," Salomon says. "Looks sick to me, that's all."

"I'm colour-blind," Jarno says. "What are you?"

"I'm a Rasta."

"And I'm not?" Jarno says.

"Not the real kind, you're not. A real Rasta doesn't eat meat, doesn't drink alcohol."

"You eat chicken," Jarno says.

"Fish and chicken, yes. But not the mammals: Jah made those like He made man."

"Was Haile Selassie divine – the Lion of Judaea?" Jarno asks.

"Africa allowed itself to be rough-ridden by white people," Salomon says. "Haile Selassie was the only one who kept his throne when the white grasshoppers of colonialism swarmed the continent."

"He allowed his people to die like flies in the countryside," Jarno says. "If that's Rasta, then . . ."

"Are you Ethiopian?" Salomon asks.

"No."

"Then don't tell me who we are."

"People always make God serve their own needs," Jarno says, spits on the ground and, getting up, walks away.

Mick

The phone in the common room rings. It's Mum.

"Mick's coming to pick you up. He'll drive you back to Tanga," she says.

"Mick?" I say. He's in a Technical School in Germany. "When did he get back?" I ask.

"It's the same thing as with Alison," Mum says, sighing. "He says they couldn't teach him anything he didn't know already."

"So what's he going to do now?" I say.

"He works for the lodge as their driver on the luxury safaris for American tourists to Ngorongoro and Serengeti," Mum says.

Mick is the only boy I've ever . . . done it with. Yes, because Christian doesn't count – that all came to nothing.

"Alison has arranged for him to come and do the repairs to all our outboard motors," Mum says. None of the motors for our boats works. We have them so our guests can go sailing, or fish, dive, water ski. That is, if there are any guests at all – Tanga is a bit off the northern tourist trail.

"Is Alison there?" I say.

"No, she's still in Dar, but I think she's coming home soon."

"O.K.," I say, feeling relieved. I'm not being picked up by the folks, and I don't have to get the bus. I am driving down with Mick, who is a real human being. And he at least will be a part of my holiday.

I go out to find Christian without having much luck. Then I bump into Panos.

"Where's Christian?" I ask.

"What do you care?" Panos asks.

"What do you mean? Is he mad at me?"

"No, I think he likes you a bit too much for that."

"But where is he?"

"He flew back to Denmark yesterday," Panos says.

"Is he coming back?" I ask.

"I think so."

The next day all the boarders go out to the car park with their luggage as soon as we've had lunch.

"Have a nice holiday, Samantha," Truddi shouts, jumping into her parents' Land Rover.

"Die in Hell," I say under my breath as I smile and nod at her. Holiday – at long last. The others are getting into the school's bus, which will take them to Kilimanjaro Airport, out on the plain between Moshi and Arusha. They're flying to Dar es Salaam with A.T.C. – Air Tanzanian Cooperation, a.k.a. Air Total Confusion. I hope the plane breaks down – in mid-air. Come on, Mick.

Beach buggy

Long before I see him, I can hear that he's driving the beach buggy. Brilliant. The bus has started its engine, and here comes this little yellow car flashing into the car park with an open top, huge exhaust pipes and a spare set of fog lights at the front. The motor roars and rumbles in its place between the back tyres.

"Samantha," Mick shouts. "Jump in." He's put on weight again but is still slender. Seppo comes over and asks about the car. Mick doesn't turn off the engine but offers me a cigarette. I've already put my sunglasses on. I'm loving this. Mick lights my cigarette with his petrol lighter.

"Wankel engine, 1500 c.c., fibreglass body," Mick says, revving the engine, doing a wheel spin right in front of the bus, and then off we go, down Lema Road, giving it our dust-spraying all.

"It handles well," I shout above the wind and the roar of the engine as we drive to the Y.M.C.A. roundabout en route out of Moshi. All the children shout and wave when they see the car.

"I've just given her a once-over: paintwork, engine, the works." The cigarette almost smokes itself because of the wind that whips my hair into the back of my neck. I wonder how Mick is being paid for the work in Tanga. I ask him.

"The stay is free," he says. "Food, booze, everything." Everything? What is everything? Me or Alison? "Plus, I get your dad's best rifle, and he's going to owe me a stay at your hotel for some of our tourists when we have some in who want to go diving."

"Have you spoken to Alison?" I ask.

"No, it was my mum who spoke to her. What's she doing in Dar?"

"She said she wanted to go there to look for a husband," I say without looking at him, aware that Mick turns his head to look at me.

"Oh," he says. Maybe he's disappointed, but she is a year older than him.

"So you might be out of luck," I say.

"Plenty of fish in the sea," Mick says. I don't say anything to that.

The tarmac ends when we turn right at Road Junction. The fine red dust on the road explodes in clouds from the tyres.

"Are you going to stay at the lodge?" I ask.

"No," Mick shouts over the noise of the engine. "My brother and I don't see eye to eye. I'm going to need some money first. But then I'll probably set up my own garage for safari companies in Arusha. Maybe I can import used cars from Dubai. I had a stopover there. Loads of good used cars – and cheap too. So if they ease up on the import restrictions, that's the way to go."

Fish on the hook

We arrive at Tanga covered in dust, turning down the dirt road by the coast and stopping in front of Baobab Hotel. Mum comes out of the house. She hugs me and Mick.

"Douglas will be back in a few days," she says. "And Alison's here."

"She's back?" I say.

"Yes, she's gone down for a swim," Mum says smiling. "We don't have very many guests at the moment so you get a bungalow each." Mum goes into reception and gets our keys – then she tells us that there will be sundowners on the patio at six as usual. I dump my bag in my room and skip down the broken stairs to the beach. Alison is swimming way out, so I drop all my clothes except for my knickers and vest and throw myself into the water, starting to work my way over to her.

"Hello you," she calls and waves – swimming towards me and hugging me in the water, so our heads are submerged and we splutter. "Is Mick here?" she asks.

"He's gone over to look at the motors," I say. "How did it go in Dar?" Alison smiles and winks at me while we tread water.

"I caught one," she says.

"You're kidding," I say.

"A really big fish, this one," she says.

"You're taking the piss," I say. Alison raises her eyebrows because I'm swearing. Dad doesn't want us to swear, and Alison feels the same.

"Frans," she says. "Dutch. The new head of K.L.M.'s office in Dar."

"But," I say. "Is he nice?"

"He's lovely," Alison says.

"But when are you seeing him again? When am *I* going to see him?"

"Soon, Samantha. But I'd like to sink my claws a bit deeper into him before he meets our darling parents."

"Of course," I say. "That makes sense." I swim back to the shore, have a shower, meet the others on the patio. Mick points to himself when we start talking about Frans:

"What am I going to do, then?" Mick says. Alison smiles:

"Make a go of it with Samantha?"

"But I don't want Mick – he's just a big boy," I say.

"And you're just a little girl," Mick says.

"No, I'm a big girl now," I say, grabbing my tits, pouting.

"Don't make a scene," Mum says.

Cleanliness

I help Mick with the motors. We take everything apart, clean it, grease it, adjust it. Mick sacrifices the least salvageable one so as to have spare parts for the others.

We put the first one together. Afterwards we give it a try. I waterski. We dive for squid with harpoons and beat them against the rocks until they're tender.

"You really should go, Mum," Alison says at lunch. "You deserve a nice holiday."

"I really should stay and help you out, darling," Mum says – her hangover from last night has almost gone, but she looks a mess – worn out.

"I know my mum would appreciate a visit," Mick says. In the end we manage to talk her into going, and she drives off to pay Mick's mum a visit at the lodge.

And then we have the place to ourselves. Alison is busying herself with plans for getting the hotel up and running. She's on the phone non-stop making arrangements with travel agents in Arusha – among them, Jerome, Mick's stepfather. And she gets new mattresses in, and mosquito nets, and gets painters to work.

Alison is to oversee the daily running of the hotel and will serve as head of catering in the evenings to get customers back to the restaurant. She needs a reliable head waitress who can enforce discipline among the serving staff so the guests are treated properly.

Applicants are told to lay a table and serve Alison a meal. I stand by and watch as a woman from the village, wearing her Sunday best, puts the cutlery in all the wrong places and knocks over the glasses from sheer nervousness. She is sent packing. Afterwards a tall, attractive-looking lady has a go at it – Halima is her name. Everything is placed correctly on the table – she knows what she's doing. After that Alison drags her to the toilet where the toilet seat is missing.

"Tell me what's wrong in here," Alison says. An ordinary woman would notice that there's water in the tap, and that there's a tin of water next to the toilet bowl so that you can wash your bottom; everything is as it should be – what more could you wish for? Toilet paper, soap and a towel are not something you expect in a Tanzanian toilet. When a European tourist uses a toilet where there's no soap, his subconscious will immediately ask itself what the standard of cleanliness is in the kitchen. But the employees here have grown up in village huts with mud floors – they just can't see it.

"There's no toilet seat, there's water on the floor, there's no toilet paper, soap or towels. And a good clean wouldn't go amiss – the walls and the ceiling as well. Maybe you should have it painted."

"You're hired," Alison says.

I don't understand why it's so important to get the hotel up and running, before Dad sells it. He's never had it for the money. It's only a cover to account for why he lives in Tanzania. I ask Alison.

"His other businesses aren't doing too well," she says. "He needs to get a decent price for the hotel. And he can only get that if the hotel is bringing in a nice profit."

"Couldn't you take it over? Run it?"

"No. I want to go down to Frans in Dar."

"Frans, Frans, Frans," I jeer.

"I miss him," Alison says.

"You've only just met him."

All she does is smile.

Mango flies

Whatever time we have off we spend swimming, sailing, eating, drinking and going for drives in the beach buggy. I sleep like a log at night, wake up early and go for a swim. As I come up the slope, I can hear Alison screaming inside the house. I run.

"Out, out – get out," she shouts. I hurry out into the kitchen; the maid is standing at the door, looking scared. Alison grabs a knife from the worktop and walks towards her. The maid yanks open the door and flees.

"My, my," I say. Alison turns around. She's looking thunderous. She lifts up her *kanga* so I can see her naked arse; there are boils – larvae.

"*Tsk*," I say. Mango flies lay eggs in damp laundry when it's hung outside to dry. If the clothes aren't ironed properly, the eggs survive and hatch – the larvae leave the fabric and penetrate the skin, where they grow. Then you have to squeeze them out of the boils on your skin. They're the colour of maggots.

"You have to do it for me," Alison says.

"Yuck! No."

"But I can't reach," she shouts.

"Can't you just wait until they open the skin themselves, crawl out and take off?"

"Samantha . . ." She covers her face with her hands and sobs.

"There, now," I say and go over to her.

"Yes but . . ." she says with her face still in her hands, "if Frans comes up, and I . . . Then I'll have boils on my arse – it's so gross." I put my arms around her.

"There, there," I say. "I'll do it." I slap her bottom.

"Ow," she says.

"Do you think he'll come here?" I ask.

"I hope so. I miss him."

"Jesus!" I say and pull her into our parents' room. I sit astride her back and start squeezing larvae out of her buttocks while she complains.

"Are you sure you don't want me to leave one in there?" I ask. "Then it can make its way out when you're shagging, and fly home like a good little ladybird."

"You're really not a well person, Samantha," she says, biting into the pillow.

"O.K. Just an idea."

Discipline

It seems that Frans misses Alison as well. One afternoon he shows up at the hotel in a big, new Land Rover. He's come 350 kilometres from Dar es Salaam – most of it on a dusty road – to see her. Alison drags him off to her bungalow as soon as he gets here.

"What are they doing?" I ask.

"Shagging like bunnies," Mick says. He is attaching a new nylon cord to the starter of a motor. Then Alison and Frans come out. He stays outside with Mick while I have to go and help Alison with dinner. I'm standing next to her, teasing her until Frans and Mick come in. They sit down with cold beers and cashew nuts at the table where they can watch us work.

"Good-looking sisters, aren't they?"

"Yes," Frans says and gives an awkward laugh. I turn to him.

"Do you really mean to live with that one?" I ask, nodding at Alison.

"Yes, of course I do," Frans says. "Don't forget, she's the love of my life."

"That's just something you think. You don't know her at all," I say.

"You're just jealous," Mick tells me.

"Not of Alison, I'm not," I say, winking at Frans. Alison is standing next to me, chopping veg – I just need to get her to turn around. I say: "But maybe I'm jealous of Frans because my sister is one hell of a fuck!" Alison spins around to say something to me. My arm is already moving. *SMACK!* The slap lands squarely on her cheek while I shout:

"Who are you fucking?"

"What are you doing?" Frans shouts, jumping out of his seat, knocking it over, while the sound of the slap is reflected drily from the walls – he takes a long step towards me, but stops when he sees that Alison is keeping her head still, her arms still, the hand with the knife in it still, her feet still; she blinks twice very fast, but looks me in the eye, totally indifferent, while the marks of my fingers glow white on her tanned cheek. Frans has frozen awkwardly in the middle of the room and is looking dumbfounded.

"You've still got it," Mick says, smiling – he's seen it before. The moment has passed. Alison smiles at me.

"Just you wait," she says, holding up an admonishing finger and wiping a single tear from the corner of her eye.

"What . . . what's going on?" Frans asks.

"You're crazy, you are," Mick says.

Alison walks over to Frans with a smile:

"Don't worry, darling – it's a family tradition." She holds on to his neck and kisses him hard on the mouth. He looks shaken.

"Slapping each other?" he says.

"Practising the art of receiving a blow without reacting," I say.

"But why?" Frans asks – he wouldn't be able to do it. Alison explains to him that our dad would alway hit us when it was least expected, like while asking a question or barking out an order; it was his way of disciplining us.

"It's important to be able to take it without breaking down. He despises weakness. We trained each other to cope," Alison says.

"But that's . . . mad," Frans says.

"He doesn't do it anymore, our dad," Alison says.

"Not to you, he doesn't," I say. "But I always have a slap coming."

"Your mother – did she put up with it?"

"She wasn't exactly holding the reins," Alison says.

"She left the disciplining to the beast," I say.

Lab rats

After we've eaten, we sit on the patio, knocking back gin and tonics and getting stoned on Mick's Arusha-*bhangi*, the highest quality from the slopes of Mount Meru.

"Have you ever thought that it might all just be a set?" Alison says.

"That what might all just be a set?" Mick asks.

"Everything around us," Alison says with a gesture that encompasses the sky and the earth, and the sea, and the hotel, and us. "The world, and the people, and everything that is going on, it's all so absurd that it can't be real. I know I'm real. I'm here and I'm trying to . . . manoeuvre my way through it all. And people keep trying to influence me and tell me what to do. They judge me. And the things I really want to do, they tell me those things are wrong. And the things I don't want: Those are the things they want me to do. Going to school and working hard, being well behaved . . . all sorts of things," she says and her face is one big question mark. I look at Frans. He smiles at her, looking happy, but underneath the happiness he is nervous. She's never been like this at the cocktail parties in Dar es Salaam. Mick clears his throat:

"People try to manipulate each other all the time – sure. That doesn't make the world a set." Alison tries to focus:

"No, but . . ." She points at herself with both hands, "I am a biological experiment, a lab rat. I am the only human being that exists. The beings found me and they thought . . ." Alison changes to a lecturing tone: "'This is a one-off. It's the only one of its kind that we've managed to resuscitate. And now we're going observe what she's like, so we'll create an environment and put her in it. And in order to find out how this species works,

131

we'll continue to cook up the most extraordinary things and throw them in her path.' That's the feeling I've got."

"We're out to get you," Mick says.

"You're robots, that's all," Alison says. "But those beings really ought to take the experimenting down a notch. It's too much. Parents, school, a useless hotel, a crazy little sister and . . . men. Everything's weird."

"Is it so hard where the men are concerned?" Frans asks. Alison looks at him with surprise, leans forward and puts a hand on his thigh.

"No, not you, darling. I think they've decided – the beings, that is, that I am allowed to be happy now." She smiles at him. But that's exactly what she's saying about men. Babies – swashbuckling braggarts one minute, insecure weaklings the next.

"It's quite simple, really," Mick says. "You just do what you want to, and then the beings can put that in their pipes and smoke it."

"That's what I think," Alison says. "Should I give it a go? After all, morality is just a part of their test set-up. What do you think, Samantha?" she asks.

"To me reality's really real," I say. "But I'm not sure that actually matters."

"But it does matter to you, I mean whether you're happy or . . . Like at school," Alison says.

"Yes, but that's not something you can control," I say.

"What isn't?" Mick asks.

"Well . . . feelings and that."

"No but . . . Personally I like things fast-paced," Mick says. "And sex too. What worries me most is that there are such long intervals where I have to do all sorts of pointless nonsense before I can get back to what really matters: things that are fast-paced. And sex."

"Mick," Alison sighs.

"You know what I mean," Mick says.

"Yes, but that's not everything, is it?"

"No, but it comes bloody close."

"Yes well, alright then," Alison says and takes Frans' hand. "We're out of here," she says.

"Goodnight," Frans says and they leave us there, after a conversation about fierce and full-on sex. I look at Mick who lights a cigarette.

"Full-on sex," I say.

"You know where to find me," he says and empties his glass in one gulp. He gets up. "And I'll be in." And then he leaves as well. I sit there for a bit. I put out the bat lights, carry them inside and lock the house from the outside. Then I go over and knock on Mick's door.

"Yes?" Mick says.

"Can I come in?"

"Yes." I open the door.

"I don't mean to . . . I'm just tired of sleeping alone," I say.

"Come in, will you," Mick says.

Stooping to Dad's level

Two days later Dad returns. Frans is visibly nervous at the prospect of meeting him. We're standing by the patio.

"So, you're going to take my big girl from me?" Dad says.

"Yes," Frans says. "I already have."

"Really? Yes. Fair enough," Dad says and turns to Mick, patting him on the shoulder.

"He's alright, that Frans of yours," I whisper to Alison.

"My point exactly," she says.

"Mick," Dad says. "Seems I can't offer you anything but my youngest daughter."

"Come off it," I say.

"Not quite as good, but she's showing promise," Dad says.

"I'll go and get the drinks," Alison says and goes inside, followed by Frans.

"I bumped into Victor. He might come down in a week or so," Dad says.

"Victor!" I say. "How long's he staying for?"

"Just a few days – then we have to be off," Dad says.

"But, where are you going?" I ask. Dad looks at me.

"Why?" he asks.

"Oh, it's . . . I'm just curious," I say. At Hotel Tanzanite Victor touched my thigh when I got out of the pool. And I kissed him when he came to see me in Moshi. Who knows what could happen . . . "It's just that I promised to teach him how to dive," I say.

"I don't think we'll have time for that," Dad says. Alison comes out, carrying beer and fizzy drinks. We have lunch together, and then Mick and Frans have to go. Mick wants to go to Dar to pick up some spare parts to get all the motors up and running. And there's something about a job he wants to enquire about. Frans has to return to mind his job. They drive off bumper to bumper – Mick in front in the beach buggy and Frans behind him in his Land Rover. The place feels empty after they've gone. Dad and Alison sit down with the accounts and go around the place discussing what needs to be done. Mum returns; she looks rested and is completely out of the loop when it comes to the running of the hotel. Alison introduces Dad to Halima, who is licking the waitresses into shape.

"That Halima seems very able," Dad says.

"Yes. And that means I don't have to worry about that part of the business," Alison says. She is going to stay in her bungalow even though Frans has gone. I have gone back into the house because we've got more guests now – a herd of elderly Swiss people. I'm lying alone in my room, and I can hear the folks when they return late at night from the Yacht Club in Tanga.

"If you don't behave, I'm going to go home," Mum says in the sitting room – her voice is slurred.

"Then go," Dad says.

"You really are stupid," Mum says.

"No, you're stupid," Dad says. That's the level of their conversation.

"You can't do this to me. I've given you two children."

"That was a long time ago now," Dad says.

"You're such a swine," Mum says.

"And you're an old cow," Dad says. I put my pillow over my head. But I can still hear Mum go to their bedroom to sob herself to sleep, and in my mind's eye I can see Dad sitting in the sitting room, stiff as a board, squinting. Why did he even have us – Alison and me? What does he want with us? Finally I hear him go to bed. I get up. I take my blanket, my pillow and my cigarettes – and then I go over to Alison's and knock on the door.

"It's me," I say.

"What's wrong?" she asks sleepily and opens the door.

"It's Mum and Dad – they're being stupid," I say as she pulls me inside and closes the door.

"Are they having a row?"

"Yes, but Mum's cried herself to sleep now, and Dad's passed out from drinking."

"What were they rowing about?"

"Nothing – they were just talking rubbish." I've lit a cigarette and am lying on the empty bed. Alison is smoking as well, blowing up smoke rings that soar through her mosquito net and continue on the other side only slightly distorted. It looks pretty.

"Do that again," I say. She looks at me – assessing me, I think, before blowing out another fat smoke ring.

"He'll shag anything with a pulse," she says.

"What?"

"Anything. All the young waitresses. If they don't want to, they're sacked. And when he's away on business – who knows?"

"You're kidding," I say.

"No. I'm not."

"But . . ."

"But what?" Alison asks. Yes what? I light another cigarette. Look up at the mosquito net.

"Yes well, he won't be doing that anymore," Alison says. "I've told him that if I'm running the hotel, he can't interfere with the management. And not with the staff either."

"Did you tell him he couldn't bonk them?" I ask.

"No, but he got the point."

Afro

The next day there's no water. Mum calls me; she is sitting in the bathtub in just a drop of water and wants me to wash her. She looks worn: her breasts sag, the skin on her arms and legs has been made all leathery by the sun. Her buttocks have shrivelled, her tummy has swollen with the drinking, her thigh muscles are slack. It's a sad sight.

In the afternoon she makes a pathetic attempt at doing a Jane Fonda aerobics routine from a book Alison brought back from England. But Mum lacks the stamina to do even the warm-up. The next day she is even more hungover and doesn't get up until after lunch. She wants me to curl her hair with some chemicals my aunt has sent her. It's called a cold perm. Put in the perming lotion, roll up the hair on curlers, put in something else that make the curls last. She looks like a poodle. Just then Dad comes through the door.

"Are you trying to grow an afro?" he says. And she goes to their room to cry. They make me feel . . . ashamed.

Mick calls to tell us it'll be a while before he returns. Alison takes the car and goes to Arusha to meet with some safari companies. I could go with her, but that would make Mum sad – it would be like I was running away from her.

Mum is lying in, feeling crummy. I take a blood sample and drive into town to the hospital to have it looked at: malaria parasites. Dr Jodha returns with me and fills the car with his stench of betel nuts and mothballs. He spits red splatter out of the window and wipes his mouth. He gives Mum a dose of Klorokin and a load of tablets, smiling his rust-red smile at her: "I'll come look at you again tomorrow, Mrs Richards."

Dr Jodha returns and gives Mum another shot, so she really ought to start feeling better now, but somehow she doesn't really. She doesn't have an appetite. She's running a fever. Dad carries her to the car, and I drive her to the hospital where she's admitted and treated with Fansidar, which works like chemotherapy. Later that day I go back with food – people will starve to death in hospital if they don't have someone on the outside to help them. She's completely lost her appetite, her mouth is raw, she's as sick as a dog. All the mosquitoes on the coast are resistant. Quinine doesn't work any longer, so Mum's daily efforts with the gin and tonics are a complete waste.

Bloodshot

Alison returns. She's all geared up, full of exciting new plans for the future of the hotel.

Mum's back from hospital and is feeling better. She starts doing things again and seems normal.

She invites the Whitesides round for lunch one day. We get off to a good start when I get up to take a shower that morning. Mum comes running through the door.

"You can either do the dishes or the vegetables. The Whitesides will be here in three hours," she shrieks.

"Then call someone from the hotel," I say.

"I don't want any of them in my kitchen," she says – determined to have a function in life.

"They're not my guests, you know," I say. She stops on her way out of the bathroom and stares at me:

"You're having that food as well, so you'd better chip in." She's been drinking half the night and slept late. Her face looks like the backside of a dog that has got tired of shitting. I feel sorry for her, but really, it's not my problem.

"I'm bleeding. I need a shower," I say. She leaves.

"Where's Alison?" she shouts. But Alison has got up early and gone to Tanga to find some workers who can build a new staircase for the slope down to the beach.

She returns in time for lunch, which is alright.

"Maybe you should get it together with that Mick," Dad says.

"What the hell are you on about?" I say. The Whitesides stare at me.

"Mind your language," Mum says.

"He's a nice chap – very able," Dad says.

"Don't worry your head about what I do."

"Oh really?" Dad says.

"Stop it, you two," Alison says.

"Why would I get together with him?" I say.

"You're going to need someone who can provide for you when I can't be bothered any longer," Dad says. I get up from the table abruptly and leave.

"You're so bloody sensitive," Dad says behind me. When I return, the Whitesides have gone. Through the windows I can see the folks sitting, drinking in the sitting room. Alison is there as well. She's got her perfect life all mapped out. First a stint at the hotel – the daughter who saves her parents' hotel. Then down she goes to her hubby with the fancy job in Dar. Eew! I pile some leftovers onto a plate and go to my room, listen to music on my headphones and leaf through magazines that have been left behind by German tourists. I go to bed, fall asleep.

"Come in and sit with your parents, o daughter of mine?" It's Dad. He's popped his head through the door. He puts the light on. I am holding a hand to my eyes. His own eyes are bloodshot.

"I'm sleeping," I say.

"You can sleep when you get old. We're talking about the future. We're making plans."

"I'm still at school – what do you want me to do?"

"Don't be such a sourpuss, Samantha. We're having a big family meeting – come on."

"I'm sleeping."

"Awh," he jeers and shuts the door without switching off the lights.

The next day Mick returns covered dust from the road.

"New job in Dar in two weeks," he says. Mick is going to be supervisor for a construction company. "I'll just have time to drive you back to school, Samantha."

"School," I say. "Ugh."

"Let's go for a drive," he says. And off we go, tearing down the dusty roads.

"Want to join me in the shower?" Mick says when we're parked behind the hotel again.

"No – I'm not in the mood," I say and walk up to the house.

Soldier of fortune

It's late in the afternoon. I go down to the beach for a smoke, because Mum doesn't want me to smoke even though she is puffing like a madwoman herself. When I return, I see a Land Rover I've seen before. Victor! He's sitting on the patio with Dad.

"Hello, Victor," I say.

"Samantha," he says. "How are you?"

"Good," I say, smiling.

"We just need a quiet chat here," Dad says.

"O.K.," I say and go over to the garage where Alison is talking to Mick about how to get Baobab Hotel included as a stopover on package holidays.

"Dad has a visitor," Alison says.

"Yes, I noticed. I said hello to him," I said.

"What do you think that Victor wants with Dad?" Alison asks.

"I don't know," I say.

"A soldier of fortune," Mick says. Alison laughs at him.

"What does that mean?" she asks.

"Another white man looking for a shortcut to happiness, adventure and wealth in Africa. But it has to be easy – he doesn't want to work for it," Mick says.

"One of us, then," Alison says.

"Yes," Mick says. "Except that we know it can't be done. We're working for it."

"But not too hard," Alison says.

"We will, though," Mick says and looks at me.

"What?" I say. I wonder whether Victor's going to spend the night? Will he have his own bungalow? If he did, maybe I could go over to his bungalow at night and sneak in. But I wouldn't dare – I know that.

"Almost time for a sundowner," Alison says. Mick wipes his hands on a rag. I go outside. Victor is packing things into the boot of his Land Rover. Dad is nowhere to be seen. I go over to Victor.

"Leaving so soon?" I ask.

"Yes, I'm afraid so. Maybe I should come and see you in Moshi again," he says.

"Maybe you should," I say.

"I'll send you a telegram before I come to let you know where I'm staying."

"Then you'll have to wait and see if I show up," I say.

"Oh, I think you will," he says as Alison and Mick come out of the garage.

"Bye," I say and walk over towards them – but slowly, because my cheeks are burning. They stop and wait for me. I swallow and go over to them.

"What did he say?" Alison asks.

"He asked if I knew where he could buy some cigarettes," I say.

"Tsk," Mick says. "Can't the man even get his own cigarettes?"

Alison grins and shoves Mick who says, "What?"

"You're a grumpy git," she says.

"I'm just sick of freebooters, and passengers, and fucking tourists," Mick says and walks towards the patio and his sundowner – the daily gin and tonic injection.

Tanzania Revenue Authority

I go up to the house for lunch. A fat black man in a suit is sitting with Alison on the patio, having a beer. My shorts and T-shirt are stained with oil. Alison sends me a warning look.

"*Shikamoo mzee*," I say. Alison introduces me, tells me that the man is from the T.R.A. – Tanzania Revenue Authority – he's the taxman, in other words. I show my hands and say that I'd better not shake his hand.

"So your little sister is a mechanic," the man says, laughing. The hotel accounts are on the table, but the books are not open.

"Bring out some more beer," Alison says. I hurry into the kitchen and wash my hands, carry out beer, pour it into their glasses and go back inside.

"Which is why the hotel is experiencing some difficulties at the moment," Alison tells the man.

"We are all having some difficulties," the man says. Tax is fixed here every six months when the taxman comes to visit – it's one of the best jobs around. Sometime later I see the man getting into his car and driving off. Alison is sitting quietly on the patio.

"Alison?" I call. She doesn't budge. I go out to her. She is sitting in her chair as if paralysed.

"Dad owes so much money you wouldn't believe it," she says.

"How much?"

"They could confiscate the hotel."

"Are they going to?" I ask. Alison sighs.

"They might. I've paid the man to bury the case for four months – and then we'll talk it over again. But . . . I don't know what Dad's thinking." She shakes her head.

We fix the last outboard motors. Mick eats loads of food and drinks lots of beer – he's getting his padding back. I don't go over to knock on his door at night – he doesn't knock on mine either. I don't know why. He doesn't say anything about it.

"What about Mick?" Alison asks.

"What about him?" I ask.

"He's moving to Dar," she says, raising her eyebrows.

"No, not Mick."

"Why not?"

"I mean, he works for his mum," I say. "Now he's going to work for a construction company. He's . . . porky."

"And?" Alison says. "I work for my dad and have tiny tits."

"Yes, but . . . he just doesn't fancy me," I say.

"I think he does. But you're not showing him that you want him to, and so he lets you be. He's a nice guy."

"Stop it, Alison," I say. "What's the matter with you people? Am I a cow to be sold or what?"

Generator

I wave goodbye to Alison as Mick drives the beach buggy out onto the road. We're heading towards Moshi and the school. Alison has made us a packed lunch, and we've brought bottled water. We don't speak – just whizz down the dirt road while Mick concentrates on getting us around the worst potholes. Late in the afternoon we make a stop under a tree and have our sandwiches and smoke cigarettes.

"I don't want to go to school," I say.

"It's only for one more year, Samantha," Mick says.

"It's torture," I say. Mick drops his cigarette on the ground and steps on the lit end.

"Let's go," he says, and we get back in. Mick turns the key. No response.

"What the hell?" he says and tries again. Nothing. He gets out and goes to have a look at the engine.

"Please don't tell me the damned thing is broken," I say.

"Don't worry, Samantha," he says and pokes at the engine with a screwdriver. I smoke in silence, fanning off insects.

"Shit," Mick says.

"What?" I say.

"The generator's bust."

"The generator?" I ask.

"It's a generator system – D.C. – it's got no alternator, so now the battery won't charge when the car's going."

"And what does that mean?" I ask.

"That the car won't start," Mick says.

"Damn it, Mick."

"What?"

"Why doesn't your car work like it's supposed to?" He looks at me.

"Because we're in Africa," he says.

"Jesus!"

"We'll need to be towed to Moshi," he says and looks back to the road we drove on earlier. It's Sunday – there's no traffic. "If we see a bus, you get on it," Mick says.

But there's no bus. A couple of boys appear and look at us. Mick explains to them that the car's broken down. They ask for sweets. We don't have any. They ask for money. Mick tells them to get lost. After the better part of an hour a heavily loaded pickup appears in the heat haze and slithers towards us at a snail's pace. We wave, the man stops.

"I'm sorry," he said. "I can't tow you. My load's too heavy as it is."

"Yes, I can see that," Mick says.

"Where are you going?" I ask.

"Himo," the man says.

"Can you give me a lift then?" I ask.

"Yes," the man says.

"No," Mick says.

"Why not?" I ask.

"Because I say so," Mick says.

"But why?" I ask. Mick has stepped up to the man in the car.

"Thanks for stopping. Have a nice a trip," Mick says, and the man drives off.

"Why couldn't I go with him?" I ask.

"Because I said I would drop you off at school."

"But I could have got on a *matatu* from Himo."

"It'll be dark in an hour and then you'll be the only white girl around – no."

"I can handle myself."

"If you can't, then it's my responsibility."

"I'm not your responsibility," I say.

"Right now you are," he says. I sit in the car's passenger seat. Dusk is closing in on us. Mick is standing, looking down the road. "Where are the cigarettes?" he asks.

"Don't talk to me," I say.

"Don't be such a spoiled brat," he says. A train is slowly gliding past on the rails that run parallel to the road – its locomotive spews clouds of steam. Dusk is settling.

"I'm thirsty," I say, because the water bottle is empty; we have no food left; it'll be completely dark and really cold soon. Mick laughs. "What?" I say.

"You're being waited on hand and foot, Samantha, and you still complain if there's so much as a pebble in your path – that's bloody amazing, that is," he says.

"*Tsk*," I say. It's another half hour – not much light left now.

"A lorry," Mick says. I look. It's coming closer. "It's empty," Mick says.

"How do you know?" I ask.

"The sound of the engine," he says and waves his arms. The lorry stops. Mick introduces himself. The driver's name is Yasir. He's going to Moshi. His young helper, Qasim, gets out and finds a pair of long wooden boards in the back of the lorry so we can push the beach buggy up. We sit in the cabin with the two men, driving through the darkness.

"Good job you were passing," Mick says.

"Yes," Yasir says. "Tomorrow you'd be nothing but bones." The three of them laugh. I light a cigarette. What's there to laugh about?

Mick and the car are unloaded outside Chuni Motors in the middle of town. I grab my bags.

"Mick," I say. "Thanks for taking me."

"No problem," Mick says. I take a taxi up to school.

Halima

Back in hell. Year Ten. The days drag their sorry feet. The weeks crawl on the ground. The months go on forever.

Alison calls. She sounds tired.

"Mum's gone home," she says.

"Where's she gone?"

"Home," Alison says.

"Home where?" I ask. "To the house in Dar?"

"To England. She's gone home to England."

"Why?"

"You know, Dad's been . . ." Alison starts. I interrupt her.

"She hasn't even called me," I say.

"The phone lines have been down," Alison says.

"Maybe I would have liked to come," I say.

"You've told us so many times you don't want to go to England."

"Maybe I've changed my mind," I say.

"Samantha," Alison says.

"Yes," I say.

145

"She found out that Dad's been having it off with Halima – the new . . ."

"I know who she is," I say.

"They . . . were going at it in one of the bungalows. Mum went inside to pack and just left," Alison says.

"What did Dad say?"

"That she could go if she wanted to."

"What did you say?"

"I sacked Halima."

"What are you going to do now?" I ask.

"I'm going to stay here – at least until you've been back for Christmas."

"But Christmas isn't for another three months. Where's Dad?" I ask.

"I don't know. In Dar, perhaps."

"What about half-term? We've got a week off. You could come up to Mountain Lodge. Please?" I ask.

"I haven't got a car," Alison says.

"You could take the bus."

"I have to mind the hotel."

Waves

I don't want to ask Tazim and I don't want to call Mountain Lodge and ask Sofie. It seems pathetic, and I don't actually want to stay at someone else's – I just want to see Alison. But half-term isn't for another few weeks and being at school is simply more than I can bear. I steal a pair of Truddi's Levi's and sell them to a taxi driver and go off on a weekend alone at Hotel Tanzanite – luckily Mum had given me a Weekend Exeat Permit.

Angela isn't at Arusha Game Sanctuary but staying with some Germans in Lushoto, so . . . I'm all alone. When the tourists have gone Friday night, I go for a swim. Later I go to my room and read a Harold Robbins novel full of violence, sex, drugs, deceit and love.

*

The next day I go to Arusha and have a walk about. I go down to see the Strand brothers, who are at home for the weekend. We have lunch. Their parents aren't home. The elder, Emerson, wants me to stay until Sunday, but I know what he's thinking and I don't want to. His little brother, Gideon, is too stoned to want anything. I get on a bus and am about to get off to go to Mountain Lodge, but then I feel like I would be showing up like a beggar, so instead I stay in my seat and get off at Hotel Tanzanite. I have chicken and chips, take a bath, smoke cigarettes, drink gin and wait for it to get dark.

The tourists have finally left the pool, and I get in. I swim on my back, do front crawl and laps underwater – the water is nearly dark now – it's only lit by the lamps above the doors to the changing rooms. I've come up for air in the shallow end when I see a man step up onto the diving board, jump once and cleave his way into the water. And that's it – he's gone. Who is he? Where is he? I take hold of the edge of the pool and am pulling myself out of the water when something grabs onto my ankles and pulls me down. I scream as a body starts to rise up right in front of me.

"Samantha," the voice says. Victor! I throw my arms around his neck, clinging to his body.

"You really scared me," I say, folding my legs around him, grasping his neck underwater, kissing him hard, shaking. His hands are on me underneath the water; they squeeze my buttocks, press my thighs.

"You're so lovely, Samantha. I've missed you," he says and lets his thumb rub across one of my nipples, sending hot flashes into my chest. I can feel his thingy against me under the water – he's hard.

"What's that I'm feeling, Mr Victor?" I say, putting my hand down his swimming trunks, gripping his cock and pressing it. There's a humming noise in his throat. "I have a room," I say.

"Yes." We go to my room. Big waves crash against the shore, making the earth shake and the water sizzle between the rocks, only to gather new speed and crash against the shore once more.

Victor is lying on his back. I have thrown one leg across his body, and I

147

feel really cool – the way I handled him like I actually knew what I was doing. We smoke cigarettes. He turns his head and smiles at me.

"I've never felt better than I do right now," he says. I smile.

"I feel exactly the same," I say.

"There's something I have to tell you," he says.

"Yes?"

"Your dad's coming tomorrow." I laugh. He laughs.

"What he doesn't know won't hurt him," I say.

"Atta girl," Victor says and nibbles my earlobe. "Samantha," he says.

Rabies

"Hi, Dad," I say from my seat in the deckchair by the edge of the pool. Dad turns his head.

"Samantha?" he says. "What are you doing here?"

"Just here for the weekend – I'll have to get the bus soon," I say.

"Have you seen that Victor?" Dad asks and sits down in the deckchair next to mine.

"Yes, he showed up yesterday," I say. "He's staying next door at Arusha Game Sanctuary."

"Good," Dad says.

"Want to have dinner with me tonight?" I ask.

"I can't tonight," Dad says. "I have an important meeting."

"Oh," I say.

"I'm sorry," he says and gets up. "I've got to go as soon as I'm done."

"Bye," I say.

The afternoon lingers on. I don't pack until I absolutely need to if I don't want to miss the bus to Moshi before it gets dark, then I fling my clothes into my bag.

"Samantha?" Someone is calling outside. It's Dad. I open.

Behind him is Victor who says, "Hi there, Samantha."

"Dad. Victor. What are you doing here?"

"I've come to see my daughter," Dad says, smiling – sheepishly, I think.

"But I'm off to Moshi now," I say.

"Yes, yes. I'll drive you. We've got just enough time for dinner in Moshi."

"Are you coming, Victor?" I ask.

"No," he says. "I'm going inland. I just wanted to make sure the old man remembered to visit his daughter." I smile.

"Yes, yes," Dad says. "It's not easy to find time for it all." Victor says his goodbyes, and Dad goes to the bar while I finish packing. We're taking the Land Rover. Luckily it's leaking and noisy, so it makes no sense to talk during the hour it takes us to drive to Moshi.

"Where should we eat?" Dad shouts when we reach the Arusha round-about on the outskirts of Moshi.

"Newcastle Hotel – they have a roof terrace," I shout and direct him to the hotel. We go up, order food and beer.

"You have to learn to drink these things," Dad says, smiling.

"Oh, I know how to drink," I say. We fall silent. What are we going to talk about until we can stuff our mouths full of food? Halima? Mum?

"Alison is doing really well with the hotel," Dad says and starts telling me about the various changes and improvements she's making. I am sure he's trying hard not to imply they are things Mum ought to have done a long time ago. Luckily our chicken and vinegar chips come not too long after. Dad offers me a cigarette – lights it for me. We smoke.

"I had better get back to school before it gets too late," I say. Dad nods and pays. We're off. We drive up Lema Road. Dogs are barking savagely in the night – they come closer. Dad looks over his shoulder – four dogs come running up alongside the car, baying furiously.

"Dogs," I shout. "The window!" Dad's right elbow is resting on the edge of the door – the window is rolled all the way down. I scream as Dad pulls his elbow back just as a dull sound is heard – the dog at the front has jumped up and slammed into his door – its jaws snap through the open window, its teeth are shiny and it's frothing at the mouth. Dad reaches into his khaki jacket, pulls his pistol from his shoulder holster as he brakes; the dog jumps up again, he shoots it in the mouth, making the back of its head explode in blood, bone and brains. I quickly roll up my window as he shoots twice more, curses, puts the car into gear and rolls up his own window. A dog's snout knocks against my window, trailing froth and saliva.

"Rabies," Dad says, stepping on the accelerator, trying to hit a dog in front of us. It jumps up onto the bonnet. A mangy dog with crazy eyes. Dad brakes again, looks in the side mirrors.

"No," I shout, but he is already halfway out of the car. Pumps the dog full of lead. Gets back in. Steps on it. He honks his horn before we reach the school gates. The guard opens the gate to us and we get out in the car park where Owen is standing, looking worried, with Ebenezer and one of the other guards – they've heard the shots.

"What happened?" Owen asks. I tell him while Dad lights a cigarette and curses.

"But who fired those shots?" Owen asks.

"I did," Dad says. "Three of them."

"Oh. Well I'm glad to have run into you – I wanted to see you anyway," Owen tells Dad who looks at him, then at me, then back at him.

"About her?" Dad asks.

"Yes, well, you know, Samantha is . . . What I mean to say is that . . . she plays truant and is quite boisterous," Owen says.

"Well, that's not on," Dad says.

"No, and in the end, we may have to employ the disciplinary measures at our —"

Dad cuts him short. "But then you bloody well shouldn't have pupils walking around in an area where there's rampant rabies. It may well be that Samantha should get a grip – she probably should. But you damn well should too." Dad glares at Owen – it's embarrassing and thrilling at the same time.

"The authorities are having it . . ." Owen starts and is cut off again.

"The authorities? The Tanzanian authorities?" Dad says. "You must be off your trolley." He turns away from Owen and comes over, hugs me and says, "You behave yourself, Samantha." Letting go, he digs into his pocket and hands me a packet of cigarettes. "You'd better take these," he says and jumps back into the car. Tooting the horn he drives off. I've already started walking back to Kiongozi House – I can actually feel how Owen is rooting around in his brain to find something that can make up for his humiliation. Nothing's coming. I continue walking. Then it comes.

"Do you have a smoking permit, Samantha?" he calls.

"Goodnight," I call back and stroll on. He doesn't try anything else.

Community service

"We are privileged. We get an education and we have options in life, so we really owe it to the world – and to our local community in particular – to give something back. We have the energy and the ability. You are going to leave this school as citizens of the world, free to choose your path in life. Our neighbours don't have those same options."

Owen just keeps going. Is he trying to convince himself? He's standing in front of us at assembly in Karibu Hall, waffling on and on about why we must do community service. But we're not part of that community anyway, not really – except for Jarno who forms part of *mama mbege*'s clientele.

"It's our duty. We owe it to the locals to make a contribution in return for their having made us so welcome, even though they don't have the possibilities we do."

It's a requirement to have completed a set number of community service hours in order to pass your final exams in Year Twelve, but you can start putting in those hours as early as in Year Nine so you won't be too busy those last two years when you're going to have to cram like there was no tomorrow. But doing community service makes no sense unless you stay at school until the bitter end. Could I actually endure two more years after

Year Ten? The others from my year want to start now, and of course it is a way to get to hang out with the oldest pupils.

We can play with the kids at the orphanage. We can help build a school in *mama mbege*'s village, or build a new bridge across Karanga River right next to the school so the women west of the river don't have to go all the way down to the old Karanga Bridge to go to market in Moshi with their produce. There used to be a bridge here, but it was built too far down the slope, and it was slowly gobbled up by the water when the river swelled during the long rains.

All that shit. They want us to save the world while always travelling First Class. Does building that bridge make us good people? Like hell it does.

I walk around looking for Christian, but he isn't there. He's off sick. All week. He's not at school at any rate. Instead I meet Panos.

"My mum has gone back to England, because my dad is shagging the waitresses at the hotel," I say.

"*Tsk*," he says.

Shebeen

Sunday afternoon I go down to Mboya's *duka*.

"Let me have a beer brought round to the garden," I say.

"The teachers sometimes come here to keep an eye on it, you know," Mboya says.

"Do you let them into the garden now?" I ask.

"No, I tell them it's private property. But sometimes they post a guard on the street outside – and then I can't see them and warn you."

"I'll take the back way out when I leave," I say and put the money on the bar . "Let me have a beer." Then I walk through the shop out into his garden and sit myself down at one of the tables in the shade. You can't look into the garden from the road, because Mboya has a tall fence behind the hedge. And there's a secret passage through one of the hedges into the garden of a house on one of the streets running parallel to his. Mboya comes out to warn us if a teacher shows up – you have to be quiet then.

One of his daughters brings out my beer and a glass. I light a cigarette, wipe down my sunglasses, listen to the rattling highlife from Mboya's transistor radio – and feel almost like a real human being.

When I return to Kiongozi House, Minna grabs me by the arm and sniffs my breath.

Hair of the dog

Monday afternoon I go down to Christian's to pass the time.

"I got done for drinking," I say.

"When?" he asks.

"Yesterday," I say.

"Are you out?"

"They're meeting later today. They're letting me know tomorrow," I say.

"What do you think?" he asks. I smile.

"First they caught me behind the kiosk. Then I called Minna a despotic whore and slapped Truddi. I think I'm out."

"Out for good?" Christian asks. I shrug.

"Hair of the dog, what do you say?" I ask.

"It'll have to be with Coke in it. My dad might come home."

"I don't mind," I say, and Christian says:

"But he's probably going to the school."

"Is he still on the board?" I ask.

"Yep."

"You must have been a blot on his reputation," I say. We drink our Coke-coloured beers, smoke cigarettes. A car stops in front of the house. Christian's dad comes in.

"Hello, Samantha," he says.

"Hello, *Mzee*," I say, and he smiles and says something to Christian in Danish, raising his eyebrows like he's asking a question and looking from Christian to me. He says a bit more in Danish and says to me, "Bye for now."

"Yes, bye now," I say and look at Christian.

"He didn't know who they were meeting to discuss," Christian says.

"As long as I can drink the man's beer, I'm not fussed," I say and take another of Christian's cigarettes.

The upshot of the meeting is that I get two weeks' quarantine: this week plus the one right after half-term – a total of three weeks away from school. The suspension isn't going to make keeping up academically until exams next year any easier.

Insha'Allah

"Is your mother away as well?" Owen asks when he gives me money for the bus fare as he promised Alison over the phone that he would.

"No," I say. Strictly speaking it's true. She is in England – not away from home. But it's none of his business. Obviously Owen is worried that I'll be all alone in Tanga and go crazy in a drinking-smoking-sex-and-madness frenzy.

"Are your family all at home in Tanga?"

"Alison's there. Dad might be there as well. We're just going to relax, do a bit of diving, waterskiing, fishing," I say.

"You're going to have to do some looking at your schoolbooks as well," Owen says. "Or you'll not be able to catch up."

"I'll see what I can do," I say.

"Look after yourself," he says.

"Bye," I say and go out to the school pickup, which drives me to the bus station. Then the long drive to Tanga – excruciating.

I make my way down the aisle in good time and get off at the little marketplace on the outskirts of Tanga. The taxi drivers call to me – I ignore them. I just stand there – feeling the breeze. I'm just me again; on the other hand I stink to high heaven. I look at my watch. 350 kilometres in seven hours – not bad for a bus. I go over to a kiosk to buy a Fanta.

"*Baridi?*" the girl asks – do I want a cold one?

"Yes." They always ask that, about beer as well. Many of the locals drink beer and fizzy drinks lukewarm, because they're used to *mbege*, which is always drunk lukewarm. It's a question of health as well. Ten cold pints will wreak havoc on your stomach when it's hot; they'll make you sweat and dehydrate. The same goes for fizzy drinks. Boiling hot tea is the best drink when it's hot outside.

I gulp down the Fanta greedily. Smoke a cigarette. The young taxi drivers honk their horns at me and wave at me to come over. I shake my head, because I can't be bothered with their crazy driving all the way to the hotel. I go over to the oldest driver on the lot – an old Moslem, almost full-blood Arab. I've seen him many times before – he's one of the legendary taxi drivers. He drives well, safely, looks after his car. He knows everything there is to know and that allows him to actually make a living off his driving; most drivers don't own the car they're driving – they pay a set fee for renting it for a day and have to return it to the owner with a full tank after they're done. The driver keeps the profit, if there is one.

I greet him politely.

"Are you holidaying at the hotel?" he asks.

"It's my home. I'm on holiday from the International School in Moshi," I say.

"Ahhhh, now I know you. You're *bwana* Douglas' daughter. You're almost grown." The man smiles. I get in.

"Yes," I say. "What about your children? Do they live close to you?" He's so old he will soon need his children.

"Yes, two daughters. They live close to Doda where I live with my wife," he says. Doda is on the coast north of Tanga.

"And they're well?"

"They're fine," he says. "But it's hard when the husband's only a fisherman. Not a lot of money."

"Do you have sons?" I ask.

"Yes. Shirazi – my eldest. He has gone to Zaire in search of his fortune."

"Zaire? That's a long way away. What's he doing there?" The man grins:

"Not Zaire with Mobuto Sese Seko. My son works in the mine at Merani Township where they dig for tanzanite. It's close to Moshi, isn't it? Close to the big airport?"

"Yes, it's not far. Is he a miner?"

"Yes, it's hard work. Difficult working underground. We hope Allah will smile on him."

"Maybe he'll come home a rich man," I say.

"Insha'Allah," the driver says. If the taxi were his own car, the son wouldn't have had to go underground. The driver sells me three packets of cigarettes that have been smuggled in from Kenya – they're much better than the local ones.

One big, happy family

I get off in front of the main entrance, and Alison comes running out from reception and hugs me.

"Good to see you, naughty sis," she says. "I just have to sort out these German tourists – they need a lift to Dar – but we'll have dinner together tonight."

"Yes," I say. I go through the hotel's kitchen and say hello to everyone. I have a fizzy drink in the bar – the German men gawp at my legs. Then I go inside and change into my bikini, and go down to the beach for a swim. I have a shower. I eat chicken and chips and pass out on my bed for a couple of hours. That night I just manage to have dinner with Alison before the electricity stops working. And then we sit ourselves outside with a bat light, smoking and drinking gin and tonics.

"Want a refill?" Alison asks.

"Yes, definitely. Otherwise the mosquitoes will bite my head off."

"Of course," Alison says. The quinine in it keeps the mosquitoes off. You need six, though; one for each of your arms and legs, plus one for your torso and one for your head. Mum always used to say that if you drink more than six, it's because you're a drunk. We smoke the smuggled Kenyan cigarettes that were brought across the border by the fishermen.

"There's something I have to tell you," Alison says.

"What?"

"It's about . . . I told you about Halima, remember?"

"The waitress Dad was bonking and who you sacked."

"Yes," Alison says. "He's got her pregnant."

"What?"

"Yes."

"How do we know it's his?"

"I don't think it's something she would lie about. I mean, you'll be able to tell when the baby's born anyway. Besides, he was shagging her non-stop last time he was here," Alison says and looks at me. I breathe in.

"Jesus buggery Christ."

"Yes."

"Does Mum know?"

"Yes."

"Was it here – that they were doing it?"

"In one of the empty bungalows. I've asked him. He says he's going to marry her."

"Like hell he is."

"I think he is, actually," Alison says.

"I thought the two of you had agreed he wasn't going to interfere with the running of the hotel. Isn't he breaching his promise if he sticks his cock into your head waitress?"

"What do you want me to do?" Alison asks.

"I don't know. You could always go down to Frans, I suppose."

"You know, I do want Frans. But I don't want to come running now and tell him I don't have anywhere else to go – it's not the thing; besides it would give him too much power. Men with power, they stink."

"So you're staying?"

"I don't know," Alison says.

"What if he suddenly says she's going to come and live here?"

"She's got a small house in Tanga."

"Oh. And here was I thinking we were going to be one big, happy family. I've always dreamt of having a stepmother who could be my big sister."

"Give it a rest, Samantha," Alison says. "What about you? Are there any nice boys at school?"

"No," I say. I don't tell her about Victor. I know Alison would freak out if she knew. But she's got Frans – it's so easy for her. I don't have anyone.

Happy days

"Get up," Alison says and shakes me in my bed. "I need you to help out."

"It's my holiday. Just relax, will you?" I say.

"It's not your holiday – you're suspended," Alison says. "Come on out into the kitchen." I splash some water onto my face and putter out to the kitchen. Alison has already been to the market to buy peanuts, which she is now shelling. I help her with the rest. She sprays them with salt water and pops them in the oven on a baking tray with the skin still on them. After ten minutes in the oven, the water has evaporated and the peanuts have a thin salt coating. She tells me to cut coconut into thin flakes that are then chucked into the oven in the same way.

"Time for our gin and tonics now, is it?" I ask.

"It's for the guests in the bar," she says.

"That's no reason not to get a taster now."

"Now?" Alison says. "Don't start doing what your mum does."

"She's your mum too."

"Yes," Alison says. "And I plan on doing exactly the opposite of what she's done – that way I'll have a good life." She starts making pancakes for us and puts me to work making fruit salad – no rest for the wicked.

Dad comes home late in the afternoon. He gets out of the Land Rover with a big smile on his face. We go over to him.

"Hello, girls," he calls. All's well: he can't know until he reads the letter from school, which I've burned. And I don't think he has a clue as to when it's really my holiday and when I'm supposed to be at school.

"Did you have a good trip?" Alison asks.

"Yes, it was fine," he says, sounding relaxed. I just have enough time to think that . . .

"Did you two have a good time?" he asks. Alison says:

"Yes, we've been fine . . ."

BAM – the taste of blood in my mouth, pain, flashes before my eyes.

"You're an idiot," Dad says flatly, pulling his hand back. I blink very quickly to hold my tears back.

"What?" Alison says.

"Kicked out of school for drinking," Dad says. "Bloody stupid, that's what it is."

"Where do you think she picked up the habit?" Alison asks, raising her eyebrows.

"It's only two weeks," I say, gritting my teeth, swallowing the blood in my mouth.

"How the hell could you be so stupid and get caught?"

"I'm your daughter," I say. "So I can't be stupid when you're so clever, can I?"

"My good genes must have been diluted. Diluted by your drunken mother," he says.

"You two stop it right now, or I'm leaving," Alison says.

"I stop by the school to visit my youngest daughter, and what do they tell me? *Tsk*," Dad says and, spitting on the ground, he goes over to the car and starts unloading it.

Alison doesn't say anything – we don't show any emotion when he's around. I look at his back. "Don't you get that I didn't get caught on purpose?" I say. "Are you that thick?" I start walking away as he replies:

"The day I put you on a flight back to England will be a truly happy day."

Guerrilla tactics

Dad disappears the next morning, and Alison goes off on safari with two elderly English couples who are going to Dar to see Bagamoyo and on to Ruaha, where Panos' older brother is taking them on a safari. I'm left alone to my own devices. Later in the day Dad comes back, bringing his whore, Halima. They get out. While Dad's not looking, I note that his whore's tummy is plump without bulging – you can't actually see that a seed has been planted. After that I only look at Dad – I won't dignify her with a single glance.

"I don't want her living here with me," I say. He comes over and sticks his face down close to mine.

"Don't say another word," he says. I feel no fear, because I know he never hits when it makes sense to. The blow has to come as a shock – his child-rearing methods are inspired by guerrilla warfare. He carries her bags and suitcases into the house. That way he can piss into her whenever he wants to.

I go inside and pack my things – drag them over to one of the bungalows. I stay away from the house and fetch food from the hotel's kitchen.

When it's dark, another car arrives. I go outside and look around the corner. Dad comes out on the patio.

"Victor," he says. "Welcome."

"I want you to meet Mary," Victor says. Standing next to him is a chunky-looking white woman. I choke up. Who is she? How can he do that? But then, we're not . . . anything, really. But we've got something secret. That can't stop. I start crying. I lie on my back and think about whether Victor will sneak out of his house during the night and come knocking on my door. It's a long time before I fall asleep.

Early next morning there's a knock on my door.

"Yes?" I call.

"Open the door," Dad says. I creep out of bed and open. He grips my jaw with his big hand, which has so many scars that it looks like it's been through a mincing machine. I used to be proud of his hands, but that was before I realized what he does with them.

"What?" I say as he turns my face to his.

"My partner Victor and his girlfriend Mary are staying in the big bungalow for a couple of days. If they need any sort of assistance, you help them out."

"With what?"

"Anything. If they want to go fishing or diving – that sort of thing. You behave yourself while I'm away. If I'm not back before it's time for you to go back to school, you take the bus or, if Alison is home, she will drive you. I don't want to hear that there's been any trouble," he says.

"No," I say.

"What?"

"O.K.," I say.

"What's that?"

"O.K., Dad. I'll behave."

"Good," he says and lets go of my jaw, rummages in his pocket and hands me a wad of banknotes held together with a rubber band.

"You be well, darling," he says and gives me a quick hug.

"Have a safe trip," I say to his back as he walks towards his Land Rover and drives off.

Essex girl

I go to the hotel's kitchen and make myself breakfast, then eat it standing up. I light a cigarette. Going over to the boathouse, I open the padlock and, removing the chains, loosen the mooring lines of the best speedboat. It'll be tide-out soon, so I'll have to punt the boat out.

"Can I come?" someone says. I turn around. Victor. I swallow – what am I supposed to say?

"Don't you think that . . . that you'd better stay with your girlfriend?" I say. He smiles a big, toothy smile.

161

"She's not my girlfriend, Samantha. She's just a girl I know from England. She's come for a visit," Victor says. "It's got nothing to do with you and me. Are you going diving?" he asks. Should I say more about it? What?

"Just with a snorkel and flippers. And a harpoon," I say.

"Can I come?"

"O.K.," I say. "Maybe your friend wants to come."

"I don't think so," Victor says.

"I'll go and ask her," I say and head up to the hotel, because I won't let him take complete control of the situation.

"O.K.," Victor says and smiles – a bit strained, I think. Or at least I hope so. But he stays by the boat. I skip up the staircase, which Alison has had mended. The woman whose name is Mary is sitting under a sun-shade outside the restaurant, drinking iced tea. Pale, short, chunky, with bleached hair and long pink nails. Your typical Essex girl. It occurs to me suddenly that she reminds me of how Mum used to look when I was younger. I introduce myself and ask her if she's coming out to dive with us.

"No, ladies don't do these things," she says with more than a touch of affectation, I think. Lady, my arse; she's a helpless passenger. I skip back down. The water has pulled back almost altogether.

Below the surface

"Well, go on then," I say.

"I'm pushing," Victor says. He's wearing sneakers so the corals won't cut his feet. Ten metres out there's enough water under the keel to allow me to lower the outboard motor into the water. We sail further out, while he asks me about school. I tell him as little as possible, glancing at him when he's not looking. He's good-looking: well-built, slim, tanned, the golden-blond hair on his chest is curly and bleached by the sun. He doesn't tell me anything about what he does for a living, and I don't ask. I drop our small anchor and hand him one of the harpoons; we pull on our flippers.

"There'll be squid," I say. He smiles.

"I'll see what I can do, Samantha." We jump overboard, spit into our masks and distribute the spittle on the glass to stop it from fogging up, breathe in the surface and dive down. I move towards the bottom more slowly than he does, but I also use less energy – less oxygen. His movements in the water are too abrupt, too angular, restless and without rhythm. You have to use your body like a fish would. There are plenty of moraine eels baring their teeth at us from the caves – you don't want to get too close. I see a squid between some stones. As I get into position, I notice a touch on my arm. Victor is pointing up – he's running out of air. Then, up he goes. I stay, catch the beast, and rise to the surface with the animal speared on the tip of the harpoon. He's waiting on the surface.

"Blimey, you are good at that," he says and swims up close. It feels odd when that Mary person is waiting back at the hotel. Maybe she's looking for us. "Can you teach me?" Victor says.

"Of course." And I show him how you have to let yourself slide into the water, use your flippers gently with your legs kept together, economize your oxygen. I teach him to swim on his back right below the surface so that you see the underside of the waves, glinting – vibrant blue silver in the sunshine.

"That Mary doesn't mean anything," he says as we sail back with our catch.

"She doesn't worry me," I say.

"Why not?" he asks.

"Because I am so much hotter than she is."

"True," Victor says. "Are you upset about that woman who's staying with your dad?"

"I don't think it's on," I say.

"No, I can see why. But you're almost grown-up; soon you'll be able to do whatever you want. You might want to get yourself a man like Alison has," he says, winking at me.

"I'm looking high and low," I say. "But I'm not happy with what's on offer." We pull the boat ashore so I can moor it by an iron post that has been knocked into the sand. Victor puts his hand on the small of my back. I turn to face him, put my arms around his neck, parting my lips. We kiss. His hands start roaming on my body. "That's enough," I say and let go of him, turn around and wriggle away.

"I can't wait to see you again," he says behind me. I don't know how to respond to that, so instead I flip him the bird without turning to face him. The rest of the day I make sure to stay out of sight.

Calculator

Victor and Mary leave the morning after. The hotel is a mess now that Alison isn't here. I don't want to be the slave driver. Halima swaggers about. She makes the staff do things around the house – I have no idea what. Removing all traces of my mum perhaps. From whore to self-appointed divinity. She's already behaving as if she owned the place, even though she's only twelve years older than me and barely knows how to read. But she's got a head for maths – she's got everything worked out. Her calculator's between her legs.

I stay in my bungalow, eating food from the hotel kitchen, going for swims, sleeping, reading, smoking cigarettes and a little *bhangi*. I refrain from answering when Dad's whore speaks to me.

There are only a very few guests here, and watching how the staff just let everything go to the dogs when there isn't anyone to keep them busy is painful. I'm not going to keep them to it. If his bitch is going to go around like a queen, she's going to have to look after the business as well. When she was working here, she was perfectly able to get things done. But now she's with the boss and above lifting a finger. It's a typically African attitude.

The receptionist comes to fetch me. Alison's on the phone. She's calling from Dar. I give her an account of the state of things. I am not due back at school for more than two weeks, because this week is half-term and after that I have to stay away for another week – my suspension for drinking. But right now people from school are holidaying in Dar.

"Come on down," Alison says. I go in and pack. Then I get a taxi, go to the bus station and get on the first departure south and bump along for 350 kilometres. The bus has two punctures on the way; changing the tyres take forever, and after fourteen hours I arrive in Dar feeling completely dazed.

White man's club

We're staying with Alison's friend, Melinda, who is married to an American who works at Philip Morris. He is a buyer in the Iringa area, and his company is putting itself into a prime position to buy up all the processing plants in Tanzania when the political climate changes from nationalization to privatization. The change is inevitable, because the country is on the way down. African socialism – the degree of corruption involved is ludicrous.

We're at the Yacht Club. I'm bored. It's full of people living like lords. The place is teeming with all their snotty brats. The mothers act as if they're miniature goddesses simply for having shat out a baby; the men cringe and crawl, fetching this and that, sending furtive looks at my breasts and legs.

"Let's go sailing," I say to Melinda – I suppose they must have a bloody boat when they're members of the club; after all it is a requirement.

"I don't actually sail. My husband uses our boat sometimes," she says and returns to Alison. Melinda has shat out a baby; Alison plans to sink her claws deeper into Frans so she too can sod off to Dar es Salaam and shit out a baby – they have loads to talk about. I get up and go for a walk across the square where the boats are parked, down to the beach, towards the bar and restaurant area.

"Sam?" I turn around – there's a boy with sunburn, wearing shorts and mirror sunglasses.

"Jarno," I say.

"Almost," he says.

"What are you doing here?" I ask. He shrugs, pointing at the beer bottle in the sand. I smile and sit down.

"Yes, not much else to do, is there? Have you got a cigarette?"

"Yes," he says, with a sweep of his arm. He's been home at Msumbe, has kicked up the dust for a few days and now he's staying in the Norad guesthouse for the last few days of half-term. Norad are the people his dad works for. The house isn't far from the drive-in cinema. "You can come round for supper," Jarno says.

"Do you have a cook?" I ask.

"Yes, of course I do. A live-in cook. He does the shopping and the cooking. It's like being at home – only without Mum and Dad, which makes it bloody perfect." He's pretty well plastered, or he wouldn't be able to say so many words in one go.

"Is there a bar cabinet as well?" I ask.

"Sorry, no." Jarno shakes his head.

"Is there a party anywhere tonight?"

"Just the one at Marine's Club, as far as I know," Jarno says.

"That's so bloody tedious," I say.

"White, that's what it is," Jarno says, looking around. The only blacks in sight are waiters, bartenders, cooks, the man with the broom. "We come to the blackest part of Africa, and then we go to the whitest club."

Endless Love

That night I go to the drive-in with Jarno on a motorbike he's borrowed. There's no chance of rain, so not being in a car is fine – it saves me from being locked in with a randy teenager.

"Hey, Sam, Jarno," someone says. It's Aziz, who thinks he's a playboy; tinted glasses despite the darkness. "Come over and park next to us – we've got booze," he says and explains where they are parked before going over to the kiosk to buy crisps. Jarno gets the bike started and we go over – some of the cars honk their horns at us, because the film has already started. I give them the finger. There are a couple of young local girls in Aziz's car – their clothes aren't expensive enough for them to have come from Msasani. In the car next to them is Diana with some Italian girls who go to the international school in Dar.

We chat for a bit, watch the film "Endless Love", which is so inane that the Africans, sitting in their cars, laugh out loud – and I laugh with them. White people's idea of romance with its soft music and hazy shots. As if there was no animal in the human being. The couple in the film don't even look like they're having fun. *Oohhh* – it's all so serious.

"It's not funny," Diana says sharply.

"No, it's a good film," Jarno says. But then, I've seen him gawp at Diana's bosom several times. He's totally in line with the film – gentle and romantic. He doesn't seem to have caught on to the fact that Diana needs to be taken in a way that allows her to think that she is safe in the arms of a conquering male.

Africana

I drink some of the *Konyagi* that Aziz has brought. Salomon shows up with his dreadlocks and asks if we want to come up to the Africana – the big tourist hotel on the north coast where there's a disco at night – pretty grotty, and they're completely undiscerning about who they let in. The only other option is Kilimanjaro Hotel down by the harbour where the Bar Keys are playing, but the entrance fee is steep. Hotel Africana it is. Jarno tries to lure Diana along, but she doesn't want to go. We drive there when the film is over – a long drive along the coast in the darkness, the smell of the ocean. Africana is full of fat white men with lissom black ladies. The music's not bad, but Jarno won't dance until he's drunk, and then he'll just stand with his eyes closed, swaying. Aziz wants me to come over to a corner with him.

"I've got a treat for you," Aziz says, pulling out a little bag of white powder. "Cocaine," he says. "Really high quality stuff it is too. It'll give you a buzz." I'd like to try it.

"What do you want for it?" I say.

"Hey, it's just . . . if you want a taste – strictly between friends. It won't cost you anything."

"O.K. then," I say, taking the line he cuts for me on the table. Great buzz. I dance. Aziz comes over and dances with me – pressing his groin against my hip in circles, thinking he's really intense. Tries to kiss me.

"No, Aziz. You said it wouldn't cost me anything. There'll be no kissing."

"Will you kiss me if I give you some more?"

"Fuck you," I say.

"Happily," he says.

"In your dreams." The effects of the coke are wearing off. I'd actually really like some more, but not like that. I go around for a bit. Victor! I smile. Victor is sitting at a table outside. I get my drink, touch my hair, start to walk towards him and am almost there, about to say hi when I suddenly see Mary out of the corner of my eye, wearing a skimpy pink dress that is tight across her boobs. I stop in my tracks. They haven't seen me. She sits down with a sullen look on her face without looking at him. He says something, looking fed up, gesticulating. She answers curtly, shaking her head. It looks like he's cursing as he gets up – coming straight towards the bar. I back in between people – but I can't get away in time. He's seen me.

"Samantha," he says.

"Hi," I say. "Is everything alright?" He chuckles while shaking his head.

"I should have got myself a real woman. Someone like you," he says, winking at me naughtily.

"You don't know me," I say.

"Not yet," he says. I'm aware that I'm blushing; I just hope he can't see it in the dimly lit room.

"Is . . . Mary alright?"

"Yes, yes. She's just upset because I won't come back to England with her."

"She's going to England?"

"Yes, she doesn't like it here. Look, Samantha; I don't know why she even

168

came. I didn't invite her. She's just someone I knew a bit about a year ago. You're welcome to come out and sit with us, but it's not likely to be much fun."

"No thanks, I'm alright," I say.

"Good," he says. "See you some other time, yes?"

"I'm still waiting for that telegram," I say.

"Good," he says and, taking the drinks he ordered, goes back out to Mary. I go to look for Jarno and Salomon.

"Jarno, we're leaving," I say. "And I'm driving." I manage to get the key from him. Even though he's pretty well plastered, I can still feel his stiff cock up against my arse as I drive us back to town. I get off in front of the gate to Melinda's house and call the security guard.

"Don't you want to come round to mine?" Jarno asks.

"No thanks. Goodnight."

The Lion of Zion

I return to Tanga. A week of mind-numbing boredom. Halima the Whore reigns supreme in my childhood home. My schoolbooks gather dust, despite the fact that I ought to be reading in order not to fall too far behind. I'm staying in the biggest of the bungalows with Alison. She's in a huff because of Dad, but he isn't here, so instead she takes it out on me. And she misses Frans. Luckily he can get a flight to Kilimanjaro Airport, so they arrange a romantic rendezvous in Arusha, and so the Alison who drives me there is a happy one.

Back at school. Everyone else has been at it for a week. I see Christian's back in the hall one morning. I walk up behind him and put my arm under his.

"Hello," he says, sounding surprised – people stare; they always do.

"How was your half-term?" I ask.

"All week my Dad insisted that I stay home and swot. Death, that's what it was."

"Did you, then?"

Christian grins, shrugging. "I was stranded. He chained the motorbike to a tree in the garden. Sometimes he'd unlock it when he came home from work."

"You should have cut down that tree."

"I didn't have an axe. How about you? Suspension for drinking. In Tanga?"

"Tedium. But then I went to Dar," I say. "It was nice. And then last week, back in Tanga. Tedious." The bell rings. "See you," I say and let go of his arm.

"Yes," he says and stays where he is while I wriggle down the corridor in front of him.

In the snack break I see Salomon – he's completely bald.

"So, you're not a Rasta anymore?" I say. Dreadlocks are supposed to symbolize the mane of the lion – the Lion of Zion – they say that when they're gone, you're weak.

"Rasta isn't in your hair – it's a state of mind," he says and adds, "My scalp started itching, so they had to go." He walks away. Aziz is standing with a nasty smile on his face.

"What?" I say.

"Salomon was sleeping, and his dad came in and chopped off a bunch of dreads. Salomon was a very one-sided Rasta when he woke up," Aziz says.

"Not much of a Rastafari that Ethiopian ambassador, is he?" I say.

"Nope," Aziz says.

A bit further down the corridor I bump into Jarno, who is looking sad even though he still has his dreads. Diana hooked up with an American marine before half-term was over – the soldier hadn't bought into the message of "Endless Love". I don't say anything about it to Panos, because now she's going about snogging him again.

Telegram

A secretary comes to fetch me in the middle of our history lesson. What have I done this time? Owen is sitting in his office with a grave look on his face.

"A telegram has arrived for you," he says. I smile. He looks confused. "Were you expecting a telegram?" he asks. I realize he thinks it must be bad news: an accident, a death, shipwreck . . .

"Yes," I say and tear open the envelope. "Am at the Y.M.C.A. V.," it says. "My cousin has had a daughter – they're going to call her Samantha." I smile at Owen.

"Congratulations," Owen says.

"Thank you," I say, fanning myself with the telegram as I leave his office. After the next lesson I skip lunch. I go straight to the car park, but when I hear Christian's motorbike I stop and stay where I am until he's gone. Then I get a lift with some Germans who live close to the police school. I walk the final bit down to the Y.M.C.A. Victor is nowhere to be seen.

"My uncle is staying here," I say. "Victor Ray – what room is he in?" The receptionist tells me the room number, and I go up to the third floor and find the room; my knees feel weak, everything seems really clear. I knock on the door. Victor opens – naked chest and boxer shorts. He steps into the corridor.

"Samantha," he says and lifts me up, so that I'm lying in his arms. He bends his head and kisses me. "Let me carry you to where you belong," he says.

"Yes," I say. And he carries me to his bed.

"I've missed you," he says, undressing me, kissing every new bit of skin – little tongues of water lapping at the beach until they grow and the waves crash heavily and suck my body out to sea.

I take a taxi back to school – I just pretend everything is as usual. No-one can tell from the way I look that I've got Victor. It's my secret. It's great.

A private person

Christian's dad is away on business, so he's constantly skiving off. He goes to the toilet to smoke cigarettes, is caught – gets a warning.

Friday there's a party at Kilele House. I go there with Tazim. It's not much fun until I hear a motor bike. It's Christian. He stops on the road outside the Kilele fence, gets off and lights a cigarette. I go out to the fence. It's not an ordinary cigarette.

"Hi, Samantha," he says. "Fancy a little *bhangi*?" He comes over to the fence and sticks the end of the spliff through the wire.

Seppo, who has seen him, comes out of the gate and says:

"Christian. I'm going to have to tell you to leave school premises right now. Monday morning at eight you report to Owen's office."

"Hey, you can't tell me what to do. I'm a man on the street, smoking my own weed. I'm a private person. You have no rights over me." Christian takes another puff, sucking it deep into his lungs looking straight at Seppo and blowing smoke in his direction. Seppo comes towards him. Christian raises a fist with the spliff stuck between his index and middle finger.

"If you hit me, I'll hit you," he says. Seppo stops. Christian grins and, putting the spliff back in his mouth, gets back on the motorbike and tears down the road until he is swallowed by darkness.

I ask him about it that Monday. He's due a week's suspension, but they can't get hold of his dad, so for now they keep him on because they've finally realized that he's living on his own in the house while his dad is away. And what would Christian do without someone to look after him? Later they manage to get in touch with his father who arranges for Christian to stay with some Swedish friends of his. And then the father has to report to school as soon as he gets back to Moshi. Christian really ought to have been expelled, but his school fees are being paid in foreign currency and the school can't afford to lose more income.

A week later Christian is lodged in Kijana House as a boarder.

"It was a fucking requirement, because the old man is away from home so much of the time," he says. "Either he had to sign me up as a boarder, or they wouldn't keep me on."

"So the next time you do something like that, you're out on your ear," I say. Christian smiles.

"Exactly," he says.

"Well you don't have to be in such a bloody hurry," I say.

"No, but it's nice to be in control of the situation."

"Yes, but it'll be so boring if you go."

"You can't do anything here," he says. "It's like a prison."

I go down to Kilele House and lie down on the bed in my new room and look up at the ceiling. I have been moved from Kiongozi House down to board with the oldest girls because I was constantly rowing with Truddi.

Staying here is better. I share a room with Adella, a girl from Uganda who barely says anything at all. Her parents and two older brothers were murdered by Idi Amin. Adella and her little brother were sent off to Tanzania and told to survive. Idi Amin murdered almost every other member of her clan. She and her little brother are at school on scholarships paid for by the tribe's exile community in Europe. I like her. When it's lights out in the evening, she sits at the desk and rolls a spliff. Before she lights it, she presses a towel into the crack under the door so nothing seeps out. We smoke in silence. It's really nice.

During the day I try to mind my own business and stay out of trouble.

Trouser thief

It's my seventeenth birthday. After lunch I go to my compulsory tennis lesson. Sally makes me play some Indian tart called Naseen. She totters about in her high heels and hits none of the balls I deliberately aim at her to scare her.

"*Mwizi, mwizi!*" The call comes from the teachers' houses on the far side of the tennis court. I throw down my racket and run over with several others. In one of the gardens we see ten or twelve men and women – cooks and maids from the teachers' houses and some of the school's gardeners. They shout and kick at a man who is lying on the ground. My English teacher, Mr Cooper, comes running up to them.

"Stop. Stop!" he shouts. They stop reluctantly and stand aside, but only so much. A man is lying huddled up on the ground, bleeding from wounds to his head and on his face. "What are you doing?" Cooper asks. A maid bends over and holds up a pair of jeans that are lying on the ground.

"He tried to steal your trousers from the clothesline," she says in Swahili.

"What's she saying?" Cooper asks. I translate. The man on the ground is bleeding from his mouth – maybe he has internal bleeding.

"You're all mad," Cooper says in English and shakes his head.

"We've saved your jeans," the maid says with visible pride – at the bus station you could sell jeans like that for what a man makes in a month. I explain it to Cooper. Owen has arrived. Cooper asks him to get the school's pickup.

"Yes, he must be taken to the police," one of the gardeners says in English.

"He must be taken to the hospital," Cooper says.

"Police first," the gardener says. Cooper doesn't answer.

The pickup arrives – they drive the battered thief away while the crowd cheers with excitement at their own good deed.

Fish

In the dining hall Panos sits at the same table as Sandeep the Cat Man and Adella. I walk over to them. Today's main course is fish – a rare treat inland because there are next to no refrigerated cars in Tanzania. Nile perch from Lake Victoria. It smells good. I pile some onto my plate and pass the bowl on to Sandeep, then I take a mouthful. It tastes nice as well.

"No thanks," Sandeep says.

"Don't you eat fish?" I ask him.

"I come from Bukoba," he says.

"Yes. By Lake Victoria. Don't you eat fish in Bukoba?"

"Not after Idi Amin we don't – my mother has never let us have fish after that again," Sandeep says. His dad is Indian, and Idi Amin threw all the Indians out of Uganda, but Sandeep's mum is black – he's the only person I've met who is half Indian, half black.

"Try to explain why fish and Idi . . ." I start when I suddenly realize. Idi Amin: mass murderer. He had deep freezers with the heads of his victims so he could take them out and talk to them. He killed 300,000 people. Countless bodies were thrown into Lake Victoria, the crocodiles feasted and the fish population soared. "Cannibalism," I say.

"Well, very nearly," Sandeep says:

"Would you eat a fish that has eaten a man?" I push away my plate.

"It's been years," Panos says.

"Five years," Sandeep says. I point at Panos' plate:

"So, do you like your Ugandans?" I ask.

"*Tsk*," he says and says and spears another piece of fish with his fork. And suddenly I remember Adella and look at her. Adella only eats chicken – no other meat. Her face looks all wrong. Panos holds up his fish and looks at it, "The fish ate the enemies of Idi Amin, so what? They were men of honour – good people. Tasty people," he says, popping the fish into his mouth and starting to chew it. Adella giggles hysterically, then starts crying and coughing violently and, getting up abruptly, runs out of the dining hall. "What?" Panos says.

"Her parents were killed by Idi Amin," I say, eyeing his fish. Panos nods:

"Good people," he says and continues eating.

That night I have to crawl into Adella's bed and hold her. She can't stop crying, but in the end she does stop and speaks calmly:

"We were sailed off at night from Port Bell by a fisherman. It was dark and there was no wind. He rowed out from the shore, and then he started the motor and navigated by the stars and lights on the coast. It was just me and my brother in the boat, and I was afraid because I didn't know him. He had been paid, so really he could just throw us overboard. My brother fell asleep, but I wouldn't allow myself to drop off. After a long time the horizon started to seem a bit more grey – it was almost morning. And then the boat bumped into something so big the fisherman had to slow down, and I asked him if it was crocodiles, because I couldn't see anything – the water was still too dark. He told me to close my eyes, but I wouldn't close them, because I was afraid of him. And the boat kept bumping into things, and there was a strange smell, and he asked me if I had closed my eyes, and I said yes. And then the dawn came just as he speeded up the boat and things were being pushed away from the hull of the boat, and I looked – it was light enough to see now. The surface of the lake was full of bloated bodies, floating in the water – some of them had been partly eaten by crocodiles and fish. Idi Amin liked to feed the fish." Adella hugs my arms close to her chest.

"Shhh," I say. "It's over now."

"I always think about my family," Adella says. "I should have been there with them."

Mum's dog

Christmas is fast approaching. Dad is in Uganda or Zaire or . . . He's sent a letter, telling me to get the bus home to Tanga like some peasant. How can he treat me like that? The phone is disconnected, so I can't get hold of Alison and ask her what's going on. Or whether she's even there.

"Sam. Phone," Adella calls. I jump up from my bed and run over.

"Who is it?" Adella simply smiles and hands me the phone.

"Samantha here," I say.

"Darling – do they call you Sam?"

"Mum!"

"Hello. How are you?"

"Are you coming down for Christmas?" I ask.

"No. I can't. I have to work."

"But . . . Come on."

"How's school?"

"It's shit, really. It's a school. Why can't you come down on holiday? Dad would pay, wouldn't he?"

"I don't want to be with your dad any longer. It's nice here. When you've finished school, I want you to come and live with me."

"In England?"

"England isn't that bad, Samantha."

"It's bloody freezing and the people are weird."

"We'll be together," Mum says.

"So it's been decided, has it? Don't I get a say?"

"What would you rather do?" she asks. I don't answer.

"What do you do for a living?" I ask.

"I've found work."

"What kind of work?"

"I'm . . . at a hotel." She sighs. "I'm the night clerk."

"Isn't Dad sending you money?"

"Yes, but there's trouble at the hotel in Tanga. He's short of cash."

"Yes, of course he is. He's bonkers. But are you . . . O.K.?"

"I don't drink anymore," she says.

"That's good. But . . . aren't you going to see him again?" As soon as I ask the question I realize how ridiculous it is. Dad is shagging the waitress.

"We're getting a divorce," Mum says.

"But . . ."

"Why do they call you Sam?" she asks.

"Sam – a man among sheep."

"But is school alright?"

"Yes," I say. "It'll be fine."

"I know I promised to send you some clothes, Samantha. But it'll have to wait a little."

"Don't worry about it – I can always steal some from the white girls here."

Mum chooses not to hear that.

"What would I do in England?" I say.

"You could get an education," Mum says.

"What sort of education?"

"Any sort you like."

"You know I'm not bookish."

"But there are vocational training courses as well. We'll worry about that when you get here," Mum says. "Have you got yourself a nice boyfriend?"

"No," I say. "Have *you* got yourself a nice boyfriend?"

"After your father I've had enough of men. I'm thinking about getting a dog," Mum says, and we laugh. Then she can't afford to talk any longer.

The Seychelles

I'm told to go to the Headmaster's office. What did I do this time? I haven't done anything wrong in weeks; at least I haven't been found out.

Oh bugger. Dad's in there.

"Samantha," he says, taking me in his arms. "It's been such a long time since our family has spent any time together," he tells Owen. "After their mother went back to England . . . And I've been so busy; Mozambique, Uganda – I'm constantly on the go. So, now's the time."

"Yes," Owen says and nods empathetically. I wonder if he knows what it is Dad does for a living. What it is that pays my school fees.

"What?" I say. Owen smiles at me. What's going on?

"We're going to the Seychelles on holiday – you, me, Alison. And Frans. We're staying the night at Tanzanite, and then we're flying out tomorrow from Kilimanjaro Airport."

"O.K.," I say and go to do my packing. I suppose it's common for psychopaths to be unpredictable. Tomorrow is the last day of term; I'm cool with it as long as Alison is there.

The next day Mahmoud from the lodge drives me and Dad to the airport where we catch a flight to Dar where Alison and Frans get on.

We arrive in the Seychelles. A tiny island group a thousand miles east of Dar es Salaam. It's startlingly beautiful.

The guesthouse is quite some way up the mountain on the main island. Dad rents an open car for us so we can drive around, get into town, get down to the beach. I don't care much about food, but the food here is just . . . wow; it's an abundance of seafood. Alison gives Frans a two-day diver's course for Christmas. In the week leading up to New Year's Eve we do nothing but eat, drink and lie on the beach. It's lovely, really lovely.

1985

Birder

A couple of days into the new year, Frans begins his diving course at a hotel on the beach. Me and Alison lounge by the pool, gin and tonics in hand, while a big, hairy-backed man with a handlebar moustache gives Frans a crash course in how to check his equipment, the diving signals, how two people can share one oxygen bottle, different manoeuvres. Tomorrow Frans is going to try it out in the sea.

After the course we drive into town. Every nationality and race is represented: Indians, Africans, Arabs, Whites – even Chinese. Everyone's interbred with everyone else for generations – they look amazing. Except for the Chinese, who are superior to all the others and who consequently have only mated with each other – inbreeding taken to a whole new level.

We sit ourselves on a roof terrace and order drinks and lunch.

"Is Mick still in Dar?" I ask Alison.

"Yes," she says. "He's become the daytime manager at a security guard company that's responsible for K.L.M.'s security in the airport among other things."

"And he's good at it," Frans says, nodding.

"Good for him," I say. Mick – I do like him, but he's a boy, an oversized baby.

"You'll see him when you come down and stay with us in Dar," Alison says.

"Your dad and birds – that is strange, isn't it?" Frans says. Dad went off as soon as we got up with his bag and his binoculars and his camera in the car he has rented for himself. "I'm going birding," he said when Frans asked him about it. Alison sighs and smiles.

"He's not really birding, you know," she says.

"Then what is he doing?" Frans asks.

"Preparing a *coup d'état*," Alison says.

"A coup? Against which government?"

"The government here in the Seychelles."

"But . . ."

"On behalf of a group of oppositionists in . . . London, I think it is," Alison says.

"But . . ." Frans looks disoriented.

"He's out having a look around: drawing up maps, taking pictures, calculating how much time they would need. Then he and his men can take over the key spots on the island – electricity and water supplies, communications, the harbour and airport."

"Are they here now?" Frans asks and looks around very quickly – I almost laugh out loud.

"No. I don't know when it's going to happen, but it won't be while we're here. It's not even certain that it will happen at all – he's just looking into it."

"Has he told you that?"

"No," Alison says. "He doesn't have to – I can think for myself."

"Doesn't it bother you?" Frans asks.

"Doesn't what bother me?"

"That he's . . . involved in that sort of thing?"

"He always has been – all his adult life. What do you want me to say?" Alison says. I laugh.

"Is it funny?" Frans says.

"No, but he's the one doing it – not us," I say and point at myself and Alison. "We're just trying to get away from the man."

"Isn't there a risk he could end up in prison or . . . be killed?"

"Of course there is," I say. "The latter seems preferable to me."

"But if he pulls it off, they'll probably allow him to settle down here," Alison says.

"This is crazy." Frans shakes his head.

"Maybe," Alison says.

"I don't think so," I say.

"But is he . . ." Frans starts.

"A mercenary," I say. "Yes. He's a former S.A.S. officer. He was booted out in 1969 because he used extended leave to go to Nigeria and fight for Biafra in the 4th Commando Brigade during the civil war."

"Does he just go about waiting for his next assignment, then?" Frans asks.

"No." Alison explains it to him, "The last few years he's dealt mostly in training guards for mining companies in Katanga, advising the military and that sort of thing. And he owns a couple of businesses in Tanzania."

Dad doesn't come back that evening. He's not there the following morning. We drive down to the hotel and sail out to the coral reef with the hairy man. Frans does his first scuba-dive. Alison has rented the full gear while I just have a snorkel, a mask and my flippers. The boat has a glass bottom; the seabed slopes downwards until – suddenly – an explosion of colours: a huge coral reef with an abundance of shoals. We drop anchor. They dive down while I smoke a cigarette in the boat with a local boy. We watch the others through the glass panel in the bottom of the boat. They get as far down as ten or twelve metres.

"I'm going to swim down to them," I say.

"I'll come with you," he says. We jump off the boat – pull on our flippers and masks, lie breathing for a while on the surface until we swim down. Nice and easy, through the water – saving our breath. Frans' eyes are enormous when he sees me. I wave at him and swim around a little before rising to the light.

Women and children

Dad is there when we return to the guesthouse. That evening he takes us out to the best restaurant – we sit outside and look out over the city and the sea. Alison asks Dad what it was like when we were little.

"What do you mean?"

"Having babies?" Alison asks.

"It was hard work," he says.

"Like you would know," I say.

"You were still in the military then, weren't you?" Alison asks.

"I was," he says – not adding anything about how he got the boot for going to Biafra as a mercenary.

"I suppose Mum must have been the one who looked after us," I say.

"It was your mum who made having you so difficult," he says grinning and, turning to Frans, says, "It's not until your woman has children that you find out who she really is. Everything that once was goes away – the children change her character and personality. She's no longer yours – she's theirs."

"It can't be as bad as all that," Alison says.

"It must change the man as well," I say.

"Yes, but not nearly as much," Dad says. "A man can't breastfeed – he's on the outside. But it changes his relationship with his woman. It's the lack of sleep. Once the woman hasn't slept for six months, civilization is peeled back and the real monster peers out at you. Not sleeping is torture; it can break almost anyone." He looks at Frans again. "You have no idea what you're getting yourself into," Dad says. Frans smiles without saying anything. "Your mum almost lost it," Dad says.

"And yet you spawned another," I say. He looks at me as if not understanding. "Halima," I add. Does the fool even remember who he has impregnated?

"African women aren't like that. They work until they go into labour, and then they go back to work when the child's come out – none of that whingeing."

"Oh, come off it," Alison says.

"It's God's honest truth," Dad says.

"I don't want you to sit there and spill your bullshit stories about women when Frans is here – I don't want him infected with that sort of thing."

"Don't worry," Frans says. "I'm not like your dad."

"No," Dad says. "You're not." Alison folds her hands and looks heavenwards: "Thank God. Amen."

"What would you have done if Alison had found someone like you, Dad?" I ask.

"Alison is my daughter," he says, looking at her. "So I think she has more sense than to find someone like me."

"Why haven't you brought your partner?" Alison asks.

"My partner? Juma?"

"No, not Juma," Alison says. "That Victor."

"Why would I bring him?"

"The Seychelles seems like just the place for you and him."

"What would you know about it?"

"I'm not half-witted, you know," Alison says. "What does he do?"

"I think Victor's in Angola."

"But what does he do for a living?" Alison asks. Dad bends his head and looks at her with knitted brows.

"What do you do for a living?" Frans asks.

"That's my business," Dad says.

The head of the family

Alison and Frans get off in Dar es Salaam – I wish I could stay with them. The aeroplane takes off again. We approach Kilimanjaro.

"Is someone coming to fetch us?" I ask.

"You'll just get a taxi back to school," Dad says.

"But I'm not going back to school so soon, am I? There's more than a week left of the holiday," I say.

"Yes, but you can't come with me. Mahmoud is coming to K.I.A. with the Land Rover, and I'm going to straight to Lake Victoria."

"I could stay at Mountain Lodge until term starts," I say.

"No," Dad says. "We can't keep banking on their hospitality."

"But there might not be any pupils at school," I say.

"There are a couple of pupils who stay at the school during holidays," Dad says. "I've spoken to Owen."

"But . . ." I start.

"No," he cuts me off. Bastard. What's he doing at Lake Victoria anyway? They dig for diamonds in Shinyanga. Copper in Zambia. Gold and diamonds and copper in Zaire, Uganda and Rwanda. Too many people, good soil for farming, and minerals galore. Maybe he's going to train guards for a mining company or teach weaponry to a herd of ignorant villagers who have been forced to enlist in the lastest tribal war. The rebel soldiers can neither read nor write. "The most advanced equipment they've ever dealt with is a bat light," Dad usually says. He teaches weaponry and weapon maintenance as well as basic tactics. I'm not supposed to ask about his work – I'm not supposed to talk about it at all. Those are the rules I was brought up with. He will hit me if I break them. Not today, but when I least expect it. Maybe that's over now – I'm a big girl after all.

"What are you going to do there?"

"It's just business," he says. When he returns from his business trips, he always tells us a little, but it's invariably perfectly innocent. I yawn. I need a cigarette.

At school we don't talk about what our parents do either. *Why do you even ask? Does it matter? They're old. It's got nothing to do with me.* People get offended if you ask – I get offended. The Scandinavian boys all think that they're Rastafaris, Africans. Rasta – what's that? An excuse to smoke *bhangi*? A bunch of bleached Jamaicans with bad hair and positive vibes who think Africa is the best? But we're still our parents' passengers. We're children. I was dragged here when I was three years old. We have lived on the skills my parents brought from England. We're not Africans. And now Dad says I'm going home to England when I finish school. It's ridiculous. A foreign country.

Dad's sitting on the plane trying to look like a civilian: a pale blue shirt and trousers with knife-edge creases. Who does he think he is, really? A former S.A.S. officer – the British special forces. Currently a mercenary and businessman, and head of a family. A crook with a heart of gold? He always gets up at five in the morning to "make the most of the day", which is how he puts it. It's not a problem because his evenings start with a sundowner before 6.00 p.m., and by 10.00 p.m. he has drunk himself into such a stupor that he passes out. Onwards, onwards, onwards. Does he ever think about anything but the next thing? I don't want to be like that. Everything he does in his life is wrong – nothing good will come of it.

Crashing hard

Taxi from the airport – I'm a week early. What am I supposed to do at school? I hope Adella is there. I make the driver drive me through town to the market and tell him to wait. I go over to Phantom in his little kiosk by the entrance and have to pay through my nose before he gives in and hands me some, wrapped in newspaper.

My houseboss at Kilele House is Mrs Smith. She's hasn't been told I was coming, and Adella isn't here either. Mrs Smith sighs: "You can have supper in the dining hall at school – they serve supper to the guards at 6.30. Breakfast and lunch you'll have to have with us." No way am I going to sit down and eat with the Smiths.

"I wouldn't want to trouble you," I say. "Can't we arrange it so that your cook gives me a plate of food?"

"O.K. – I'll tell him to expect you."

So, I'm on my own at Kilele House. I sit down outside behind the small *kibanda* in the garden where some of the pupils have sex. I roll myself a huge spliff and smoke until my tongue feels green. I go back inside and lie down on the bed. It's not good *bhangi* – I feel heavy and out of sorts; my engine is coughing and spluttering. I let my fingers glide over the bricks in the wall as I wobble down the hall and into the toilet. I sit down. What a strange sensation . . . Bugger it . . . I haven't pulled down my knickers. *Oh no*.

"Shitting-pissing-sick-shit." I start sobbing. I wail as I toddle out of the cubicle and start bashing the door into the wall over and over. There's a loud crashing sound; the door splits at the top. I lean against it, holding on to the doorknob and try to get my knickers off without getting shit on my fingers, and my legs go all wobbly while I have the soiled knickers down around my ankles, and I slide to the floor. Someone's coming. Mrs Smith – the gardener has heard my wailing. It's so humiliating.

"Malaria," I say, because malaria can fuck you up completely when it hits hard, and it's common in the Tanga area – the hardcore sort. And then you can't think straight.

The white people

Mrs Smith manages to shove me into the shower and fetches a towel for me. Afterwards she drives me to *mama* Hussein's sickbay at Kijito House.

Mama Hussein supports me to the sickbay and puts me in one of the beds. She feels my forehead, looks me into the eyes and takes my temperature.

"You're high," she says, stating the fact. No malaria. "Why did you get high, Samantha?"

"I just had to . . . get out of my head."

"Why did you have to? Isn't your head a good place to be?"

"No, it's so . . . confusing. Because my mum has upped and gone to England, and my dad . . ." I start crying again – telling her more than she needs to know: "He wants to send me to England after Year Ten, and his whore is already moving into our house."

"His whore?"

"A waitress from the restaurant that he's started pissing into."

"Why do you call her a whore? She's a human being too, isn't she? Maybe they like each other." I look at *mama* Hussein:

"What would you like me to call her? A dreamer?"

"So, you're going to England after Year Ten – in six months or so?"

I sigh: "Yes."

"And what will you do there?"

"Die."

"What do you mean?"

"They'll kill me."

"Who will?"

"The white people."

"Which white people?"

"The English. The white people in England."

"Why?"

"Because I am . . . I am too much of a negro."

"You are white," *mama* Hussein says. "They can't tell that you are a negro."

"White on the outside. Inside I'm all . . . grey."

"What are you going to do?"

I shrug. I do not know.

Haze

Mama Hussein keeps me with her. I'm thinking about Victor, but what good does that do me? I don't know how to get in touch with him. I don't know what to do if I bump into him. I don't know anything. I get a terrible cold and diarrhoea. After a week they let me go back to Kilele House. It starts raining. It buckets down. Everything is sodden. Sweat pours from my body if I so much as chew on a piece of toast at breakfast. The towels are never dry. Everything smells of old dampness – fusty.

The boarders are supposed to return today, but not many of them do. It turns out that everyone from Dar is stranded at the airport because the president has taken the aeroplane to Kampala, and the other planes have broken down.

School starts the following day – the classrooms are half empty. Late in the afternoon the others show up. Tazim hasn't spoken to me in a long time. Now she's speaking to me like nothing's happened. I don't answer her. I ignore her. And then school's up and running again; everyone cramming like mad – exams are closing in on us. Tazim and Salomon are having problems – she's running to that priest of hers again. In a couple of weeks they'll give us time off to revise. Being here is unbearable. I can't pull myself together at all. Revising, sitting exams . . . it means nothing to me. I walk about in a haze.

The condemned man

Reading week is fast approaching. Christian has been moved down to be with the oldest pupils at Kishari House because a place has opened up. One weekend there's panic among the teachers responsible for him. Christian has disappeared. Of course he's in town with his local friend, Marcus. When Christian returns on Sunday afternoon, there are a number of meetings in Owen's office. It's only been a few months since he was made a boarder. Now he's expelled. There is no mercy.

"Last K.C. of the condemned man," Christian says and drinks *Konyagi*-Cola from a Coke bottle. We're standing outside Mboya's and have bought a couple of the small plastic bags of *Konyagi*, which we pour into the Coke bottle after we've taken a few initial gulps. Just to give it a bit of kick – to get a buzz. Diana and Truddi are sitting on a bench not far away staring – we stand as far from them as we can in the courtyard. The Bultaco is clicking away in the shade under the trees while the engine cools down. It's Saturday. Christian is going to Shinyanga with his dad tomorrow. Later he is flying to Denmark. He's going to live in his mum's sister's basement and retake Year Eleven of the Danish school system in a few months' time.

"You'll be fine," I say.

"Yes," he says and lights a cigarette, holding it for me so I can take a puff. "I'm looking forward to getting out of here – living just for me." He lets me have another puff, and I blow a big, fat smoke ring at him. Christian lifts his hand and pops his middle finger right through it.

"You'd like that, wouldn't you?" I say.

"Been there," he says. I punch him on the shoulder.

Truddi sneers at us from her seat on the bench, "You two are sick."

"Shut it," I say. Christian is standing there, swallowing. His face looks like mine feels: tortured.

"I'll just get it started," he says and grabs the motorbike. Something's wrong with the kick starter. He runs along next to it and jumps on it when it starts, then turns it and returns to me. I bottle it up inside. Now he's dead too. Like Gretchen when she left. The roar of the engine means that Diana and Truddi can't hear us. Christian takes off his sunglasses and looks into my eyes for a second before he puts them on me. I smile. Ray-Bans. We hug.

"Do you feel the emptiness?" I ask.

"Yes," he says into my ear. "Pretty grim, isn't it?"

"Yes."

"I'll see you around," he says.

"Yes," I say and am glad that the sunglasses are covering my eyes now. He lets go of me and revs up the engine. His eyes are watering. He doesn't smile. Then he's off, the engine roars through the gears, the dust explodes from the back tire; he's round the corner, down the dirt road, out of sight, gone. I am left standing, looking in the direction of a sound that only gets fainter.

"So, Sam," Truddi says. "Soon you'll have no friends left."

I walk up to her. She looks scared.

"I am not afraid of you," she says. I punch her in the ear. She screams.

"You're crazy!" Diana shouts. Yes, I am. I walk away. Heading up towards the school, kicking at the ground so the dust rises in cloudlets around my calves, colouring them red. What now? Then I hear the sound of a motorbike. It's probably just Osbourne. No, it's Christian. He is coming back. He flings the bike on the ground, his eyes are full of tears. Mine mist up. He throws his arms around me. His voice trembles in my ear.

"I'll come down in a year – on holiday. I promise," he says.

"I don't know if I'll be here."

"If you're in England, I can . . ." Christian starts. I cut him off:

"Yes, but . . ." I stop. Stand still. He lets go of me, bends down for the motorbike. Runs next to it to get it started and jumps onto it. Drives away.

Hitchhiking

Thursday Panos tells us that he's going to Arusha the following weekend to drink. He's going to stay over at the Strand brothers'. "Svein and Rune might come as well – they want to go to Hotel Saba-Saba for the disco."

"Alright," I say, nodding. We both have Weekend Exeat Permits from our parents and can leave school on the weekends when we want to. Even though Dad has told me not to visit Mountain Lodge. The Norwegians say they want to catch the bus. Panos shakes his head:

"I've got double detention first," he says.

"For doing what?"

"For leaving in the middle of a lesson."

"When was that?" I ask.

"Yes, you wouldn't bloody know, would you?" he says. "You didn't even show up."

"Ohhhh, that's right – I was ill."

"Ill, my arse."

"It was that time of the month," I say, smiling.

"It's that time of the month every week," he says.

"Can we get a bus then?" I ask.

194

"I'll hitchhike," Panos says. "I can't be arsed to sit with three Maasais on my lap while a goat shits on my shoes."

Friday afternoon I sit outside the library and wait while Panos takes books down and dusts the bookcases for two hours. Afterwards we stomp out onto Lema Road. We grin at each other when we see the first car approaching. On our side. But it doesn't stop for us.

"Fascist," Panos says. Sometime later a pickup comes clattering along. Once again we hold out our hands, palms down and thumbs wiggling – that's how you hitch in Africa. The car doesn't stop, but it's going so slow we can jump into the back. The man looks out through the rear window of the driver's cabin with obvious surprise.

"Thanks a bunch," Panos calls in Swahili. We get off on Kilimanjaro and walk across the golf course down to Arusha Road where we quickly get a lift with a political apparatchik in a brand new Land Rover, complete with chauffeur and air conditioning. We talk about our school and the nation. Panos tells us about his Greek father, a former sailor who went ashore in Dar in the early 1960s because he was fed up with the sea. These days he runs an enormous tobacco farm in Iringa. Panos' mother is half English, half black Tanzanian, born here and works as a schoolteacher. Panos says that his father has difficulties expressing his feelings. When he wants to tell his wife he loves her, he puts on a record with a sappy song and asks her to dance.

"Then what does he do when he's angry?" the careerist asks.

"Don't worry, he knows how to punch," Panos says.

We're set down outside Mount Meru Hotel and go into town and grab a bite to eat before heading to the Strands' house in the well-to-do area southeast of the city centre. It's getting dark already.

"Where are we going to sleep?" I ask Panos.

"I think I'll crash with the Strands," he says. I don't want to – an entire night of having to ward off horny boys.

"What about the glue sniffers?" I ask.

"They probably have a room at Arusha Hotel."

Saba-Saba

When we arrive Svein and Rune are sitting in the garden with Emerson and Gideon Strand. They've already had a few beers, and Emerson is rolling up a spliff.

"Aren't we having any bitches round?" Svein asks.

"Sam's here, isn't she?" Emerson says.

"Shut up," I say. Panos has drained his first beer and started on number two. He doesn't care about bitches – he just wants to get shitfaced.

"Shall we go to Saba-Saba then?" Rune asks.

"I'm not fussed," Panos says.

"Of course we're going," Svein says. We drink some more and then we go. Saba-Saba is Swahili for seventy-seven. It's a large conference hotel built for the meeting of the Group of Seventy-seven Nations in 1979. Mount Meru Hotel is right next to it and is slick by comparison. But Saba-Saba has big disco nights – the biggest in Arusha. We get in, and after only three seconds Svein is talking to a couple of whores. Rune wants to hook up with me, but luckily he's too scared to make a move. Emerson knows he doesn't stand a chance – he won't forget that until he's had a lot more to drink. Thirteen-year-old Gideon feels me up under the table until I threaten to pummel him. Panos I've known for years. It would be like snogging your brother. Besides he's very much in love with Diana, the fool, and she's giving him hell for having messed around with Truddi, who he used to be in love with. I go up to the bar and squeeze in next to Panos.

"Can't you ask Rune for the key to their room? Tell him you want to sleep there."

"Why?" he asks.

"I can't be bothered to stay."

"Why don't you ask him yourself?"

"He'd just follow me there."

"Yes, I should think he would," Panos says, grinning. He gets me the key and tells me that Svein has one as well, so I don't have to wait up. I take a taxi – I don't fancy walking alone at night, thank you very much. I plod straight through reception – I'm white, of course I have a room. I let myself in. I think about taking one of the beds, but they're the ones paying for the room, so I just grab a blanket and lie down on the floor by the window.

One kick only

"No, you have to wait outside," Svein says.

Where am I?

"I'm tired, damn it," Panos says. "I want to go to sleep."

Arusha Hotel.

"Just give me ten minutes, yeah? Then you can have a go as well."

On the floor? With a blanket over me.

"You're sick, you are," Panos says.

What's going on?

"Just get it over with, Svein," Rune says. The door is shut. I'm lying completely still.

"Karibu," Svein says.

"*Lete shilingi*," a female voice says – give me the money. Who is that? The sound of money being counted out. "*Sawa*," she says – alright then. The sound of . . . clothes. Being taken off. Oh bugger. A little bit of light is coming through the curtain from a lamp outside. I turn my head so I can see the beds. Four legs. Then the springs in the bed by the door give – loudly – and two of the legs are suddenly off the floor.

"*Njoo Bwana*," the woman says – come, man. Christ almighty, he's paid some fat mama at the disco to come back here with him. Svein's legs go as well.

"*Nzuri sana*," he says – very nice. The numbskull. What do I do? My eyes are getting used to the darkness. The springs are squeaking – none of them will be able to hear me moving. I prop myself up on one elbow, lift my head above the bed so I can see the other bed where . . . Svein has her enormous breast in his mouth as he groans pathetically and thrusts into her – you almost can't see him for her enormous thighs.

"*Wewe, fanya kazi!*" she says – do the job. Yes, I suppose he is doing his humble best. I suppress a giggle, lowering my head just as Svein groans. That didn't take him long. He gets up, puts on his boxers, opens the door and calls to Rune.

Svein says something in Norwegian while the mama gets up lazily and reaches for her dress.

"*Mmoja Mwegine,*" Svein says – one more.

"*Sawa,*" the mama says. "*Lete shilingi ngine.*" She can do another, but she must be paid more money. Svein says he's paid for everything. She raises her voice and says he's only paid for one kick. Two kicks are going to be almost twice as much, but she can offer them good price until tomorrow morning. Rune says something in Norwegian – his voice is nervous, probably because the woman is speaking loudly. Apparently he's run out of money.

"O.K.," Svein says, sounding resigned. The mama pulls on her dress over her head, slips her feet into her shoes and leaves. Panos comes in and puts on the light. I roar with laughter.

"WHAT?" Svein shouts. Panos starts laughing.

"You weren't so hot at that, were you?" I say and look up over the bed. Svein goes bright red. Rune starts laughing as well.

"What. . . ?" Svein repeats. "What-err . . . ?" He picks up his clothes and walks out of the door, which he slams shut behind him.

"Damn it," Panos says. "I'd completely forgotten about you, Sam."

"Er," Rune says. "Did you see them?"

"Yes," I say.

"Er," he says again. I tell them how it was. We laugh again. Smoke cigarettes. Go to sleep. Rune goes out and finds Svein who comes in and goes to sleep in the bed where he mounted the mama. What a pervert. I think I'll split tomorrow. I fall asleep.

Mountain Lodge

I wake up Panos. We leave the sleeping glue-sniffers and go down to the Strands' to have breakfast.

"Where are you going now?" Panos asks.

"Either Mountain Lodge or Arusha Game Sanctuary until tomorrow," I say.

"Did you hear about Angela?" Emerson Strand asks. I shrug. "She's made off with her mother's boyfriend, the Italian big game hunter, and has moved in with him," Emerson says.

"You're kidding," I say.

"I'm not," Emerson says. "First he had the chicken, now he gets the egg."

Panos walks with me into town. I go over to Mick's stepdad, Jerome, at his travel agency.

"Is Mick at the lodge?" I ask.

"No, he's still with the security company in Dar," he says. "What are you doing in Arusha?"

"I went to a get-together yesterday, but now I don't actually know what I'll do."

"You could always come up with me," Jerome says. "We've got plenty of room." I say yes, feeling relieved. If nothing else I can always . . . kick back. Saturday is a short day at the office; Jerome shuts up shop at two, and off we go, out of town and turn left, up the slopes of Mount Meru.

"Have you seen Angela?" Jerome asks.

"No," I say. "Why?"

"Oh nothing, I was just thinking," Jerome says.

The chicken and the egg

They are busy at the lodge, so I borrow Mick's little Bultaco 125cc and drive to Arusha Game Sanctuary, but Angela isn't there. Her mother's in Reception so I ask her.

"I think she's in Arusha," she says.

"Where?" I ask even though I already know that she's probably with her mum's ex-boyfriend; the Italian big game hunter – a man with an appetite for both chicken and egg.

"I think Angela is staying with friends," her mum says; it seems like she can read something in my face, because suddenly she looks ill. "But I really have to get back to work now," she says and turns away.

Back at the lodge I sleep for an hour and dream that I'm naked, straddling Svein with my hands behind my head, while he bonks the big mama, and then I piss all over them. And laugh. I wake up feeling very happy.

I play with baby Anton in the garden as the night falls, and after dinner Sofie and I sit in the room with the open fireplace. We open up the big Zanzibar chest; inside is an amplifier and a record player as well as some records – the wood smells intensely of camphor. Sofie puts on some piano music. She asks how I'm doing. I don't say very much, so we mostly listen to the music.

Sunday I borrow their phone and call home in Tanga. The maid doesn't know where Dad is. She hasn't seen him for weeks – nor Alison, for that matter. I call Frans in Dar.

"Dad's locked up," Alison says.

"What? Why?" I ask.

"The military police arrested him in Arusha, and now they're keeping him locked up somewhere in Dar," Alison says. "Something about the Seychelles."

"But . . . have you talked to him?" I ask.

"Yes, he has a lawyer. He's not really under arrest, just detained while they investigate. But there is a risk of him being booted out."

"But . . ." I start and then I stop again.

"He maintains that he was on holiday with his family. I'll call you at school if something happens, I promise," Alison says.

"Have you talked to Victor?" I ask.

"Victor? Why would I talk to him?"

"It's just . . . Maybe he knows something," I say.

"I don't know where he is," Alison says. If Dad is expelled, I'll lose my residence permit. I am seventeen, and there's no way I can stay without a job. I can't even get married, not even if I did have someone I wanted to marry.

Breaking the rules

At school I walk around in a haze that is mine alone. The oldest pupils break all the rules. They're about to sit their final exams in Year Twelve, and they know that they won't be expelled for some small misdemeanour – the school needs to be able to prove that they have a good percentage of pupils who complete their education in order to attract new pupils. We hear about several incidents; Salomon is constantly stoned and was caught with a decent-sized bag of *bhangi* in his room. He's been smoking forever, but now he is getting careless. Everyone knows you can buy *bhangi* from the Strand brothers; they grow it on their parents' farm somewhere in the Arusha area. Alwyn sells it as well – his father has a cattle ranch on West Kilimanjaro. Strands and Alwyn – the big farmers. Salomon is busted but not expelled – he is the son of the Ethiopian ambassador. Aziz is caught with a local girl in his room; Jarno is found, shitfaced and snoring, on the flat roof of Kishari House. Those are the stories. None of them are booted out, and that's why the Kijito and Kijana boys start running amok as well.

I myself am called to the Headmaster's office for a serious talking-to:

"Your attainment in almost all subjects is, quite frankly, deplorable, Samantha," Owen says. "Your grades are going to be dismal. It's doubtful whether you'll be able to write and hand in all the papers you've got behind with. If you don't, you will have to retake Year Ten."

"I see," I say.

"What do you mean?" Owen asks. I point over my shoulder:

"I'll go straight to my study to write those papers," I say.

"Good luck," he says.

"And to you," I say. And I try desperately to write the papers, I really do. But it's hard.

Five capital sins

Thursday all the boarders who have become teenagers are called to assembly in Karibu Hall. Owen gets up and talks about discipline and the five capital sins: sex, gambling, drugs, alcohol, theft.

There are no real gamblers here; what would we play for? And what would we use? There are no real drugs here either. Alcohol and sex and *bhangi* – yes, alright, in moderation. Theft . . . Of course I did nick a pair of Truddi's jeans from the laundry basket, but that wasn't because I actually needed the jeans – it was just to tick her off. And I couldn't really spend the money once I sold them in the town – you can't buy anything around here. I mean, I did spend it – but it took a while.

"We all have a right to be here, and the teachers are not here as police. But if you pupils can't control yourselves, we will have to come down harder on you. You have to understand that your parents have transferred their responsibility to the school, and we as teachers take that responsibility very seriously. And the recent lapses in discipline will no longer be tolerated. We will dispense house arrest, warnings, suspension and – if the worst comes to the worst – you will not be allowed back."

Transport

Adella calls me to the phone in the common room at Kilele House.

"Yes?" I say.

"Hello, gorgeous," Victor says. "I'm going to Kampala. Do you want to come?" I hesitate for a second.

"No," I say. "I need to revise if I ever want to finish school."

"Where are you going to do your revision?"

"I might go to Mountain Lodge or home to Tanga. But I think it'll be at Mountain Lodge."

"Alright, gorgeous – I'll try to call you on my way back. Then we can meet up."

"Er, do you know what's happening with my dad?" I ask.

"Don't worry. Nothing's going to happen. There are people in the government who need him," Victor says.

"For what?" I ask.

"He does some work with the A.N.C. training camps in Tanzania – with the government's approval."

"That wouldn't stop them from giving him the boot if they were certain he was up to something in the Seychelles," I say.

"No. Now they know where they've got him," Victor says. "I'll be back in a month and will try to get hold of you."

"Yes, alright," I say.

Baltazar

One of the Indian girls comes to tennis in the proper white get-up: long-sleeved T-shirt, full-length trousers and white tennis shoes. It's that little tart Naseen, who had given up the game. Now she actually wants to learn how to play. The other Indian girls are still dressed in saris and high-heeled sandals. Their leader, Parminder, tells Naseen off. But Naseen doesn't care. She comes out on the court and tries to hit the balls.

"That's what I said," I say.

"What?" she says.

"You're a tennis player," I say and hit a ball so hard it breaks one of her nails, but she keeps playing. It's great. Out of the corner of my eye I see Baltazar appear.

"Looking good, Samantha," he says on the other side of the fence.

He's hanging about with his hands lacing into the wire mesh. Naseen glares at him, surprised.

"I know I look good," I say and bounce from one foot to the other while I wait for Naseen's serve. Baltazar sits down on the grass and watches the game.

"Nice," he says when I hit a sharp passing shot right past Naseen.

"What are you doing here, Baltazar?" I ask without looking at him.

"I want to see you play," he says.

"No," I say. "What is it you want?"

"I want to . . . talk to you," Baltazar says.

"Then talk," I say.

"When you're finished," he says. I shrug and go on playing.

When we've finished, I walk out to him.

"What?" I say. He makes a gesture towards the fields. "Do you want to go up for a smoke?" he asks.

"No. What is it you want?" I ask.

"Well, you know, I . . ." he starts and then stops.

"I don't want to be with you," I say. "Not ever." And I turn my back on him and strut away so he can see what he's missing out on. Tosser.

Minefields

Swot, swot, swot. Panos has no time for hanging out – he's going out with Diana and she thinks I'm a psycho. I'm so far behind – now I pay for all the papers I didn't hand in, and all the papers that didn't pass muster. They have to be O.K.'d by the teachers before I can sit my exams, and reading week is almost upon us.

Every day is a minefield of problems. Today the only bright side is English, because Cooper is actually pretty cool. But then Owen comes through the door to cover the lesson – Cooper is in court to testify about the attempted theft of his jeans. It's been three months, but the thief has been fighting for his life at K.C.M.C. – it's only now he's fit to be brought before a judge.

I call Alison, who is back in Tanga, and ask her if Dad has got out. Yes, he's out – no problems. "Some *bwana mkubwa* in the government must owe him a favour, because they're letting him stay in the country," she says.

"Maybe he's paid his way out," I say.

"He hasn't got that kind of money at the moment," Alison says.

"Are you going to stay in Tanga, because then I'd like to come home to revise, but if not . . . I can't stay there with Dad's whore in the house," I say.

"I'll think of something," Alison says. I'll just have to wait and see. I sweat over my homework, because . . . if I do end up in England, I have no idea what I'll do.

The next day Cooper's back again.

"Did the trouser thief go to prison?" Panos asks.

"Yes," Cooper says and sighs. "It was quite surreal." He looks out over the class and starts telling us about it: "The judge arrived at court in a Mercedes which costs five times his official annual salary. And in the courtroom I couldn't identify the thief. When I drove him to K.C.M.C. his face was covered in blood and dust. The man I saw in the courtroom was freshly washed and using crutches, with a face covered in scars and one arm in plaster."

"How much did he get?" Panos asks.

"A year in prison," Cooper says. "Steal a little, they throw you in prison – steal a lot, and they make you a king."

"Did you get your trousers back?" I ask.

"No," Cooper says with a wry smile. "The evidence had mysteriously disappeared during its stay at the police station – maybe it's out taking a walk." Henry puts up his hand – his dad is friendly with the regional commissioner:

"Are you suggesting that the judge and police are corrupt?" Henry – whose school fees are certainly come by through large-scale corruption – asks.

"I'm not suggesting anything," Cooper says. "I'm just explaining what happened."

A couple of days later we hear a story about Owen having been summoned to the Regional Commissioner's office, where he was reprimanded because his teachers imply that the Tanzanian judicial system is corrupt. The Regional Commissioner supposedly threatened to give Cooper the usual twenty-four hours to leave the country – a procedure Tanzania picked up from the Soviet Union. They didn't actually do it – Owen probably gave them a discount on Henry's school fees.

Conned

Alison is sitting on one of the benches outside Kilele House when I get back after my last lesson Friday afternoon.

"Fancy coming to Tanzanite?" she asks.

"Yes, of course I do," I say and run over to hug her. She's driven up from Tanga. Sunday she is meeting Frans at Kilimanjaro Airport, and then they're going to Holland for a week so she can meet his family. I hurry inside to pack. Alison has already been to see Owen and told him that I am coming with her for the weekend. Owen has probably said a lot about how different we are and asked Alison if she could try to rub some of her talent for order and some of her diligence off on me. She was always well-behaved at school.

"Are you going to move in with Frans, then?" I ask as we're heading towards Arusha.

"Yes. I mean, Frans doesn't know that I've speeded things up because Halima has moved in. But she can run the hotel for Dad now. And Halima is actually not so bad, Samantha."

"What do you mean?" I say.

"She conned the old man," Alison says. "She wasn't actually pregnant when she said she was."

"Did she just say it to get into the house then?"

206

"No, no. She was much cleverer than that. She said it to see how he would react. And what he did was to move her into the house, so now she's made sure she really has got pregnant."

"How has she made sure to get pregnant?" I ask.

"Come on, Samantha, you can only get pregnant once, so once Dad thinks Halima's pregnant there's no reason for him to use a condom – he can spray away to his heart's content. And then, she got pregnant."

"Eeeew!" I say. "Does he know?"

"Yes, he's the one who says that's how it was." Alison giggles.

"Does he think it's funny?" I ask.

"It's the sort of thing he respects, isn't it? – that she could con him. I mean, the man's a freak."

"Do *you* think it's funny?" I ask. Alison becomes serious.

"Mum's left him. It's certainly better for her."

"If it's true what you say that he's been shagging everything with a pulse for years, then why has he stayed with Mum for so long?"

"I suppose he wanted us to be settled, and she was the one who was supposed to make sure we were."

"I'm not settled."

"No, maybe not," Alison says. "But now you can stay with Mum in England until you are."

"But I don't want to."

"I know. But you can get an education and then return afterwards – like I did."

"How?"

Alison sighs, "Samantha, you keep asking: what will happen? With me, with you, with . . . everything. I don't know. I just know that we don't need Dad any longer. He'll pay if you want to go on and finish Year Twelve here, and you can stay with us in Dar during holidays. Or you can go to England. I'm just glad Mum left. If she had stayed in Tanga, she would have drunk herself to death."

I still haven't heard from Victor and reading week is fast approaching.

Countermanding

While we're at Tanzanite, we go to Mountain Lodge. Alison arranges with them for me to stay there during my revision.

"I'll write a letter to Dad about it – so he knows," Alison says.

Frans arrives on Saturday night.

"Mick says hello," he says. "To you too, Samantha."

"Thanks," I say.

"It's a good job that he's got now. He's saving up so he can open his own garage in Arusha," Frans says.

"I know," I say.

We relax, and on Sunday Alison and Frans drive me as far as Moshi. They put me down at the roundabout by the airport. I'm standing by the roadside where the buses to Moshi stop, watching their car disappear. Alison is nipping off to Holland. Far out. She's struck lucky. What have I done?

A couple of days later Dad calls me.

"You're not going to Mountain Lodge for reading week," he says.

"Why not?"

"You're coming to Tanga," he says.

"But I don't want to go to Tanga. Alison is in Holland, and the only person who'll be home in Tanga is . . . her."

"This isn't about what you want. In our family we manage on our own, and we don't encroach on other people's hospitality. I've called the Lodge and told them you're not coming. And don't you dare go anyway." Dad lets the words hang in the air. "Got it?" he says.

"But . . . are you coming to pick me up then?"

"No, you'll have to take the bus."

"But will you be there – in Tanga?"

"I don't know – maybe."

"But why can't I stay at the lodge then?"

"You'll do as you're told." He slams down the phone.

I go down past Christian's, but the house is empty. His dad is supposed to have got a new job in Shinyanga. Maybe Christian is there, or maybe he has already flown to Denmark.

Handiwork

The Strand brothers are throwing a party in their parents' house to celebrate the beginning of reading week. I go along. Tazim and Truddi don't go – they've gone straight home to start revising. But the others are there: Diana, Panos, Baltazar, Stefano, the glue-sniffers. Music is blaring in the sitting room. I've had a couple of drinks and am standing on the patio with my back to the wall, smoking some of the Strand brothers' potent Arusha-*bhangi* – it goes straight to my head. Baltazar is standing so close to me that I can feel his cock against my hip.

"So, still missing me, are you?" I ask.

"When I'm away from you, Samantha, it's against the laws of nature," Baltazar says. I slip a hand down and squeeze his cock.

"Yep, the laws of nature certainly are hard," I say.

"Do you want to go somewhere?"

"Fancy a little handiwork, do you?"

"I fancy anything you've got," Baltazar says and nibbles my earlobe.

"You can forget that," I say. He starts touching my inner thigh – moving his hand up between my legs.

"Just a little handiwork then," he says. I swallow.

"Tit for tat," I say.

"You first."

He slips his hand down my knickers – finger fucks me and tries to kiss me on the mouth. "No," I say. "No kissing." I look straight ahead into the darkness – enjoying the sensation, the movement. Baltazar . . . I don't care about him. I almost go all the way. That's enough. I push his hand away.

"Let's go down to the garden," I say and walk in front of him. Baltazar follows me. At the bottom of the garden I turn around – he comes up to me; I get out his cock and start wanking him. "Do you like it?" I ask.

"Oh yes," he says. I keep going – it doesn't spill. Maybe he's too drunk. The absurdity of it hits me: I'm standing at the end of a garden, yanking some bloke's cock. Laughter bubbles into my throat. And then his hands are on my shoulders, and he knocks me over, and suddenly he's on top of me.

"Don't," I say, pushing his upper body away from me; his hands catch my arms, one hand grabs both my wrists, his other hand presses up between my legs. "No, Baltazar. Stop it!" I shout.

"I want to make love to you," he says.

"I don't want to," I shout, thrusting my head up towards his to bite him, but he pulls his head away while he rips off my knickers, spreading my legs with his knee. "HELP – damn it. HELP me!" No-one can hear me because of the music – Baltazar presses my one leg to the side with his free hand; I try to kick his side with my knee, but I can't seem to put any strength behind it – I twist as hard as I can.

"Lie still, you whore," he says and slaps me across my mouth.

"Stop. Please stop," I say.

"You know you want to," he says, and at the same time I feel his cock against my inner thigh – I am completely dry now and cold. And I see . . . something moving, behind him.

"*Help me*," I shout. The shadow comes closer. Stefano. He has started going out with Shakila, but I don't think she's here. Maybe they're not together anymore. "Help me, Stefano." He stops. "For God's sake, help me!" I shout – a stabbing pain flashes into my body.

"Fuck you, Samantha," Stefano says, and he smiles.

Baltazar groans. "I'm in, man."

Stefano stays where he is. I let my body go slack. Baltazar is pumping away; he's starting to feel something, forgetting himself. I tear my arm out of his grip and hammer the heel of my hand into his Adam's apple; he keels over, I jump up and take two steps back. Baltazar is holding his neck, he can't breathe. Stefano is standing still, looking at me. I can't think of anything to say, so I turn around and walk up towards the house but walk around it, through the streets to Mount Meru Hotel and up to my room.

It doesn't wash off, no matter how long I stay in the shower.

Baseball bat

Not long after there's a knock on my door. I don't answer it.

"Sam?" It's Panos. "Are you there?" I open the door slowly.

"Where did you go?" he asks. "What happened?" he says when he sees my face. My lower lip is swollen.

"I . . ." I say and start sobbing.

"Tell me, Sam – did Baltazar do that to you?"

"Yes."

"But you hit him back," Panos says, laughing. "His neck is really hurting." Panos comes over with his arms wide open – he wants to put them around me.

"Don't." I turn away – a sob is welling up in my throat.

"What is it?" he asks. "What happened?" I look at him:

"He raped me. Do you get that, Panos? He raped me down in the garden. And Stefano was standing there, watching him do it. I called for help, but he didn't do anything – he was just standing there watching while Baltazar raped me on the lawn." Panos looks at me.

"Why didn't you come and get me?"

"How could I get you?" I wail. I make myself take a deep breath. "I couldn't get away," I say.

"Afterwards."

"Panos – they all think I'm a slut. They would laugh. They would say that it was my own fault – that I had it coming."

"Are you O.K.?" Panos asks.

"No," I say.

"I'm going to have to go down to the bar to get Diana, but . . . Do you want us to come up?"

"No," I say. "Go down to Diana. I'm leaving as soon as it's light."

"But . . ."

"Just go," I say, pushing him towards the door.

"I'll get them for you, Sam," he says. I don't say anything. He can't get them for me – it's too late for that. I curl up on the bed.

An hour and a half later Panos is back. I open the door. Diana is standing in the hall, a couple of metres away. She's looking pale beneath the skin.

"Baltazar had made himself scarce," Panos says. "Stefano . . . I don't think he'll be in school for a while."

"What did you do?" I ask. Diana looks at us wearily.

"He bashed Stefano up with a baseball bat," she says.

"What should we do about Baltazar?" Panos asks.

"I don't know," I say.

When the first light comes, I go up to the main road and take a bus to Tanga.

Music on strings

"Your dad tells me you must be put to work – you're not a guest at the hotel," Halima says. "If you're going to be staying, then you must work." She is standing there acting the queen in the kitchen in her fancy frock with her pregnant belly poking out – upsetting the cooks.

"Don't you bloody tell me what to do," I say while I grab some food and load it onto a tray.

"That's what your dad says."

"My dad is full of shit – as you'll soon enough find out." I turn my back on her and carry out my tray, shaking inside and with my knees going wobbly and my nose going all snotty. Damn. There are no letters from Mum. The phone is down. Dad isn't home, and no-one knows when he'll be back. Alison has gone to Dar to be with that Frans – she doesn't care about me at all. And Victor doesn't come by like he said he would.

Halima says that someone called Christian called, but that he's gone back to Europe now. I write him a letter, telling him that I want to kill myself, that I hate life, the world and everyone in it.

I'm supposed to revise. I've tried – but I can't read a single line. Nothing matters to me. I can't eat anything either, only drink Coke and smoke cigarettes. I'm sick with hunger. As soon as I eat anything, I have to go to the toilet to be sick. My head hurts. I can't . . . I feel disgusting on the inside; I don't want it to be me who has had filth pumped into my body, slimy, rough, squeaky, corrosive, vile. No water, and my hair is greasy, the cigarettes feel like slimy weeds and diesel on my tongue – in the burning sun there are crisp layers of salt under my eyes.

A car appears in the yard and honks its horn. I lift my curtain and peer out. The police. A waiter comes running out. The police officers ask him a question. He points to my bungalow, and they start walking towards me. I quickly pull on a pair of trousers. There's a knock. I open.

"What?" I say, squinting.

"Samantha Richards?" one of them asks.

"Yes?"

"We're looking for Panos Koukinas. Is he here?"

"No."

"Do you know where he is?" the man asks.

"No."

"Is he in Tanzania?" the man asks.

"I don't know – he might be," I say.

"Are you sure? Hiding a fugitive from the police is a criminal offence," he says.

"I wish I knew where he was," I say.

"O.K.," he says. Stefano's dad would have paid him far more if he had found Panos, but the police officer has earned a couple of days' wages just by trying. I wonder what Panos did that morning. And where he went to afterwards?

I drink K.C. – more *Konyagi* than Coke. I go up to the house. The whore is out. I get some more *Konyagi*. Take the pills from Mum's cabinet. I carry it all down to my bungalow, focusing on the job at hand – my knees are wobbly. I wash down the pills with Coke. I can't even cry. Look what you're doing to me. The tape recorder is playing reggae. I turn it off. There's only the gecko barking on the wall, the chickadees playing their crackling strings, a bit of a wind moving, and I don't say goodbye, because there's nothing worth saying goodbye to. I notice the chemicals starting to kick in, I doze off, the muscles in my back become as heavy as lead – everything else is a grey sludge, drying up and becoming grey dust; I can't move my arms – I'd love to smoke a final cigarette. How could you do it to me? Do you see it now? What you're feeling; it's what you need to feel; it's the result of . . . You know you love me. You've just forgotten it. Now you'll remember. I'm helping you to never forget. My body is disintegrating, my flesh is separating from my bones, my skin from my flesh, my hair from my skin – I soar, as the weight of my bones slowly makes its heavy way through the mattress and through the bottom of the bed; my flesh is blooming in colours of red – rotting away. My eyes go dark.

Rusty red

Burning. Through my throat – up, up. Something sticks in my mouth; I am choking in darkness; bile is spilling up, corroding me. My muscles are wood, cramping. There are voices: a woman:

"She has to drink it. Now." My upper body is lifted, slumping back into arms that pick me up. Light is cutting into my eyes. A cool liquid is tumbling into my mouth. My throat feels closed and acidy. It rushes out across my chin, down over my breasts. "Hold her nose." Rough fingers on my face, and I drown – I can't . . . must swallow, the river keeps coming, must spit it out, swallow, breathe. Choking, drowning, drinking, swallowing, breathing. "Make her throw up," the woman says. And fingers are thrust into my throat, which contracts, my stomach is thrusting back, the fluid is pouring out over me from my throat – an acidy, chemical stench.

My head is pierced by thick, rusty metal bars; my body is aching – heavy, sluggish, grey. A hand on my forehead – a scent of mothballs mixed with cotton fabric ironed with a splash of rosewater. Betel nut. I force my eyelids apart – it feels like breaking open a wound; my mother's bed – an Indian man in a suit with a stethoscope feels my forehead. I'm alive. The skin in the corner of his mouth is bright red, and his lower lip. Dr Jodha. Halima comes into the room.

"Tsk," she says, turns around and goes back out. I look after her. She comes in again. Looks at me.

"I . . ." I start and then stop.

"You need some rest," the doctor says; his teeth – brownish, rusty red.

"Stupid girl," Halima says. "I want you out of here as soon as you can walk."

"Yes," I say. She brings me a thick soup, feeds me with a spoon. I can smell her warm skin.

"You think everything is about you," she says. "But there are other people in the world." I swallow the soup. It is about me – to me. But I can't say anything. Faeces are running from me in a steady stream, and I'm crying, closing my eyes, unable to bear her seeing me like this.

Three days I'm in bed, and then I can move – I go out and stand under the shower. Smoke a cigarette.

"What am I going to do with you?" Halima says.

"I'm going to Dar," I say.

"When?"

"Tomorrow."

"O.K., I'll drive into town and get you a ticket on the good bus," she says and gets up from the table. That's it. I stumble over to the bungalow – I have to force myself to go inside and get my things. I go back to the house. I sit on the patio for the better part of the night – it's the last time I'm here; that much is certain. Goodbye, Baobab Hotel.

Halima drives me to the bus.

"Look after yourself, stupid girl," she says.

"You too, stupid woman," I say. I go in, sit down. Drive off.

Congratulations

I take a taxi through Dar es Salaam, across the Selander Bridge and out to the Msasani peninsula. The corals, the sand, the roar of the ocean. Out on the very tip is the Yacht Club. I drive past the diplomatic quarter and on to where the ordinary rich people live. It's late in the afternoon. My stomach hurts. I hope Alison will look after me.

The taxi drops me off. I go to the front door.

"Alison?" I call. She comes round the corner from the garden. She's radiant.

"Samantha," she says. "Why didn't you call?"

"I'm ill," I say.

"Oh, darling. Come on in. What's happened?"

"It's my stomach," I say. "How are you?"

Alison starts giggling, looks at me, looks away and looks at me again.

Alison shows me around the house and garden. Frans has all the good stuff: stereo, European furniture, Carlsberg in the fridge. Alison has brought great clothes for me back from Holland. We sit down in the sitting room to avoid the heat. She looks at her hand in a dreamy way. I follow her gaze: a ring – tanzanite.

"Did you get that in Holland?" I ask.

"Frans gave it to me. He had it made up in Holland. The stone is one he's bought through Mick."

"Why did he give it to you? Is it like . . . an engagement ring?" I ask. Alison sighs:

"Don't be upset now, but . . . we were married at a Register Office in Holland."

"Oh wow," I say, getting up, going over to hug her. "Congratulations. That's fantastic. Are you happy?"

"Yes," Alison says, looking relieved. "Yes, I am. I just know . . . I called Mum and told her, and she was a little upset, and I know that Dad is going to be really ticked off, but . . . if Dad were to stand in a church and give me away to Frans – I thought that would be too far out."

"Never mind," I say. "It's you who got married – not them."

"Yes, well, I think they were once, but it doesn't seem to be working for them," Alison says, and we laugh.

"Did Frans carry you through the door to your wedding bed?" I ask. Alison giggles.

"You know, he did actually."

I manage to keep it all in – she's as blind as a bat. Frans is a K.L.M. man. He could easily have got an extra ticket for me. It wouldn't have cost him anything. But all he wants is to take Alison away from me. I can see why Alison doesn't want to sully her new family with our parents. But me . . . That's a real blow: Fuck off from our new family – we're eradicating the contamination. I don't ask if Frans' family was there – of course they were.

"Are you pregnant?" I ask.

"We're working on it," she says, laughing.

In the shade

Dad. It can't be long before he shows up, and I simply can't face telling Alison what happened. She takes a deep breath. Sighs.

"What about your exams?" she asks.

"I can't revise," I say.

"But do you want me to call them and say that you're ill? Maybe they'll let you sit the exams later."

"I don't know," I say.

Frans works a lot, and when he's not working he leaves me alone. Alison is busy looking into becoming a travel agent arranging various specialized trips in Tanzania that can be sold by companies in England as part of a larger package holiday. She's betting on the southern safari trail, which is less busy and not as smooth as the northerly one, and then of course on Zanzibar.

Most of the time I stay in bed, or sit in a chair in the shade on the patio. After a couple of days Alison comes home from town with a very strange look on her face.

"What's with Stefano?" she asks.

"What's what with Stefano?" I say.

"Apparently Panos beat him up with a baseball bat."

"I . . . I don't know."

"Yes, you do." Alison has spoken to Aziz, who's heard that Stefano was beaten for something he did to me. Stefano had a fractured skull, his arm was broken and three of his ribs; he's lost his sense of smell and something's not right with his sense of balance. I start crying very quietly. What am I supposed to say?

"He tried to . . . rape me."

"No," Alison says and squats next to my chair, hugging me awkwardly. And I cry – I can't seem to stop. "But. . ." she says.

"No." I shake my head. I don't know if it means that he didn't succeed or that I don't want to talk about it. Why don't I tell her that it was Baltazar? Because he is black, and Dad would have him killed. Stefano, well, kill away. Strictly speaking, Stefano would probably have raped me that time by the stables if Ebenezer hadn't come. But Baltazar, he did it – Stefano was watching. She keeps asking.

"But Samantha, nothing happened, did it? Tell me."

"Please don't tell Dad – he'll have him killed," I say.

"But did something happen?"

"No."

218

Sister

"You're sick!" Dad roars – as if I didn't know already. "You're a sick little brat!" He keeps at it – on and on. Alison is standing diagonally behind him with her mouth open – I haven't told her anything about . . . the pills.

"You can't stay here mooching off your sister," he says. "In our family we take care of ourselves."

"She can stay," Alison says, but he chooses not to hear her.

"I haven't raised you to be like this," he says.

"You haven't raised me at all," I say. "You sent me to a boarding school in Arusha when I was ten."

"There's nothing wrong with being at a boarding school," says the man who went to one for his entire childhood and was beaten to within an inch of his life.

"Yes, that makes sense. You are a splendid example of the great people that come out of that sort of school."

"Don't be cheeky," he says.

"Oh," I say. It seems a bit silly if he hits me – it's been a long time since that made an impression on me.

"Stop it," Alison says.

"Going there didn't make Alison an idiot," Dad says.

"No, because Alison is a bloody saint," I say and look at her. She blinks, swallows and looks away.

"Sorry," I tell her.

"You're going to go back and finish school," Dad says, index finger held high and everything.

"Dad," Alison says firmly. "Come here." She turns around and goes inside.

"I'm not done with you," Dad says and follows her. I can hear Alison inside:

"She can't sit an exam right now – she has to stay with me until she's back on her feet."

219

"And then what about her exams?" Dad says. "She's as much use as tits on a bull. How do you think she'll manage when she returns to England? Your mum can't provide for her." Alison doesn't say anything for a while.

"She can retake Year Ten," she says. I'm not retaking anything.

"You want me to pay school fees one more year because the girl is bonkers?"

"Maybe she can do retakes – I can call the school and talk to them," Alison says, trying to smooth things out. She can tell him that Stefano tried to rape me. I can tell him that Baltazar actually did . . . How would he react then? Alison doesn't know, so she's afraid to say anything.

"Alison," Dad says. "I don't know how much longer I'll be here – in Tanzania. I can't look after her for much longer." What will happen then to the seed he planted in Halima?

"No, but I'll be here," Alison says.

"I don't want her to be a burden to you," Dad says.

"She's not a burden," Alison says. "She's my sister."

I think about Panos – where is he now? And Baltazar? The others are back at school after their weeks of revising – busy sitting exams. Will I ever get mine? I call the school and speak to Tazim.

"What's going on?" I ask.

"You know, exams," Tazim says.

"Oh, well, but . . . what about Panos and Stefano? And Baltazar?"

"Er," Tazim says, sounding hesitant. "There are some really crazy rumours going about."

"Like what?"

"Like you paid Panos to beat Stefano up. Or that you're pregnant with Baltazar's child, and that's why he's gone back to Angola, and that you're not coming back to school."

"Is Baltazar in Angola?"

"He certainly isn't back from reading week," Tazim says.

"And Panos?"

"But Samantha," Tazim says. "What happened?"

"What do you mean?" I say.

"At that party at the Strand brothers'?" Tazim says.

"Baltazar tried to rape me," I say.

"Then why did Panos beat Stefano up?" she asks.

"Because he was watching," I say.

Lull

Once again Dad is nowhere to be found. He has a little house in Dar, which he bought a couple of years ago. He's having it done up – maybe he means to sell it. If nothing else, we don't see much of him, and that in itself is a relief.

I spend my mornings wandering around the neighbourhood, going down to the beach, having a Coke at Oyster Bay Hotel, smoking cigarettes, looking into thin air.

I really should to write to Christian. I have suddenly remembered that I wrote to him from Tanga and I haven't answered any of his letters. He wrote something about coming down. On holiday. But I can't . . . And why should I go to all the trouble of writing to him? It's awkward – all that stuff I wrote about everything being over. It's only when I'm on my own that I have bad thoughts. When I'm at places where things are good, I'm fine. I can be good too then. And Christian is nothing, really – he can't help me anyway. Maybe it's better if he stays where he is. But it's all so far off, and I keep putting it out of my mind. If he did come down – would I have to spend time with him? And what is it he really wants? Is that good? No.

Accounts

Alison and Frans have gone to Bagamoyo with some Dutch friends of theirs. I am sitting on the patio, smoking. I hear the sound of a car stopping on the other side of the house. The cook goes to answer the door.

"Samantha, Samantha," he calls. I go inside and go to the door. A squat man with pitch black hair is standing outside. Damn.

"Tell me what happened to my son," Stefano's dad says.

"You can ask your son that," I say and puff on my cigarette.

"I want you to tell me right now," he says. Stefano's and Panos' dads both run tobacco farms in Iringa and Morogoro.

"Your son got beaten up because he was behaving like an animal," I say.

"Tsk," Stefano's dad says, looking away. "I know it was Panos who did it, but I need to know why. My son is broken – he won't speak to me. And Panos has gone away, so I can't reach him. I need answers."

"Ask your son – he knows why he was beaten up." Stefano's dad takes a step towards me.

"You will tell me right now," he says, pressing me up against the door – exactly the same way Stefano pressed me up against the stables.

"You bloody son stood by watching while I was raped – do you understand that? I was screaming for help, and Stefano came and just watched." The man is silent for a moment.

"Maybe he couldn't do anything," he says.

"He stood there, laughing at me," I shout. The cook appears.

"Do you need help, Samantha?" he asks. Stefano's dad takes a step back – away from me.

"But . . . I don't believe you," he says. I start crying.

"He was standing right next to me, watching while I was being raped," I say. The man turns around and leaves.

Blood

We're driving home from the restaurant in Frans' Range Rover, which bobs and rocks lazily on the road; the suspension is too soft by far. I get out almost before he stops the car and am sick in the bushes by the drive.

"What's the matter?" Alison asks, holding me from behind while I spew. I can feel her stomach against my lower back.

"It was probably the prawns I had at the restaurant," I say.

"Were they not alright?" Frans asks.

"Yes, but when it's curry you can't really taste it if they're not," Alison says. I get myself to bed. Drink a little water. Then I get up again and am sick. Alison pokes her head out of her door when I come out of the bathroom.

"It's alright," I say and go in to lie down. It's not alright. I'm scared. It's several hours before I fall asleep.

I'm lying curled up in bed. It's almost noon. Alison comes in.

"What's going on, Samantha?"

"My blood isn't coming."

"Your blood?"

"My blood," I shout. "I haven't had my period." Alison stands quite still and looks at me for a second; then she turns around and walks out. I can't hear anything. Sometime later she comes in, her face completely dissolved in tears. She's been out to think about what to say, whether to scold, or cry, or something else altogether. She's newly wed, and they're trying for a baby. What does the situation call for? She squats next to the bed, taking a deep breath. Suddenly she raises her hand over my face.

"Who did it?" she shouts. But she doesn't hit me. She starts sobbing.

"Does it really matter?" I ask, and Alison lowers her forehead onto my arms.

"No," she says. "But Dad is going to ask you about it, and you mustn't tell him."

"It was just someone from school," I say.

"Stefano?"

"No."

"Then who?"

"I don't want to say who it was, because . . ."

"Because what?"

"Because it was just a boy, and it was an accident – the condom broke. And when he asks me, I don't want the child."

"He won't ask," Alison says.

"No," I say. She gets up.

"I'll tell him, you are . . ." she says.

"I can do it myself," I say.

"No," she says and then she leaves. I can hear her speak quietly on the telephone. Then the door opens, the car starts and she drives off. I go out into the kitchen and try to eat a little. I'm sick in the kitchen sink. The cook is very worried.

"It's only a stomach upset," I tell him. "Nothing worse than that." But the man probably understands more English than he lets on – he heard Alison on the phone. Maybe he's snuck up to the door on his bare feet and has heard us speak inside my room. He puts a bucket in my room. And a jug of water and a glass. I eat a little more. And am sick again. I drink some water. Go for a lie down.

The second-rate daughter

The car returns, but it's Alison's car, which means that Dad didn't come with her – he never drives in anyone's car but his own. She comes in.

"I've left several messages for him, so he'll probably be here later," she says.

"Yes," I say.

And he is. A couple of hours later I can hear his Land Rover. Alison starts crying in the sitting room before he's switched off the engine. My stomach becomes a tight knot.

"What's happened?" Dad barks in his most commanding voice, and I try to swallow the lump in my throat, it's moving into my stomach. The roar of the ocean is in my ears; I can't hear what Alison says. His steps come down the hall, and as he grabs the doorknob, I lean over the edge of the bed and spew bile into the bucket, spit, look up at him and let me head fall back onto the pillow. He looks at me, puts his big, rough hand on my forehead. His palm is dry; my forehead is clammy and cold. I snivel and a sob escapes my mouth, even though I try to hold it back.

"There now, darling," he says and gets onto the bed next to me, lifting me up into his arms and holding me close, rocking me. "Who did this to my little girl?" he asks in a calm voice – too calm by far; it's not like him at all. Maybe he'll hit me next. I tell him the story, sobbing about a condom that broke. "I'll have it taken care of," he says.

"Yes, but how?" I cry. "If I go to England . . . And Mum . . ." I go all to pieces.

"I know someone," he says. "A really clever doctor. Don't worry." He smiles. "When I saw Alison. You know, I thought it'd be something far worse. I thought that . . . that maybe it was a serious illness." All I hear is the pause. He thought that perhaps there was something wrong with Alison. But it was only his second-rate daughter causing trouble. "These accidents happen, you know," he says. "It's just so unfair that it's always the girl who has to deal with it." I'm so happy he says that. I start crying with relief, even though it's stupid because I know he's pretending; he's a man – crap like that pours from him in a steady stream. Where do they pick it up? "You should have told me at once," he says. "Instead of taking those pills."

"I . . . I couldn't," I say. He smoothes down my hair. No, because I didn't know that I was . . . pregnant. But now he sees my pregnancy as the reason for my taking the pills, and then it's alright – that makes sense to him. All is forgiven, as long as I have the embryo yanked out of my body.

Mulatto

How many young black girls has he got pregnant across the length and breadth of the continent in his time? You never see a mulatto – almost never. They're called "market dust" because their skin is the colour of dust. What do you do if you're having a baby like that? Live with the shame? No. When the whores have their babies, they go home to their families in the villages. The shame is great, but in the city they can't have a baby without a man to support them for the first couple of weeks after the birth. If the child is flawed – handicapped, that is – you strangle it at once and tell everyone it was stillborn. Then you bury it behind the house. You do the same if it's a mulatto. No-one can see its colour because it's wrapped in a sheet. No authority comes to look at a dead child. They would be too busy to do anything else if they did. And the child has to be buried at once before decomposition sets in in the heat. My mulatto brothers and sisters are rotting away below ground. My dad has only kept his white children. But despite that, I'm not surprised he comforts me. He wants to help me as he's supposed to. Maybe I can pull through.

"But in England," I say. My mum.

"No," he says. "Not in England. I know a doctor here. It's not a problem. He's very good – trained in England." Shakila's dad – I know it's him. Who else would it be?

"But then . . . I could keep it, couldn't I?" I say.

"Keep what?" Dad asks.

"The baby."

He smoothes down my hair.

"You're not old enough for that at all."

"But . . ."

"You have to make a life for yourself first. How could you possibly look after a baby when you're still a child yourself?"

And he's right. How could I possibly make that work?

From my bed I can hear Alison and Dad talk on the patio.

"And what about Halima?" Alison is saying.

"She lost the baby," he says.

"And now what?"

"She's staying in Tanga." Alison doesn't ask him about anything else. He's paid Halima, of course he has – like the whore she is. Maybe he's passed the hotel on to her. But is it true – did she lose the baby?

"Samantha doesn't want to go back – I don't think she does," Alison says.

"Back?"

"To England."

"That's not for her to say," Dad says.

"Are you sure?"

"I'm sick and tired of all the trouble that girl causes," he says.

"She's staying with me until she's back in shape," Alison says. I can hear the same insistent tone in her voice – I can picture how she must be looking at him.

"Yes, alright," he says. And then, "Do you really think it was an accident?"

"She won't tell me anything," Alison says.

"Damn it – she's not stupid. When she was suspended for two weeks, she did it on purpose."

"But can you . . . help her?"

"To have it removed? Yes," Dad says. They don't say anything for a while. "I damn well want to know who it was," he says.

It can only be a question of time before he hears about Stefano. But Stefano has been beaten up – I suppose that's enough. And Baltazar: he dies if I tell Dad about . . . if I say the word: rape. Dad wouldn't be doing it for me – he'd be doing it because that's what you do in his world. He wouldn't even be doing it himself, just handing in an order, paying for it – as if it weren't a big deal at all.

Scrub room

I'm lying in front of the toilet, sick as a dog, when Dad returns. Dad said the doctor has said I mustn't eat for five hours before, so I haven't. I cry all the way to the hospital. I make Dad stop by the roadside and am sick out of the window. People honk their horns at us. We get there in the end. I go towards the door, bent double by stomach cramps – that's how nervous I am.

"Aren't you coming?" I ask.

"No," he says. His voice sounds gravelly. I stay where I am, looking at him. He looks away. "I can't," he says and lights a cigarette. I am sick in the bushes, but nothing comes up. Then I go in. Never have I been as nervous as I am now – compared to this, everything else . . . was nothing.

A nurse takes my arm and leads me quickly down the hall, past the closed doors that lead into the wards towards one end of the hospital, through an office and into a scrub room where the staff keep their clothes. I am tucked into a scuffed iron bed. Paint is peeling off the spindles at its head and foot. Abortion is illegal here. There's a searing pain in my abdomen. Red hot strings of lava shoot through my insides. Shakila's dad comes in. They take me through to the operating room. The hospital looks like an abattoir: brightly lit, with bare walls and scarred concrete floors. They put a mask on me and tell me to count down from ten. I wake up in the scrub room. It's dark outside. Is it evening or night? I'm alone. They've left the light on – I can hear sounds, but there's no-one around. My head feels like it's full of cotton wool, my abdomen feels mauled, and my stomach is reeling. The baby isn't inside me anymore. I jerk away so I won't be sick on the blankets. There's a bucket on the floor. Bile is pouring from me. They said that it would: that the anaesthetic might make me sick – that's why I had to fast. The sound makes the nurse come in.

"Where is it?" I ask.

"Where's what?"

"The baby." She puts a hand on my forehead and takes my pulse.

"It wasn't a baby," she says. "It was a tiny seed. It's gone now."

"But . . . It can't just . . . I have to see it."

"I don't know where it is," she says. "It's better this way. It's over now. I'll get *mzee* for you," she says and leaves. Shakila's dad comes in:

"Everything's fine," he says. "Nothing to worry about." As a matter of fact there's everything to worry about. He smiles at me. "You can get on with your life now," he says. Get on?

"Get on?" I say.

"I know it's not easy to be young," he says. "But you're already a bit of a legend at school. I've heard stories about you. You don't take nonsense from anyone. You'll be fine, Miss Samantha," he says. I try to smile at him. He pats me gently on the cheek: "Your father will be here soon – I've called him. And if you feel anything not right, you just come and tell me. Yes?"

"Yes," I say. "Thank you."

"Good," he says and leaves. Shakila's dad. He is unbelievably rich. Their house is nothing special, the hospital looks like the backside of a dog, but that's the way it is. You must never flash anything worth having in Tanzania unless you are incredibly powerful. Otherwise it'll be nationalized or torn from your greedy, grubby grasp in some way or other. And the better it looks, the more greasing of palms it'll require to get the necessary permits. But the man has two children at boarding school. His operations must be expensive. I wonder if they're all foeticides – ordinary coils are hard to come by, pills are nigh on impossible to get; and even if you did find a condom on the market, African men don't want to wear a mac when the heavens open.

Pet meds

Alison has talked to school. They have agreed that I will return after New Year to retake the second half of Year Ten and finish by sitting my exams. New Year isn't for another five months. Until then, I'm free. I lie in as late as I can every morning. I putter into the sitting room and sit down at the dining table, fiddling with a few things to let the cook know that I'm there. He comes in.

"Do you want eggs?"

"Scrambled eggs. And some bacon as well."

"Certainly," he says, even though he hates frying bacon – he's a Muslim. But it's part of his job. I pour juice from the jug on the table and smell it. Passion juice from a tin mixed with fresh oranges. Good. I grab a piece of toast from the rack, but it's been there too long – it's gone soggy in the humid air.

"And some fresh toast," I shout. Why do you have to tell them everything? He brings me my plate. Scrambled eggs, bacon, fried tomatoes.

Fresh toast. I poke at it and manage to get some down. I hear Alison's car in the drive. The door opens.

"Mum called," she says. I look at her. She looks at me. "No," she says. "I didn't tell her. I told her you were ill, but that you're doing better."

"Thank you," I say.

"What else could I tell her?"

"What did you say was wrong with me?" I ask. It's useful to know in case Mum asks me.

"Malaria and intestinal worms." When we were little, we were both infected with intestinal worms from the dogs.

"Give me some of those pet meds," I say, and Alison laughs. Dad wasn't home, and dog meds was the only thing Mum could get her hands on, so that's what she gave us; we shat and vomited out pale little worms for two days.

Rockwool

I get a letter from Christian in Denmark, forwarded by the school in Moshi. He writes that he . . . loves me. "I want to kiss you, caress you. Everywhere." Does he now? Completely round the bend he is. And he misses me, misses Tanzania. He wants to come down – on holiday. Maybe he had better stay where he is. What does he want here? He writes that he works, insulating houses against the cold; something about sheets of something called Rockwool – it has the texture of tough cotton wool and is made by heating up granite until it's liquid and then blowing it through a machine to make it into a gazillion thin hairs like candyfloss; then it's pressed into mats that are put above the ceiling to keep the heat in during the winter. The thin stone hairs pierce the skin, making it itch like mad. He writes that to get it out you have to shower, alternating between really hot and really cold water to make the pores open and close. He moonlights, so he doesn't pay any taxes. He doesn't really know anyone. Denmark is very nice, and tidy, and tedious. He has to cook his own food, do his own shopping, wash his own clothes, clean up after himself. He has no money. He has to bike like an impoverished negro whenever he needs to get from one place to another. He doesn't have money enough to get a taxi and barely enough to buy cigarettes. All sorts of shit like that. And they want me to go to England – over my dead body.

Off kilter

It's entirely possible to smoke so much that your poo smells of nicotine. It's a matter of stamina, that's all. I secretly drink from the bottles in the cabinet. A Dry Martini is made by mixing half a drinking glass of Tanqueray Gin with the thought that there might be a bottle of vermouth knocking about somewhere in the country. No olives – I don't hold with veg in my drinks. The mornings – I potter about in the garden. No, I have to . . . get out. I find a cap, and hide my eyes behind sunglasses. I trot around the residential neighbourhood, but am constantly afraid of bumping into someone I know. They finished their exams ages ago – I have been in hibernation for a long time. Some of them, the ones who live in Dar, must be here for their holidays. Or has school already started again? But it's almost noon – too hot to move around outside. I go as far as the kiosks at the exit to the drive-in cinema – find a bloke with dreadlocks and buy some spliffs from him. I go all the way down to the sea – there's not a soul there this time of day. I sit down and smoke. The sea is breathing. I breathe – I get some help from the waves – we breathe together.

Lying on my back in the warm sand. The smell of seaweed, dead crabs, salt water. The palms that are actually a kind of grass are, er . . . vegging out, drying up. I stagger over to Oyster Bay Hotel, through the empty restaurant and out to the bar in the back. I order two Cokes and a packet of Sportsman. I drink the first one quickly and burp. Then I wait. For what?

"You're hard on your men," the voice says. What? I look up. Aziz is standing in front of my table.

"Aziz," I say, and it sounds like a question.

"Yes, it's me, you weirdo," he says and sits down. "That was one serious going-over Stefano got."

"He got beaten up – he didn't get anything he didn't deserve," I say.

"Perhaps, but his head's messed up for good," Aziz says.

"What?" I say.

"Haven't you heard?"

"What?"

"He's lost his sense of smell and his sense of balance. He can't taste what he eats. And he'll never play sports again – he falls over his own feet. He can't drive a car either. And Panos has gone missing."

"Oh," I say, looking away. A couple of expensive whores sit at the bar, waiting for white fish; they're not interested in Aziz – they don't fancy Indian take-out.

"'Oh'," Aziz says. "Is that all you can say?"

"Yes."

"And what's that thing about Baltazar?" Aziz asks. I shiver.

"What's what with Baltazar?"

"Why has he been sent home to Angola?"

"Has he?"

"Yes. He didn't return for his exams. He has been sent to a boarding school in Angola even though his dad is still commercial attaché here in Dar."

"I haven't the foggiest," I say and think about Panos. I wonder what Panos is doing. He must have threatened Baltazar, or perhaps Baltazar is afraid I'll go to the police. Or to my dad. Perhaps Panos has been shipped off to Greece. Or to his mother's family in England – I don't think he speaks any Greek. He once talked about taking an agricultural course, so he could become a tobacco farmer like his dad. But now he can't ever return to Tanzania, because Stefano's dad is out to get him.

There's a letter for me from Tanga. I think it must be Halima's handwriting on the envelope. Inside the envelope is a postcard from Panos:

"I caught a bus to the other side of the mountain and crossed the border at Ronagi with a group of cattle smugglers until we got to the abattoir in Oloitokitok. From there I hitch-hiked to Nairobi where I borrowed some money from some friends of my dad and flew to Athens, where I stayed with his older brother on Lesbos for a while, and then I went back to Athens and thumbed it through Europe and got on the boat to England where I'm staying with my mum's sister and her husband in London and go to an agricultural school. I work at a petrol station and am broke but otherwise fine – you Brits are a strange lot. My mum has my address if you want to write. Call me when you get here yourself. Jah Love. Panos."*

What he did for me – this is how much it's cost him. Against his will he's gone to Europe. He's living on the mercy of some distant relatives of his. Working as a coolie at a petrol station. Was it his choice? Yes, he could have let Stefano be, but then what? What sort of person would he have been then? I put him in that situation. I hope Mick hasn't heard about it – he would never forgive me.

Alison comes barging through the door:

"I'm . . . me and Frans, we're . . . we're *pregnant!*" she shouts.

"Oh wow, really?" I say, making my eyes wide and forcing myself to smile: "Congratulations." I hug her so she can't read my eyes.

Sewer

I am almost eighteen; Christmas is in six weeks; I haven't seen my mum for more than a year, and in a couple of months people expect me to return to boarding school and retake Year Ten. And no-one cares about any of those things. All anyone cares about is Alison's baby bump. She's sitting on the sofa, looking at it lovingly. Frans goes over and pets it. He speaks to it. She giggles.

"Come, have a feel," Alison says. "Right here – it's grown." What is she talking about? You can't see a bump yet. Maybe it's just gas.

"I think he's a footballer," Frans says.

"Maybe it's a girl," Alison says.

"Then she'll be beautiful like her mother," Frans says.

They make me sick. I get up from my deckchair on the patio and pull the dressing gown tight around me – I can feel my bones sticking out, I've got no padding left. I've got no appetite. I go inside. Frans pretends to look at some papers. Alison asks me if I want anything to eat. She's happy. When she looks at me, she's ashamed of being happy. It's sick, that's what it is. And we can't talk about it. I'm the one who has to break the pattern, and I have to do it now. So I go over and smile and put my hand on her tummy and say:

"Is it awake?"

Alison smiles with relief.

"I think so, but it's not moving right now. Or maybe it's eating."

"Or pooping," I say. Aren't I just funny, or foul-mouthed, or hiding behind the attempt?

"Eew," Frans says.

"Yes, but think about it: where does all the poo go?" I say. "The baby's pooping away inside my sister. That's gross, that is." Alison gives me a slap.

"They don't start pooping until they come out, you know. As long as they're inside, it all comes out through the umbilical cord."

"So it's like a sewer?"

"Samantha," she says.

"Yes, alright," I say. "Yes, I'd like something to eat, but I just have to . . ." I say and point towards the toilet. I go out, have a bit of a cry, but very quietly so they won't hear, and then I go back in and sit down and force myself to eat a little.

"Samantha?" Alison says.

"Yes?" I say.

"Dad's having some problems at the moment."

"And?" I say.

"And they may suddenly decide to kick him out of the country," Alison says.

"What . . . does that mean?" I ask.

"It means that any children of his who are not yet eighteen are going to lose their residence permit as well," Alison says. It's me she's talking about.

Original sin

Alison bakes an enormous cake for my eighteenth birthday, and Mum has sent new clothes and sandals. And Dad doesn't show, so all in all it's a lovely day.

Staying with Alison is starting to bore me, but I make a real effort to seem O.K. to her so she won't worry. It might make the baby strange or something if she worries too much while she's pregnant. Being strange can happen soon enough. I go down to Oyster Bay every morning. I kick at the sand. Smoke a cigarette. I'm wearing the Ray-Ban sunglasses Christian put on my nose right before he left. Through their tinted glasses I see the water wiping out my footsteps in the sand. And then what? I'm gone without a trace. After that, I go for a swim – keeping the sunglasses on and my T-shirt; what else can I do? If I leave them on the beach, some kid will come along and nick them. It wasn't like that when I was little, but these days Oyster Bay is littered with human filth. I get out of the water and start wading back towards a grassy patch where I've buried a packet of Sportsman and some matches under the shell of a coconut.

"Hi, Samantha." I stop. Shakila is sitting on a knocked-over palm trunk. Oh bugger, what am I supposed to say to her? "How are you?" she asks. "Did you have malaria?" That's what I look like: too thin by far, and worn out to boot.

"Yes. And intestinal worms," I say. "How about you?" She shrugs.

"I started university."

"O.K. – did they give you the day off?"

"Skiving off," she says. Shakila skiving off – what's the world come to?

"What are you studying?"

"Medicine." Of course – a doctor like her dad.

"How's that? Good?"

"No," she says and fishes a packet of cigarettes out of the pocket of her dress and holds it towards me. I go over and sit down next to her, take a cigarette and look at her as if asking a question. "My dad," she says, sighing. "They hate my dad – the lecturers. And they take it out on me."

"Why do they hate your dad?"

"Because he used to teach there as well. And then he opened his private clinic and they're envious, so they take it out on his daughter."

I know that Shakila's dad was educated in England at the same time Tanzania won its independence. Her mother is a Jamaican nurse who her father met in London. They're divorced, and Shakila's mum lives in the States. Shakila's stepmum is supposed to be terrible. Shakila was sent to the boarding school in Arusha from Year One, whereas I didn't start until Year Three. I only went because Alison was already there and the school in Tanga was simply terrible. Shakila and her brother went because her stepmother didn't want to have them living with her in Dar.

"How are they taking it out on you?" I ask.

"*Tsk*," Shakila says. "For one, I fail exams even when what I do is O.K. And then when I re-sit the exam with a lecturer who doesn't know my dad, I pass with flying marks."

"Shit," I say.

"And when we do a petition as a class to complain about the teaching standards, and everyone signs it – I'm the one who's called to the chancellor's office, because he thinks I'm behind it, and because I supposedly think I'm something special because my dad owns a private hospital – there's no end to his blithering."

"Then what are you going to do?"

"Try to get a scholarship somewhere else."

"Abroad?"

"Yes, absolutely." Shakila digs a little hole in the sand, dumps her cigarette butt in it and covers it. "How about you? What do you get up to?" she asks. Maybe she knows that her dad has . . . removed my pregnancy. But then . . . maybe she doesn't know.

"I've been ill – for a long time. I'm staying with my sister right up there," I say, pointing back towards the residential neighbourhood.

"Yes, I know where that is: with the K.L.M. man. But you never returned for your exams?"

"No," I say. I don't want to talk about it, so I add, "Maybe I'll sit them later, as retakes."

"Are you going back to Tanga?"

"No," I say.

"Why not?" she asks.

"I'm just not," I say, because I don't want to talk about my mum, my dad, old England . . . all that shit.

"What are you doing now, then – in Dar?" Shakila asks.

"I'm bored rigid."

"Maybe we could, you know . . . do something?"

"Do you go to Marine's Club?"

"Yes, sometimes I do," Shakila says.

"Then maybe I'll see you there," I say. It's not like I don't want to, but . . . And I know where she lives. I can always stop by, if I want to, can't I? But then, I don't want to, in case her dad is there. So I don't know.

Marines

I go to a film night at Marine's Club on Laibon Street. It's right across the street from the American Embassy and the ambassador's residence. The soldiers live in the house, and at the end of the garden there is a big screen made out of white boards where they show films every other Thursday night. In the bar you can buy Heineken, which the ambassador has special permission to import for his own consumption. I go right in – a young filly – and although I'm still skinny, my arse has started to plump up again. I walk around the garden for a bit, having a look; Shakila isn't here – there's no-one I know. Only seemingly brain-dead marines who give me hungry looks. I buy a Heineken at the bar. There are rows of white plastic chairs in front of the screen. No-one has sat down yet. I grab a seat to one side – on the third row. A marine comes over – his muscles bulging and his head practically hairless. He puts a foot up on the empty chair next to me and leans forward, introducing himself.

"And who might you be?" he asks.

"Sam the Man," I say. He offers me a Marlboro, which I take.

"Do you want to go inside? I've got something stronger than that," he says, nodding towards the beer or the cigarette – I'm not sure which. I turn around in my chair, looking up towards the bar and the people standing around it.

"Do you want to let down the local girls?" I ask. He looks where I'm looking.

"I like you better," he says.

"You know what?" I say.

"No."

"My dad's an army man," I say. "That's enough as far as I'm concerned."

A boy comes along the row of chairs from the other end to where the soldier is standing. He flops into the chair next to me, putting his feet up on the chair in front of him; he looks at me and then looks straight ahead with the ghost of a smile on his lips.

"What kind of army man?" the soldier asks. I drop my cigarette on the lawn, stubbing it out with my foot and look at him – he is visibly annoyed with the little chap who's sat down.

"A mercenary," I say.

"Really? Where?"

"In Africa," I say. "He eats guys like you for breakfast."

"I don't think so," the soldier says.

"Don't let that worry you," I say. "I know so."

"What kind of training does he have?" the soldier asks.

"S.A.S.," I say. The soldier stands up straighter.

"I'd like to meet him," he says.

"Would you?" I say. "Personally, I'd rather not."

Flaming

"Marine," says the bloke who's sat down next to me, "can't you see you've been blown off?" The soldier takes a breath as if he was going to say something, but then he just sneers, takes his foot down and leaves. I throw an indifferent look at the guy.

"I'm Jack," he says.

"Hi, Jack – do you have a smoke?"

"I sure do, gorgeous – I've got more than that," he says winking at me.

"Who are you?"

"American. The new ambassador's son," he says.

"Yes, I suppose that explains why that fathead didn't beat you to a pulp."

"It does."

"Are you trying to get into my knickers?"

"No – I don't swing that way," Jack says.

"I thought there was something."

"Do you mind?" he asks.

"Not at all," I say. "It makes life a lot easier."

"What do you mean?"

"I don't have to be raped by you, then."

"Want to come?" he asks, jerking his head towards the ambassador's residence.

"Yes, why not?" I go over. Jack racks up two lines of cocaine on the kitchen table.

"Where did you get this?"

"Someone called Aziz," he says. "His dad's import–export company does some work for the embassy."

"I know him," I say. We take a line each. Not bad at all. We drink Heineken, smoke Marlboro, listen to A.B.C.

"I want to see your room," I say, starting to walk through the house.

"Right . . . Right . . . Left . . ." Jack says, following me like a dog. The room: sports magazines full of semi-naked men, posters of men, L.P.s with gay pop, and the clothes in his closet are a bit fey – flaming queer, that's what he is. I throw myself onto the bed, rubbing my tits.

"Are you sure you don't like girls?" I ask.

"No offence," he says. "But that really doesn't do anything for me."

"Good," I say. "Shall we go and see that film?"

Put a sock on it

"Can't you go and see Mick at the garage and ask him to come eat with us on New Year's Eve?" Alison asks.

"Can't you just call him?"

"Come on, Samantha. You need to get out and about more. He'll be pleased to see you." She gives me the address. Mick has started working as head mechanic at a big logistics company – he's sorting out their lorries. The private transport sector is incredibly well paid – no-one with any sense would ever send perishable goods by freight train, because they're always late. And even if the train were to leave on time, there's no way you could be sure the goods would still be in the carriage when the train arrived at its destination.

I drive down to the garage. I ask for Mick. One of the mechanics says he is in the office – and shows me in. Seeing him at the desk makes me feel suddenly happy. He's bent over some papers. I knock on the glass pane and he looks up, and I can't help smiling when I open the door.

"Samantha," he says, standing up. "Close the door, will you?"

I do.

"Hi, Mick," I say. He is standing behind the desk, leaning forward with both palms on the table, looking at me.

"What the fuck do you think you're doing, Samantha?"

"What do you mean?"

"Suddenly I've got your dad in my face because he thinks I've knocked you up."

"No . . ."

"Yes. You have to start looking after yourself, missy," he says. I put my hands on my hips:

"Who says it was my fault?" I ask.

"Then find yourself a bloke with enough sense to put sock on it before he pumps you."

"But, it was . . ." I start.

"Yes, and Panos is paying the price for it. Stranded in sodding England," Mick says.

"*Tsk*," I say and leave. There's a lump in my throat. I walk all the way back to Msasani.

"He couldn't come," I say when Alison asks me.

1986

Kigamboni

Alison and Frans are at the Yacht Club. The cook calls me to the phone.

"Yes?" I say.

"I've missed you," a voice at the other end says.

"Victor!" I cry.

"Hello, gorgeous."

"Where are you?" I ask.

"I'm so close I can almost taste you," he says. I giggle. "We can meet if you want to," Victor says.

"If I want to – what's that supposed to mean?" I ask.

"Maybe you're tired of waiting for me," Victor says.

"Oh, I am. But I'd like to see you. I'm bored. Where are you?"

"Kigamboni," he says – a peninsula just south of Dar es Salaam. You take the ferry from the fishing harbour. Kigamboni isn't particularly densely populated. There are a few little hotels dotted along the beautiful coast, but there are almost no guests because the ferry is far from reliable, and if you take the main road, you have to take an enormous detour inland before you can cross Mzinga Creek to go there. The hotels on Kigamboni are where the Dar es Salaam jet set have their wedding parties.

"But . . . are you coming for New Year's Eve here at Alison's? Have you been invited?" I ask.

"No, no-one knows I'm in Tanzania. No-one except you, that is," Victor says.

"I thought you were in Angola or England," I say.

"I was in Angola and England, but now I'm back to see you."

"But what about . . ."

"I'm all alone," Victor says.

"I'll be there tomorrow morning. I'll be there at nine," I say.

I tell Alison that I'm going with Shakila to visit some friends of hers in Bagamoyo. And the next morning I get on the ferry. Victor picks me up on his motorbike in the small harbour on Kigamboni. We kiss for a long time – long, deep kisses. He's staying at a small hotel outside the village. As soon as he has closed the door behind us, he starts undressing me – it gives me goose pimples. "Careful," I say. It's my first time since the rape, and I'm afraid I won't know how to any longer. My body is tense. "I'm a bit nervous, actually," I say.

"Just relax," Victor says. "There's no rush." He holds me close and kisses me for a long time, stroking my entire body, squeezing me, caressing me everywhere until I'm soaking wet.

"Lie down on your back," I say and sit astride him – taking him into me carefully. I've still got it. His cock is red hot and alive as I ride it and slam my fingers against the bean between my legs.

We make love and drink gin and swim together and ride the motorcycle and eat grilled corn on the cob and make love and smoke *bhangi*. I tell him I've been ill and that I'm going back to school.

"What did you do with that Mary?" I ask.

"I left her in England. She was no good in Africa," Victor says.

"But where are you going to live?" I ask.

"I've been to Angola, Zaire, Uganda, here – there are an awful lot of great places," Victor says. "I just need to sort out a bit more work before I make up my mind. I'm going back to Zaire for a while. How long are you going to be in school for?" he asks.

"Just six months. I missed my exams because I was ill, so now I'm doing the last six months again."

"Yes, I heard you were ill. But you're alright now, aren't you?"

"Yep, right as rain."

"Don't tell anyone you've seen me. It's our secret," Victor says, touching my tummy.

"Yes, of course," I say, grabbing on to him.

Barbecue

Frans is minding the barbecue while Dad sits on the patio regaling him with tales of how you fry steaks in the bush by packing them in tin foil with a bit of grease and some herbs, opening the bonnet and tying the parcel of meat onto the exhaust manifold with steel wire then driving full throttle for a number of minutes determined by the species and age of the animal in question, the thickness of the slab of meat, the diner's appreciation (or otherwise) of red meat, and whether the engine is cold when you start or already warm.

"It takes experience," Dad says. Hmmm . . . I keep a low profile, in fact I simply keep my mouth shut. It turns out I've got quite a knack for that. We eat and drink beer. I think about Victor and shiver.

"How's the hotel?" Alison asks.

"I've got a buyer, but he's a bit iffy," Dad says.

"Why?" Frans asks. "Can't you offer him a discount?"

"He's afraid the authorities are going to seize the property."

"But why would they?" Alison asks, even though she knows from the time the taxman came calling – but she probably hasn't told Dad that.

"They think I'm in arrears with the taxes," Dad says. "And there are some other things as well." You're not supposed to ask about those other things.

"How's the renovation of the house going?" Frans asks. Dad's little house in Dar, which he is probably going to sell as well. At least, I assume he is, unless he's gone soft and wants to play at being a granddad when Alison has had her baby.

"We're making good progress – it'll be done soon," Dad says.

"But are you moving then?" Alison asks.

"Why do you ask?" Dad asks. Alison points at her tummy, looking inquisitive.

"No, I won't move until after it's born," Dad says, smiling. I get up.

"Where are you going?" Dad asks.

"To wash my hair," I say. I go to my room. Smoke a cigarette. Then I go out and wash my hair. I am bored witless, but feel tense at the same time. Move? To him Tanzania is just something you can leave. But I don't want to leave.

Child soldiers & cannibalism

When I come out again, Frans has had a few too many – enough at least to want to hear about what Dad does for a living.

"In Africa," Frans says. "Child soldiers. Have you come across child soldiers?"

"Yes. There are always child soldiers," Dad says.

"Why?"

"The younger the soldiers, the better. Young men have no understanding of their own mortality. And in Africa, ignorance and religion play into it as well."

"But . . . have you fought children? Shot at them?"

"What choice do you have when twenty or so twelve-year-old boys come at you, machetes drawn and A.K.47s at the ready? Are you going to call U.N.I.C.E.F.? Those boys know that my bullets can't hurt them. The medicine man has told them so, and he's an authority figure to be reckoned with."

"But surely they see their comrades fall?"

"Yes, but they also know that they'll be killed by their own officers if they don't go through with the attack," Dad says.

"And they're stoned," Alison says.

"Yes, there's that as well: drunk and stoned. You see, Frans, you think of them as boys who could be playing with train sets – kids that are fundamentally good. But these boys have seen their families murdered. They

248

have been encouraged to rape grown women from their own villages. They have been forced into cannibalism. They're not boys anymore."

"Cannibalism?"

"Yes. In Central Africa, when everything collapses, cannibalism kicks in. You eat the meat of your fallen enemies to acquire their power. If you can see it from their perspective, it makes perfect sense. I've seen it happen."

"What did you do?"

"I shot them."

"But don't all human lives have some value?" Frans asks. Dad laughs:

"Some more than others," he says and points at the security guard doing his tour of the garden. "Your life is worth more than his. Don't try to tell me you don't think so."

"Don't try to argue with Dad," Alison says. "He has no soul."

"I beg to differ. It may be a bit tainted, but this is where we are," Dad says with a sweeping motion of his arm. Does he mean Africa? Or the world?

"How can you . . . live with yourself?" Frans snivels. Alison gets up, goes over and puts her hands on his shoulders.

"Bedtime," she says.

"I don't get it," Frans says.

"Up you get," Alison says.

"No, wait," Frans says.

"Dad, why do you always have to . . ." I start but stop myself, because it's wasted on him.

"I'm answering the man's questions. It's easy to have a heart of gold when you're flying first class."

Politics

"But . . ." Frans says. Alison has sat down again – ever the good wife: if her husband is drunk and doesn't want to go to bed, she won't make him go. "But how can it be that unrest in Africa is always so . . . over the top. I mean . . . it becomes so bestial – so barbaric." Frans' voice is somewhat slurred.

"No more barbaric than anywhere else, I would think," Dad says.

"Child soldiers, rape, cannibalism. Surely that's . . . inhuman," Frans says.

"No," Dad says. "It is perfectly human. Do you think white people aren't capable of these things?" Frans doesn't say anything. I don't know a lot about history, but even I have heard about World War II.

"It's just hard to understand," Frans says.

"Imagine yourself, here in Tanzania. You're a young man – fit and able. You've no money to live on, less than a dollar a day. You can't read or write. You don't know anyone with any influence on anything. You have no prospect of finding work. All you can do is stand on the street corner and look with envy at each passing vehicle and each smart pair of shoes. And then some authority figure comes along who points out the enemy responsible for your misfortune and orders you to kill and tells you to rape first, and tells you that once you're done, you can take your victims' possessions. What would you do? Rape and murder – of course you would."

"But then why don't we do something to help – us westerners? Why . . . don't we change the system?" Frans asks.

"This is politics in practice – the politics of power. Africa is rotten from the core out with corruption and nepotism. They have raw materials we want, and we take them as and when we want. We westerners are invited to a party, and at parties you don't worry about the ones that haven't been invited. We simply don't care how the average negro is faring, as long as we have our fig leaf in the shape of aid, which is more than outweighed by what we steal with the other hand. We've got them by the balls."

"But it still seems more . . . bestial. Here. When there's a war," Frans says.

"It's no more bestial to kill with a machete than with a rifle – it's just closer to hand and more messy."

Frans gets up without saying anything and starts staggering towards the door. Dad shouts at him: "The world is entirely logical, you know. It's all connected. The Soviets need foreign currency; the military air carriers are rented out to humanitarian organizations from the West; the pilots take

Russian weapons along to sell to the rebels. Which rebels? There are always some to be found."

"Goodnight," Alison says calmly and takes hold of Frans' shoulder and goes inside with him. I follow them while Dad sits complaining that we're all going to bed. I'm not sitting alone with him, thank you very much.

Going back to school

"You're going back to school in two weeks," Dad says. Everything has already been arranged – I don't get a say in it at all. I have to start again halfway into Year Ten – the year below my own – and then I have to sit my exams.

"I don't want to go back," I say. "Alison left her school in England as well."

"Yes, but she finished Year Twelve. With you, all I insist on is that you complete Year Ten, but I do insist on it," Dad says.

Prison looms ahead. I go down for a swim, buy a bottle of *Konyagi* and sit in the garden with a glass and some cigarettes. The phone rings in the house and the cook calls me in.

"Yes?" I say into the phone.

"Hey – it's Panos here," he says.

"Panos! Where are you?"

"England. Agricultural school," he says. "I'm learning about soil." Panos laughs. "You Brits are a strange lot," he says. "I'm working at a petrol station. I'm one of the poor ones."

"But when are you coming back?" I ask.

"I don't know. My mum says Stefano's family might move back to Italy or perhaps go to run a tobacco farm in China. Once they're gone, I'll come back," Panos says. Yes, Stefano's dad could have him killed if he came now.

"Panos," I say. "I'm sorry that I . . ."

Panos cuts me short. "I'm not. I've wanted to kick that bugger's arse since I was four." He laughs across the intercontinental connection. I laugh as well – that's the *Konyagi* working. "How about you, Samantha?" he asks.

"I've been ill," I say. "And now I have to do Year Ten all over again."

"Tough luck," Panos says. "But it'll be cool, though, finishing it and coming up here. It'll be cool."

"But where are you staying?" I ask.

"In a basement – the temperature is what I'd call moderate," Panos says, laughing again.

"But how do you live? Do you have a car? Where do you eat?" I ask. Panos laughs.

"Christ, Samantha. In Europe you have to do everything yourself, you know that. I ride my bike, cook my own pasta and smoke hand-rolled cigarettes. I mean . . . I've thought about it. I'm half black, but I had to come all the way to England to live like a proper negro," he says.

"Do you have money?" I ask.

"No money," he says.

"That's not good," I say.

"Oh well. I'm hanging in there. But Samantha – are you O.K.? I really miss . . . you know, having a cigarette with you, downing some of that K.C.," Panos says.

"Yes," I say. "Me too."

Waiting

I'm waiting. What am I waiting for? Victor. I'm hoping Victor will show up again, but he doesn't, and I don't want to run the risk of asking Dad, because he mustn't know that I'm fooling around with his partner. The days limp on. In the end I even have a look through my schoolbooks. I could sit that exam so easily. If that's what it takes to make them happy. But I need my own life. How can I have that? With Victor? But he's always on the road, and is he really serious about me? Panos, when he returns? But then, Panos is Panos. I mean – it's too weird, I think. And Mick, he doesn't like me anymore. He doesn't come by; he doesn't ask if I want to do something with him. I don't know what to do anymore.

A couple of days before the new term starts, I call Tazim.

"It'll be fine," she says. "It's only a couple of months, and then you'll revise and sit your exams and it'll be over."

"But . . ." I say. "People think that . . ." I don't actually know what people think. "What are they saying?"

"You know, people say that Panos was in love with you and that he beat Stefano up because he was jealous."

"And what about Baltazar?" I ask.

"Baltazar?" Tazim asks. "What about him?"

"He . . . Nothing," I say. Baltazar has left school, so he's already been forgotten. He's dead and gone, just like Gretchen and Christian.

Pariah

I carry my bags into the room I'll be sharing with Adella –that's something, at least. We smoke a spliff just like we used to. We sleep – at least, she does. I'm thinking about packing my bag and going down to the Y.M.C.A. – getting a bus in the morning. At school – it's as if there's some invisible boundary around me: no-one dares come too close, no-one dares to speak to me. I'm sitting in class with a bunch of babies a year younger than me – I don't even know their names. But this is my year now, and I leaf through books I've already worked through once, and it's . . . What am I supposed to do here, really? I go up to Kijana House and sit down on the smokers' bench, lighting a cigarette, but who am I supposed to talk to? It's not like I am being given the cold shoulder – people just don't talk to me. My friends have all gone. Panos has gone. Gretchen. Baltazar and Stefano weren't my friends exactly. Christian has gone. Shakila is in Dar es Salaam. Diana and Truddi shun me like I was a leper. I go up to Diana during break.

"Have you heard from Panos?" I ask.

"You stay away from me," she says.

"I only wanted to tell you . . ." I start.

"Get lost," Diana says.

Tazim goes out of her way not to see me. I think she thinks I'm over the top. I make a point of seeing her.

"You create a lot of problems for yourself. And you create a lot of problems for the people who are close to you. I don't want that in my life," she says and walks away from me. I think there are a lot of rumours about me. People respect me, or else they just avoid me, maybe they're afraid of me. I go to the smokers' bench every break time – this is where I belong.

Jarno sits down next to me.

"Welcome back, Sam," he says.

"Yes, thanks a bunch," I say.

"It'll be fine," he says.

"Will it?" I ask. He smiles, shrugs and smokes his cigarette.

Manual

I decide on swimming as my games activity – that way I don't have to talk to anyone, and I can outswim almost anyone. I need someone. I go all the way up to *mama mbege*, but Jarno isn't there. I bump into a Sikh from Jarno's year – Bramjot. He smiles and offers me a cigarette, but he doesn't speak to me. The following afternoon I go down to Kishari House and inside the building, where I'm not allowed. Jarno is sitting by the desk in his study. I step inside and lie down across his bed. He looks at me and smiles, but he doesn't say anything. I don't say anything either. His smile goes a bit stale. He doesn't get up from his chair.

"Christian might come down in June," he says.

"Oh," I say. Jarno doesn't say anything else. Everything stands still. I can't stand it.

"Why don't you do something?" I ask.

"Do what?"

"I'm right here."

"What do you want me to do?" Jarno asks.

"It's not like there's a manual," I say.

"What would you like?"

"How would I know?"

"Yes well, I don't have the manual either," he says and gets up from his chair. He's standing in the middle of the room.

"Then bloody think of something," I say, getting up as well. I'm standing in front of him, looking at him. He's looking at me. We're standing still like that without speaking for several seconds. "*Tsk*," I say and leave the room.

Violence

I end it in late March, right before the end of term. It happens in the library. I'm studying for a biology assignment, and Gulzar sits down across from me and whispers:

"I can pay you, if you'll do it with me." I look up at him to sneer, but he looks so excited. Like I might actually do it – that the world works that way, that I would touch him for money. I want to be sick, but somehow I have already got up and have the back of the chair in my hands and am swinging it up and across the table, so that its legs crash into Gulzar's head, and he flumps sideways off his chair, knocking his head against the concrete floor. He lies there groaning. Blood is running from a deep cut on his cheek – one of the legs of the chair must have cut it.

"You're mad!" the librarian cries and kneels next to Gulzar. Mr Harrison comes running in.

"What happened, Samantha?" he says. The librarian looks up:

"She hit him. With the chair." Harrison grips my arm firmly. He looks down on me.

"Why did you hit him?"

"Because he's a pig," I say.

"Headmaster. Now!" Harrison says and leads me towards the buzzing crowd that has gathered in the library. "Make way," Harrison tells them, and they pull back a little to let us through. I see Diana and Masuma and

Voeckler, the teacher. In the Headmaster's office, they dump me in a chair in the front room. Owen is almost running when he shows up.

"You're not likely to get away with this, Samantha," he says and goes into his office to make calls. I see the librarian and a teacher help Gulzar walk down to the car park. I suppose they're taking him to see a doctor. I sit there for more than an hour and a half, while Owen makes his various phone calls.

"I need to go to the toilet," I tell the secretary. She goes in to see Owen.

"Come along, then," she tells me and walks me to the toilet. "I'll wait here," she says out in the hall, and I go in, light a cigarette, sit down and pee. When we return, I am called in to see Owen.

"You're lucky," Owen says. "Gulzar's father is not going to press charges, but as of now you're no longer a pupil at this school."

"O.K. I'll go pack," I say.

"No," Owen says. "We've packed your things for you. They're in the back of my car. I'll drive you to the bus station in a couple of hours."

"Then what am I going to do now?" I ask.

"You're coming home with me to have your supper," he says. I follow Owen to his house. He usually eats in the dining hall, but he has had food brought over to his house from the school kitchen. His wife and children aren't there – they're probably in the dining hall.

We're sitting across from each other at the table and eating silently. I'm not hungry at all.

"Coffee?" Owen asks.

"Yes, please," I say. He gets a thermos, cups, a tin of Africafé and bowl of sugar. We each make our own coffee. "Can I smoke?" I ask.

"Patio," Owen says and goes out. I follow him. I drink my coffee and smoke my cigarette, looking over at the school. That life is over for me now.

"Hmmm," I say.

"What?" Owen says.

"Shall we go?" I ask.

"Let's," he says. Not a word is said. He buys my ticket, then hands me some cash. "Good luck," he says.

"You too," I say and get on board. I sit down, wait. I'm out.

Life, it's hard

"Don't cry now," Alison says when she opens the door and sees me.

"They've expelled me," I bawl.

"I know," Alison says. "Owen called. Why did you hit that bloke anyway?"

"He offered to pay me to . . . to . . . touch him," I blub.

"And?" Alison says.

"And I completely lost it," I say. Frans appears behind her.

"You could have just ignored him," he says. I look at the floor.

"Come in, will you?" Alison says.

"The bump is showing," I say.

"Yes – impressive, isn't it?" she says. The baby is due in two and a half months. I could have had a bump just like that – only bigger. I do the maths: I would have given birth a month ago. A little baby the colour of a Cadbury's bar.

Frans is none too pleased to see me.

I sit down on the patio and have a smoke. We're in the middle of the long rains; it's 35° Celsius in the shade, and humidity is 94 per cent – the cigarette will extinguish itself if I'm not puffing on it constantly.

The next day Dad shows up. I can hear Alison in the drive.

"Don't touch her."

"No, of course I won't."

"If you hurt her, you'll never see your grandchild."

"I won't hurt her," he says and she lets him in. I'm sitting in one corner of the sofa with my legs pulled up under me. He comes over and sits down next to me. He doesn't say anything. He simply offers me a cigarette and lights it for me.

"Let's go out for supper," he says.

"O.K.," I say. We drive down to Oyster Bay Hotel. What is he up to now?

"When I was young and angry, like you are now, it got me into trouble," he says, looking at me. I don't say anything. "It turned out to be really hard – life, I mean."

"What was hard about it?" I ask.

"I got into the army, the S.A.S., and was disciplined. I got myself sorted out."

"Sorted out how? For killing negroes?" I say.

"You have to have discipline to get your life together. Self discipline," Dad says. "You have to make sure you get it, Samantha."

"What are you talking about?" I ask. Dad looks at me then looks away, sighing.

"I don't know," he says. "I'm trying to tell you something."

"What?" I ask.

"I'm damned if I know."

"If you don't, then who does?" I ask. Dad looks at me.

"You can't be like me," he says. "If you want a happy life, you can't be like me."

"I know that," I say.

"Do you?" he asks. I don't say anything. "I'm going to have to send you home to your mother," he says.

"But not until after Alison has had the baby, right?" I say in a small voice. He looks at me sceptically. "It's only two more months," I say.

"Alright then," he says.

Itching for a boy

I wake up early and go down to the beach for a swim. Then I go over to Jack's. The maid opens the door slightly. I greet her in Swahili – asking her whether the boy is in.

"The boy isn't up yet," she says, holding the door, ready to close it again.

"I'll go wake him up then, shall I?" I say.

"I'm not sure . . ." she says, looking nervous.

"You don't know if you're allowed to let me in to wake up the ambassador's son?"

"I don't know," she says.

"You do know that the boy is *msenge*, don't you? Otherwise he would have tried to cop a feel a long time ago." She titters and looks at the floor, raising her hand to hide her smile. I'm standing there telling her the ambassador's son is as queer as a chocolate orange.

"The ambassador wants you to let me in," I say. "He's hoping I can make the young *msenge* normal." Now she's grinning quite openly, opening the door and letting me in. I find the room and throw myself onto Jack's bed, waking him up.

"Hi, Sam," he mutters. "Do you want some breakfast?"

"I want a shag," I say, grabbing his hand and guiding it towards my groin.

"Cut it out," he says, giggling, trying to pull his hand back.

"Come on, Jack – just bonk me, will you?" I throw myself on top of him.

"No, Sam. I don't want to – I mean, you're a girl." He struggles to get out from underneath me. I pull up my T-shirt to reveal my tits.

"Don't you even like my titties?" I ask. "You can fuck me up the arse," I say.

"Stop it," Jack says.

"How about if we turn off the lights?"

"*Stop*," he says.

"Surely one arse will serve as well as the next?"

"Bitch," he says, pushing me away. I groan.

"I just need a shag," I whimper.

"Have a cigarette," Jack says and jumps out of bed – his cock not the least roused. He goes to the door and called loudly in his pidgin Swahili, "Please to ask for food for two in the morning, please."

We eat. Then Jack drives me home. He's going scuba-diving: but I don't want to – too much water above you for my liking.

The days and weeks continue like that and nothing much happens. Alison doesn't say anything about England. Dad wants to send me to live with Mum when Alison has had her baby. But I don't want to go. I'm hoping something new will pop up – some new opportunity or other.

The imperialists

Range Rover, Land Rover, Land Cruiser, Nissan Patrol, Cherokee Jeep, some new Peugeots, Mercedes, a bleeding Porsche – the cars, all recently polished by the staff, are parked in the drive at the Swedish ambassador's residence. Frans parks his shining Range Rover.

"We'll all be good, won't we?" Alison says to me as we walk on the fine shingles of the drive, past the chauffeurs in their poo-coloured uniforms, smoking and polishing the vehicles while they wait for their lords and masters to get drunk enough to want to be carted home.

"Of course," I say. The embassies are allowed unlimited tax-free import of goods – I have seen the catalogues both at Christian's in Moshi and recently at Jack's – the same Danish companies selling everything: furniture, clothes, sweets, food, booze, jewellery, curtains, bog roll, cigarettes, tents – everything. A uniformed waiter hastens towards us with a tray – he's carrying long-stemmed glasses containing the welcome drinks. I take one and saunter off. There's food aplenty, but luckily it's not a formal do – you ask the waiters for whatever you want on your plate and sit down at one of the small tables in the garden. We eat. Afterwards I stay close to Alison, who's moving around, saying hello to people in the garden. It's lit by torches and has a marquee where they serve cocktails.

"However did you teach your maid to do this sort of thing?" Alison asks the Swedish ambassador's wife.

"Maria's very quick to learn," the ambassador's wife says. "I only have to show her the steps two or three times, and she's picked it up." We've had *crêpes suzettes* for pudding. But, really, it's just pancakes. And here they are, talking about the maid like she was some sort of a dog who was good at performing the tricks you'd taught it. The entire relationship between master and staff is like the one you would have with dogs who depend on their master and who know it – and who behave because behaving is the way to be fed. And, of course, there are those who fear their dogs. They think they might bite.

I walk away from them before the woman can speak to me or start talking about Alison's baby bump. Alison and Frans get asked to an unbelievable number of these embassy dos because of Frans' job at K.L.M. – he can always get last-minute tickets.

The place is full of Swedes. The bar is made up of long tables covered in yellow and blue tablecloths like the Swedish flag. The men are in their forties, too fat by far and looking tired. Some of them have brought black women who stay in the background or speak to other black women who have also caught themselves a white beastie. And then there are the white women.

"Does your cook steal as well?" they ask.

"Yes, they all do. But as long as they don't overdo it . . ." someone else says.

Frans shows up next to me, taking my arm and leading me away from the gossiping women.

"Complaining about one's staff is stupid," Frans says. "Just like complaining about the traffic when you're on the road in Africa is stupid, because you'll end up having a nervous breakdown or a hernia if you let it get to you. Probably better to go home in that case," he says, in a low voice that no-one but I can hear. Frans is alright.

"Nothing wrong with the traffic here," I say. We stroll around the garden for a bit. I get him to give me a cigarette.

Alison comes over.

"Shall we go?" Frans asks. Alison puts her hands on her tummy.

"Soonish," she says, nodding at a beautiful, local woman with large breasts.

"Is she still with that German trade attaché?" Frans asks.

"Yes, I think she's bagged him," Alison says.

"I'll just go get us some drinks," Frans says and goes towards the bar where the black waiters are standing in their dark trousers and uniforms.

"Bagged?" I say. Alison tells me that the woman is a widow with two young children and that for three years she's done the tour – working on finding the perfect white man who can pay for it all.

"Hi, girls." It's Jack.

"Jack," I say.

"Let's get this party started," Jack says.

"We were just going," I say.

"Noooo," Jack says, as Frans returns with our drinks and a fruit juice for Alison.

"I have to watch myself," Alison says, looking at her bump.

"If Sam stays, I promise to get her home safe," Jack says.

"I'm not sure how safe you'd be behind the wheel right now," Frans says.

"I've got a chauffeur," Jack says.

"Ask Samantha – I'm not her mother," Alison says, grinning.

"Well, yes – I'd like to stay," I say. Shortly after Frans and Alison leave, me and Jack go to the toilet to powder our noses. We drink like fishes and go around listening to people talking, tittering until Jack's dad shows up and asks us to keep it down. After that we have a couple of cans of beer and let the chauffeur take us to Oyster Bay where we skinny-dip and sit on the sand, drinking, smoking, chatting.

The next morning: I brush my teeth; my head is killing me after last night. Alison calls me – she wants me to come out shopping with her and go to the hairdressers.

"I just need to brush my hair," I call back. My head hurts. I've got a bit left from yesterday. I flip down the lid on the toilet. I quickly scoop the powder onto it, give it a chop with a nail file, roll up a banknote and snort it. I look in the mirror, sniff again and wipe my nose, shaking my head. Then it's out in the car.

"Are you alright?" Alison asks.

"I'm fine."

"You look a bit rough."

"I'm just knackered – I'll be fine."

"O.K.," she says, asking me about last night.

"I got in around five," I say.

"But then you've barely slept."

"I can sleep when I'm dead."

Jarno

One day the cook has a note for me: "I'm staying at the Norad guesthouse – come see me. Jarno."

O.K. He was in Year Twelve. That means that the exams have to be over. If I had stayed in school, I would have had my exams now. What difference does it make? I go outside and find a taxi. I go there. There's an old Yamaha 125 parked out front, the cook is sitting in an alcove outside the staff quarters speaking to the gardener. I greet them and ask about Jarno.

"He's through there," the cook says. I go in. The stereo is playing brain-dead rock music, and I can hear the shower. I go over and open the bathroom door.

"Jarno," I say. He's in the bathtub as naked as a baby.

"What?" he says and half turns to look at me.

"Shall I wash your back?" I ask, because I really want to get my leg over.

"Be my guest." Afterwards we go to his bed. He's got condoms. He kneads my tits as if they were dough. We do it, and he comes after precisely twenty-seven seconds – I'm counting, that's how boring it is.

"Sorry about that," he says.

"Never mind," I say.

"Over-pressure," he says. "I'll do better next time." His cock has already started stiffening again. I'm not interested.

"I have to go," I say.

"Stay a bit," he says.

"I'm meeting someone."

"I'll give you a lift," he says. We get dressed and go into the kitchen and get two Cokes from the fridge. The cook is standing with his back to us, muttering an almost inaudible "*tsk*" while he chops his veg and shakes his head almost imperceptibly. We're behaving scandalously. And if we are, how is that any of his business?

It's too hot outside, so we sit ourselves down in the sitting room and have a smoke.

"I think Christian will be down soon," Jarno says.

"Here? In Dar?"

"He wrote to me in Morogoro. He asked if you were dead . . . ?" Oh bollocks. Suicidal – I wrote all that stuff to him. And I just know he's in love with me, and now he's coming down, and then I'll have to . . . I just don't know what to do about it.

"What do you think?" I ask. "Am I dead?"

"You don't seem dead to me."

"You can tell him that then."

"I have. He's looking forward to seeing you."

"I'm not sure I'll be here – I'm leaving soon."

"Yes, I know what you mean," Jarno says.

"You do?"

"Yes. Africa – it doesn't belong to us."

"That's not what I mean," I say.

"Then what?"

"Europe – does that belong to us?" I ask. Jarno shrugs, defeated.

"Finland?" I ask. "Is that where you're going?"

"Military service," he says. "Compulsory."

"Eew!"

"You said it." He chuckles. "I'm starting off behind bars."

"Why?"

264

"I was supposed to have been there a week ago. The embassy people are looking for me."

"Don't they know you're here?"

"I suppose they will soon, but what can they do about it? They can't arrest me. They have to ask Tanzania to do it officially, and they don't want to." I get up.

"I have to go," I say. Jarno gets up as well, comes over and puts a hand on my hip.

"Why don't you stay a little?" he says – randy bastard.

"Is Christian going to stay here when he comes down?" I ask. Jarno removes his hand.

"Yes," he says. I was actually thinking about asking if I could crash here for a while, but then Jarno would be constantly . . . And if Christian is coming, then he'll be – it's no good.

"You won't tell Christian about this, will you?"

"Of course not," Jarno says. Of course he will. A secret is something you tell someone – if you don't, it doesn't exist. Jarno can't do anything for me – he's just another passenger.

Fatheads

Alison and Frans are going to Zanzibar on a long weekend, and quite a lot of people have returned to Dar now that school is over. I make some calls and ask some people round on Saturday evening. I instruct the cook to prepare some food that can be passed round. I put plastic containers full of water into the freezer to make lots of ice to cool beers in the bathtub. Frans and Alison have said I can. It's a brave new world.

Jack is coming. Aziz has brought Diana. Jarno and Salomon, whose hair has grown back. A couple of the nice marines Jack goes diving with. Some of the local girls who usually go to Marine's Club. I go with Aziz and Jack to the bathroom to powder our noses.

In the sitting room they're all sitting talking about their plans: Diana is going to study in Canada; she says that Tazim might be going to Portugal; Jarno is going back to Finland, prison and military service. Aziz has started working at his father's import–export company – his grades were too poor for anything else. Salomon is due to go to university in Milan. The marines are going back to the States to do whatever one does in the States – the local girls think they're going too, but they're wrong. And me . . . I have no idea. Soon they'll all be dead. Soon I won't ever see them again, and they'll be dead. Like Gretchen is dead – I don't hear from her, she doesn't hear from me.

I haven't had enough to eat, so I get drunk too quickly. I go out to the garden to have some air and a smoke. Jarno comes and puts his arm around me. The darkness of the garden makes me shiver. The memory returns: Baltazar in the Strand brothers' garden at the party in Arusha.

"Don't touch me," I say sharply. My voice breaks ever so slightly. "I'm not feeling very well," I add. He lets go. The music from the sitting room has got louder. I go inside. Salomon is sitting by the table, rolling spliffs – some of the guests are dancing. I want to lie down. I go to my room. One of the girls has her head glued to Aziz's groin. He's lying across my bed. Her head is moving up and down his cock like a piston.

"Out!" I bellow – going over and kicking her arse. She moves away. I kick Aziz. "You complete twat. I want you out – right now," I say.

"Relax," he says, pushing me off when I try to kick him again. He gets up and does up his flies. The girl has made herself scarce. I push him towards the door while I shout at him. I follow him into the sitting room and turn the music off to make sure he can hear me:

"I don't bloody want you to use my bed to get laid in," I shout. Aziz turns around. Everyone's staring at us.

"I wasn't getting laid. I was getting a blowjob – there's a difference, you know," he says and goes into the hall where Mick is standing right inside the door. I left a message for him with his cook. Mick looks at me. Aziz walks past him to the girl, who is waiting for him outside. Someone has put the music back on.

"Come in," I tell Mick.

"What are you doing, Samantha?" he asks.

"Getting rid of that bastard," I say.

"Why did you even let him in?"

"It's a . . . a party," I say.

Mick looks past me into the sitting room. "And pseudo-Rasta-Salomon – another twit. Jarno – as much use as tits on a bull." It's my dad's favourite expression. "A bunch of fatheads from America and their local whores . . . It's not a party, it's a bummer." He turns around and heads towards the door.

"Mick?" I say, running after him. He gets into his car. I'm standing at the driver's side. He rolls down the window.

"Victor," Mick says. "He smuggles weapons and drugs. And he's got some sort of hold on your dad. That's the situation in a nutshell." Mick starts the engine.

"How do you know that?" I call. He turns his head and looks at me.

"Your dad told me," he says, looking over his shoulder now, reversing down the drive before I have time to say anything. Out on the road. Out and away.

Help

Alison and Frans are having people round for dinner: a Dutch couple. And Dad is there. I have dressed up and am on my best behaviour. We eat at the table. Then we move to the sofa area. Dad gets up and goes to the drinks cabinet to get a refill. I go over to him, because we have to talk. I need to know what will happen if I go to England. Whether that's it. Whether he's going to stay here. Whether . . . all sorts of things. I stand next to him.

"Dad," I say.

"Yes, darling," he says.

"Are you going to stay in Tanzania – a long time, or . . . ?" Two of the bottles are knocked over as his arm swings forward and to the side; it continues towards me as I jolt backwards and away. The arm hits me. Hard. Right in my face.

"Stefano got you up the duff, didn't he?" he says. There's a taste of blood in my mouth. The shock drowns out how much it hurts. So many of the nerves in his hands have been cut that he doesn't even realize how hard he hits. I look him straight in the eye and say:

"Hit me again if you like it so much."

"I'm your dad. You should have told me," he sneers. "You don't understand anything, Samantha. You're a stupid girl."

"I understand more than you do." He shakes his head. They're dead silent on the sofa – I take care not to look at them. Dad looks strange when he speaks:

"I'm trying to help you. We're a family – we're supposed to help each other," he says. I have no idea whether he's drunk or not – what will happen next? Alison speaks in a cold voice from her seat in the sofa:

"How exactly is hitting her going to help?"

"I wouldn't spit on you if your face was on fire," I tell Dad. Tears well up in my eyes – completely unexpectedly. I turn abruptly, yank open the mosquito net doors, go into the garden and around the house, as far away from him as I can get. Alison is shouting in the sitting room:

"What do you think you're doing, you absolute idiot? Do you think you can come into my house and behave in that way? You go out and apologize to her RIGHT NOW."

I hurry on. An apology from him? No thanks. Stefano – no, it wasn't him who got me pregnant, it was Baltazar. But does it really matter now? It all happened such a long time ago.

When I return three hours later, I see my swollen cheek in the mirror in the hall. Alison comes out and hugs me.

"Where is he?" I ask.

"The brute passed out on the sofa," Alison says. We go into the sitting room. There he is, snoring away. I continue out into the kitchen and help myself to a Coke. Alison lights a cigarette, even though she hasn't smoked in months.

"He's not what he once was," she says.

"When was he ever?" I ask.

"We have a real problem," Alison says and looks at me with something not unlike anxiety. I don't say anything. "They won't extend your residence permit when it expires," she says.

"But . . ." I say.

"Dad has provided weapons for the A.N.C. training camps in Tanzania, but the final shipment is almost sorted now and the authorities know he was up to something in the Seychelles. So he's getting the boot, and you won't get an extension on your residence permit when it expires."

"But I'm eighteen," I say.

"Yes, but you don't have a job," Alison says.

"But you don't either," I say.

"I don't need one – I'm married," Alison says.

"So I have to get married, is that it?" I ask.

Dad's voice says through the open door:

"If anyone will have you."

"*Tsk*," I say and turn my back on him.

"Get out," Alison tells Dad.

"I'm sorry, Samantha," Dad says, and then he goes out and drives off.

Thirty-two carats

Aziz comes over to us in the bar at the Kilimanjaro Hotel. He sits down next to Jack.

"Have you got some?" Jack asks.

"Loads," Aziz says. Jack fingers Aziz's gold bracelet.

"Do you like it?" Aziz asks.

"Yes," Jack says. "How many carats?"

"Thirty-two," Aziz says.

"Twenty-four is as high as it goes," I say.

"In India we have thirty-two carats," he says.

"You've never been to India," I say.

"I'm from India," Aziz says.

"No, you're not – you're from Africa."

"I come from Indian tradesmen. I'm a Hindu. I'm from India."

"You're a negro with bad skin," I say.

"And what are you?" Aziz says.

"Out of your league."

"Are you buying?" he asks Jack.

"Don't buy any here," I say.

"Why not?" Jack says.

"It's been cut with all sorts of crap – fertilizer; it's great for plants, but not for you."

"It hasn't been cut. It's clean," Aziz says.

"I'll get you something decent," I tell Jack, even though I have no idea where.

"Just one then," Jack says and hands a few banknotes to Aziz discreetly, who presses a folded banknote straight into his hand in the middle of the bar. That's how it's done these days. Tanzanian money isn't worth the paper it's printed on; the printing press keeps rolling, and cocaine is delivered to the customer wrapped in a crisp 100 shilling note so you have the requisite tool handy when you want to powder your nose.

Aziz leaves. A large waiter comes round to change the filled ashtrays.

"Look at him – isn't he gorgeous?" Jack says.

"Simmer down, Jack."

"We're having dinner at Marine's Club."

"I don't want to – they keep trying to get into my knickers."

"Sure they do, and I think one of them is trying to get into mine."

"But they're as dumb as bricks."

"And as hard."

"You have a one-track mind, you know," I say.

"You bet, girlfriend. You and me – we're two of a kind," Jack says. We go out to the car. Jack is driving.

Traffic

"Let's see if we can get something somewhere else," I say. "That shit Aziz gave you will fry your frontal lobes." We're driving around town, checking a couple of places, asking the bartenders discreetly whether you can buy something for your nose. No joy. It's late, and we're hungry; we race back along Upanga – there's a power cut, so the only light comes from cars and lorries. The traffic is dense and quick – you have to be on your toes. Jack whizzes past the pedestrians walking at the side of the road – risking their lives to avoid getting their feet dusty.

"Aaaiiiihhhh," Jack cries. Du-dum, go the tyres. There's just enough time for me to see . . . a dead man. We've just driven over a dead man, his fingers spread, rolled flat on the tarmac by the cars, his torso spread thin by the lorries.

"Shit," I say, looking back. When I look back at Jack, he has started shaking. Typical poofter.

"Why hasn't anyone moved him?" he shrieks.

"They'll be run down if they go out on the road."

"But that's so . . . so sick."

"It won't make any difference to how dead he is, Jack."

"I can't drive any further," Jack says.

We are coming up to Selander Bridge. We're in the middle lane, on the far side of several very long lorries, because we're turning right at the crossing – it's impossible to pull over here.

"You have to wait until we've crossed the bridge," I say. The smell of rotting seaweed and sewage comes through our open windows from the stagnant waters west of the bridge. Jack turns down Kenyatta Drive with a trembling lower lip and pulls over straightaway. He snivels.

"What are you doing?" I say.

"I just can't drive," he says.

"Alright," I say and step out and walk around the front end of the car. Right away there are two boys there, trying to sell me peanuts and cigarettes – they normally work at the crossing when the traffic grinds to a halt.

"*Toka!*" I say – get lost. Jack scooches over – he is sobbing melodramatically. "Don't hump the gear," I say. "I won't have your shit on my hand." He laughs through his tears.

"Big and hard," he says, falling into the passenger's seat. I release the handbreak, guiding the car into the traffic – big engine, good acceleration: a Cherokee Jeep. I drive along Oyster Bay. The wind whips through the windows. There's no electricity here either, so the large villas seem like sinister castles, except for the ones that have generators. Out on the ocean I see the lanterns on the freighters that are anchored in the bay.

Appetite

"Let's get something to eat," I say.

"Eat?" Jack says. "I couldn't eat now."

"But you just said you were hungry?"

"Yes but . . . it's that dead guy. I really can't eat anything now." I brake and make a U-turn to go to Jack's dad's house on Laibon Street.

"I'm hungry," I say. I can't remember when I was last this hungry. We get there. Light is pouring from Marine's Club and from the embassy – it goes without saying that they would have an independent electricity supply, and it's the marines' film night tonight. We're let in through the gates of the ambassador's residence, park and go inside. There doesn't seem to be anyone home.

"I really don't want anything," Jack says as I head towards their enormous kitchen.

"Then what am I going to have?" I ask. I can't cook.

"I'll fix you something." Their Indian cook is coming from the staff's quarters – the guard has told him there are people in the house.

"What do you want?" he asks in English.

"We'll be fine," I tell him in Swahili.

"It's so weird how you just speak the language," Jack says. How is that weird? I've lived here for fifteen years. The larder is full to the brim with all sorts of canned food; there's chips, pizzas, lasagne, pies and all sorts of stuff in the freezers. Jack is taking things out of a fridge that resembles a showy 1950s American car – it's so big you could stand four people inside it.

"Beer?" I ask. He turns around and throws me a can of Carlsberg. I open it carefully so it won't spill. Jack has got the oven going and a pan; he starts chopping up cocaine on the worktop – Dar is humid, which makes the powder clog. It's Aziz's stuff – maybe it clogs because he's cut it with all sorts of things.

"I'm just going to give it a go," he says when he sees the look on my face. He snorts a small line, shakes his head and blinks his eyes. "Something's not right with that stuff." With a quick movement of his hand he sweeps the rest of it onto the floor. There are footsteps – the ambassador's coming.

Manoeuvres

"Hello, Sam," Jack's dad says and smiles with his big, square teeth, so white it seems off. But then everyone has white teeth – the negroes as well. He's like them – a skeleton behind his flesh and blood. But he doesn't seem to think about that. He's just hoping his son has developed a taste for the obvious talents of this girl; that a tomboy like me can fix his little problem.

"Hello, Mr Ambassador," I say.

"How are you?" he asks.

"Brilliant, now," I say, raising my beer.

"Yes. Er – what are you guys up to?"

"Sam needs to get something to eat," Jack says.

"O.K., then. Are you going to Marine's Club later?"

"We might," I say.

"How's your dad doing?" he asks, even though he's only met him once, out at the Yacht Club. But the ambassador probably knows who my dad is – and has probably also heard that he's in trouble.

"He's looking for a war," I say.

"What . . . what do you mean?"

"You know what I mean. He's a mercenary. Tanzania has had it with him because they think he was up to something in the Seychelles. Plus he owes a lot of tax on his hotel in Tanga. They might extradite him."

"I see," the ambassador says. "Hmmm," he adds. "And then what about you, Samantha? Where would you go?"

"I'm going to England, it would seem."

"Are you going to school?" he asks. I titter.

"You haven't seen my exam records, have you?"

"Are they bad?" he asks.

"They're non-existent," I say.

"Hmmm. But as long as the two of you have a good time together," he says.

"And where are you going?" I ask, looking him up and down – he is wearing a dark suit and a tie.

"Dinner at the Saudi Arabian embassy."

"No pork and no alcohol," I say.

"Hopefully it won't be as bad as that," he says.

"What? They drink like the infidel dogs?" I ask.

"They follow the Koran," he says. "It says that you can follow the way of life of the people you live amongst while you live among them."

"Clever," I say. "And your wife?"

"She's still at home," he says. In the States. According to Jack, his mum is an alcoholic and in rehab at a Betty Ford clinic in California. People say the ambassador is a regular at Margot's – the most expensive whorehouse in

274

Dar es Salaam.

Jack doesn't want to eat. He goes to the sitting room and puts on Billy Joel: gay pop. And then, still looking glum, he grabs a fork and eats more than half of the food on my plate.

"Shall we go see that movie, Sam?" he says.

"Alright then," I say. What's the alternative? I can't be bothered to drive all the way to Africana where there won't be anyone we know anyway – everyone will be trying to get into Marine's Club, which is considered hip and where there is cheap Heineken and that sort of thing.

String puppets

We slob through the gates towards the two fatheads who guard the sacred entrance to the holy of holies that is Marine's Club.

"Sam," Salomon shouts. He's coming out of the darkness from somewhere a bit further down the garden wall. "Good job I found you." He nods at Jack.

"I thought we were going to meet up inside," I say, but I can't actually remember Salomon telling me he would be there, or that it had anything to do with me.

Salomon licks his finger and rubs it on his skin. "See? The shoeshine won't come off," he says. "They won't let me in unless I'm in the company of a beautiful, fair-skinned girl."

"That's because you're acting up," Jack says.

"Acting up? It's an embassy – I'm only trying to have a chat about politics with the soldiers."

"You're calling them names," I say, laughing.

"No. I'm telling them something intended to rouse their awareness to the fact that they are feckless lackeys to the arrogance of Power. Without that awareness they're just string puppets – worse than dogs, because dogs have limited intelligence – they can't help it. Marines can think and they really should."

The two fatheads have started looking over at us.

"They're not here to think," Jack says. "They're here to kill anyone who threatens the safety of the embassy."

"My point exactly," Salomon says. "How fucked up is that?"

Jack looks Salomon up and down:

"You just let me know if you need help getting in," Jack says.

"Your help might come at a price I can ill afford," Salomon says.

"You won't know until you've tried it," I say. We continue to the entrance and in Jack's company we are let straight through.

Every negro's dream

I spot Shakila standing with a couple of local friends of hers, and Aziz, who is probably supplying the fatheads with powder. I haven't seen Shakila since that day at the beach; I haven't felt like it because she probably knows that . . . But it wouldn't be nice of me to ignore her. I go over and introduce Jack to her, and then Jack goes to the bar with Salomon to get us some Heineken.

"I didn't think you came here," I say.

"It's only my third time. And it won't happen again – I can promise you that," Shakila says. She sounds angry.

"Ah well, but the films are good, don't you think?" I say.

"They see me as a gullible negro believing in the dream. But I'm not that at all," Shakila says. She *is* angry.

"The dream?" I ask. Shakila gestures towards three local girls who are talking to some of the fatheads.

"The dream that they are going to marry me and take me back to America with them. Of course they're not going to – they're white." She's right: the marines trick the local girls who come here wanting to be married and become Americans. And the guys get what they want. They know what's what. They are forced to come to Tanzania, and the only thing they can do about it is try to have fun while they're here and then get the hell out.

"Yes, building your future on the promise of what some man might do for you is a bad idea," I say. "Because it's bound to be either too little or the wrong thing altogether." Jack shows up and distributes cans of beer.

"Exactly," Shakila says.

"What happened to your plans?" I ask.

"Nothing, yet," she says. And then the film starts and we sit down. They're showing "Shaft" on the big screen in the garden. Cool. Salomon washes down his Heineken and lights a spliff which he shares with me and Jack – no-one says anything about it, even though the smell is pungent. When the film is over, we sit down at a table in the garden: Salomon, Jack, me and Shakila.

The United States of America

"America out of Afghanistan," Salomon says, squashing the beer can against the tabletop. "America out of Iran." He chuckles and, taking my beer, drains it and squashes it. One of the marines comes over and leans over with his hands on the table, looking at Salomon:

"This belongs to the Embassy of the United States of America. I'm going to have to ask you to keep it down," the soldier says. And Salomon repeats it word-perfect with an exaggerated American accent. The soldier blinks – a film slips over his eyes and his knuckles go white.

"Otherwise we're going to have to ask you to leave the premises," the soldier says. Another soldier is standing not far behind him, muttering:

"Fucking socialist assholes." It's the same guy who came on to me the night I met Jack, I think.

"Otherwise we're going to have to ask you to leave the premises," Salomon says.

"Cool it, Salomon, or you'll be out on your ear," I say. Jack nods at the soldier and says:

"It's alright. We'll get him to keep it down."

"I don't like these people," Salomon says. "They're not nice. Ignorant and horny. Racist. They're just here in their fortress. They don't want to be with the people. I miss *ngoma* – the real Africa." *Ngoma* means partying with lots of dance, the way you do it traditionally in the rural countryside.

"They're not *allowed* to rub shoulders with the people," Jack says.

"Only with the whores," I say under my breath.

Jack continues:

"They're not allowed to beat you to a pulp either, and they won't kick you out because you're sitting here with me."

"They killed Bob Marley," Salomon says.

"What are you talking about?" I ask.

"They had him irradiated with plutonium in the U.S. – it was the C.I.A. who did it, because Bob had a lot of power as a popular artist; he pointed out the evils in the world. And the evils came from America."

"I don't think Bob Marley made much of a difference," Jack says.

"Two albums after 'Uprising' would have made him bigger than ABBA. They just gave him a grain of dust – the same way they shot John Lennon and blamed a mentally sick man. They just keep doing it."

Poontang Garden

"I'm going to the bar to get us another round," I say.

"I'll come with you," Shakila says. She looks around as we walk.

"Where's Aziz?" she mutters.

"Are the two of you going out?" I ask, feeling surprised.

"No," she says, laughing. "But he gave me a lift, and he did promise to drive me and the other girls to the disco in town when the film was over, but I can't see any of them anywhere."

I buy us a round and offer her a cigarette. We light up. I'm pretty doped up and slightly tipsy to boot.

"We should try and look round the house now we're here," I suggest.

"Yes, I suppose we'll have to," Shakila says – the house is where the soldiers are billeted and it's where they lure the girls to when they try to get lucky.

We walk up the stairs to the entrance.

"*Poontang* Garden," a white bloke says. He's lounging about outside. *Poontang* means cunt in Vietnamese – I learned that from a war film.

"Shut it," I say. The house is quite dark – there's music playing in two or three different places. Downstairs there's a common room and a kitchen, but no Aziz, so we take the stairs to the first floor and walk down the corridor. A scrawny white soldier comes out of one of the rooms with his vest hanging out of his trousers and a filthy grin on his face which goes a bit stale when he sees us. He slips past us quickly, going down the hall and down the stairs. We continue. There's a sound of . . . screams? Punches? I take three steps forwards and open the door. And then I fly at the man in the middle. The girl is lying on the bed with her legs spread open. Two blokes are standing on either side of her, each with a hand holding her torso down on the mattress while the other hand is pulling her legs out to the side. The third soldier is pumping her. I'm on top of him, punching my fist into his throat. The two others let go of the girl, who leaps from the bed, and Shakila is already by her side, holding her, trying to pick up her clothes, and the man is moving backwards with me on his back, and the two others are closing in on us to help him, and I hit him again while I try to get my head down to bite his ear. My back – the pain of it, when he slams me against the wall. I let go of him, falling to the floor, the air knocked out of me. I wave my arms in front of me – but he's pulled back to pull up his trousers, buckle his belt. The two others soldiers are stooping over me.

"Get out of here, you crazy bitch," one of them says. My old flame from the night I met Jack. Out of the corner of my eye I see that Shakila is getting the girl dressed. I have enough of my breath back to speak again and I look to the bloke who has zipped his trousers.

"You're not getting away with this – we're going straight to the police," I say. He grins:

"We're on American soil – the nigger police can't come in here."

Pimp

We're escorted straight out of the house, down through the garden, out through the gate. No chance of getting in touch with Jack. And what good could he do now? Shakila is holding the girl, who is crying. We have to get her home to wherever she lives. I go over to them.

"Let's go out to Bagamoyo Road and get a taxi, so we can get her home," I say.

"Yes," Shakila says.

"I'm with Aziz," the girl sobs. "You have to get Aziz."

Aziz . . . ?

"Why?" I ask.

"It was Aziz who brought me here. He must pay me – I can't leave," the girl says.

"Pay?" Shakila says.

"For . . . what they did." Just then Aziz comes out of the garden and comes towards us very quickly.

"I'll take it from here," he says, putting an arm around her shoulder.

"You're one sick bastard, Aziz," Shakila says.

"We can't all have a daddy who takes care of everything for us," he says and moves towards his car with the girl. Shakila starts walking down Bagamoyo Road. I follow her.

"But his dad's rich as well, isn't he?" I say.

"Yes," Shakila says. "But Aziz is getting no help from his dad – he's found out that Aziz is out of his depth, and he's giving him the cold shoulder."

"Now what?" I say.

"We hit the town," Shakila says. "Some of my friends are at Black Star."

"What kind of friends?"

"Just a couple of people from Msasani – and maybe a few people from uni."

Black Star

We leap into a taxi, driving towards the city centre. We arrive at Black Star, which is a high-end disco. Pulsating lights, reggae music, Nigerian high life, Zaire Rock, the works. Several girls and a few blokes come over and say hi to Shakila who introduces me. We get a large, rather low table, buy our drinks, smoke our cigarettes. There's no-one here I know.

"How was Marine's Club?" one of the blokes at our table asks.

"Boring," I say.

"Heineken?" the bloke asks.

"Yes," I say. "Enough to fill an ocean."

"Tsk," he says. "What about Aziz? Isn't he coming tonight?"

"I think he has his job cut out for him at Marine's Club," I say. "How come you didn't go?" The bloke looks at me with surprise, pointing towards himself with one stiff finger:

"Do you think they'd let me in? The white men want our women to themselves."

"They're not being let in," Shakila tells me.

"They let Aziz in," I say.

"He's an Indian. He performs favours," the bloke says. A good-looking girl with large breasts and an arrogant look on her face comes over and drops into the chair next to the guy we're talking to – staring at Shakila:

"Ah, the American negro is here at last," the girl says. Shakila sighs:

"What's your problem?"

"I've had it up to here with you – daddy's pet. The way you dress. The way you speak," the girl says with a dismissive gesture: "You think you're better than the rest of us."

"No, I don't," Shakila says. "But I know I'm better than you." Shakila gets up, looking at me. "I just can't be bothered," she says. "Shall we go?"

"Absolutely," I say.

"Going about with white folk isn't going to make you any more white, you know," the girl says somewhere behind us.

"Just ignore her," Shakila says, but I've already turned around, taken two steps back and slapped the girl. She tries to get up but she can't find her balance, so I shove her into the bloke – she falls over on the floor. I point at her:

"Come outside, and I'll kick you seven shades of shit." I turn around, making my way through the people on the dance floor – who are staring at us – down a tiny corridor, past the bouncers and outside. Shakila is standing shaking her head with a cross between a smile and a sneer on her face.

"Samantha, you're too much," she says. I shrug.

"Do you think she'll be coming out?" I ask.

"No," Shakila says. "She's all talk that one."

White negro

"Why doesn't she like you?" I ask.

"Well, according to her, I'm not a real Tanzanian."

"Because your mum's from Jamaica?"

"No – because I went to the International School and don't speak English with an African accent. And because I wear jeans and smoke cigarettes and speak my mind. That makes me . . . like you."

"Oh, shut up," I say.

Shakila laughs:

"You know, white. You're white. White people . . . we smile at them, because they have something we want, and we hope smiling will help us get it, but . . ."

"I know," I say. "It doesn't really, though." I stub out my cigarette with the tip of my shoe. "There's bound to be a taxi down by the port," I say, and we saunter off. The smell of rotting seaweed and fish refuse comes from the market on the fishing quay. She must know about my abortion – how could she not? There's a taxi. The driver calls us over. The door handle is covered in greasy salt deposits from the humid air.

"Go," Shakila says.

"Where to?" the man asks.

"Msasani," she says. The windows are open, there's the smell of tar and the beating of the air on our bodies.

"Are you going home now?" I ask.

"No, I'm going to the beach."

"O.K." She asks the man to stop at Oyster Bay Hotel. We pay and, getting out, go down to the beach. The Msasani peninsula is one big coralline formation. We're walking on coral covered in sand.

"Now what?" I ask. Shakila unbuttons her shirt, dropping it on the sand. I yank my long-sleeved T-shirt over my head so my breasts poke at the air. We kick off our shoes and pull off our jeans. Shakila opens her bra. I drop my knickers and wade into the water. We swim.

"This is great," I say.

"It is, isn't it?" she says. The wind starts to pick up. The light from the moon is bright enough to allow us to see if anyone is coming. There's not a soul in sight. The beach rises from the sea, so you can't see the road from the water. The crowns of the palms are lit ever so faintly when a car passes. Shakila gets out of the water, black against the pale beach. I follow her. She puts her knickers and shirt on with her back turned to me, so I do the same. Then she pulls something out of her bag and turns around with a half-filled bottle of *Konyagi* in her hand and, taking a sip, hands it to me. I drink while she lights cigarettes for us.

"Are you going to England?" she asks.

"I don't want to, but I can't see how I can avoid it. How about you? Scholarship?"

"Nothing yet, but . . . my dad is pulling all the strings he can."

I sit on my jeans so I don't get sand everywhere – the wind picks up even more and dries us.

"Bugger it," I say. "Why does it all have to be so bloody . . . hard?"

"I don't know," Shakila says. The beach is lovely at night. The palm leaves make a dry rattling sound in the wind. I remember from some biology

283

lesson or other: palms are really a sort of grass – coconuts are seeds.

"Do you come here a lot?" I ask.

"Swimming? Yes. We usually come here when we've been out. But that girl really has it in for me."

"Why?"

"Her father's a doctor like mine, but he teaches at uni where he makes no money at all whereas my father's rich. And that, of course, is all my fault."

"She's on to something there," I say. We sit for a while in silence.

Storm

"Ow," Shakila says, rubbing her thighs – the wind is making the grains of sand sting. We get up, pull on our trousers and start walking up towards the road. Two cars are coming from the south, quickly. One is Aziz's Peugeot; the other a jeep. The American fatheads have a boat lying in wait at the Yacht Club and they'll invite girls aboard if they think they'll get into their knickers. Aziz brakes hard when he sees us in the headlights, so the car behind him slams on its brakes and pulls to the right to pass him – but a thin layer of sand has blown onto the tarmac, and the jeep skids. We jump back. The jeep leaves the road and slams into a palm tree with a bang. Flames burst out from under the bent bonnet. I grab on to Shakila and pull her back while the door is opened on the driver's side and someone falls out onto the sand and scooches backwards, away from the car – it's him, my old flame. The smell of petrol. Aziz has got out of his Peugeot – he's standing as if paralysed, looking at the whole thing – the girl who was raped is peering out of the rear window of his car. Shakila tries to pull out of my grip and head to the jeep.

"No," I say, holding on to her, "It's going to blow up." And just then, an airy gust, the flames engulf the jeep and rise higher in a pillar of fire that caresses the palm leaves high above. They are lit with a dry, crackling sound, and sparks fly up like a large group of fireflies making their way through the darkness. On the passenger seat of the jeep – a man burning.

The wind is making the palms sway, which carries the fire further – from palm to palm, fire in the sky. The flames are beautiful – the wind carries them, blowing them ever higher. The soldier is lying sobbing on the ground, staring in at his dying friend.

Shakila pulls out of my grip and runs to the soldier, squatting down next to him. I look at Aziz whose eyes are wild as they meet mine. He leaps into his car, gets it in gear and drives off. I go over to Shakila, putting my arms around her shoulders.

"We have to go now," I say, looking at the soldier. A long, pink gash shines red on his soot-smeared cheek. Then I look over at Oyster Bay Hotel to see if anyone's looking, but no-one is.

"He's O.K.," she says.

"Now," I say.

"We'll have to wait for the police," Shakila says.

"No," I say. "I'm not talking to the police." I pull her to her feet and, putting my arm around her, move her out on the road, across it, down a side street and towards the residential area.

"Why not?" she asks.

"My residence permit," I say. "It may not be valid." Shakila looks at me. I shrug: "My dad is in some sort of trouble with the authorities."

"The mercenary," she says. And the first drops from the sky hit us with heavy splashes, right before the heavens open and rain starts tipping down.

Assistance

"Samantha. Rise and shine," Alison says.

"Why?" I mutter. I'm sleepy and sweaty. My head feels heavy. "Why isn't your air con on?"

"There's a power cut," Alison says.

"This country is bollocks," I say, sitting up, rubbing my face. I get up. Alison is at the door – I slosh towards her.

"There isn't any water either," she says.

"For Christ's sakes," I say. I lean my head against her shoulder. "What am I to do?"

"You're going to put some clothes on before you come in for breakfast. And put on a bra today, so you don't look like a hippie," she says and waddles down the corridor with her big tummy. "We have to go and buy charcoal," she says.

"But I'm going to the beach." I'm going to look at the charred palm trees.

"You're driving," she says. I put on my clothes. She doesn't want to be alone in the car, because the baby is due so soon; she needs to pull the seat as far back as it will go to fit the bump, and her arms are then too short to reach the steering wheel. I go to the sitting room and sit down. I make myself eat a slice of papaya, a boiled egg, a piece of toast that tastes like charcoal, drink coffee and juice. I light a cigarette. What to do, what to do? Oh yes – drive.

"Has Dad talked to you about your ticket home?" Alison asks.

"Why – do you want to be rid of me?"

"No, of course not, but . . ." She doesn't finish the sentence. I can't swan about in her house forever like this. But it's so nice, and if I so much as think about England and all the things I have to do . . . I feel so confused, and I can't be bothered to think about that. I want to go to parties and drink all the alcohol I can hold, and have men look at me with hungry eyes. Some of them are completely lost to the world. I want to tell them that it's alright – they should just go home. But I don't want to go. I *am* home. I just can't get an extension to my residence permit.

"No, I haven't talked to Dad," I say. "I haven't seen him since he hit me and crashed out in his drunken stupor on the sofa."

"Oh. Right. Let's go, shall we?" Alison says and goes outside. I finish my cigarette, put my shoes on and go out to the garage. The gardener and the cook are loading a wooden crate into the boot of the car. They're struggling to get it in.

286

"What's that?" I ask.

"I'm supposed to deliver it for Dad out at the Africana," Alison says. That's the large tourist resort on the beach north of Dar.

"To who?"

"Victor Ray – former S.A.S. – do you know him?" Alison asks. I look away so she can't see me blushing. Victor is back – that's great news.

"I've met him," I say.

"When?" Alison asks.

"I met him in Tanga when Mick was there fixing the outboard motors," I say. Blimey – that was more than a year and a half ago. I have fancied him for so long, but I've only seen him a handful of times – I must be off my trolley. And now everyone wants to cart me off to England. What am I supposed to do?

"Oh well," Alison says. "But he's up to something with Dad. I don't even want to know what it is."

"Weapons for the A.N.C.?" I say.

"Could be. Or something up in Zaire," she says.

"Victor Ray," I say. "It's a cool name."

"*Tsk*," Alison says. "It's not his real name. Victor Ray – *victory*. Phoney name – probably phoney passport."

"What's in the crate?" I ask and go over, taking hold of it – it's heavy.

"I don't know," Alison says, sounding testy. Weapons. Many of the white mercenaries camp down in Dar, because Tanzania always was one of the most peaceful countries in tropical Africa. Then they make sure to have a few businesses of a nature that will account for why they are here. And they make lots of money. My dad has been everywhere: Biafra, Angola, Mozambique, Congo and especially Rhodesia, of course, before it became Zimbabwe – and after that it was Zambia. But the last couple of years haven't been good to him. Business is bad, and there are no wars where they use expensive white mercenaries. With the exception of the South African soldiers who are financed by the Apartheid regime and who fight in the neighbouring countries. Dad's last job was as a military advisor in Uganda, but that's almost at an end.

Panic

Palm trees and mango trees along the road north – the occasional banana tree, looking a little parched. We stop and buy two sacks of charcoal by the roadside. Africana looks like shit. We send a boy to look for Victor. He comes out. Tall, good-looking. His shirt open, his chest hairy, his skin tanned, his muscles clearly defined, joints large, eyes a watery blue, and sun-bleached, unkempt hair.

"Alison, Samantha," he says. "Good to see you. Come and have a drink."

"I've brought your things," Alison says.

"Shit," Victor says. "Can't you hold on to it a little while longer?"

"My husband is starting to ask questions about it."

"He does know who he married, doesn't he?"

"Yes. Frans married me. Not my dad."

"Right, point taken," Victor says and opens the boot. He takes out the crate and, lifting it onto his shoulders, starts walking.

"Come and have that drink anyway," he says. We follow him. Alison sits down under a sunscreen next to the pool. I should have brought my swimming gear, but I can swim in my knickers and bra. I drop my shorts and T-shirt and get in. Victor returns and sits down. No. I shouldn't have done that; I'm still far too skinny. A waiter returns with fizzy drinks and beer. I get out of the pool. Alison is making eyes at me. I look down. My bush is visible and dark in my wet knickers. I hope my hipbones aren't looking too bony – or my pubis. I go to the table quickly – Victor is looking at me, first at my tits, then at my crotch – I sit down, crossing my legs. You'd like that, wouldn't you? He smiles. Victor. He asks. I tell him I've left school.

"So, are you going to study in England, then?" he asks. I titter.

"I left before my exams, so I don't think I'll be doing any studying anywhere. No, I want to be a beautician – I mean, it's just a maker-upper, but it sounds more impressive, don't you think?" I babble about my latest fancy. To be honest, I don't want to do anyone's make-up. He looks straight at me – into my eyes, and I fidget and light a cigarette because I have forgotten the one I lit seconds ago, which is lying in the ashtray, and I wonder whether he can see my cunt through my knickers, and whether it looks nice, and what about my tits? He takes a couple of cashew nuts from the bowl on the table and pops them into his mouth, chewing them with his lips slightly open, so I can see moisture and tongue and teeth. That mouth has eaten me out; I want it to do it again. He's at least thirty-five, he could be my dad – well, almost. When I first met him, I thought that Stefano – that maggot of a man – was God. Victor takes the extra cigarette from the ashtray as if it were the most natural thing in the world and talks to Alison. The sound of his voice is at once soothing and arousing. I want to shut my eyes and just listen to him. It makes me feel weak. Silly. Alison gets up to go to the toilet. There are two black girls sitting at the bar looking over at me and Victor; they're on the lookout for a nice white fish. I jerk my head at them, looking at Victor:

"Which one of them is yours?" He looks in the direction I indicated, and then back at me:

"Neither," he says. "I only like skinny white girls with a nice bit of bush on them."

"That Mary wasn't particularly skinny," I say.

"No, and that always was a problem, you know," he says. I blush and am about to ask him where she is. And when can we meet? But then Alison comes back towards us.

"We have to go now," she says, and even as we turn to walk towards the car park, I start to miss him; I panic on the inside, because. . . when will I see him again? I want to cry – I want him to hold me, force me – just a little. What's going on? Victor walks us to our car. We say goodbye and get into the car, drive off. How am I going to get out here tonight? And has that Mary really gone for good?

"Didn't he have a girlfriend?" I ask.

"Yes," Alison says. "Mary. But she is in England having their baby." I shudder.

"Baby?" I say.

"Yes, she's due a month after me," Alison says, sounding irked. But I was at Kigamboni four months ago – I had sex with Victor for two days, non-stop. I had his cock in my mouth. At the time Mary must have been . . . three months pregnant. Of course he knew. I look straight ahead at the tarmac in front of us while Alison continues to speak: "I dread the thought that she might come down and think that we'll be new mums together. That Mary . . . she's an Essex girl if there ever was one – there's not one independent thought in her head." I force myself to say something, so Alison won't find out that something's not right. So she won't turn her head and discover how off I look.

"Couldn't she have the baby here?" I ask. "Like you?"

"She can't have the baby in a negro hospital, see?" Alison jeers.

"English women – what are they like!" I say.

The threshold

The taxi is winding its way down the dark road north – the breeze is coming in from the sea, smelling of salt and seaweed. Everything is dark – another power cut. It's not till we get to Africana that there's light. They must have their own generator. There's almost no-one here. Victor is doing laps in the pool. I stand at the edge of the pool until he sees me:

"Samantha," he says. "You came."

"You . . ." I say and stop as he lifts himself out, his arms on the edge of the pool, right next to me. He is dripping wet as he stands up.

"Come here," he says and sweeps me up in his arms – I can see the waiter behind the deserted bar looking at us. Victor starts walking. He carries me across the threshold of his bungalow like a bride. "I miss you, Samantha. No other girl can make me happy."

"But . . ." I say as he lays me on the bed in the dark room. He bends down and kisses me.

"No buts," he says and unbuttons my shirt – my nipples are buzzing.

"Mary," I manage to say. I had expected him jolt at that, but he almost doesn't react, simply opens the last button, caresses my breasts, squeezing one nipple just a little with his strong fingers and kissing it. He speaks slowly and calmly as he opens my shorts.

"I don't think she'll come down again. Getting her pregnant was a mistake. And I'm not even sure it's my child. She knows it's over." He peels off my shorts and my knickers in one go and buries his face between my legs. We make love.

Raid

I wake up early, because Victor is being noisy. He is packing. I look around the room. There are weapons in here, a rifle and two machine-guns – the wooden crate has gone.

"I've got to go – a job," he says. I get out of bed and hug him from behind, putting my cheek against his back, letting my hand run through the hair on his chest. "Good morning, gorgeous," he says. I get into the shower. The guns and the rifle are on the bed when I come out. There's a knock on the door.

"Who is it?" Victor says loudly.

"Police. Open the door."

"Get on top of them," Victor says in a low voice and points towards the weapons on the bed. "You're awake." He turns his head: "Just a sec," he says towards the door. I'm naked, and the sharp edges of the steel are cold and hard against my thighs, arse and back. Victor is standing at the door, ready to open while I lie all the way down and pull up the blanket to cover me and the weapons – my head is resting against the pillows at the headboard, and I am holding the blanket close to my breasts. Victor opens the door. The police come in and stare at me – I'm naked under the covers and they'd like to see it. They look around, want to see Victor's papers, root through his bags. I don't say anything. The police can't see how young I am compared to Victor, because I'm white and most Africans have a hard time assessing white people's ages.

"Is there a problem?" Victor says.

"We're investigating," the police officers says, looking round the room – they haven't found anything.

"Let's go outside so my lady friend can get dressed," Victor says, and they go outside. I get out of bed, arranging the blankets so no-one can see the weapons underneath, and put on my clothes. I'm fully dressed, sitting on the edge of the bed smoking a cigarette when Victor returns. "I think they came mostly to have their palms greased," he says.

"Is someone after you – are you going to be kicked out?" I ask.

"No," Victor says. "But maybe someone has been talking when they shouldn't have."

"Who?" I ask.

"It could be anyone. You?" he says, smiling.

"No, I'd much rather keep you here. What would they have talked about?" I ask.

"Maybe Alison, because she wants to keep me away from you," he says.

"Alison doesn't know I'm seeing you," I say.

"Maybe your dad," Victor says.

"Why would he want to have you deported?" I ask.

"Because he owes me money," Victor says. "Or because he wants me to leave his daughter alone." He smiles again as he slowly comes towards the bed.

"He doesn't know anything either," I say.

"Are you sure?"

"Yes, if he did he would have thrashed me," I say.

"Really?"

"I think so."

Hospitality

Victor has gone – maybe for weeks even. Perhaps it's Mick who has reported Victor to the police. I think about that a lot. Mick.

My sister has asked a lot of people round for dinner. I've asked Jack.

"Is anyone else coming, anyone I know?" I ask. Mostly to find out whether Dad will be there or not.

"I told Dad he could bring that Victor," Alison says. Victor! Perhaps he's back already.

"What do you want to see Victor for?" I ask. I know Alison is tired of us living off Dad's job. Victor is in the same line of business. And Alison is tired of us almost never having seen Dad when we were little. She's married a thoroughly potty-trained man for that very reason. She'll be able to see as much of Frans as she wants and the baby will as well.

"It was probably a really bad idea," Alison says irritably. "But I can't just sit and chat to Frans' friends' wives; I mean . . . they're so unbelievably dull."

"Then how about Mick?" I say.

"He couldn't come."

"Why not?"

Alison looks at me, "Don't you think it might be because you're always so dismissive of him?" I don't say anything to that.

"Dad?" I ask.

"I don't know, Samantha. I . . . You live here, so you'll just have to put up with the people who come here as guests, and if you can't, then . . ." she says, rolling her eyes, shrugging, turning her back on me and waddling out of the kitchen. Her hospitality has worn thin.

Standstill

"My dad's sending me home," Jack says. We're standing outside the house. He doesn't want to come in, even though he's been invited to dinner – the guests will be here in half an hour.

"Why?" I ask.

"That barbecued marine out at Oyster Bay."

"But that wasn't your fault," I say.

"No, but I know those people. I do drugs with them. Hang out, drink. He doesn't like the fact that I sleep with men either."

"That's none of his business, though," I say.

"He's ambassador of the United States in Tanzania," Jack says. "And I am his son in a country where homosexuality is forbidden by law. And it doesn't look good that my best friend's father is a mercenary and seems to have had plans to overthrow the Seychelles government, whose security is guaranteed by Tanzania."

"I'm sorry, Jack."

"Me too," he says. He hugs me, goes to his car, climbs into the back and is driven away. I go inside.

Alison sends me to an Indian corner shop, because she has forgotten to buy snacks. When I return, Victor is standing on the patio, talking to Frans. Should I go over and talk to him? What should I say? I go to the bar in the sitting room and ask the cook for a gin and tonic; I light a cigarette and stand there, bouncing on the balls of my feet while I wait for my drink. How should I play this? There's a hand on the small of my back. I turn my head, blowing out smoke. Victor. He leans against the bar next to me.

"What sort of undies are you wearing today, Samantha?" he asks.

"What makes you think I'm wearing any?" I say and suck on my cigarette again as I look at him. Out of the corner of my eye I see the bartender put the drink down in front of me; I take the drink and sip it while I continue to look into Victor's eyes.

We're called to the table. I sit across from Victor. Should I do it? Or would that make me a slut? And so what if I'm a slut? Is being hard to get really that great? I could run my foot across the floor and up along his trousers, along his inner thigh until my foot reached its destination.

The door opens and Dad comes in – I leave my foot where it is, on the floor, still.

Moving house

How am I going to go and see Victor again? I don't know where he's staying. The air in the house is thick and stale – all sounds seem to come from far away and travel through mats of mud and cotton wool. Alison is pregnant, heavy and sluggish. She doesn't say it, but I know: she's fed up with having me here. And when she's happy, with Frans, when they're talking about the baby . . . when I come in, they stop. Because I had that abortion. And when she strokes her tummy and says that the baby is kicking – crap like that – I go outside. I know it's not fair on her, but I can't stand seeing her so happy about this. Why did I become like this?

"Dad's house is finished," she says.

"Right," I say. "Is he selling?"

"No," she says. "We've talked about . . . Dad says you can stay there for a while."

"When did you talk to him?"

"I asked him this morning. It won't be for long. I just can't . . . So much is happening right now, and . . ." She stops herself.

"But I won't have to live there with Dad, will I?" I say.

"No, no, of course not – he won't be there. I think he's staying at a hotel, or else – or else he's got someone somewhere."

"Someone what?"

"A woman. You'll be there alone," Alison says. "Juma and his daughter are in the servants' quarters."

"O.K. No problem, then," I say. "Of course. As it happens, I'd be glad of some time to myself."

Alison drives me to the house when I've packed. We don't say a lot on the way. The house is not as close to the beach as Alison's – it's on the cheap side of Msasani. Juma opens the gate to us.

"Samantha! *Karibu sana*," he says with a smile that shows all his brown teeth. His daughter is staying with him – she can be my cook, do the washing – it'll work. Juma shows us round the house. It looks fine inside – recently painted, new bathroom, new sockets, air conditioning. We're standing outside, saying goodbye.

"How am I going to get anywhere?" I ask. Alison sighs.

"Dad said he would get you a motorbike," she says.

"Cool," I say.

"You're always welcome to come round," she says before she drives off. "You do know that, don't you?"

Birthday

I'm in Dad's house – alone. I have neither a car nor a motorbike. What am I supposed to do? I drink *Konyagi* and smoke weed, listen to my tapes on a tiny tape recorder. I am bored witless. There's a man still going around outside fixing the outer walls – the foundations of the house have deteriorated in several places. I'm standing inside in the air-conditioned room looking out at him; the sun is baking down on him, there are beads of sweat on his naked torso, his tools have been put into a bucket of water to stop them from scorching his hands when he picks them up.

A couple of nights later a taxi appears at the gates. Juma comes to my door.

"*Mzee* has sent the taxi for you. Your sister is having the baby." I go straightaway – leaping into the car. It's happening. Dad is sitting silently, drinking coffee, looking at me in a strange way, but looking away when I try to catch his eye. Then the baby comes. It's a boy. Dad makes a big hoo-ha. Frans is teary-eyed. Shakila's dad comes out of the bedroom, and his brow is sweaty. I smile. I go in and have a look – it's a pink lump, and it's moving. The skin in my face feels like bark. Everyone is happy. Everyone goes into the garden. Everyone except me. They smoke and they spit. That could have been me.

The next day I force myself to take a taxi and go and see them, hand over a prezzie, look at the baby, make silly sounds. Dad is standing there, chucking the boy under the chin, carrying him proudly around the room. Alison comes across and sits next to me.

"He's behaving like a human to the new generation," I say.

"Yes, he only skipped that one generation," Alison says.

"Oh, come off it," Dad says.

"It's strange that," I say.

"Girls. I may not have been the best dad ever," Dad says. "If you want to be good parents, you'd probably have to be different from what I was. But I'm your dad, and . . . I love you. And I love this little guy." He blows on the baby's tummy and makes loud farting noises – the brat starts howling, and Alison gets up to take him from Dad. It's comical and I can't bear it. What's happening with him? What an old fool.

"Did you speak with Mum?" I ask Alison.

"Yes," she says, sighing. "She can't afford the ticket."

"Can't Frans get her one?" I ask.

"Only for the immediate family – or he'll get into trouble."

"But you'll give her a ticket, won't you, Dad?" I ask.

"She couldn't get time off from work anyway," Dad says.

"Won't you?" I say again.

"He hasn't got any money," Alison says.

"I've got debts," Dad says. He owes Victor money, I think. Maybe it'll be Victor's money that will pay for my ticket back to England. Because apparently Frans' immediate family doesn't include me or Mum, even though he's married to Alison. I tell them I'm meeting someone and leave.

Flatmate

Two days later Alison and Frans bring the baby round on their way to the Yacht Club.

"Why don't you want to come?" Alison asks.

"I just don't feel like it today." They leave. I go to the bar cabinet and take the gin bottle. That's it. I sit down on the patio. Shit.

A Land Rover has slowed down on the road on the other side of the house. Dad? Someone honks the horn.

Juma calls, "*Shikamoo Mzee.*" Yes, it is Dad. I get up, go out into the kitchen and start filling ice cubes into a jug so he can have some water. I can't be bothered to argue with him. The door is opened.

"Samantha," Dad calls. I wander down the corridor. Dad and Victor are standing in the middle of the sitting room. Victor is carrying a couple of bags. What?

"Hello, Samantha," Victor says.

"Hi," I say.

"Victor is going to have to stay here for a while," Dad says. "He needs to keep a low profile until we've sorted everything out."

"I see," I say.

"Too many eyes and ears at the Africana," Victor says.

"You can move back to Alison's if you want to," Dad says and adds, "Even though now's probably not the best time."

"No, no, it's alright," I say.

"Then Victor will be able to keep an eye on you and make sure you don't go to the dogs altogether," Dad says. I'm not falling for that.

"How about that motorbike?" I say.

"I'll pick mine up later today – you can use that," Victor says. Dad is standing there, smiling, obviously pleased with the situation, and with my reaction – it's all good as far as he's concerned. Is that man completely clueless? He probably doesn't care that I'm having an affair with Victor. Why should he? He doesn't care about me, after all. Victor goes out to get his bags from the car. Dad puts his arm around my shoulder.

"You can flirt with him as much as you like. But remember, he has a wife back in England, and she's having his baby any day now."

"I'm not a complete idiot, you know," I say. Dad says:

"I'm sorry to do this to you, Samantha, but I owe the man some money and I have to do him this favour."

"Don't worry about it. Did you talk to Mum?" I ask. Because I know I'm going to have to go to her before long. But I'm still hoping she'll be down to see her grandchild and that we can go back together.

"She can't come," Dad says.

"Alright then," I say. Victor reappears with his bags.

"Good," Dad says and claps his hands, looking around the room. "I'll be off, then."

I show Victor to the empty bedroom, tell him that if he needs anything he can just give Juma some money and he'll get it for him. That Juma's daughter will serve breakfast around 8.00 – and if he's up earlier, all he needs to do is tell her.

"Do you have a beer?" he asks. We sit down on the patio, drink our beers. His movements are precise; he looks at me calmly, squinting slightly.

"What?" I say, tittering.

"Do you mind me being here?"

"Not at all, as long as you don't imagine I'll go all housewifely on you, because I won't."

"It wouldn't suit you," Victor says. "I'm sure you have lots of other talents."

Sometime later he leaves to get a taxi to pick up his motorbike. I traipse all the way to the beach for a swim. Then I walk back. I let the shower wash the greasy feel of salt and sweat off me. I wash my hair. I hear the motorbike arrive. I wrap one towel around my hair and another around my body. I go into the sitting room in direction of the kitchen without looking to the side where he's sitting on the sofa.

"Hi there," he says.

"Oh, hi," I say. "Did you get that motorbike for me, then?" He laughs:

"It's not for you. But you can borrow it if you're good."

"Just how good would that be?" I say as I continue out into the kitchen. When I return, he isn't in the sitting room. I go down the hall towards my room and he comes out of the other room, wearing nothing but his boxers and a towel over one shoulder. We approach each other there in that narrow hall. The scent of him, the long, lean muscles under the tanned skin, the frizzy blond hair on his chest that continues down over his stomach towards his thingy.

"I'll just get a shower. Shall we head out to the Yacht Club for a bite to eat afterwards?" he asks.

"Can we go to Oyster Bay Hotel?" I ask.

"No, I have to talk to someone who wants to buy a boat," he says and starts to move past me.

"Your treat," I say and get what feels like an electric shock when his hand slaps my arse as he says yes and turns into the bathroom.

"Watch it!" I say.

Mistress

The next day we eat at an Indian restaurant. Victor pulls out my chair for me at the table.

"I'll be back in a sec, Samantha," he says and goes up to the bar where he speaks to Aziz's dad, who gets stuff in and out through Customs in the harbour. I'm wearing a tight skirt that stops right above my knees. No knickers. I'm sitting there, getting nervous that Alison might turn up – but she's just had a baby, so she probably won't. Victor returns to the table. We drink beer while we wait for the food. He asks about my plans.

"England just isn't for me," I tell him. "I can do things here. I understand people, I understand how things work. In England . . . my mum's working as a night clerk at a hotel and lives in a tiny flat. I'm too much of an African to be able to live there. Or, of course, I could live there, I just really don't want to."

"You're right. It's no place for a free life. You're spot on," Victor says. I may as well go for it.

"What about Mary?"

Victor sighs. "I don't know. She likes it here, but only if everything is done for her. She doesn't know how to do anything for herself. And she gets jittery."

"But is she going to come down when she's had the baby?"

"I'm not so sure. She wants me to come home."

"Do you want to?" I ask.

"No. I want to stay here."

"Me too." I say.

"You understand it. Mary doesn't. You know how to behave around here – I can see that. You're the right sort of girl to be with in Africa."

I push my high-heeled shoes off under the table and start to run one foot up his leg.

"And what does that mean?" I ask.

"I want you," Victor says.

"Do you want me to be your mistress?"

"Yes."

"Why?" My foot is headed towards his groin.

"Because you're amazing. You're absolutely stunning – not just pretty, but . . . you have a lot of gumption. I like that."

"I'm not sure that's enough for me," I say. "To be your mistress." I look at him as my foot reaches his stiff cock. Then our food arrives. I take away my foot. Victor groans. I start to eat, chewing with my mouth slightly open.

It happens when we return from the restaurant. Victor has opened his shirt; he's sitting by the coffee table. He pulls an envelope from his shirt pocket, opens it and taps on it with one finger, making the powder jump out and onto the table. I sit myself in an easy chair, sipping a Coke. I have taken off my skirt and wrapped a *kanga* around my waist – under the fabric I'm naked. Victor hands me his lit cigarette, pulls a banknote out of his pocket and starts rolling it up.

"Just enough to adjust the mood," he says, smiling.

"Of course," I say, smoking his cigarette.

"Do you want some?"

"Yes, of course I do."

"I didn't know you were into that stuff," he says.

"I'm into a lot of stuff," I say.

"Come here," he says. I get up, go over and sit down next to him on the sofa. He hands me the banknote. I take a line. I lean back against the back-rest and his arm. His hand grips my neck and starts massaging it.

"That's good," I say, handing him the note.

"The best," he says and leans towards the table. Then he sits back on the sofa, turns towards me, puts a hand on my thigh, kisses me, takes me – just like that.

Zanzibar

I wake up in my own room. Victor must have carried me in during the night so the maid wouldn't see me in his bed. She would tell Juma. Who in turn would tell Dad. I get up. There's no-one in the house, but there is a note on the dining table – written in squarish, copperplate letters. "Back around noon," it says. I grab a bite to eat, smoke, shower.

"We're going to Zanzibar," he says when he comes through the door.

"Zanzibar? What are we going to do in Zanzibar?" I ask.

"No questions," Victor says. "We're going, now – two nights, pack a bag."

"I think I'd better tell Alison," I say. Victor is headed down the corridor.

"Better not tell her you're going to Zanzibar with me – she wouldn't like that."

"No," I say, smiling. I get Alison's cook on the phone. I tell him I'm going to Morogoro to visit Jarno for a few days.

"Shall we get going, then?" Victor says.

"When's our flight?"

"Our boat, you mean."

I throw a few things into a bag. We're getting a *dhow* from the harbour to

Zanzibar – how great is that? I get up behind him, but Victor is going in the wrong direction.

"What sort of boat are we getting?" I shout.

"We're going from the Yacht Club," he says. "Speedboat." Twenty minutes later we're sitting in a large rubber boat with two heavy-duty outboard motors – black, the sort the military uses. We whip across the surface of the water. It's only 50 kilometres from the harbour in Dar to Zanzibar.

"Is this the one you were selling?" I ask above the whistling wind.

"Yes – I'm delivering it today. We're flying back."

"Were you going to use it in the Seychelles?"

"Yep," Victor says.

"It was a shame you were found out, wasn't it?" I say.

"We should have gone through with it anyway, even though the politicians got cold feet," Victor says. "We could have settled down very nicely there."

"But if the Tanzanian forces knew you were coming . . . ?"

"They didn't have a clue until your dad went there on a scheduled flight," he says. "Before that eight or ten men with twenty local supporters might have taken the entire island group – electricity and water supplies, radio, newspapers, telegraph, harbour and airport – in one fell swoop, nothing to it."

"Was the money good?"

"Yes. And we could have lived there when it was over."

"And we've lost everything in Tanzania," I say.

"We're going to lose everything here no matter what we do," Victor says.

"What do you mean?"

"They've nationalized your hotel – and a lot more besides. Your dad may well be expelled."

"How about you?" I ask.

"They don't know me. But I'm thinking about living in Zambia – close to Zaire."

*

We're racing into Menai Bay between the little islands and land on the beach in the bay just north of Bweleo. An Arab comes down to meet us and pays Victor for the boat. His helper gives us a lift into town.

We have dinner at a restaurant in Stone Town – then we go back to our hotel. Victor goes to the bar and gets us a couple of gin and tonics. I'm already tipsy. He uses an ice cube on my inner thighs and labia. He moves his face in between my legs. His stubble scratches me, and he opens me with his warm tongue, thrusting it into me.

Later we're lying on the bed, smoking.

"We could be a good team," Victor says.

"Yes," I say. "But I'm not sure my dad would approve."

"What he doesn't know won't hurt him," Victor says.

"He's not stupid," I say. "He has a habit of finding things out."

"He'll be out of the country soon enough."

"How do you know?"

"He hasn't got any more favours to call in."

Poisonous dreams

Back in Dar es Salaam. Alison nips over with the baby. Victor is sitting at the dining table, smoking, looking through some papers.

"Come on in," I say. "Do you want a drink?" Alison says hello to Victor and follows me out into the kitchen.

"I'd like you to move back with us," she says in a low voice.

"Why? I'm very comfortable here." I open the fridge.

"You're better off with us," Alison says.

"First you give me the boot, and now you want me to . . . *tsk*." I turn my back on her and pour out juice for us, so she can't see my face. Alison almost whispers:

"Do you think I'm stupid, little sister? Do you think I can't see you're flirting with him?" she says to my back.

"It's a laugh, that's all," I say.

"You do know what will happen if Dad sees it, don't you?"

"Oh come off it, me flirting a little bit isn't going to tick him off," I say.

"He'll put you on the first flight back to England, that's what he'll do."

"The cranky old bastard is going to do that anyway," I say and turn to face her. Alison looks angry.

"Mary is in England to have their baby. Then she'll be back. What exactly do you think will happen then?" she asks.

"Alison," I say. "I don't think anything. She's in England – not here. Maybe she'll come down. Maybe I'll be sent home. Maybe all sorts of things. What do you want me to do about it?"

"You're being stupid," Alison says. And it's not true what I'm telling her. I do think . . . certain things. Victor says: "I don't think she'll be down here again. She didn't like it here."

And I'm thinking . . . that I'm here.

Christian

Victor has told me he might be able to get some work in Goma – he has to leave for a few days to look into it. I'm alone in the house. Goma. He leaves. What am I supposed to do, then? I feel lonely already. Luckily the motorbike is here, so I go over to Jarno in Norad's guesthouse. He's still there – has just got out of bed.

"Christian came yesterday – he's out looking for you, I think."

"Oh shit," I say. Jarno comes over and puts his hands on my hips.

"Fancy joining me in the shower?" he says.

"In your dreams," I say and push his hands away.

"I know you want to."

"You don't know anything of the sort," I say. "And how do you think your good friend Christian would like it?"

Jarno doesn't say anything. Christian – he thought that I wanted to kill myself.

I give Jarno a lift to the Yacht Club. I see Alison's car in the car park. I go inside. Bollocks – she's sitting with Christian at a table. They've never met before. Someone must have told him that she's my sister. But then he probably hasn't told her . . . all the things I wrote to him. We hug. He asks me about all sorts of things, tells me a load of stuff, but I can tell he really wants to get me on his own, so I stay at the table. Alison asks us all round to hers for a garden party to celebrate the baby. In two days.

"Angela will be there as well," Alison says, smiling.

"Angela?" I say.

"Yes, she's holidaying in Dar. It'll be fun seeing her again," Alison says. I keep my mouth shut. I don't think it'll be fun at all. I ask what time it is. They tell me.

"I'm going to have to dash – I'm meeting someone."

"How do we meet?" Christian asks. "Where are you staying?"

"Can't we just meet up at that garden party?"

"How about tomorrow?" Christian asks.

"I can't. I've got plans," I say. Alison gives me a strange look, but doesn't say anything.

"How do I get back, then?" Jarno says to me.

"I'll drive you," Alison says. "That way I can show you where we live – it's on the way."

"See you later," I say and go out to my motorbike. Damn.

Mum

The next day I'm on edge. What if Christian has found out where I live? What if Alison has told him? Or . . . it's . . . What happens when Victor gets back? The phone rings, and I get the maid to pick up. She's supposed to say I'm not here, unless it's Victor. It's not Victor. It's Christian, Alison, Dad. I have a root through my papers and find Mum's number. I call her.

"I'm having an affair with a man," I say. "I don't know what I'm supposed to do."

"A . . . man?" Mum says.

"Yes, he's a bit older than me," I say.

"How much older?" Mum asks.

"It doesn't matter – his girlfriend is pregnant."

"Samantha," Mum says with a deep sigh. "Is he . . . white?"

"Yes," I say. "He's . . ." I say, but then I stop, because what is he really?

Mum says, "It's a bad idea."

"Please don't tell anyone," I say.

"Then you have to promise me to end it," she says.

"I don't know if I can," I say.

"I know you can. And you'll be here with me soon," she says gently, and I feel stifled by her gentleness and the thought of England: the cold and the rain. I have to do it abruptly, in the middle of a sentence; then she'll think the connection was cut.

"Alright Mum, I promise I'll . . ." My hand pushes down the hook. I don't know why I told her. Maybe because it's been a year and a half since I last saw her, and suddenly she seemed so close on the phone; maybe it's because . . . she's my mum.

Powder

Victor returns home.

"I'm just popping down to Bimji's to pick up some goods," he says. Bimji is Aziz's dad, the Harbour Master – he's in charge of all the permits and papers you need to have to get things in and out of the country. Most especially, he's in charge of having all the appropriate officials bribed.

"I want to come," I say.

"It's not your sort of thing," Victor says.

"Drugs," I say. He opens his eyes wide.

"Where did you hear that?" he asks.

"It's what I hear," I say.

Victor smiles:

"I'm going to have to know where you heard it," he says.

"I don't want him to get any trouble, the guy who told me," I say.

"Fine by me," Victor says.

"Mick," I say.

"Hmmm. He was a lot less sanctimonious when he was snorting it himself," Victor says.

"I want to come," I say.

"It's not entirely safe," he says. I shrug. We go down to the harbour in the late afternoon. I'm supposed to stay in Bimji's office while he and Victor go down to the docks. Half an hour later they return with a wooden crate the size of two beer crates. They draw up the last documents. The papers attached to the crate state that they contain spices.

"Is it heroin?" I ask when we're back in the car.

"Never you mind," Victor says.

"I do though," I say.

"It's cocaine. Most of it is going off to Europe, but there's a market for it here as well."

"Cocaine? Where from?"

"Asia. I've got a new route up and running. The customs officers in Europe don't check things from Africa."

"So, what's going to happen now?" I ask.

"I'll pack it into large cans, with cashew nuts around the package of powder. The cans will be sent to Germany and Holland."

We return to the house. I follow Victor out to the kitchen. He sends the maid away, opens the crate, takes out a couple of little plastic bags full of white powder. "The rest is going to be packed and shipped on tomorrow," he says.

"What about the stuff you've taken out?" I say.

"For the local market, to give me some cash to live on," he says.

"Are you going to sell that?"

"I'm selling the whole thing to a guy – that's all I do," he says and takes a small sample. "Perfect," he says and gets out a large bowl.

"What are you doing?"

"I need to cut it." Victor puts on some thin plastic gloves and fetches a bag of some other white powder, which he mixes into the cocaine. I've heard about this – you can mix ground-up painkillers or sedatives or potato starch or broken glass, fertilizer – all sorts of things – into the powder.

"How do you feel about . . . selling this sort of thing? Drugs, I mean."

"It's a commodity," Victor says and looks at me, stopping his work. "Samantha," he says. "Your dad doesn't get it. There aren't any lucrative wars left. There's nothing above board about it any longer – whenever there's trouble, it goes haywire. There used to be soldiers, armed forces. These days it's ordinary peasants and farmers with machetes and Kalashnikovs. They don't need us. It's over. So this . . ." he says, gesturing towards the worktop, "this is the new business. If we get involved, we can grow; if we don't, we can just sod off."

"But it's . . . drugs."

"Is it better to kill or teach people to kill than to move some drugs from one place to another?"

I don't say anything.

The next day Victor is busy. He drives into town with one of his partners. The cocaine is packed with cashew nuts into big tin cans, which are then sealed and provided with labels and the proper export papers before he returns them to Bimji. We make love when he returns early in the evening, but he seems . . . preoccupied.

"Is something wrong?" I ask.

"No no – I've got a lot on my mind, that's all," he says. "I need to drop off the stuff I mixed."

"Where?" I ask.

"I'm meeting the guy at Margot's," Victor says and looks at his watch.

Margot's is the most expensive whorehouse in town, catering for embassy employees, the corporates, politicians, businessmen.

"Shall we head out then?" I ask.

"You're not going, Samantha," he says.

"We're in this together. Of course I'm going. I'll wait in the car."

"O.K. then," Victor says and starts getting dressed. I want to ask him, but I don't: Had he meant to use the services offered at Margot's?

Colour

The guard at the gates to Margot's is intelligent. Not the type who would work for the usual pennies – he has had a proper education and is well-dressed.

"I promise you she won't get out of the car at any point," Victor says when he grills him. The guard bends down and looks past Victor at me.

"Do you agree, Miss?"

"Yes," I say, and the guard signs to his coolie to open the gate before he goes back to his guardhouse. We drive up the shingle drive with conches along the borders. The villa is large and well-kept and has gorgeous flowerbeds and a luscious lawn. Victor gets out as the uniformed doorman comes down the steps.

"Shall I park your car in the back, sir?" he asks. Of course – that way people can't see it from the street; you're paying to bonk pretty girls at Margot's.

"No," Victor says, grabbing his shoulder bag with the stuff. "I won't be a minute." The doorman lets him in. I light a cigarette, smoke it to the butt. He still isn't back. I open the car door, get out, have a good stretch. The doorman looks at me. I go over to the stairs and up the steps. The doorman isn't expensive – it seems to be the guard who does the sorting. On the other hand, he looks like he might pack a punch. He's probably their bouncer as well. I'd really love to go inside – just to see it.

"What are they hiding in there?" I ask.

"Nothing you'd care for," he says.

"Do you have all shapes, sizes and colours?" I ask.

"Not your colour, I don't," he says, smiling wanly. I suppose I could just try trotting over and opening the door. Maybe he wouldn't know what to do, because I'm white. Of course he's ready to stop a white person, but he'd probably hesitate because you never know what the consequences might be – who's her husband, who's her father? Is it dangerous to lay a hand on her? But the lobby probably wouldn't be full of wild goings-on anyway. And, come to think of it, my dad might be in there.

"Is there no entertainment to be had for a lady?" I ask.

"No – men only," he says.

"But maybe I want to buy myself a girl to play with. Doesn't Margot cater to girls with that sort of fancy?"

He smirks and looks around nervously.

"Alright then," I say and shrug. I offer him a cigarette, which he takes and puts in his pocket.

"Thanks. I'll save it for later," he says.

"Take care," I say and go back to the car.

"You too," he says.

Children & adults

The garden party at Alison and Frans'. Victor and I go together. A couple of streets from their house, he pulls over and stops the motorbike. He turns around and kisses me.

"Just be cool," he says. "Can you do that?"

"Yes, of course I can," I say. We drive the last little stretch. Christian and Jarno are already there – white T-shirts, blue jeans, Carlsbergs in hand. Angela is there. And Dad.

I ought to take Victor to talk to Christian and Jarno – introduce them as if it was the most natural thing in the world. But . . . I just can't. I don't want to go over to them. I don't want to talk to Christian. I think he sees right through me. There's lots of food, and beer, and alcohol. Dad is on barbecue duty. Victor goes over to him and they chew the rag. They make me want to be sick. Christian is standing there, staring at me – any second he'll be over to talk to me. I hurry to the bathroom. I sit out there for a while, but it's no good. I go out again. Alison comes over.

"What's wrong?" she asks.

"That time of the month, that's all – I'm not feeling so hot," I say.

"Oh well, that'll pass," Alison says. She goes over and introduces Victor to Christian and Jarno. I pull away from the others, going to the corner of the house where they've put the pram. Like I'm really caught up in watching the sleeping sprog. Christian comes over.

"He's a lot like your dad, isn't he?" he says, nodding at Victor.

"No," I say. "They're nothing like each other." What? How? They're not the same.

"He could be your dad," Christian says. How can he know that . . . ? I realize that Christian has had a few too many – quite a few, as it turns out.

"But he isn't," I say. "And he couldn't be. He would have had to start very early to be my dad." Why do I even bother to answer?

"He's just using you," Christian says.

"And you would too if you saw an opening," I sneer.

"Nice comeback," Christian says and leaves.

Victor is standing with Angela at the bar, laughing. I go over to them. Angela puts her arm around my shoulders and steers me out into the garden, towards the furthest end.

"No harm in trying out a grown man, Samantha," she says in a sugary tone. "Experience does matter. But you're going have to face the fact that you can't trust him." I shrug off her arm.

"Stay away from me," I say and look around the garden, and there's Christian talking to Victor, and . . . what am I supposed to do? Where am I supposed to go, and what am I supposed to say to who about what? And why? I'm approaching them from behind when I hear Christian say:

"So when is your wife coming down?"

"I'm not sure. The baby is due tomorrow, but she may well be late. And then I suppose it'll be a few weeks before they can fly down together."

How can he call Mary his wife and say she's coming down when he keeps telling me that they're not together anymore and that he doesn't think she'll be down again?

I head straight towards the house, blinking furiously to keep the tears back, going through the sitting room, down the corridor. I try the bathroom door, but it's locked, and I can hear whoever's on the inside opening it. Tears are streaming down my face now, so I hurry through the nearest door. It's Frans and Alison's bedroom. And Alison's sitting on the bed, next to the crib where she's just put the baby – and there's a scrunched-up nappy next to her. Alison has either fed or washed the baby, and . . . I'm sobbing. She looks up at me, at once cool and caring. I cover my face with my hands.

Nightmare

"You little idiot," Alison says. "And what do you think will happen when his wife comes down? Tell me that, please."

"She's not his wife. He loves me," I say through the gaps in my hands.

"He's lying to you," Alison says calmly. "I simply can't believe that you're as stupid as that. But maybe I'm wrong. You're letting him fuck you, and you dream of how you're going to live together happily ever after in Africa. Of course he's lying to you. His wife is holding their baby in her arms, and you're out on your ear."

"He's divorcing her," I say, but . . . I don't even believe that myself.

"Did he say that?" Alison says.

"Yes."

"But he'll have to wait a bit, because his wife is having the baby, and it wouldn't be fair if he just called her and told her, and of course you understand that, don't you, and so on and so forth," Alison says and looks at me. Oh no.

313

"She might not come down," I say.

"Explain that to me," Alison says.

"She's just some girl he picked up and went out with for a while, and she got pregnant by accident and insisted on keeping the child. They're not even married," I say.

"It wasn't an accident," Alison says. "They've been married for five years."

"No," I say. How can she say that?

"Yes," she says.

I freeze up.

"And Dad – what exactly do you think he'll do to Victor and to you if he finds out you two have been having it off? Let me – you know – hear your best guess?"

"But . . . he must know," I say.

"He's your dad, and you don't even know him," Alison says, shaking her head.

I don't say anything. It was Dad who introduced me to Victor. What did people expect me to do with the man? I stare at Alison. Dad doesn't know. Alison nods.

"Exactly," she says. "So you better be careful that Dad doesn't find out what you've been up to."

"But . . ." I start and then stop.

"Go and wash your face." I leave the bedroom. Christian is leaning against the wall in the corridor.

"There's a queue," he says without looking at me. He might have been there for several minutes – then he'll have heard it all. I go back to the bedroom. I dry my eyes as I hear the bathroom door being opened and someone coming out; Christian goes in. I take Alison's arm, and together we go out into the garden. Luckily it's getting dark. I am shivering on the inside. I sit myself down and talk rot with Jarno about old times at school. Then the phone rings. Frans goes inside to answer it. He calls for Victor who goes inside. Frans comes out.

"That was Victor's sister-in-law calling from the hospital. Mary is having the baby."

"That's fantastic," Victor shouts into the phone. "Call me as soon as anything happens." He comes out, grabs himself a beer. "Cheers," he bellows into the garden. "I'm having a baby." Everyone raises their glasses or bottles. Everyone except me. I light a cigarette. I go to the bottom of the garden. I turn my back on the others. I hear steps.

"Are you O.K.?" It's Christian.

"No," I say.

"What are you going to do?"

"I don't know. I don't care. I'll think of something. What do you want me to say?"

"Something that isn't completely inane," he says. He's never spoken to me like that before.

"Everyone's lecturing me. Everyone," I say. "Now you are, too. I can't be bothered." Christian stares at me. "*Tsk*," I say. Suddenly he looks sad – he shrugs.

"It's so fucked up," he says. He walks away through the dark garden. I follow him. His eyes are teary. I put my arms around him – trying to comfort him. "No, don't do that," he says, pushing me away. Because he knows I don't mean it. He feels it too keenly. Or does he? I hug him again. If he stays and has a place to live, and if he gets himself something to live on . . . I could go with him to Moshi.

"Stop it," he says, twisting out of my arms. "You've . . . You're just using . . ." he says and points at my body. "It's the only thing you know how to do."

It's the only thing I'm not afraid of. I miss Mick. Christian is just a child after all. If his dad wasn't here, he wouldn't be here either. He isn't his own person. He's . . . lost. I don't want to go to England. I could live with Mick, here. He understands how it is. I insulted him last time I saw him. How could I possibly go to him now? I don't even know if he wants me.

Upheaval

The sitting room is dark. I'm waiting for Victor. I left the party pretending to have a headache. And now I'm going to give it to him straight. I'm going to tell him he's a bastard, a twisted beast, a wanker . . .

My mouth glued up, I wake up on the sofa – the maid is bustling about in the kitchen. It's light outside. I totter to the front door and look out. The motorbike is there. I go to the bathroom to brush my teeth, and then I go to Victor's room. He looks the same as he always does. I give him a shove. He opens his eyes.

"Some soldier you are," I say. All that nonsense about always sleeping with one eye open. "I could have killed you in a heartbeat." He doesn't say anything. "You're a real pig, you are, Victor."

"No, Samantha. I'm fond of you. But you're very young – you need to live your own life," Victor says.

"It was you who said you wanted to be with me. But that was just a lie. You just said that to . . . get into my knickers. To get into my knickers," I say.

"No, Samantha. You'll understand in time . . . You'll have a great life. We've had a good run. It's been fun, but —" I cut him short:

"You've used me."

"I've given you exactly what you wanted," Victor says, and it's true, but . . .

"You've been using me, that's all."

"Well what did you think?" Victor asks.

"That . . . you liked me. You said you did." I start crying.

"You're a tough cookie on the outside, Samantha. But wobbly on the inside. You need to get a hold of yourself, my pretty."

"Don't say that," I sob.

"You're a stupid little bitch who wanted a bit of rough. You had it. Stop whingeing."

"Are you proud of yourself?" I ask, snot running from my nose.

"I am the proud father of a son," he says and shrugs, smiling coldly. I wipe the snot from my nose.

"Then . . . why did you say all those things?" I ask.

"Time to call it a day, Samantha. Your dad is on to us. And it was fun. But my wife is going to be bringing down my son, and that's that. That's the end of it."

Dog on heat

I pack a bag. Victor stays in his bed. I go in and take the keys to the motorbike in his trouser pocket without looking at him once. I drive over to Alison's. They're at the Yacht Club. I go there instead. They're sitting under a sun screen, surrounded by a host of other families. Brunch. I stand some way from them, watching them. Mum, Dad, Baby, Granddad – eew! Then I go over to them.

"Hi," I say and catch a warning look from Alison. I sit down. I look at Dad – he leans back in his chair, breathing in, and then he speaks in his most commanding, piercing voice.

"You run around, flashing your cunt to the man – what did you think would happen?" What? Did Mum tell him after all? But she couldn't have. All conversations at tables around us drop to whispers; I feel faces turning to look at us. How does he know? I don't look to either side.

"What are you talking about?" I say.

"I'm not blind, you know," Dad says. "I saw you last night when he got the call about his baby."

"Calm down, Douglas," Frans says, but Dad ignores him.

"You're not a fool, Samantha. I know you've got brains," Dad says. "But you're out of your depth. I understand that – I was out of my depth too when I was young. But then I went into the army and sorted myself out," he says. I finish his sentence for him:

"And became a murderer."

"And sorted myself out," he says. "Focus, discipline. You need that."

317

"You used it to become a murderer," I say.

"I was no different from Victor Ray," he says. "You think about that."

"You were the one who brought him. You didn't have to plant the man right next to my bed, did you?" I say.

"He's a married man," Dad says.

"You owe him money. I thought I was a down payment," I say. Dad shakes his head:

"Isn't it time you stopped behaving like a dog on heat?" he says and gets up, trying to look menacing. There's nothing scary about him now.

"Who do you think taught me to be that way?" I ask. And then . . . my cheeks sting with his slaps, which land suddenly and unexpectedly – first left, then right with the back of his hand as the arm moves back. Frans has got up, snatching Dad's arm, his shoulders, trying to pull him off. Tears spring to my eyes. Dad has changed. He thrusts Frans away, making him crash into the table next to us; people scream, glasses and plates are broken, children howl, Frans collapses on the tiles, covered with juice and egg. Alison gets up and shrieks:

"We won't speak again until you've apologized to all of us." Frans has got up as well. Alison picks up the moses basket, Dad is standing silently, stooping – his arms are hanging down his sides, and the big hands are like dead shovels. "Samantha," Alison says. "Come on."

An hour later I'm sitting on their patio when Dad comes through the door. Alison is in the sitting room, nursing the baby.

"Calmed down a bit, have you?" Dad says.

"What was that again?" Alison says.

"The girl has to learn self-control."

"I don't seem to be able to hear you."

"Oh, come on, Alison," he says.

"Get out," she says.

"Now listen here . . ." he starts. But Alison has got up – she has gone to the phone, she's standing there turning the dial, holding the phone in one hand and the baby with the other. Dad stays where he is. Then he turns and walks out. Alison puts down the phone. Dad's car starts on the other side of the house. Alison is standing with one hand on the phone and her back turned to me so I can't see her face – she is holding the baby up to her face. Maybe she is kissing the baby. Her back is shaking.

Residence permit

I need my clothes, my cassettes.

"Shall I go over there?" Alison asks.

"No. I'll do it."

"Shall I come with you – in the car?"

"No," I say. "I'm fine. Maybe I'm an idiot, but it's not me who's the arse-hole."

I go over. I go there on Victor's motorbike. But he isn't there.

"He's gone for a few days," Juma says smiling – he doesn't know anything.

"What about his wife?" I say. "Has she arrived?"

"His wife?" Juma says – a blank look is spreading on his face. The me-no-understand strategy: an African classic.

"Yes, his wife and his new baby who are due to come down." Of course Juma knows I've been shagging Victor. He's an old soldier, alert and attentive.

"I don't know anything about that."

"Juma," I say, sighing. "Please, tell me."

"That wife isn't coming until the baby's a bit older," he says, looking embarrassed.

"Thank you," I say. "I'm just going to fetch a few things." I go inside and pack the rest of my gear into a bag. When I return to Alison and Frans', the police are there – two officers.

"What's going on?" I ask.

"Who are you?" the older of the two policemen says.

"Who are you?" I ask.

"They're looking for Dad," Alison says.

"I don't know where he is."

"We need to see your papers," the policeman says. He's already holding some passports – they're Alison's and Frans'. I dig into my bag and hand the man my passport.

"I've called Frans and told him to come home," Alison tells me.

"Your residence permit has expired," the policeman says.

"She's flying out next week," Alison says.

"You were supposed to have left two months ago," the policeman tells me. "That's going to be a big problem now," he adds and puts Alison's papers down – they're fine, because she has a husband who is allowed in the country. We don't even have the same surname anymore.

"What are we going to do about it?" I ask.

"We're going to have to issue a fine for illegal residence in Tanzania. You are going to the airport and must be on a plane out of Tanzania in twenty-four hours," he says.

I speak to him in Swahili:

"I've been here for fifteen years." And then I stop myself – what else can I say? I've been here all my life, as good as – and now I'm not allowed to stay. And the man ignores me. He refuses to speak Swahili with me. He takes my speaking in Swahili as an insult to his speaking in English. He continues in English.

"You must come to the station with us," he says with that smug, dead look in his eyes that all African officials adopt when you're at their mercy – passed down in direct line from the British colonial civil service.

The door opens – Frans comes in. He greets the policeman humbly. Suggests that we go down to the K.L.M. office so he can issue a ticket for me straightaway. I can come along. And of course I'll pay the fine as well, Frans promises. The policeman doesn't want me in the car. What he wants is to go to the K.L.M. offices and have Frans grease his palm without anyone seeing how much money he is being paid.

I sit in my room, staring at my hands – they're shaking.

"Did you get her a ticket, then?" Alison asks when Frans returns.

"Your dad had already bought one for her." There's three seconds of complete silence.

"When did he do that?" Alison asks and her voice is freezing. Frans hesitates:

"Yesterday. Yes, I know," Frans says, bowing his head. "But he asked me not to say anything until he had spoken to you himself. And he apologized." Alison's voice is icy:

"You will never put that man ahead of me again. Not ever. If you do, we're over."

"Yes," Frans says.

"And it isn't you he should be apologizing to. It's Samantha."

"Yes," Frans says. In her dreams. I put on my headphones and listen to music. They keep singing about love. But it isn't working.

Time to go

I drive to the Norad guesthouse. Jarno is there. He's due to fly out tomorrow. Christian is at the beach with Shakila. Oh, so now it's her he's chasing. We drive down to the beach to join them. Christian looks confused when I show up. It doesn't matter. I hide how I feel. I ask him what his plans are. He's going to Shinyanga to see his dad, or perhaps he's going to Moshi to see his dad there.

"How about you, Shakila?" I ask. She smiles.

"University in Cuba," she says.

"Did you get a scholarship?"

"Yes. My dad performed the Cuban ambassador's hernia operation and got him a *particularly cheap* summer cottage in Pangani. They play golf together," she says, smiling.

"But that's great news," Jarno says.

"It's quite common, really," Shakila says. "If Canada offers Tanzania twenty university places as development aid, you'll have all the Secretary of Education's best friends lining up at the airport, waving goodbye to their kids who are going off to Canada to study. And the Secretary will have all sorts of juicy bones to gnaw at." Shakila shrugs.

"Why does everyone want to leave?" I ask. All anyone thinks about is getting their children out of Tanzania. To Canada, the U.S., England, Australia, anywhere as long as it's out of Africa. The young Indians at school studied like mad in order to get scholarships, and once they leave, they never come back.

"We want to leave," Shakila says, "because God has forgotten about Africa."

"Do you still go to church?" I ask.

"Yes," Shakila says.

"Why?"

"It's nice having God on my side."

"Christian. Did you know Shakila sings like an angel?" I say.

"No. Do you?" he asks.

"Yes. So did Samantha when she was younger – at the boarding school in Arusha."

"You went to the boarding school in Arusha?" Jarno asks, looking at Shakila. He doesn't ask me – he's ticked off that I didn't let him have it.

"From Year One," Shakila says.

"How could they send you to boarding school from Year One?" Jarno asks.

"I can only suppose my father doesn't love me."

"Did you go as well?" Christian asks, looking at me.

"Two years with the Catholics in Tanga, and then boarding school in Arusha from Year Three," I say.

"Do you remember the uniforms?" Shakila asks, smiling. We all wore uniforms: bottle-green undies, bottle-green or black socks, khaki-coloured skirts and white shirts – little soldiers we were. When we went to shower late in the day, we went to the shower room in a long crocodile, washed, and brushed our teeth, and then back to our dormitories. During the weekends we were allowed to wear our own clothes, except for church on Sunday: the boys in white shirts and black trousers and shoes that were polished until they shone, the girls in white dresses and white shoes.

"And the Makumira clergymen's naughty children and the missionary teachers," I say. Shakila laughs:

"They didn't make much of a Christian out of you." She can say that again. Makumira is a theology centre with European and African teachers whose children went to Arusha School – mostly we just taught each other how to smoke.

"What are you going to do, Christian?" I ask.

"What do you mean?"

"Are you going to Denmark and school, or are you staying here, and if you do, what on earth are you going to live on?" I ask.

"I might train to be a diving instructor in Denmark and then start a diving centre for the tourists here in Dar or somewhere along the coast," he says.

"You won't get any customers," I say. "We had one in Tanga, but Moshi and Tanga are both too far from the northern tourist route – it just won't work. People who want to dive go to Mombasa or the Seychelles."

"I've also thought about setting up a disco in Moshi," he says.

"You haven't got a stereo," I say.

"Yes, I do – in Denmark. I'm looking into the options now, and then I'll have it sent down," he says. I don't think he can manage here, but I say no more. It's none of my business – and besides, I know fuck-all about how to manage a business.

"But what are you going to do – the next few days?" I ask.

"I'm going to swim," he says and gets up – wading into the water. Shakila and Jarno follow him. I light a cigarette. They splash each other. Shakila gets out of the water, wet and luminous and black, rolling on the beach so the little grains of sand make her skin white in big patches.

"Do you like me better like this?" she asks.

"What?" Christian says.

"If I were white?"

"No, damn it – get it off." He goes towards her, grabbing her, starts dragging her to the water. She escapes from his grip.

"Is it because I'm black that you like me?"

"I like you just the way you are," he says, glancing up at me. Maybe it's supposed to make me feel jealous. But I don't feel anything.

Underestimated

"Here's your plane ticket," Dad says, putting the ticket on the coffee table. Alison isn't home.

"I want to stay," I say.

"Samantha," he says. "They're expelling me. Do you understand? They're taking away my businesses. They've already taken the hotel. You can't stay – what do you think you would live on?"

"I can take care of myself," I say. He looks at me. Go on, say it, you old fool. Call me all sorts of things. But he doesn't say anything. He comes over, bends forward and grabs me by the neck, tries to tickle my tummy, and I try to wriggle my way out of it. We used to wrestle when I was younger. "It's not funny," I say. He lets go and goes to the window to look out.

"No," he says. "It isn't."

"What about Victor?" I ask.

"What about him?"

"Is he being kicked out as well?"

"They don't know about him," Dad says.

"But he was supposed to have been involved in the Seychelles coup," I say.

"*Nothing* was supposed to happen on the Seychelles," Dad says.

"Is that right?" I say. "Then we didn't go so you could plan a *coup d'état* on behalf of a doctor of Arab origin, currently living in London, planning to end the collaboration with Tanzania, which currently guarantees the security of the Seychelles?" Dad looks at me:

"Maybe I have underestimated you after all, Samantha."

"But you flew to the islands from Tanzania which made them suspicious. Apparently blacks aren't as stupid as you think," I say.

"Your mum knows you're coming," he says, nodding towards the ticket.

"But . . . why can't I stay here? With Alison?" Dad sighs.

"Alison has a husband and a child of her own. She has a life to live. She can't look after you. You have to go home and get an education – get qualified."

"Home?" I say.

Mick giving me what for

I take a taxi to Mick's garage. I cross the large yard, which is crammed with broken-down lorries – some of them taken apart to get spare parts for the others. Mick is standing beside a lorry, his upper body leaning in across an engine, shoulder to shoulder with another mechanic. A young bloke spots me.

"*Bwana* Mick," he calls, and Mick looks up.

"Samantha," he says. He comes towards me, wiping his hands on a dirty rag.

"How are you?" I ask. Mick looks at me silently, then at the office and back at me.

"I'm well," he says. "I'm always well. And you?" he asks.

"Is it a good job?" I ask, nodding towards the lorries.

"It'll do," Mick says. "I'm saving up for a place of my own in Arusha – a garage. But what about you? Are you O.K.?"

"I . . ." I say and stop.

"When are you flying back to England?" he asks.

"England," I sneer. "I just don't think I'll . . . you know, be happy there."

"Are you happy here?"

"You know, I've got friends here. People I can hang out with, people I can party with . . ."

"Samantha, I don't think that partying in Dar is going to make you happy."

"Why not?"

"Because it isn't your own life. You're staying at your sister's; you're staying in your dad's house. There's no future in that."

"I'm eighteen. I'm in no hurry to get myself a future – I just want to have fun."

"Is shagging every berk in Dar fun?"

"What?" I look at him. He has put on weight again since he was ill. I look him up and down:

"And what would I be better off doing? Shagging you? Some bloody, porky mechanic," I say.

"Hey hey hey," Mick says, holding his hands up in front up him. "I don't want you."

"You're so damned sanctimonious, but you're sneaking about pumping black holes like everyone else. You don't have a chance with me – not one."

"Samantha – someone ought to give you what for," Mick says, turning around – going back under the lean-to. I'm left standing there, frying in the sun. He leans in across the engine. Damn. I sit back in the taxi – the plastic seat is scorching, so I have to sit awkwardly on the edge of the seat.

"Drive," I say. That leaves me only Christian. I can disappear – go to Moshi with him. His dad is probably giving him money. Then I'll be off. They'll look for me, they'll be worried, they'll have to face the fact that they're treating me like a piece of furniture and they need to find a better way of going about it. But it'll only postpone the inevitable. And I ruined that friendship two and a half years ago at the boarding school in Moshi – because of sex. All Christian can think about is shagging me. And he's useless. He left for Europe, but he couldn't cut it there. And now he's returned with all sorts of hare-brained schemes for making a life for himself in Tanzania without having the know-how. He's like me. We're the same.

Escape

The taxi is approaching Valhalla – the residential area where the Scandinavians live. It's surrounded by a tall wall, at the top of which a series of two-foot-tall V-shaped flat bars poke into the air, linked to each other with barbed wire. It's like that everywhere in Msasani these days – there's been an explosive hike in the crime rate since I was little. Dad says it's because of the invasion of Uganda in 1979, when Idi Amin was deposed by the Tanzanian army. The soldiers didn't get any pay – except from what they could filch. They continued in the same vein when they were sent home. We drive to the gate and the guard's house. The guard lets us in – after all, I am white. The streets wind between the European-looking houses with the gardens framed by flowering hedges. I stop in front of number twenty-eight – I see a uniformed guard come down the street. I ask the taxi driver to wait. I ring the doorbell. The maid answers the door. Inside the floors are dark, gloomy. Christian comes down the hall. He's borrowed a room at one of his dad's colleagues' since Jarno flew home to start his life behind bars.

"Hi there," I say. "I just need to use your toilet." The bathroom has grey tiles; everything is streamlined and cold – very Scandinavian. I sit on the toilet for a bit. Then I flush. I turn the tap. I wet the soap, dry my hands, go out.

"Do you want a drink?" Christian asks, holding up a Carlsberg.

"I need to go straightaway – the taxi's waiting outside," I say, gesturing towards the street.

"But, I thought . . ." he says, but stops himself. Damn it. But I can't just . . .

"I have to pack and stuff. I simply can't stay, Christian." He's standing still, looking at me. "I'm sorry," I say. He's not as easy to read as he used to be, but I know the dead look from myself. On the inside he has been blown to smithereens. "But I'm having dinner with my dad tonight, before he drives me to the airport. You could come and have dinner with us . . . ?"

"Do you think he'd think it was a good idea?" Christian asks.

"No, but he's already given me a piece of his mind. Come on – it'll save him having to repeat himself."

"O.K.," he says.

"Oyster Bay Hotel, 8.00 p.m.," I say. I go over and hug him, kissing his cheek. He doesn't lift his arms – he's just standing there, stock still. "I'll see you later – 8.00 p.m.," I say and go back to my taxi.

Objects

Why must I pack these clothes? They'll be useless in England – too thin, too flimsy, too laid-back, too African. I take a couple of *kangas* that I've bought and put them into my suitcase. *Kangas* in England? Wrap one around you in the morning instead of a dressing gown and you'll have double pneumonia in a week. The *makonde* sculptures on the windowsill – I put them on top of the *kangas*; I need to have something with me to remind me of home. I start blubbing now. I make sure I make no sound, because Alison is in the sitting room. Here she comes.

"Samantha," she says, hugging me from behind. "Samantha, darling." She rocks me from side to side, and then suddenly I'm bawling like a baby.

"Don't be scared," she says. "It'll be alright. Mum's there, she'll keep you safe."

"I know," I say.

"And you'll be down here again soon. It won't even be a year, then you'll be down to see me. And if Dad can't afford the ticket, I'll make sure you get one."

"I know," I say.

"Do you want me to go with you to Oyster Bay – would you like that?" Alison asks.

"No," I say. "I'll be fine. Christian will be there. And besides, you can't leave the baby." Alison turns me around, so we're facing each other. She wipes the tears off my face. There are tears in her eyes as well. We smile a little.

"I have a present I need you to give to Mum," she says.

"I need to finish up here anyway. I've promised to pop by Shakila's before I go to Oysterbay," I lie.

"O.K." Alison leaves and comes back with a parcel containing coffee, cashew nuts, a bottle of *Konyagi* and a packet of Sportsman. "Just a little something to stop her forgetting Tanzania," Alison says and gives me an envelope. "And that's for you."

"Money?" I ask.

"Just a little – so you can get some clothes and that sort of thing." We lug my suitcase and bag into the drive. The chauffeur loads it into the car. Alison hugs me for a long time, but then the baby starts crying in his pram, and she lets go.

"I'm going to have to . . ." she says.

"See you, sis," I say and get into the car. She waves and starts walking to the baby. We drive off. Down to Oyster Bay Hotel. I tell the chauffeur he can go back. I leave my bags in Reception, so I can take them to the airport after I've had my farewell dinner with Dad. He will be standing on the roof, staring at the plane until it's in mid-air to make sure I am really gone.

Saying my goodbyes

I look out across the ocean. Should I go for a swim? I look at the palm trees – some of them are a bit scorched. I have some time to kill; I go up the road and flag down a taxi, telling the driver to take me to Dad's house. Victor. Everyone knows except his wife, but she isn't here. I want to see him one last time. Even though we're not . . . anything to each other, I want to tell him that I think he's wonderful – and an arsehole. And that's sad, but it doesn't mean I can't say goodbye like a decent person. I won't make it back to meet Dad on time. He'll just have to wait for me. I've waited for him for years. I'm in a daze as I drive back through the dusky streets, feeling the heat rising from the sun-baked sand on the street come rolling through the open windows.

Juma comes trudging down to open the gate.

"*Shikamoo mzee*," I say and ask him if Victor's in. Yes. I pay the taxi driver and go through the gate. As soon as I walk through the front door, I can hear Tom Jones blaring out from the tape recorder. Victor isn't in the sitting room. On the coffee table is a metal bowl, covered by a plate. It's the bowl Victor always used to mix his stuff in – his ridiculous cocaine enterprise. It's not a real life – it's going nowhere. Victor is dealing in drugs; Dad is playing at being a soldier. What is real life? Frans – selling airline tickets; Mick – fixing engines? Is that all there is?

"Victor?" I call, but he doesn't answer. I undress but keep on my knickers and vest, because I want to see him peel them off me – my knickers with his teeth. I go towards the bedroom. One last time. Who knows what it'll be like in England?

"Victor?" I call again.

"What?" Victor shouts from behind the bedroom door. I stick a coy smile on my face and open the door. Angela is lying with her head on Victor's chest, smiling at me cruelly. Victor gives a jolt. Angela raises her head and smiles down on his glistening, wet cock, which seconds ago was in her mouth.

"What the hell are you doing here?" he says.

"Finding out who you really are." I turn around so he can't see my eyes.

My first thought is surprise; why didn't Juma say anything? But he couldn't know that . . . Maybe Angela arrived at the house while Juma was out, and his daughter didn't tell him that a woman had arrived, because she didn't think of it. And Juma has to let me in – it's my father's house. And the front door was open.

Exile

The metal bowl with the plate on top is on the coffee table. I turn off the tape recorder. I go over and push the plate off the bowl, so it crashes to the floor and breaks. Cocaine. I sit down. With three fingers I lift a portion onto the table top.

"Don't touch it," Victor shouts from the bedroom.

"Screw you," I say, flatly. I can hear him moving about in there.

"I've bloody sold it," Victor shouts.

"Like I give a damn," I say. Victor is a loser. There are two hefty lines laid out on the tabletop already – and a rolled-up 100-shilling note. I take the first line. Brain freeze. Why do I always go for such arseholes? I can hear he's getting dressed – as if there's anything I haven't seen already. His voice sounds strained.

"It's too strong for you, Samantha," he shouts.

"Like all the crap I have to take from you," I shout while my upper body starts to shake. I look up. Victor is standing in the door with a sheet wrapped around him. Angela is standing right behind him, naked, with her hands on his shoulders.

"Don't take any more," Victor says.

"Take it – fuck up your brain for good," Angela says.

"You two have already seen to that," I say, lowering my head to the rolled-up banknote, holding it to the second line and snort. There are ice picks cutting into my brain, my mouth's filling with liquid glassy fire that congeals into rough shards and explodes in screeching flocks of birds. It's not cocaine, is it? Spasms shake my neck. Heroin. I lean back on the sofa. Something wet, warm is pouring from my nose. I put my hand up: liquid. I look at it. Red. Blood. Running across my lips. I put my head forward. Capillaries in my nose explode, and in my forehead. He must have cut it with finely ground glass to give it an edge. Too much. Wrong. Fertilizer – chemicals. A bloody, red haze descends on my eyes. My ears are wet as well. It's streaming down across my breasts, making the fabric stick to my skin. Running in rivulets, soaking my knickers, dyeing the fabric.

"No." The sound of my voice is choked and thick.

"Oh fuck!" The sound seems to travel through layers of dehydrated jelly-fish on a beach. There's Victor, shaking me. Shouting without making any sound. There's Angela's silent scream. "There's no pulse," he says, kneeling close to me. I'm limp when he moves me, stretching me out on the sofa, putting his mouth to mine, tasting my blood, blowing. "Come on," he says. No. Once I would have – not now. He pounds on my heart. Yes. My upper body is moving spastically on the sofa cushions. And then I'm out of the fetters of the flesh. I am standing in the middle of the room – who will light the first cigarette? Victor or Angela? Because I can't. But she's already half-dressed in the bedroom; she's trying to step into her sandals, but is too hysterical to – she kicks them off, takes them in her hand and runs out. "Where are you going?" Victor asks – his voice breaking. A whimpering sound escapes Angela until she is out of the door, slamming it shut behind her. "Fuck," Victor says. I think not, darling. He gets up, the sheet slips from his body, he looks around. Now I can see my dead body: blood from my nose, my eyes, my ears and around my lips – smeared by Victor – over my breasts, across my stomach and on my knickers. Victor grabs my shoulders and sits me up in the sofa. He gets up and turns around and goes down the corridor to the bedroom, where he puts on underpants and wipes my dried-up blood from his mouth. I sit down inside myself on the sofa – the temperature in my body is dropping. Victor is in the bedroom. I think he's packing. I can't see that far. The blood is still in my veins, starting to coagulate. Victor passes me, turns around and looks at me one last time – he shakes his head almost imperceptibly and goes into the kitchen and out the back door. I hear the key turn in the lock – then shortly after there's the sound of the motorbike starting and driving off. I am alone. My blood is coagulating – on my skin, in my veins. What's that? The sound of a Land Rover? Juma's voice outside. Dad. A key in the door. Dad comes in. He stops.

"Samantha," he says – his voice is thick. Behind him: Christian – the heart turns black. He sees me; he gives a jolt. Dad comes over to me, feels for a pulse – his fingers are warm. Christian is sick over by the door. "Close the door," Dad tells him. Christian shuts the door, and dusk spreads in the sitting room, as Dad squats down, stroking my cheek, looking into my red eyes. "Samantha," he says again, shaking his head almost imperceptibly. There's a sudden smell of cigarette smoke; Christian has lit one – in the end he was the one to do it. But I almost can't smell anything now. "I tried to report him to the police," Dad says.

"Who?" Christian asks.

"Victor. It's Victor," Dad says. The raid at the Africana while I was in bed on top of Victor's weapons. I saved him from arrest. And now he kills me. Dad gets up; he's standing with his shoulders slumped, his lips pressed shut. He removes the coffee table, looks at the sisal rug beneath it. He goes to the bedroom and returns with a sheet. He grabs hold of the rug, pulls it aside, spreads the sheet on the floor and puts the sisal rug on top – my deathbed. I look at Christian one last time. He doesn't seem to notice anything now. Dad lifts me up and puts me down. "I promise you I will kill him, Samantha. He will feel it," Dad whispers. A bit late to want to do something for me, isn't it? And it seems to be mainly for his own sake. Now he rolls me into the sisal rug like a larva in a cocoon, but I can't feel anything against my cool skin. My vision is blocked. I want to see what is happening, but I can't leave my body any longer. "Help me lift her up," Dad says somewhere far away. There's the sound of a slap. "Help me lift her," Dad says. They lift me and carry me outside, a cocooned bride on the threshold of death. I hear Juma opening the back door of Dad's Land Rover. "Get in," Dad says – is he talking to Juma or to Christian? The car doors slam shut. "Where are you staying?" Dad asks.

"Valhalla," Christian says. The car starts. I am lying behind them. We're stopping in Valhalla. Christian gets his things. We drive off again. The sound of Dad's voice is very faint:

"When we've buried her, I'll drive you to Morogoro. You can get a bus to Moshi from there. If anyone asks you, you just say . . . Just tell them the truth," Dad says. What is the truth? The car leaves the road and drives through the bush, then stops. Somewhere far away dogs are baying. They take the shovels from behind me in the Land Rover. Then they carry me out and put me on the ground. Dad and Christian dig a hole for me. "It has to be deeper, otherwise the dogs will get her," Dad says. Doesn't he realize they already have me? They put me down. The earth above me. All is quiet.